Emma Lorant lives i̶... ...
ROULETTE is her th̶... ...s two,
CRADLE OF SECRE̶... ...B̶Y OF FEAR,
were also published by̶ ...̶line.

Baby Roulette

Emma Lorant

First published in 1995
by HEADLINE BOOK PUBLISHING

First published in paperback in 1996
by HEADLINE BOOK PUBLISHING

A HEADLINE FEATURE paperback

10 9 8 7 6 5 4 3 2 1

ISBN 0 7472 5062 6

Typeset by Keyboard Services, Luton, Beds

Printed and bound in Great Britain by
Mackays of Chatham PLC, Chatham, Kent

HEADLINE BOOK PUBLISHING
A division of Hodder Headline PLC
338 Euston Road
London NW1 3BH

ACKNOWLEDGEMENTS

Thanks are due to everyone who helped with this book.

As always, to Nickie Bertolotti, Joy Cotter and especially Gillian Geering for reading various drafts, to 'The Group' for valuable comments and support, and to Joan Deitch for careful reading of the final draft.

Thanks also to Ian Hunt, Head Basketball Coach at Millfield School, Somerset, for his generous help, and Mick Byrne, Director of Basketball at EBBA Summer Camps; to Dr Jo Doust, University of Brighton; Professor Holland of the Microbiology Department at Leeds University; the St Pancras Hospital and the Hospital for Tropical Diseases; Castlemead Publications; the Communications Section of the Human Fertilisation and Embryology Authority; the Walk-In Children's Clinic of the University College Hospital Trust; the MRC Blood Group Unit; Dr Liz Wilson, Metropolitan Police Forensic Science Laboratory; John Tink of the Athletic Union at the University of Exeter; the Royal Devon and Exeter Hospital; the Paediatric Department, Queen Charlotte's Hospital, London; and Dr Daryl Cantor.

And to Tracey and Jonathan Potter, Michael Ridley,

Ros Topley, and Stuart Garland, and the many others, too numerous to name, for their generous contributions.

And special thanks to Suzy Davies for her invaluable help with the Welsh.

Any errors are, of course, the author's.

To Gissel – GGB –
an extraordinary mother and grandmother

PART 1

1

On a collection day he made sure he got up early, long before the rest of the household stirred. He liked that; the feeling of being in control, of doing what he wanted without the strain of explanations. And he preferred to sleep downstairs, on the couch in his study. He didn't care that it was uncomfortable.

His slippered feet moved, silent, along the carpeted floor. Leaning his weight against the door, he twisted the knob slowly, cautiously, and breathed out relief. No noise. He pulled the door ajar, heard the hinges squeak, and froze. The small hairs at the back of his neck prickled against his collar as he listened for a reaction. The house remained silent.

He had to be more careful. He levered the knob upwards to ease the door open enough for him to slip out of the study. Then he crept crabwise beside the skirting of the hall and on towards the cloakroom, avoiding creaking floorboards. The elaborate manoeuvre cost him precious minutes.

He stood at the bottom of the staircase and craned his neck upwards. The bedroom doors stayed shut. He tiptoed into the cloakroom, trickled water to wash his hands, didn't pull the chain. Adrenaline was already burning blood through his veins. He dipped a flannel in cold water and spread it over his face to cool himself.

3

The wrapper – his special insulating jacket which absorbed movement, one of his brighter ideas – was hidden behind the lagging of the hot-water cylinder. He slipped it inside the breast pocket of his coat and sneaked out into the hall. The wrapper kept the sample cocooned for the drive, and at body temperature.

Ready to leave at last, he inched over to the coat-stand, slipped on his shoes, eased back the front-door bolt and slid it gently out of its housing. He slipped the key into the well-lubricated keyhole and turned it. A tiny click. 'Shit,' he hissed, but held the lock lever open while he pulled back the door and stepped outside.

He watched hot breath turn to steam as it hit the frosty air, and savoured the cold. A crisp, early October day was dawning, the crimson sky a glowing backdrop for the high-rise buildings mushrooming like giants along the skyline. He aimed the remote at his car, opened the door, settled himself and shut it without a sound.

The engine purred into life and he drove north, enjoying the quiet smoothness. It was the only luxury he allowed himself, but even that was carefully concealed. The bland exterior and the subdued colouring hid a dynamic six-cylinder engine which murmured its power. He savoured the restrained opulence of muted leather upholstery, air conditioning, a CD changer hidden in the boot.

The car clock digits showed 6:38 as he beamed the entrance gates open. He felt his throat tighten; he didn't like being late, knew it would be resented. The strengthening rays of an ascending sun cast a long, pale shadow which changed into an accusing finger of darkness across the silver bonnet of his car. The donor was waiting for him, tapping his watch.

He pressed his window down, held out his right hand in a gesture of appeasement. 'Sorry I'm late.'

It wasn't shaken. 'Eight fucking minutes. What're you bloody playing at?' His blue eyes flashed anger, impatient arms waved a threat. But the sample was pressed into the offered hand.

He didn't like lying; never was any good at it. 'Lorry jack-knifed across the road,' he mumbled, knowing he wouldn't be believed. The figure had already turned his back.

He lowered the precious cargo into the wrapper, replaced it into the inside pocket of his coat and engaged drive. Left, and left again. Then he was on the main road to central London.

Gliding through empty morning streets he was struck with the exhilarating knowledge that he carried the begetting of another human being. Impossible to foretell the chances, but the odds had shortened over the years. Baby roulette, he chuckled to himself. Nurturing winners made his life worthwhile.

The semen sample, deposited into a sterile container, had to be transported without being jolted, and then frozen within the hour of ejaculation. Semen deteriorated quickly if special conditions weren't kept to. That was his expertise. Not that he'd patented his methods. He shrugged away familiar feelings of frustration and hugged his knowledge to himself. His uncrowned achievements.

He accelerated up to the speed limit and made good time. The crimson sky had changed to a brighter, harsher light which reflected in the chrome and glass of the modern office block he worked in. He slipped his identification tag into the barrier slot, backed the car into his reserved space, used his tag to operate the lift and pressed the sixth-floor button to take him to the sperm storage department.

The night porter, face grey with fatigue, eyes almost

shut, greeted him pleasantly. But he insisted on the usual security routine; he scanned his pass and checked his code before allowing him into the donor insemination centre.

He glanced at his watch. Running it fine: only ten minutes in which to prepare and exchange the semen sample. It was his job to make sure that all specimens conformed to the regulations laid down by the Human Fertilisation and Embryology Act 1990. He always followed that to the letter, prided himself on the care with which he treated each sample he accepted.

He tapped in his personal code, walked through to his office, then frowned. Something was wrong. He looked around and stared, mouth open, into his assistant's bland face.

'Good morning, sir.'

Shoulders hunched into rigidity, he pulled in his breath. Tom Dryson at this hour? He forced his features into a grimace of a smile. 'Tom!' His voice was a croak; he cleared his throat. 'You're bright and early.'

'Following your good example,' Tom said, face shining with the glow of expected praise. The soft fuzz of mouse-coloured hair was already thinning on the crown, giving the impression of a tonsure.

He tried not to panic. All he had to do was keep his head, act natural. He made the grimace wider, showed teeth. 'Any problems?'

'There's been some mix-up with the rejected specimens.' Tom's round face took on the contours of a cherubic smile. 'Thought you might need some help to clear that up.'

He closed his eyes to hide his feelings. 'Mix-up?'

'I noticed several unaccounted-for phials in the disposal bin. Suggests a serious error in procedure.'

So it was crunch time. His mind had cleared. 'That could be serious,' he announced, face grave. 'I'd like to check all

6

data for the last six months. We'll need to read the master tape.'

'That's what I thought, sir.' A fawning spaniel, wagging its tail. 'I'll see if I can get access right away.'

He watched him go, the eager tread of hero-worship padding down the corridor. It was strictly against company policy to allow unauthorised admission to the computer room. Stella wouldn't be in till nine. But it was the end of the night-shift, and the tired porter might open up her office, or argue. Whatever the porter chose to do, it would take time. He needed that.

He switched on his terminal and the label printer, brought up the specimen list of six months ago and printed a label coded to represent a tall, fair-haired, blue-eyed donor. Given a choice, the clients invariably opted for these characteristics, and that is precisely what they got.

He opened the wrapper and took out the phial containing the sample. The procedure was becoming more complicated. So much had changed since he'd first been involved with donor insemination. Modern DI centres no longer used fresh semen. It was stored, frozen within straw-shaped phials set into Dewar containers – miniature vacuum flasks – which kept the sample cooled by surrounding the phial with liquid nitrogen. Since the AIDS epidemic, all samples were kept frozen – cryopreserved – for six months before use. Donors' blood was HIV tested at the time of donation, and again six months later. It was only when they were declared free of the virus that their semen was sanctioned for use. It meant he had to keep tabs on accepted semen samples. Worse, it was becoming harder to hack into the computer. Yet it was essential to keep track of which live births resulted from which donor. His whole work was wasted unless he knew exactly where the genes had ended up.

He mixed the sample with prepared freezing medium. The formula was his, and Spermfreeze had used it to become one of the foremost DI centres in the country, supplying smaller centres, even exporting frozen semen to the USA. Not that *he* profited from that. Nothing to worry about, he muttered under his breath; he was getting his just rewards without their help.

He worked fast, then took the labelled, prepared Dewar, unlocked the storage room and exchanged it for one already stockpiled there. As he was about to put the substituted sample in his pocket Tom Dryson walked in. Why was he following him around? Blood rushed to his head as he remembered that the wrapper was lying on his desk. Had Tom seen it there?

'Shut the door, man! You'll affect the temperature. There shouldn't be two of us in here.'

'Sorry, sir.'

He steadied his hands. 'That was quick. Were you able to get into the office?'

'I tried to persuade the porter. Said it was more than his job was worth to break the regulations.'

'We'll just have to be patient, then. What time is it?'

As Tom's spectacled eyes took seconds to scan his watch he slipped the exchanged sample into his trouser pocket.

'My Casio seems to have stopped.' The young man tapped the dial impatiently.

'Never mind. First thing on the agenda, Tom: checking the sample codes against the files.'

'Of course.'

He looked at his assistant, but the ardent face showed only an eagerness to please. Bloody man was good, as well; *was* he catching on, or merely after his job? He turned, his neat figure kept trim by weekly visits to the sports centre. He couldn't afford to let himself run to seed. He flicked his

8

eyes at the blacked-out windows, saw his reflection elongated as if he were seeing it in a fairground mirror, smiled. His teeth took on the image of a vampire's fangs.

He looked away and waved his orders. 'Just check the cold-room temperature after I've gone, will you? I'll leave you to lock up. Couple of things I've got to do.'

He walked back into his office, replaced the wrapper in his breast pocket, crossed the corridor into the men's toilet. He opened the Dewar he'd removed from the storage room, took out the phial containing the sample, unfroze it by running it under the tap. It turned to liquid almost at once. He flushed it down the drain. Then he methodically cleaned the area around the basin and slipped the empty container into his trouser pocket. He couldn't afford the tiniest slip-up. Not even a sperm-sized one.

2

'Tonight's the big match,' Sally squeaked excitedly at Petra, eyes glowing, tossing her head up high. 'And Phil's going to be the star. You can't possibly want to miss it!'

Sally's enthusiasm was oddly catching. Petra agreed to go, even though she didn't really want to spend her first evening at Exeter University watching a basketball game. She was looking forward to unpacking her things, getting together with some of the other students in their hall of residence, maybe exploring the campus.

Sally Wheeler was always burbling on about her boyfriend Phil Thompson, how wonderful he was, how tall, how brilliant at playing basketball. But when, at long last, she introduced him to Petra, it turned out to be something of an anticlimax. Because, as far as Petra was concerned, Phil was eclipsed by the man standing next to him – Edward Dunstan: Phil's best friend, and another member of the team.

It wasn't difficult to identify the two athletes waiting outside the Sports Hall. They were standing, awesomely tall, smiling a greeting as she and Sally walked up to them. Petra was thrilled to see Edward focus on her right from the start, his pupils widening as he concentrated on her face. He didn't blink, didn't register surprise, though he must have noticed she had one eye brown, one eye blue. Instead, deep sapphire eyes softened as they swept from her face to her body, enveloped her. She sensed the strength of his first impressions, felt them like a force sweeping through her. Though not as tall as his friend Phil, Edward towered above her, making her think of herself as delicate, fragile. It was the way she'd wanted to feel for as long as she could remember.

'This is Phil, Petra. Isn't he just the most incredibly handsome man you've ever met?' Sally was on tiptoe, but she only just managed to get up to a height of five foot two, bringing her head somewhere near two-thirds of the way up Phil Thompson's chest.

A polite smile edged Petra's mouth upwards, hinting at the dimples in her cheeks. She and Sally had met several months before, when they'd been up for their interviews at Exeter University. In spite of the difference in their heights, they'd known they'd get on right away. When they discovered that both their families lived in London they'd arranged to meet, become close friends. Something, some indefinable but potent force, had pulled them together. But their names were the wrong way round. Sally wasn't long and tall; she was small, a petite four foot eleven and dainty with it. Petra was five foot nine and a half; not as much as five foot ten, she'd explained to Sally, measuring herself over and over again to prove the point.

'Hi, Petra.' Phil smiled, baby-blue eyes fringed by fair lashes incongruous on top of the huge frame. 'Sally's done nothing but talk about you since you two got to know each other.'

Petra forced herself to concentrate on what Phil was saying. 'Talked about me, has she? Nicely, I hope.' Her voice came out like a sort of purr as she looked at Edward through her lashes.

Phil's laugh was more like the rumble of thunder than the sharp tinkle bubbly little Sally produced so often. That's what had first drawn Petra to her: her spontaneous laugh, her gaiety, the way they had the same sense of humour. They got on so well they'd agreed to share a room in Mardon Hall.

'Very nicely indeed.' Phil's voice wasn't quite as deep as Petra had expected, but his speech was slow and authoritative.

'Neither of you said anything to *me*!' Edward's melodic baritone reverberated through Petra's body. 'Call yourselves friends?'

Phil grinned. 'And this is Edward Dunstan. He's playing tonight as well. On my team, fortunately.'

That was when Phil passed out of Petra's consciousness entirely, and Edward took over instead. It was only later that she was to realise that events followed each other with a strange inevitability. At the time she was blinded; dazzled by an overpowering love at first sight. And she was sure Edward had been struck in the same way.

Petra drank in the dizzy feeling of being looked down on. Perhaps she was so sensitive about her height because she was taller than both her parents. It had made her self-conscious. Edward, a good three inches shorter than Phil, had to be at least six foot six.

'Why have you been holding out on me, Sal, keeping Petra from me?' he said, leaning down, taking Petra's right hand in both of his and gazing right into her eyes. He must have seen by now that they were differently coloured, but he didn't react, didn't let go of her hand. He went on talking. 'You a basketball fan?'

Petra, uneasy, looked down; she wasn't an ardent supporter, she just liked to keep her father company when Uncle Jack wasn't around. 'It's my first time at an important match.' She smiled, but pulled her hand away. She was too shy for such a public display. 'I've been to a couple of games with my dad. And I've enjoyed the Harlem Globetrotters on TV. My father's a big fan. That count?'

The light colouring of his platinum hair gave the impression of a head stretching into the clouds, his alert eyes searched her from her wavy blonde hair to her shapely long legs. 'Show-offs,' Edward dismissed the world-famous team with a wave of his hand. 'We'll show the girls how the game really should be played – right, Phil?'

'I sincerely hope both of you will.' Another blond, blue-eyed giant, older than the two players and a little shorter than Edward, had come over to join them. 'That's what you boys are here for.' He sounded bad-tempered.

'Hi, Coach.' Edward looked at his watch. 'There's half an hour before the game...'

'And I was expecting to see you in the dressing room, Dunstan. You, too, Thompson. It's the big match tonight, in case you've managed to forget. However brilliant you two may think you are, we've still got tactics to sort out.'

'We're on our way, Coach,' Phil said, his voice strong. 'Just wanted a word with Sally. Be with you in a sec.'

The team coach turned and looked at Sally. Petra could see her smile and begin a greeting, but the man stared right through her, turned on his heel and strode away without a backward glance.

'That was Bruce Traggard,' Phil said, gazing after him. 'He isn't usually so impolite. Nervous because it's the big night, I suppose. My apologies on his behalf.'

Phil's look brushed over Sally, vague, almost misty, a sort of yearning playing at the corners of a gentle mouth which lowered on to her dark cap of glossy hair. She turned her face up towards him, her smile full of eager anticipation. Petra could see her lips ready for Phil's, noticed her eyes grow large with disappointment as she realised he wasn't going to kiss her. Instead, strong arms lifted her up

14

as though she were a doll and held her off the ground while his mouth, formed into an O, brushed the top of her head. Then the big man put Sally down and started talking to her.

A short, sharp stab of surprise pushed itself into Petra's mind at the way Phil was treating her friend. He'd behaved more like a brother than a lover. Had Sally misjudged his feelings for her? Wasn't he in love with her after all? Petra pushed the thought away and watched them. All Phil's attention was directed at Sally again, his huge shoulders hunched towards her, yet his head still towering above hers. He was talking earnestly, his voice low, two frownlines furrowing the space between his eyebrows.

Tonight was a turning point in his career. Basketball selectors were over from the States to watch this game. If Phil took their fancy his future would be assured. American basketball players of his calibre became millionaires overnight; he'd have no trouble getting a green card and emulating them.

'Phil's the shining star tonight,' Edward grinned at Petra. 'He'll make mincemeat of the lot of them. That's if we can get him to tear himself away from Sally. Hello there, Phil! Are you receiving me?'

The fair head levelled towards Edward. Petra was surprised to see that he looked hot and flushed.

'I heard you; hardly seems worth the bother of answering. Don't we always trounce that lot?' A large hand rested on Sally's head. He smiled down at her, pushed a few tendrils of hair behind an ear. Then he let go and motioned to Edward with his head. 'We've got to get back for that pep talk, girls. See you after the game.'

'You have brought the camcorder, haven't you?' Sally asked, putting her hand over Phil's, holding it to her cheek.

'Camcorder?' He looked puzzled, as though he had no idea what she was talking about. It struck Petra as strange

15

that he should have forgotten Sally was going to film the event. She'd taped every game since she and Phil had got to know each other. Sally was at Exeter doing Drama and English; her ambition was to become a film director. She'd already spent three years working as a freelance journalist on a local paper, had covered all the local sports events. And she'd had a short film transmitted on Channel 4. Petra had been told that even the team's coach – the surly Bruce Traggard – valued her work.

Understanding returned to Phil's eyes, though Petra couldn't see any of the enthusiasm she'd been expecting. 'I've brought it, yes. It's in the dressing room. I'll go and fetch it now.'

'I can't believe you'd have forgotten! You feeling OK? We agreed I'd tape all the action. In case it's slipped your mind, tonight's important!'

'I'd never forget to do anything you wanted, sweetheart. You know I'd lay down my life for you.'

3

'Shoot!' Petra heard Sally hiss at her, but she ignored her. She'd learned a lot about filming from her friend. She was taping the second half of the match in order to give Sally a chance to enjoy the game.

She'd worked hard, concentrating on Phil, taking action shots of his play, catching him in close-up. There could be no question about his exceptional ball skills. He dribbled with ease, moving the basketball around as though it was attached to him. He was obviously infuriating his opposite number, the player assigned to stop him, Number Five – a shorter and, it seemed to her, a rather aggressive man wearing leather strapping as a support above and below his right knee.

Phil countered him well enough. Number Five's face was set into scowls as he focused on the job of stopping Phil. He bumped and jostled him, and Petra could see his feet straying into the area which was definitely Phil's. The referee seemed content to let it go. She decided to take close-ups of the footwork just as the tape ran out.

'You got another one, Sal?'

'That one's used up?'

'Right to the end.'

Sally dug into an enormous tote and produced another tape. She reloaded, keeping an eye on the game, then handed the camcorder back to Petra. 'This is the crucial bit.

The scores are even. If they run out of time before another score they'll have to go into overtime.'

There was a roar as Number Five stole the ball from Phil, pivoted to look for the basket and saw there was no defence in line between him and it.

'Don't let him get away, Phil!' Sally shouted out, on her feet in front of her seat, jumping up and down in excitement.

Number Five took the ball in both hands, lifted his head to look for the shot, took off, and powered towards the hoop. The whole backboard shook and rattled as he thrust the ball through the basket.

'We've only got *seconds* to even up the score and tie the game!' Sally fretted, turning to Petra. 'We need that overtime if we're to have a chance of winning.' She sighed, deflated, and sat down again.

Petra, impatient for the game to end, could only think of getting to know Edward Dunstan. 'Remind me; how long would that be?'

'What? Oh, five minutes. If the score's uneven after that, the game's over. If not, they go on for as many five-minute periods as it takes to break the tie.'

Petra aimed the lens, about to film again, when the coach for the home team called time-out. She had up to a minute's grace to use the viewfinder for a better look at Edward while Bruce Traggard instructed his team.

She'd never been attracted to anyone in this way before. There was something so – *familiar* – about Edward, she told herself. Exactly the kind of man she'd always wanted to meet.

She felt the sharp jab of Sally's impatient high heel stab her ankle. 'I wish I'd never said I'd let you film the second half,' she hissed, small hands grabbing at the camcorder housing. 'Give it to me; I'll see to it.'

'That hurt!' Petra used her greater strength to snatch the camcorder back. 'I'm only waiting for time-out to end.' But the pain had the desired effect. She tore her eyes away from Edward and looked carefully through the viewfinder. The game had started again and she tried to focus on the player now dribbling the ball. Phil Thompson, naturally.

Sally was jumping up and down in her seat. 'For goodness sake, Pet. Shoot now! He's going for the jump shot!'

Phil was about twenty-five feet from the basket. If he could bring off the shot from there he'd be going for the most spectacular play of the match so far. Success would save his team *and* show the selectors exactly what he was made of.

She took aim, centred the tall, athletic body in her sights, and pressed the firing button. This was her chance to show Sally how good she was. The strength of the shot, her father had preached at her a million times, didn't come from the arms or shoulders, but from the legs. She zoomed the lens down towards Phil's feet and stayed there a couple of seconds, irritated to find that Number Five had blocked her view of Phil's legs with his own leather-braced limb. She tried to shoot round him, found she couldn't, moved the viewfinder and travelled slowly upwards, taking in the full six foot nine of sinew and muscle.

As she filmed she saw Phil set himself up for the shot. His powerful frame arched skyward, the ball lifting in front of his face, ready to be released near the top of the jump and pitched towards the basket – the classic jump shot.

She felt the crowd's thrill of anticipation, their rooting for victory. Every single spectator knew it was going to be the shot of the match. The lens caught Phil's arms extended

19

high, the basketball resting for a fraction of a second on the fingers of his right hand. She zoomed tight in on the uplifted hands and was surprised to see them waver. Instead of cocking forward like a trigger to follow through in the direction of the basket they seemed to hang there, motionless. The ball, allowed to travel without sufficient thrust, teetered upwards for a short distance, then faltered. None of the other players had expected that; it slithered between them.

Petra pushed the lens right in and focused on Phil's face. As she filmed she was horrified to see the alert blue eyes grow vacant, the mouth grow slack, the jaw drop down. Working on instinct, she pulled out the lens, caught the whole body as it froze into immobility, then filmed it as it crashed, straight like a tree-trunk, on to the court. The referee's whistle shrilled; the remaining nine men on the court looked as though they'd been turned to stone. The game was stopped.

Petra stared, stunned, her hands limp, the video camera forgotten, pointing at random. She turned towards the small, intent figure on her right and, shaken, slid back into the seat beside her. What on earth was going on?

Sally opened her mouth as anguish poured out. At first there was a sort of howl, then a crescendo of screams as her vocal cords gathered force and expelled her horror through her throat. Petra left the camcorder swinging from its strap around her neck while she held on to her friend, trying to stop her hurling herself towards the court.

Both girls pitched forward from the front-row seats Phil had reserved for them. Sally, so much smaller than Petra, still managed to wriggle out of her grasp and plunge towards the figure lying still and prone. An official, almost twice her size, caught her and held her.

'You can't go on the court,' a deep voice boomed.

'He needs me! He's my fiancé,' she shouted out, pounding her fists against a solid chest.

The man was gentle, but he held her tight. 'He needs expert help, not hysteria. Look – you can see they're taking care of him.'

Petra clutched her friend and dragged her back to their seats. As the girls watched they could see a cluster of men around Phil, his neck now encased in a collar, his massive body shifted on to a board. Then he was carried to the side of the court away from them.

'They'll know what to do, Sally,' Petra repeated over and over again, trying hard to persuade herself as well. 'You've got to let them do their jobs.'

Sally slumped back into her seat and began to sob. 'I knew something was wrong! I could tell right away that he was different.' She put her hands over her face, her whole body shaking. 'He said it was important, we had to talk. It was the last thing he wanted to tell me but there was nothing else he could do,' her agitated voice spluttered through the clamped fingers. She looked up at Petra, mascara streaks running down her cheeks. 'He didn't even kiss me,' she whispered, a look of despair in her large brown eyes.

'You mean he was ill before the game started?'

'I don't know! He said he couldn't talk about it then, he knew I'd be devastated, he didn't know what to do.' She gulped. 'I thought he meant he'd gone off me. I never guessed anything like this would happen.'

Her eyes stared, bleak, across the court. Petra could see Phil lying prone, no movement visible. Bruce Traggard was kneeling by him, covering him with blankets, waving several players out of the way.

As she watched she saw Bruce stand up and motion a substitute to take Phil's place to start the game again. She looked at Edward, saw him hesitate, staring at Phil, then, as another member of the team grabbed his arm, he left Phil's side with slow, uneasy steps. Even when he was in position on the court he glanced over his shoulder towards his friend, reluctance showing in every body movement. Both the coach's arms were jabbing towards the court – Edward had no option but to get back into the game.

Though shorter than Phil, Edward was just as muscular. He waited for the jump ball to restart the game, took the pass a team-mate tapped to him and went for the jump shot Phil had failed to make. The crowd held its breath. Petra watched, fascinated, as Edward's body replayed what Phil had attempted. This time the ball moved forward and upward in a perfect arc. It dropped into the basket as though Edward had thrust it there with a dunk. He'd evened the score just on the buzzer.

The fans stood in their seats, roared and stamped their approval. Petra put her arm around Sally now sobbing again beside her. A further five-minute playtime was called and the game began again.

'They'd have stopped the match if it was really serious, Sal. They wouldn't have called overtime. He must be all right.'

As she tried hard to comfort Sally she heard the wailing of an ambulance, then the noise stopped. She could see two paramedics slip round the perimeter of the hall, saw them file through to the side of the court carrying a stretcher. They loaded Phil on to it, heaved him up and carried him towards the exit. He lay there unmoving.

A thick lump gathered in Petra's throat as she eyed the still form with its long, forlorn legs projecting over the end, size sixteen feet moving feebly up and down in rhythm with the stretcher. She put her arms around her friend. Sally was so in love with him, so utterly crazy about him. And now her gentle giant, the man who'd told them all only a short time ago how he'd lay down his life for his little Sally, was being whisked away from them.

Sally's head lifted high as she watched, eyes now dry and blazing, mouth set into a rigid line.

'He'll be fine...' Petra began.

'He's dying!' Sally screamed at her, crashing the encircling arm away, twisting out from under it. 'Can't you even tell? I know he's dying!'

There was another roar from the crowd and Petra looked at the court to see Edward Dunstan landing on his feet under the basket. It looked as though he'd scored with a dunk. The crowd rose in their seats and cheered, and the referee whistled time. Petra noticed Edward, released from the game, straining to see what had happened to his friend.

Turning, she became aware that Sally had lunged into the crowd, determined fists forging space between ecstatic supporters, trying to get out of the hall. Most of the spectators had already left their seats and she was having trouble. Petra snatched up their things and followed her little friend, battling to catch up with her.

Someone was shouting her name; a male voice, someone she couldn't see. But she could hear the melodious tone, even above the crowd, and she recognised its reverberating timbre easily enough. Her godfather, she registered. What could Uncle Jack possibly be doing here?

The short, stocky figure was bobbing in and out of sight, hidden every now and again between the tall bodies of basketball affiliates, appearing shorter than he was by contrast. Even under the circumstances it made Petra smile.

What he lacked in height, however, he made up for in good looks. Jack Oliver was a dapper, handsome Welshman.

He had inherited his fair hair and blue eyes from his English father, but there was no mistaking his mother's Celtic heritage in the luxuriant hair growth, the dark complexion, the flashing eyes, the musical voice with its lilting inflections. No one could doubt his background.

'Petra!' she heard him sing out again. He was about ten yards away. 'Catch Sally up and get her to wait. I'll be with you as soon as I can get out of here.'

4

Jack Oliver slipped his trim little body between the huge forms and lumbering paunches surrounding him. He got all too good a view of them, then grinned as he realised how many of his colleagues had allowed themselves to go to beer pots. He stepped between the ungainly trainers in his exquisite hand-made shoes, intent on following the two girls now moving away from the Sports Hall. He could see Petra running after Sally, catching her up, tugging at her. She could be relied on to calm Sally down, he told himself; she'd see the girl waited until he could join them. Unwilling to let them take off without him, he made another effort to get through the jostling bodies.

'Hey, Jack! Gimme a break!' Earl Jennings' booming twang directed him towards the hulking body of his main rival from the States.

'Over here!' he called out. The reverberating baritone, with its unmistakable inflection, carried through the crowd.

Jack was short: barely five foot. It was more than thirty years since his puberty, but he still couldn't quite subdue his fury at the failure of growth in his long bones which had landed him with this unimpressive stature. There was no way he could compete with the other man on size, but he was way ahead on bookings. He raised his voice again.

'Can't stay now, Earl. Got to find out what's happened to Phil Thompson...'

'The doc'll see to that.'

'...and his little girl. Poor sweetie's beside herself.'

Earl managed to force himself alongside. 'Sure thing, Jack. Settle her down, or something. We need to talk.'

'Talk?' Jack's mouth widened, the lips parting. Strong, even white teeth gleamed up at Earl. Wouldn't hurt him to cool his heels; wouldn't hurt at all.

'Guess you're sweating blood about the way your shining star fucked up.' The big man had shortened his gait to the smaller man's and was leering down at him. 'Tough titty.'

Jack slowed down further. Americans were so coarse. 'These things happen to the best of us,' he said, gazing up at Earl, his eyes bright. 'And Phil's very special. Tried to play while coming down with the flu, I'm afraid. Big night for him.'

'Big night for the both of you!'

'Right. Poor boy didn't want to let me down.' His smile became broader. 'But did you see the way Joss Black was shooting?'

'Sure thing, Jack. Great play there.' He smirked down. 'Didn't I see him marking Thompson? Doing a good job, at that.'

Jack nodded, taking Earl's arm and moving him towards the exit. 'Of course; that's what he was there for.' The teeth gleamed whiter as he glinted at Earl. 'After all, the boy was playing for the opposition. He's looked very promising for several games now; I've had my eye on him for months.'

Earl roared with laughter. 'Your eye ain't going to be the issue here, old buddy!' He fished a piece of paper out of his pocket. 'All I gotta do to get the jump on you is put his name here...'

Jack stopped and patted Earl on the back. 'You're just a little late with that, boyo. I signed him up last month.'

The big man stopped, causing the crowd to jam. 'That so?' His lower jaw had fallen a good two inches. 'I have to hand it to you, Jack. You sure know how to pick 'em.'

Tonight had been a starter, a foretaste of great things to come. He'd already sold two outstanding players to the Americans, and Joss Black would make three. No problem getting top dollar for him; the boy would make multimillionaire within a twelvemonth. With rake-offs for his little Uncle Jack, of course. He deserved it. Wasn't he the one who'd spotted his talent?

'So what happened tonight?' Earl put the contract back into his breast pocket.

'That's what I'm intending to find out.' Jack winced as he thought of the many years he'd invested in the boy, starting when he was still at his primary school. 'Phil's fit as a rhinoceros; he'll be OK. They'll have taken him to the Royal...' He saw the lack of understanding in the American's eyes. He was probably thinking the Queen's personal physician was attending to Thompson. 'The Royal Devon and Exeter Hospital.'

'I guess you don't use the Health Service for your players? All taken care of privately.'

'Looking after my boys properly is an investment.' He dug Earl in the ribs.

'My spies tell me you picked Thompson out as a kid.'

'School playground; great places to find new talent.' It had taken more than that, of course. He'd forked out the cash to sponsor the boy through Millfield. Best sporting school in the country; highest standard of coaching you could buy. Even great talent needed training, and the habit of constant practice. 'He's one of my own boys – my specials. That's why you guys are here tonight.'

Earl grinned down on Jack. 'Hear you treat your players like family.'

'That's what they are – my family.' They were now walking out of the Sports Hall and towards the car park. Jack slowed down and watched the two girls ahead of them. His gorgeous goddaughter Petra; now there was another star in the making, if only he could persuade the girl to have a try. A top fashion model for sure; the looks, the height, the brains. 'Listen, Earl. It's important I sort this out, God knows what state Thompson's in. I'll catch up with you as soon as I get the chance. You got a number I can reach?'

'Here's my new card; my working day's till midnight. My mobile'll be on till then.'

'Give you a call soon as I can.'

Jack quickened his steps, came up behind the girls, slipped between them and put his arms round their waists. He'd been surprised to find that Petra was friends with Sally Wheeler. He'd had no idea that they even knew each other, let alone that they were close friends. It wasn't good news. 'Hold on there, girls. The car's parked a couple of hundred yards from here. I'll take you with me to see Phil.'

Sally had stopped and turned. 'Will you really take us, Mr Oliver? That's so sweet of you.' Her voice sounded weak and tearful, the anger spent. 'I've got to see him before his parents come. Once they arrive I won't get a chance.'

'Thanks, Uncle Jack. I told Sally you wouldn't let her down. But what on earth are *you* doing here?'

'Not spying on you for your parents, Pet; I give you my word on that.'

She giggled, embarrassed. He knew she was thinking of the way her mother had ranted on about her going to Exeter – choosing what she called 'that tinpot redbrick university' instead of taking up his offer. Or the scholarship to Oxford she'd chosen to turn down.

'Mr Oliver represents Phil, Petra,' Sally put in. 'And Edward Dunstan. Didn't you know?'

Petra's feet kicked stones aside. 'I know he represents a lot of athletes.'

'Not just athletes, my pet. Basketball players are my little speciality. And I take the greatest care of them.' He could not keep a certain irritation out of his voice. She must know what he did – he and her father talked of nothing else! 'I thought you knew all that.' He chuckled, the fruity sound of a man who knew where he was going and was enjoying the experience. 'And fashion models, of course.'

'You're not going to start on that again...'

'Well, here she is.' The light-coloured Mercedes SL 280 was gleaming in the fine October twilight. He beamed her unlocked, opened the nearside rear door. 'I expect you'll want to sit together in the back.'

The thump of heavy feet along the gravel made Jack turn. 'Don't just rush off, Jack. I've been looking for you everywhere.' Bruce Traggard inserted himself between Jack and the girls. 'I think I've got the right to talk to you.'

'Haven't you done enough?' Sally shrieked at him. 'It's because you harry him, make him play when he isn't well – that's why it happened!'

'All right, all right, Bruce, I'm here.' Jack turned towards the team coach. 'I'll be as quick as I can, girls. Just hold on a couple of minutes while I talk to Coach. Then we'll get over to the Royal. Why don't you sit in the car?'

He saw Petra put her arm around Sally and pull her towards the car. He nodded at her.

'Let's get in and wait, Sally. They won't be long.'

'So what's the problem?' Jack had turned back to Bruce, twirling the car keys in his hand.

'Keep that bloody girl away from him, Jack. She's poison for him.'

'Sally, you mean? Is that what you came to tell me?'

'That's not the half of it. Something was going on before the game; Phil wouldn't say what. Then that fucking girl turned up.'

'You didn't push him too far? Made sure he was OK?'

Bruce looked sullen. 'I'm not a damned idiot. I said take it easy, checked his blood pressure and his temperature. Nervous – what you'd expect. Keen to show the Yanks what he's made of.'

'So what d'you want me to do, Bruce? She's his girlfriend. If it wasn't her, it would be someone else.'

'That's my point. She's too old for him.'

Jack roared with laughter. 'She's only twenty-one!'

'A year older than Phil,' he snarled. 'Clucks around him like a fucking mother hen. Thinks she's the one to work out strategy. He's all steamed up about her for some reason; she'll bloody kill him off.'

Jack shrugged. 'They're young, in love. What d'you expect?'

'That isn't all there is to it. Something was bugging Phil before the game, really bugging him.'

'Such as?' He felt a flicker of irritation. These ballplayers were as tricky as primadonnas.

'Not a clue; all I know is that Sally was involved. That's the whole prob—'

'I'll do my best, Bruce. You'd better go and calm the rest of the team down. I'll ring through any news as soon as I get it.'

* * *

'Is he really your godfather?' Sally asked as soon as the car door was safely shut. She didn't wait for an answer. 'And d'you think he really will take us to see Phil?'

'Of course he will; I've never known Uncle Jack break a promise. He's one of the kindest and most considerate people around.' She put her hand over Sally's. 'He'll make sure they do all the right things. He's brilliant at getting the best for his clients. I know he'll really take care of Phil.'

Sally began to weep again. 'If it's not too late,' she sobbed. 'Just because he's so big, people think he's Superman, but he's quite fragile really. I'm always telling him to take more care of himself.' Her shoulders shook. 'I thought he looked flushed, and his hands felt boiling hot. He got mad when I mentioned it. Some kind of flu virus, he said. Everyone gets them.'

'So he wasn't feeling well?' Petra thought back to the redness of Phil's face. 'Maybe he felt he had to play – his big day and all that.'

'Even if he was dying, I suppose! It's that bloody man; he *forces* him to play, whatever he feels like.'

'You mean Uncle Jack?'

'I mean that damned coach!' Sally burst out, her voice breaking. 'Bloody Bruce they call him; blood on his hands this time, for sure.' She gulped, pulled out a handkerchief. 'I'm sorry, Pet. I just can't stand him. He hounds all the players, but Phil most of all. And he hates my guts. I don't know what I'm supposed to have done, but he's always trying to get rid of me.'

'He probably thinks Phil spends too much time with you.'

'All the boys have girlfriends, he can hardly expect to go against nature. And I'm always supportive, tape every single one of their matches.' She began to cry again, softly this time, leaning back in the car.

Petra looked out of the rear window; Uncle Jack was still talking to the coach.

Sally blew her nose and took a deep breath. 'How come your parents know the great Jack Oliver?'

'Great – that's going over the top a bit, isn't it?'

'I've had it dinned into me by Phil's parents, and even by my mum. They say he's *the* Jack Oliver, proprietor of the legendary Jack Oliver Media Agency. Started from scratch only ten years ago, and now he's right at the top. They think he's some sort of magician who can pull millions out of a hat.'

'I don't really know about all that, Sal. He's my godfather, more or less part of the family. He comes to our house all the time; he and Daddy like to talk about sport. It turns them on. For Mummy and me he's just Uncle Jack.'

'Well, you know; you live in that super house, and your mother's sort of posh. She isn't a famous actress, or someone I should have heard of?'

Petra laughed. 'You think he represents my mum? 'Fraid not; she's just an ordinary housewife. The only reason we know Uncle Jack is because of my dad. They grew up in the same street in a tiny village near Llandrindod Wells. They've known each other all their lives.'

'So you're Welsh?' Sally sounded astounded.

'My father's name is David Jones – well, that's the anglified version. Uncle Jack calls him Dewi.'

'You never mentioned that before. And I never would have guessed from knowing you. You don't *look* Welsh.'

'I suppose I take after Mummy,' she mumbled. She could hear the harsh tones of her mother's voice, the constant refrain about the backwardness of Wales, how the people there lived in a time warp, how it was impossible to communicate with them. She always felt uncomfortable when Wales came up, always guilty, torn between her parents. Was she ashamed of her father's background? Did she actually share her mother's prejudices? Was that why, in fact, she'd made sure Sally only came to visit when her father was out? She took a deep breath in. 'Daddy's the son of a slate miner from North Wales. They closed so many mines when he was young, there weren't any jobs around. The family moved to what used to be Radnorshire, Powys now. It's mostly agricultural – sheep farming and that. He and Uncle Jack left school to come up to London to find work.'

'What's your dad do? Work with Mr Oliver?'

'Nothing like that. He wanted to be a research scientist but he never qualified, so he's a manager at Jorncy's – one of those huge international drug companies. I expect you've heard of it.' It was a big bone of contention between her parents. Her mother was always angling for Uncle Jack to give Daddy a job. He couldn't do that; not with the way Daddy mumbled his words because of his cleft palate. 'He's done very well; he's head of his department. Mummy's upset because he can never rise beyond that. No formal qualifications, you see.'

'Sounds like Phil's mum. Always looking down her nose at me because my father was only a signalman.'

'I'm sure—'

'Yes, she does. They live in that enormous place in Barnes; act as though they own the world. They don't think much of basketball. They'd have preferred tennis, I expect. Wimbledon and the stupid strawberries.'

'So what persuaded Phil to go for it?'

'He got a basketball scholarship to Millfield.'

'Wow! But if they're so rich...'

'They're not. It's all Phil's money. He was sponsored by

the Jack Oliver Media Agency when he was only eleven. Mr Oliver's been very good to him, found him some advertising work right at the start. I don't know that Phil could have stood out against his parents without his support.'

'So it's a real problem, this snob thing?' Petra put her arm around her friend's shoulders once more and hugged. 'Bet Phil doesn't care.'

'I don't know what I'm going to do if Phil dies, Petra. I'll die as well.' Sally burst into further tears.

'I can't imagine why you're assuming the worst, you know. All that happened was that Phil fainted, or something.'

'Or something! I'm not assuming it; I *know* it. When you're in love, you'll see what I mean. There's a sort of telepathy. Phil's fighting for his life, and I can feel it. He's very weak; I think he's going to die.'

Petra was about to speak, but Sally turned, wiped her tears away. 'I knew something was wrong the minute we got there. I wish I'd stopped Phil playing, but I hadn't got the nerve to make a real fuss. They'll try to hush it up, but I'm going to make sure whoever did this to him doesn't get away with it.'

'You think he was *deliberately* hurt?'

'I know he was. I saw that chap with the leather strapping on his leg looking at him. I've noticed him before. He hates Phil's guts, because he's a much better player. I expect he thought he'd have had a good chance with the Americans if Phil hadn't been in the way. I think he got at him somehow.'

'But—'

The small mouth was set in a hard line. 'Forget it, Pet. We'd better not go into all that or I'll go bonkers.'

There was a short pause. Sally blew her nose and cleared

34

her throat. 'So you're reading science because you want to do what your father didn't get the chance to?'

'Well, I suppose it might have given me the idea. I do want to be a research scientist.'

'Even though you've been offered the opportunity to be a fashion model?' Sally sighed. 'You're pretty enough, even I can see that. And that wonderful figure! You don't know how I envy you.'

'I hate being tall.'

'You should try being small, like me. I'm twenty-one, and everyone still treats me like a child. It really gets to me sometimes.'

Jack Oliver opened the driver's door. 'Phil *has* been taken to the Royal,' he said at once, putting his mobile into his briefcase. 'I'll drive us over right away.' He eased the car out of its parking space. 'No need to be alarmed. They've rushed him into intensive care.'

Petra felt a jolt go through her. It was the first time she took on board that Sally might be right, that Phil was in real trouble. 'Intensive care?' She heard the tremor in her voice. 'As bad as that?'

'I'm sure it's just standard practice. They'll look after him well, Pet.' He turned and leaned sideways, his hair only just visible beyond the head restraint, and smiled at Sally. 'He's going to be all right, you know. Don't you worry yourself now.'

'What's wrong with him?' Sally whispered, the tears pouring down her face again.

'They couldn't say yet; we'll just have to wait and see, my dear.' He fished a large, clean handkerchief out of his blazer pocket and held it between the seats towards her. 'I'm sure they'll sort the problem and he'll be fine. He's in the best hands.' He swerved the car through the narrow space. When he spoke again his voice had that soothing

35

quality which always made Petra think he could change any
event, however tragic, back to normal. 'Just occasionally
the body rebels at all the work it's asked to do . . .'

'He drives himself too hard!'

The Merc eased out of the car park and purred along the
road.

'Uncle Jack, Sally thinks someone deliberately got at
Phil.'

The car surged forward, its reined-in power unleashed.
'Got at him, Petra? What's that supposed to mean? One of
the referees would have spotted that.' Petra could see
Uncle Jack look at Sally in the driving mirror. 'A whole lot
of us were watching every move Phil made; no one said
anything about a foul to me.' There was a silence as Jack
overtook a BMW which had given way to him. 'I expect he
just fainted for some reason. It happens, even to the
strongest men.'

The girls waited in a reception area, trying hard not to get
impatient. At last Jack Oliver came out of the intensive
care unit. His face was white, his knuckles clenched.

Sally was already on her feet. 'Has he had a heart
attack?'

Jack put his arms around her. 'They don't know what it
was. They've done an ECG to see if they can rule that out.
There's a chance it might be toxic shock syndrome.'

'What does *that* mean?' Sally almost howled. 'Just tell me
what's going on!'

'I'm sorry, Sally. I know you two are very much in love;
Phil told me you were about to set the date. I am so very
sorry.'

'You mean he's dead?'

'He's in a deep coma.'

'But he'll be all right?'

He squeezed her to him, but Petra saw the glazed look in the blue eyes. 'They're doing everything they can. I've made them contact the specialist I always use. He's coming over. If there's anything I can do for you ...'

'I want to see him.' She twisted out of Jack's arms and made for the door. 'It's me he'll want.'

He followed her, caught her by the arms. She tried to break away but he held her tight, almost immobile. 'They won't let you in on your own, my dear. But maybe if I take you to the—'

'I just want to be with him! If I can only talk to him, hold his hand ...'

He relaxed his grip. 'All right. I'll see they let you in.' He smiled at Petra over his shoulder, then led Sally through.

Petra shivered. She knew Uncle Jack. When he looked straight ahead like that it meant there was no kind of doubt. It was bad news.

5

Gwyneth Davies could smell the beer even before her husband had shut the front door. It made her gag, but she had to pull herself together and face him. There was no other way.

'That you, *cariad*?' she called. Her effort to sound happy at his return couldn't have fooled anyone sober. She hoped he'd fall for it, though she knew that, however drunk he was, he remained an astute judge of the meanings carried in intonations. Anyway, she had no choice but to get on with it, to tell him before he found out from someone else. She'd started the garden centre the first time Ian had ended up in prison, in the early seventies, nearly a quarter of a century ago. Her family had stood by her, scrimped and saved to help her – especially her brother Dewi. He'd never forgotten her, had sent money from London as soon as he'd found a job. He'd looked after the whole family from a distance, even if he didn't come back to see them in the flesh as often as they'd all have liked.

By the time Ian had come out of prison she'd got the centre up and running. It had done well, benefiting from the tourist trade and from incomers buying up country properties. The builders were starting on the new extension tomorrow, first thing. Ian would throw a fit, an absolute fit, if he saw what was happening before she told him.

There was a pause as her husband negotiated the door. 'Waiting for someone else, were you, *ast*? You're such a tart!'

She tensed. He was already in one of his tempers. She knew those moods, and this one sounded ominous. It had been because of one of Ian's alcoholic rages that she'd lost the baby, and with it the only chance she'd ever had of becoming a mother. Even after all these years she could still feel the power of the punch, right into her belly, hard into the womb when she was four months gone.

'By God, just look at you. Who the hell could want an old cow like you?'

Not a cow; more like a steer. Sterile and neuter. A cold anger gripped her as she remembered that it had been his fault that she'd miscarried, that she'd been damaged beyond repair.

'Well, what are we waiting for? Where's my tea?'

She gulped; she *had* to tell him tonight. Why had she left it so late?

Ian Davies staggered into the kitchen and leant against the door jamb. Short and stocky, with powerful arm muscles, he had the deliberate walk and bodily control of the manual worker, even when drunk. He was only forty-five, but his sandy hair had already receded, leaving a scalp whose pink was pockmarked with liver spots. But his eyebrows retained most of their youthful hair colour. They bushed, a deep ginger shade, hiding mean little eyes glinting on either side of a long, pointed nose.

Gwyneth turned, forcing her lips into a smile. The surgery on her cleft palate, though done when she was a child, had left a stiffness which still bothered her. Not that it hurt, exactly; but every time she smiled she was aware of the deep, rutted scar above her upper lip.

She saw her husband's right hand bunch into a fist and

flinched. God, she prayed, not now, not tonight. I've got to tell him otherwise he'll kill me when he does find out.

'Ith all ready for you, *cariad*. I got you your favourite,' she said, the lisp she'd learned to subdue always back when she was under pressure. She opened the fridge door and took out a piece of steak. He loved a thick, juicy T-bone, with chips and fried onions.

'You're not getting round me with that.'

The first punch landed in her groin, the second in her belly. She dropped the meat as she doubled up with pain. 'Thtop it, Ian,' she gasped, as she edged towards the kitchen table and tried to put it between her husband and herself. 'I've got something th'eshial to tell you.' She made a supreme effort to sound normal; some words were harder than others.

Powerful shoulders were humped as he moved towards her. 'I heard about your fancy boy,' he snarled. 'I heard all right. Real toff, this time. Posh bastard in a suit. Bought the whole place out; your Huw was the one that told us, so I know it's true.'

He jammed the kitchen table into her, moving the heavy piece of furniture with an unnerving ease. She found herself wedged between it and her new kitchen cabinets.

'He'th a new cuthtomer, Ian! Huw was only telling you about the family that'th moved into the cottage...' She cursed the way her speech deteriorated so badly whenever she was upset. Tears began to pour. 'He'th paying in cash! He'th got a wife and kidth!'

He seemed to use everything against her, even Huw. All her younger brother had been doing, in all likelihood, was telling their friends about her latest order. An unusually large one.

'Customer, is it?' He pushed the table harder into her ribs.

'He wanth to thtock hith garden . . .'

'Paid up front then, did he now? Before he even got a smell of carnation?'

She had no idea what he was talking about. Who was supposed to have paid?

'Fifteen hundred quid; pretty steep for a few plants to put in a Welsh cottage garden.'

He must have been to the bank and asked to see their statement, noticed the large credit entered during the month. Dewi had lent her £1,500 while he arranged to get together some capital to help finance the new buildings. A proper legal loan, not a gift. He was always good at sorting out deals.

'Don't think I don't know the place he's bought, I'm not that blind. Down Hundred House way, by the stream.' Ian's small eyes gleamed at her.

Oh, God. He was going to go off the deep end about the incomers again. Such a nice family, and taking over a hill cottage of the type the Welsh were leaving in droves.

'As pretty a little garden as anyone could want. Even an English bastard wouldn't find much to change in that.' He banged his fist hard on the table, jamming it into her again. 'And even if he does, he won't have it for long.' He grinned at her. His teeth were badly stained with tea and tobacco, but he still had them all. 'I'll see it's too hot for him to handle.'

What had possessed her to marry Ian, she wondered. A mixture of pity and loneliness, she told herself. And fear; the fear of being left without a man because of the deep scar below her nose. Maybe it was just as well she hadn't had children in the end. So what had stopped her leaving? Why had she stayed with him all these years? She could be free!

'What d'you expect me to do? Sit back and let you make

42

a fool of me, is it?' He lunged across the table at her, his fist finding her ribs.

He always hit her where it wouldn't show. She doubled up with pain, jabbing her shoulder against the cupboard beside her. It was guilt which had made her stand by him. She felt herself to be in his debt because he'd covered for her, taken the blame for the burning of the cottages when he'd only been interested in the burglary. But that was years ago; she couldn't go on putting up with abuse like this.

'For God'th thake, Ian. He'th a cuthtomer. I wath going to tell you. Dewi thent the money to help me—'

The table was whisked away from her and slammed into the opposite side, into the sink unit. His right fist crashed straight into her mouth, finding her upper lip. She could hear the split as the scar tissue parted. It made her feel sick, but fury against his brutality stopped the cries of anguish in her throat, turned her to ice. So often in the past she would have howled at him, thrown crockery or furniture.

Not this time. She put both hands up to her bleeding mouth, then almost fainted with what she felt. Her top lip had been torn apart, right into the palate, opening old wounds. He'd finally gone too far. She had to get away from him, to change her life. She couldn't hide what he'd done this time; perhaps she'd never be able to hide the scars she'd have after tonight.

'I'll make bloody sure no one does anything but pity you when they take a look,' he bellowed, his face contorted, his fist ready to strike again.

She leant backwards and pulled the carving knife off the magnetic strip to her left. She held it, pointing outwards from her chest. His small eyes became slits as he took in what she was doing. 'I'll kill you,' she breathed.

The mean eyes stared at her, trying to hypnotise her,

willing her to stop. She felt the blood flowing down her chin, her neck, on to her clothes. He couldn't stop her because she didn't care. She was going to finish it for good this time, she couldn't go back. '*Dos o 'ma!*' Both hands grasped the knife-handle and pointed it outwards. 'Get back!'

He dropped his fist, opened his mouth, but only a croak came out.

She walked forward, the knife pointed towards him, rage giving her strength. He'd killed their child, he'd made her barren, he'd drunk away the money *she* had earned. 'I'll *kill* you,' she said again.

He stumbled away to the sink, banged the table aside, opened the tap, pushed a teacloth under it and waited for it to soak up the moisture. He came towards her, his arms wide, holding the cloth in outspread hands. 'No need for all that fuss, *fach*. I'll help you clean up.' His voice was gruff; the beer had lost its power.

'Get away from me!' she howled at him. Blood was bursting from her, spattering the floor, the furniture.

He stood still, holding the sodden teacloth out in an attitude of supplication. She grabbed it, held it to her mouth, and pushed past him out of the house.

'Gwyneth!' She saw her mother coming out of the house next door to hers. 'Oh, my God.' She opened her front door and pulled Gwyneth through. 'Angharad!' she yelled up the stairs. 'Gwyneth's bleeding to death. Get the car keys; we've got to drive her to the hospital.'

6

Edward Dunstan walked into the intensive-care waiting room, long strides carrying him across it in four paces. He was about to head for the nurses' station when he noticed Petra sitting on her own.

His lips smiled, though his eyes looked empty as he walked over to her. 'Is Phil all right? I came as soon as I could get away.' His voice, though friendly, was husky with emotion.

Her eyes were wet. 'Not really. He's in a coma, I'm afraid. Uncle Jack took Sally in to see him.'

His eyes broadened in surprise. 'Jack's here?'

'He brought us over.'

The big man looked relieved. 'That's all right, then. He always looks after his players, makes sure we're properly taken care of.' A small, stiff smile widened his lips. 'Treats us more like sons than clients. He's really great.' He moved a little nearer to where Petra was sitting. He was wearing a tracksuit with an anorak on top. 'He's always got a sports-injury specialist on stand-by, in case of emergencies. He'll be round to see to Phil, I'm sure. Or they'll move him to the Bath Clinic.' He took his anorak off and put it on a chair, his voice less tense. 'So Jack managed to get Sally in to see him, did he? If anything can bring Phil round, that'll do the trick.' He turned to stare at the door through to the intensive care unit. 'I've never seen a player keel over like that before. Nothing remotely like it.'

'D'you often get bad injuries in basketball?'

'Not really. People injure their ankles, but it's the knees that take the main brunt. I've been playing basketball for years and I've never seen anyone pass out the way Phil did. He fell just like a log; he didn't even crumple up.' There was a catch in his voice. 'I suppose it's hard to judge when you're playing; one tends to concentrate on the game. You didn't notice anything unusual, did you?'

Petra hesitated.

'I know we've only just been introduced, Petra, but I'm sure Sally's told you I'm Phil's best friend. We're more like brothers than team-mates. Known each other for donkeys' years – both at Millfield on basketball scholarships. You can tell me.'

'It isn't that I don't trust you, Ed, honestly. It's that I don't really understand the game. I wouldn't know what *was* unusual.'

'Well, someone punching another player, or tripping him up. We're not meant to make contact. It's a very strict rule. See anything of that kind, something the referee might have missed?'

'Punch, no. I did notice one of the opposition players – the one wearing some sort of leather brace on his leg – put his foot in Phil's space ...'

'Joss Black, you mean? Strictly illegal. He had no right to do that.'

'But that couldn't have led to Phil losing consciousness.'

'Fair enough; I can't see how it could.' He stared intently at Petra. 'Any of the medics have a clue what the trouble might be?'

'They're still doing tests. Uncle Jack said the doctors talked about some sort of toxic shock.'

'Toxic shock?' He shook his head. 'Never come across anything like that. I do know Phil was feeling under the weather; wouldn't hear of not playing in the game, though. Thought he might have a bit of sunstroke, it's been so hot.'

Petra turned, her face eager. 'Sally said she was sure he was ill. Matter of fact, I did think he looked very flushed, but I put it down to not knowing him. Some people always have a high colour.'

'I know what you mean. Coach was worried, too. Took his blood pressure, but it was fine.'

'Sally keeps saying she had this intuition...'

He bent down and took her hand. 'Look, Petra. Sally's a wonderful girl, and we all know she adores Phil, she'd do anything in the world for him. All that. But she is given to paranoia. She imagines everyone's against their marrying, that Phil's parents can't stand her, that Coach has it in for her.'

'And she's got that wrong?'

He shrugged, the massive body lunging down to sit beside her. 'Phil's mum isn't crazy about Sal. Not just because she's so small; it's the contrast with Phil, I suppose. But she doesn't hate her, nothing like that. I expect she just wants Phil to wait before settling down.' He smiled across at her. 'I'd better see if I can help. I'll let the doctors know about his feeling off colour just before the game, in case they need to ask me questions. Don't go away, will you? I thought we might get together...'

'I'm at Mardon.'

'I don't think Sally mentioned your surname.'

'Really hard to remember,' she joked. '*Very* unusual. It's Jones. But my mother insists on adding her own surname, Penn, in front of it. So, I'm Petra Penn Jones, better known as plain Petra Jones.'

'I don't mind about the Penn,' he said, 'but the plain just won't do. Delighted to meet you, Miss Penn Jones. Welsh, is it?'

'Well-guessed. My father's Dewi Jones. He's from North

Wales originally, but now his family live near Llandrindod Wells.' She grinned. 'And my mother's Louise Penn Jones. She's English, from Hertfordshire.'

The door leading to the medical area opened and Jack Oliver walked past the nurses' station. 'Edward,' he said, catching sight of him and walking up. 'You've come to see how Phil is. You're a good friend.'

'What's going on, Jack? Is he OK?'

'I can't tell you that. He's still in a coma; has been ever since he collapsed. And he can't breathe without a ventilator. They've got him on a life-support machine.'

'Do his parents know?'

'I called them on my mobile as soon as I saw there was a problem. They're coming right away, but it will take at least three hours for them to drive from London.'

'Can I go and see him?'

'Up to the powers that be, Ed.' He looked over his shoulder, then lowered his voice. 'There's a dragon at the desk. See if you can charm your way in.'

The young man stood, walked over to the nurse on duty, and spoke to her. She beckoned him through.

'How is he really, Uncle Jack?'

'Doesn't look good, I'm afraid. And such a promising career. The scouts from the States were very impressed, I could tell. He really was going to be quite something in the international basketball world.'

'Has he always been one of your clients?'

'Spotted him when he was only eleven. I remember it very well; I went to see him at a Sports Day at his primary school. He was tall even then – and no question about his enormous talent right from the start.'

'I heard you sponsored him through Millfield. You're very generous.'

48

He spread his hands out in a gesture of dismissal. 'Through university as well. Just business; I get it all back eventually. With interest.'

'Sally's crazy about him. I've only just met him, but he does seem lovely. So gentle.'

Jack was nodding at her, but his eyes were distant. 'A good boy; couldn't ask for better.'

'So how did it happen? Any idea?'

He'd turned away from her and was staring into space. Uncle Jack had been a fixture in her parents' house – he came to Sunday lunch at least every other week – as long as she could remember. She knew he was trying to spare her feelings; he hated seeing her upset.

'The doctors don't seem to have any idea,' he said. The vibrant voice was low.

'But you probably had your eye on Phil all the time, didn't you? You must have seen what happened.'

He turned, looking surprised.

She stared straight back at him. 'Sally's convinced something's wrong, Uncle Jack. She saw one of the players looking as though he wanted to do Phil an injury; it was in his eyes.'

'Jealousy, you mean? Another member of the team?'

'Someone on the opposing side. He had some leather strapping on his leg.'

'Leather strapping?' His eyes concentrated into deep points, then relaxed as he took her hand. 'That isn't illegal, you know.'

She laughed; a nervous, unsteady sound. 'Even I know he wouldn't have been allowed on court if it was. But you were watching closely, weren't you?'

'That's what I was there for; Phil's big night. But I keep an eye on all the boys. And I've signed up other players in those teams, you know.'

Petra noticed that his blue eyes had grown cold. Uncle Jack could be quite sharp if he felt he was being challenged on any point. He was generous, kind, always around to help; but in return he demanded utter, uncompromising loyalty. It was one of the reasons Petra had refused all his suggestions for her future as one of his clients. She didn't want to owe anything to anyone.

'But if Sally thinks there's some sort of hanky panky going on, I'll get to the bottom of it.'

'Maybe Sally's already got evidence. She videos all the games.' A glow of satisfaction that she could be some help brought colour into Petra's cheeks.

The handsome face searched hers. 'She taped the match, did she? Now why didn't I think of doing that? That little Sally's nobody's fool.'

'She tapes every game Phil plays in. Pretty experienced by now. I expect you know she's already had a short feature film shown on Channel 4.' She knew Sally was looking for a good agent; maybe she'd ask Uncle Jack if he'd take her on.

He nodded, and looked towards the camcorder lying on the chair next to Petra. 'So – did she get footage of the actual collapse?'

'Well, no; she wanted to be able to watch without having to think about what to take.'

'Shame, that. It could have helped the doctors work out what happened.' A frown of what she took to be disappointment crossed his face.

'But I did, Uncle Jack. I think I got some very good stuff. And I did try to keep the focus on Phil. Just towards the end, unfortunately, I was being artistic, taking close-ups of moving feet. Then I swung the lens up and got the moments just before—'

'I always knew you were a clever girl, Petra. Pity you won't let me get you into modelling. Takes brains as well as looks, you know. You could make it big.'

She stopped short, her enthusiasm to help him gone. He was such a male chauvinist pig, always harping on about her looks. 'I've told you before, Uncle Jack. I want to be a research scientist.'

'Well, you certainly know your own mind, young lady.' He swept his eyes over her hair, her body. 'So: what about that video? You going to let me have it now so we can work out what really happened?'

Maybe she'd had no right to tell anyone about Sally's tape. 'I can't do that, Uncle Jack; it isn't mine. You'll have to wait till Sally comes out and ask her.' A half-smile played on her lips. Uncle Jack wouldn't like being turned down.

'She won't want to part with any video of Phil. You took it too, though, so I suppose it's partly yours?'

'She showed me exactly how to do it.'

'And you think she'd be mad at you if you lent it to me without permission? The tiny girlfriend with the big temperament.'

She didn't quite like the way he put Sally down because she was short. After all, he was pretty diminutive himself.

He sat next to her and held her hand. 'I don't think it would have worked out between them, you know. Just too much of a contrast in their heights.'

'Would have? You don't think Phil will recover?'

'The doctors are very doubtful. They could keep him on the machine for weeks, of course, and I'm prepared to foot the bill for them to do anything they can. But I don't think there's any hope.' A stare in the blue eyes, a deadened stare. 'And even if he came out of it, he'd never make a top athlete now. That's all over. A crying shame.'

He stood, took his mobile out of its holder and began to

tap a number in. 'If you'll excuse me, Pet. There are some calls I have to make.'

He walked out of the room and into the corridor beyond.

Edward and Sally came out of the intensive care unit together. Sally was weeping, her shoulders shaking, unable to stop the tears. When Petra looked at Edward he shook his head at her.

'They're waiting until Phil's parents get here. They won't really tell us anything definite.'

'But what exactly's going on?'

'They're going to let him die!' Sally wailed. 'I know they aren't even going to give him a chance.'

'I'm sure they will, Sal. They're trying something now ...'

'I heard them talking – the nurses, I mean. I heard them say there isn't any hope.' She looked, her small face smudged and red, at Petra. 'It's only a matter of form. They need his parents' permission to turn off the machine.' She gulped.

'I'll get some coffee,' Edward offered, looking at Petra. 'See if you can get her to calm down. Phil's parents aren't going to allow them to turn off the machine.'

'You needn't worry about me; I'm all right,' Sally insisted, looking annoyed. But she sat down.

Petra recognised the signs of prickliness and put her arm around her friend's shoulders. 'What about that tape, Sally? It could help the doctors work out what really happened.'

She shook Petra's arm off, and stood up again. 'You help Edward carry the coffee, Petra. I've got to go to the loo.'

'I'll come with you ...'

'I'm not a toddler, for goodness sake! I can manage that on my own.' She put a hand on Petra's arm. 'Sorry. Really, I'm OK. Could do with a nice hot coffee, though.'

7

Sally watched Petra and Edward, still awkward with shyness, walking away from her. Her heart ached as she thought back to the first time she'd met her wonderful Phil. She'd been waiting at a bus stop outside the Hammersmith Palais, late at night. He'd stopped his car a few yards beyond the stop.

'You shouldn't be out on your own at this time of night,' he'd started out. Then his whole face had reddened to the roots of his fair hair. It was obvious even in the neon of the streetlights, though the colour had shown as an unpleasing greenish tone. 'I'm terribly sorry,' he'd murmured. 'I recognise you now; we've met before. You're the girl who came to make a film of our team playing, aren't you?' He'd rumbled embarrassed laughter. 'I'm afraid I mistook you for a child.'

'Sally Wheeler,' she'd told him. 'Don't worry about it – happens all the time.' At least he'd noticed her. 'And I'm definitely over the age of majority. Over twenty, as a matter of fact.'

'Now that I wouldn't have guessed,' he'd said, his eyes softening. 'But even at twenty it's still a bit late to wait for buses on your own. Can I give you a lift? Where did you want to go?'

It clearly hadn't occurred to him that she was taking a bigger risk by accepting his offer than waiting for the bus. But she knew she had good instincts; she'd always trusted them. This giant of a man was no kind of thug. Right from the start she'd felt an immediate empathy with him. And that had been the beginning of the most wonderful romance a girl could ask for.

The tears began to gather, blinding her eyes, releasing her thoughts. She was convinced that there'd been a deliberate, sinister attempt to harm Phil, and she intended to find out exactly what it was. Someone had got at him, caused him to fall into a coma, perhaps even caused his death. She looked at the camcorder lying where Petra had left it. With any luck Petra's tape would show exactly what had happened. She would have to examine it in detail; she'd better take it out of the camcorder and put it somewhere safe.

She wiped away her tears, looked round to make sure she was alone, opened the camera housing, took out the tape and shoved it into her tote. Then she replaced it with the one she'd taken of the first half of the match. She gritted her teeth; there was no way she was going to let whoever had been responsible get away with it. Even if they'd meant no harm, even if it had been a genuine accident, she was determined to find out the facts.

Voices along the corridor outside hastened her into zipping her bag shut. No one would even know she had the tape, and it was better that way. She was putting the camcorder back into its carrying case when Phil's mother Helen burst through the double doors leading into the waiting room, her husband following behind.

The room was small, perhaps twelve foot by fourteen. Helen Thompson must have seen her sitting there, but she walked straight past and to the nurses' station without even nodding at her.

'I'm Phil Thompson's mother,' she began, then turned as she caught sight of another figure coming in from the corridor. 'Jack!' she cried out, ignoring the nurse and going over to him. 'Thank God you're here. Has my darling boy come out of the coma yet?'

'Helen, my dear...' Jack took her by the arm, placed himself between her and Sally and led her to a seat across the room from her. 'You'll have to be brave – and patient. He's still unconscious.'

'I want to see him!'

'Not right now, my dear; we'd only be in the way. They promised to let me know when we can go in.'

She pushed his hand away. 'I have to see him,' she sobbed. 'I'm his mother!'

'Easy does it, Helen. He won't even know you're there. So let's have a little chat while we're waiting, shall we?' He held out his hand to Phil's father Geoffrey and motioned him to sit down next to Helen.

Sally saw the door open again and Petra and Edward return, bearing four steaming coffees in plastic cups.

'Good to see you, Ed.' Geoffrey's voice was low as he walked over to the young people. 'How very thoughtful of you.' He sighed as he took the tray.

'Edward!' Helen Thompson jumped up and threw herself into his arms. 'You've always been like a brother to my darling.' She leaned her head against his chest. 'You were right on the spot, you must have seen what happened. What's wrong with him? Did he cry out, or say anything to you?'

Sally saw Jack, released from Helen, smiling at her. He handed her one of the plastic cups, then took another over to Phil's mother. 'It's hot and wet, Helen; it'll do you good.'

She took it, sipped, and stared at Petra.

'Helen, Geoffrey – this is my goddaughter Petra. She and Sally are great friends. They've both just come up to Exeter, you know. They were there tonight, watching the match.'

Helen swivelled round, dripping coffee all over the floor. 'Sally?' she cried, as though she could have avoided seeing her before. 'Sally's here?' She put down her cup, took a handkerchief out of her handbag and began to mop at her face, the distraught mother. She turned towards her son's girlfriend for the first time. 'Have you been in to see him? Did he know you at all?'

Sally felt resentment rising in her throat. This woman had tried to poison Phil's mind against her. That made it very hard to respond in a pleasant way. She was relieved when Petra walked over to her and put an arm around her in a determined show of friendship.

'How do you do, Mrs Thompson. I think Sally's in shock; I don't believe Phil gave any sign of knowing she was there.' She looked at her godfather. 'We're all longing to know, Uncle Jack. Did the doctors tell you anything the nurses haven't already said?'

His face looked white and pinched. 'I've been on to my sports' specialist. It would be wrong of me to say there's much to hope for. They don't know exactly what the problem is; they're still doing tests. It could be TSS; according to the ECG it wasn't a heart attack. But they're doing everything they can.' He'd taken the fourth coffee, drunk a few gulps, then put it down. 'You know I always make sure my boys have regular checkups, so it has to have been something quite unpredictable. They say such things can happen to young men under stress.' He walked over to Helen, took her hand and looked into her eyes. 'I suppose Phil was worked up about today. The penalty of success.'

'He didn't *sound* worked up,' Sally burst out. 'He was completely sure he'd make it. After all, he *is* the tops. Why would he suddenly have worried?'

'We all know how good he is, Sally.' Jack sounded conciliatory. 'But none of us can help getting stirred up at selection time.' He went over to where she was sitting. 'I know how much he means to you, what a terrible shock this must be. But you're the one who can really do something for him, you know.'

'*Sally?*' It was a shriek rather than a question. 'How can *she* help him, Jack?' Helen stopped, wet eyes staring at Sally. 'What can she possibly do?' she whispered.

'You think he'd like me there?' Sally began, her heart beating faster as she started up from her seat. Jack put a hand out to stop her, and she sank back. 'You know I'll do anything for him.'

'Petra tells me you took a video of the game. The tape could pinpoint what went wrong for the doctors.'

She froze, a feeling of unease chilling the blood in her veins. 'You mean you want me to give you that tape?' She paused, staring at Jack. 'I'll make a copy of it,' she mumbled. 'Tomorrow, in my department. They've got all the top equipment there.' She was quite clear that once she let go of that tape she'd never be able to prove someone had got at Phil.

'No one's going to deprive you of your tape, Sally. It's just that it might show us exactly what happened in those precious seconds...'

'It might give the doctors a hint,' Geoffrey put in. 'We really would be most grateful to you, Sally.'

'What's the point of talking about the *past*?' Phil's mother suddenly screamed. 'You said my boy is dying! Will that bring him back?'

'It could help the doctors, Helen.'

'I want to go and see my boy!'

Sally bent her head, her mouth set in a mulish line. For once she agreed with Phil's mother. 'No, I'm not giving you the original. It's mine.' She kept her voice low, but determined.

Jack shrugged. 'Just as you wish; it is yours, as you say. If you like, I'll copy it tonight. Then you'll have the original, and I'll get a copy to the doctors.'

'You live in London.' Her voice was tight. She clutched at the camcorder, held it on her lap, twisted the strap in her hands.

'I'll courier it over tomorrow morning. First thing.'

'For goodness sake, Jack!' Phil's mother cried out. 'Why are we sitting here wasting time? Can't you just take me in to him?' She rushed towards the nurses' station and began to demand to be let through.

Sally couldn't bear the thought of Helen Thompson with Phil while she had to stay outside. She dropped the camera, began to sob and ran out into the corridor. Then she felt Petra's arm on her shoulder.

'I just can't stand her,' she gulped at her friend. 'You saw her cut me!'

'I wasn't here, Sal. I expect she was upset, not thinking about anything but Phil. It's only natural.' Sally felt the hug. 'She was quite nice when she did notice you.'

Her nostrils widened as she tore herself away. 'She didn't behave the way she normally does. Once she's been in to see him she will.'

'She's worried sick, Sal. Why not give her the benefit of the doubt?'

Edward's voice calmed her, though her shoulders were shaking and she could hardly stand. 'You think I'm being an idiot about the tape, don't you?' she whispered. 'You think I'm off my rocker?'

'It might help the doctors, I suppose,' Edward said. 'Don't you trust them to give it back?'

She shrugged. 'Nothing to do with them. Whatever Mr Oliver says, that awful Bruce Traggard will grab hold of it. Once he's got his thick mitts on it he'll never let it go.'

'Bruce Traggard?'

'The team coach, Petra,' Edward reminded her.

'I told you how awful he is, Pet,' Sally wailed. 'He's forever harping on at Phil, trying to persuade him not to have anything to do with me.' She wiped away more tears. 'Poisoned Phil's mother against me as well. She used to be quite polite.'

'She seemed all right tonight, Sally, really she did.'

She knew Petra's smile was meant to calm her. Instead, it infuriated her. Even her best friend wasn't prepared to trust her instincts.

'Bruce told you having a girlfriend spoiled Phil's game, is that what you're saying?' Edward asked her.

She snorted. 'Worse; more personal than that. He thought I wasn't good enough for Phil.'

'Meaning?'

She hugged her arms around herself. 'Well . . . my mum's only a cleaner, I'm what they call a midget, *and* I'm adopted. There's no knowing what my genetic inheritance might be. Not nearly good enough for a famous basketball star.'

'That's up to Phil,' Edward said. 'He wasn't taking any notice.'

She couldn't stop harsh sobs racking her. 'They all said I'd cramp his style, that he was too young to settle down. They were all so desperate for him to go to the States, they didn't care about anything else. It meant glory, money, everything. I was the only one who wasn't sure it was the right thing for *Phil*. I knew it was all right for all of them, of course.' Her brown eyes were dry now, felt hard as marbles.

'You could have gone along, Sally. Looked after him.'

She turned on them, scowling. 'Very funny. Last thing they'd have wanted.'

The door behind them opened and Jack Oliver stood in front of it, holding it wide. 'Why don't I take you girls back to your digs? I'll wait while you get your gear.'

Sally blew her nose and gazed beyond him towards the seat where she'd left the camcorder. It had gone.

'Well...' Petra began.

'Phil's parents are with him now. There's no need for any of you to stay.'

Sally looked defiant. 'It's not a question of need: I *want* to stay. Phil may ask for me and I want to be here just in case.'

'I do understand, Sally, really I do. But his parents are with him—'

'I'm not getting in their way, Mr Oliver. They're in there, and I'm out here.'

He spread his hands out. 'It would be different if you were officially engaged, but you're not. So...'

Petra squeezed her friend's hand. 'Uncle Jack! You can see Sally and Phil are very close. She wants to stay.'

A nurse came over, her starched uniform crackling in the stillness of the silent hospital. 'It is past visiting time.'

Sally sat down on the bench. 'All I want to do is stay out here, in the corridor. I'm not disturbing anyone, not asking them to do anything about me. That's not against the law, is it?'

'Of course not. But—'

'She wants to stay, and I'm staying with her,' Petra said, her voice calm, plopping down on the bench next to Sally.

'And I'll stay, too,' Edward announced, standing to his

full height and dwarfing both Jack and the nurse, who began to retreat. 'Anyway, I have to wait for Phil's parents to come out. I've brought over his car.'

'No problem, Edward. That was on loan from me. Take it over, if you'd find that useful.'

The large man turned, a pensive look on his face. 'That's very kind of you, Jack. You mean keep it for Phil until he's up to it again?'

Jack held his gaze steady. 'Keep it whatever the outcome. If Phil recovers I'll get him something bigger.'

'Really? You're sure? I'm just an also-ran. You represent Joss Black now, don't you? Maybe you'd like to pass the Dolly on to him?'

'Just keep it, Edward. And get these girls home when the time comes.'

The young man sat down beside Petra. 'We'll wait for news. If he comes round and doesn't ask for Sally or me, we'll go.'

Jack shrugged. 'Whatever you like. I'm sorry, but I have to run, I really do. Nothing I can do around here. You've got my mobile number. Give me a ring as soon as there's any change.'

'Just one thing, Mr Oliver.' Sally kept her voice low and controlled.

He turned, looked at her questioningly, but did not speak.

'Phil's video camera. It—'

'His parents gave him that. I'm afraid I can't offer that to you as a – well, it's up to them, of course. Sorry I can't do anything about that.'

'I mean, have you seen it? I left it lying on one of the chairs in the waiting room. It doesn't seem to be there now.' She stood by the open door and pointed to the empty seats.

'Ah, yes.' He turned on a winsome smile. 'I saw Geoffrey pick it up.' She could see him stare, assessing her. 'It's their property; I didn't think it right to interfere.'

'The *tape* is mine.' Blood was pounding through her head, making it ache.

'You'll have to ask them for it, then.' A small, tight smile. 'I'd have thought you wouldn't grudge them the last tape of their son.'

Had the doctors actually told him there was no hope? 'You're very sure it is the last.'

He shrugged. 'Sorry, Sally. No point in my beating around the bush. He won't be playing basketball again.'

She saw Petra turn. 'But Sally—'

She pushed the high heel of her shoe into Petra's ankle for the second time that night. Petra winced, and bent down to rub her foot as Sally bent down, too. 'I don't think he knows about the second one,' she hissed.

'Something you wanted to tell me, Pet?'

'What?' Sally saw her cross her right leg over her left and rub the ankle. 'Just banged my ankle.' Her friend smiled through her pain, a real trouper. 'What I thought, Uncle Jack, was that maybe Edward could ask Phil's parents to let him have a copy of that tape. They'd do it for him.'

'Good thinking, Pet.' He kissed her, waved to the other two. They watched the small figure moving towards the exit.

'So what was all that about?' Petra asked Sally, still rubbing her leg. 'These bruises will be getting embarrassing.'

'I suppose you told him about the tape?'

'Why shouldn't I?'

'Did you say there were two?'

'No.'

'Don't either of you tell anyone – especially not Bruce

Traggard, Edward.' Sally looked sadly at her friends. 'I won't forget this, you two,' she whispered at them. 'I know there's something wrong. I can't explain it, but I don't believe what the doctors say. They're being paid.'

'But Sally, Jack's trying so hard to be fair to everyone.'

'He's been nobbled by Bruce; just like Phil's parents. He thinks I ought to get the hell out of it.'

'That's not it at all. He's got this thing about what he calls his "babies"; you just don't happen to be one of them.'

Sally kicked at the bench leg. 'So bloody what. That doesn't mean I'm of no account. I know there's something on that tape none of them want me to see.'

'Come on, Sal. You're overwrought. What could it possibly have to do with Uncle Jack?'

She didn't know who it had to do with. That's what the tape was going to show her. 'Not him, I suppose. But whatever went on tonight, I'm going to work it out,' she said, her mouth set tight. 'It wasn't an illness, or even an accident. If Phil dies, it will be murder.'

8

David Jones drove across the Severn Bridge and saw the sign: *Croeso I Cymru* – Welcome to Wales. The scars above his own upper lip began to throb as he thought of Gwyneth. Llandrindod Wells Hospital had been able to patch her up, but after that she'd been taken to Aberystwyth. Repairing the damage Ian had done was going to take extensive plastic surgery.

The car felt hot. He opened the roof window to its full extent, welcoming the cool breeze of a fine autumn morning. What had possessed his sister to marry Ian Davies? He'd always been a liar and a thief, jealous as well as stupid. His only virtue was the way he'd protected Gwyneth from bullying when she was a child.

The four of them – he, Gwyneth, Ian and Jack – had formed a gang. He smiled wryly as he thought back on it. 'The Cymreig Atoms', they'd called themselves. That was when they were children, and had just moved to what was then Radnorshire.

The trouble started much later, when Ian was seventeen and already working on building sites. He, Jack and Gwyneth were still at Llandrindod Wells High School. The Cymreig Atoms were determined to defend the heritage the soft mid-Welsh didn't take seriously. He could see the beginning of the rot now, clear and bright.

'My boss has done up another one of those cottages,' Ian

said, downing a pint outside the pub. 'Up on the roof this morning, risking my life for the bastards.'

'Did they use real slate?' Jack asked, a keen expression on his face.

Ian's small eyes were almost shut with suspicion. He'd never liked Jack, only tolerated him because he was practically part of the Jones family. 'Rich enough to be thinking of building a cottage, are you now, Jacko?'

Jack grinned. 'Give me time. Just means they're well-off.'

Ian poured the rest of his beer down his throat and started on the second pint he'd brought out with him. 'That's right, they do have a bob or two. Good furniture, see, and a brand new portable TV, is it. Real silver cutlery; I saw the candlesticks on the sideboard.'

'Better take what you want before it's burned down, then,' Jack said, his voice low and seductive. 'Won't know it's gone, will they?'

'You know that's not true, Jack,' Gwyneth piped up. 'They'll go through the wreckage, ashes and all. They can tell what's there and what isn't, even if it has been burned.' Gwyneth was always the worrier, and usually right.

'Not if we use enough paraffin. It's in the cans, all set. Who's cycling over?' Jack wanted to know.

As though it wasn't a foregone conclusion. They'd got used to not asking Jack to do it, because he'd been so tiny. And now, even though he'd grown, the habit was still there. Jack had left it to him, and Ian, and little Gwyneth to cycle over with the cans and to scatter the smelly liquid round the cottage, outside and in. Ian took the silver before they set the match, wrapped it in newspaper, and put it in the front basket of his bike.

'You take the telly, Dewi.'

Gwyneth was crying. He tried to reason with Ian. 'Put that

silver back, Ian. They'll know it's gone. You promised us you wouldn't steal.'

'Don't be so bloody soft; Jacko was right. It would be a terrible waste. We don't want that, see?' He turned to Gwyneth. 'I can get twenty pound for the candlesticks. Pity to ruin them.'

'She's not having anything to do with that, Ian! That's thieving. All Gwyneth and I want is to teach these foreigners to leave us alone. The cottages are for the Welsh. Not right to use them just for holidays.'

The trouble was that Ian didn't get rid of the candlesticks right away. He kept them in a box under his bed. The police knew well enough where to look for Ian's hoard and used it in evidence. That was why he ended up in court charged with arson as well as burglary.

It hadn't stopped there. Ian had named Dewi as an accomplice, and the police had taken fingerprints. But he'd been good about keeping Gwyneth out of it, had sworn blind she hadn't been involved. Poor little thing; she'd only been fourteen and such an innocent. What Ian had never forgiven was that he and Jack had got off, whilst Ian had been sent to prison.

Exit twenty-four at last. He turned on to the A449 to Raglan. Busy, well-kept; he drank in the sweeping views, the greens of summer turning into autumn gold and red. Pre-occupied, he missed the exit to the by-pass and drove through Abergavenny. The town was choked with roadworks, juggernauts twisting in and out, dust coming up in clouds. He sighed. So many 'improvements'; the Wales he'd known was slipping into bland uniformity with the rest of the UK.

He went through the town and on to Brecon, past the Cathedral and on to the B4520 to Upper Chapel. He always chose the glorious drive across Mynydd Eppynt. The Army used it as an artillery range. When the red flags were up he couldn't park and roam around the hills as he would have liked, with nothing but the speckle-faced sheep for company. They kept the hillsides cropped short, making the undulating waves of turf challenge a bowling green. He loved the chance to put on boots, get deep into the turf and forget the present. It gave him the illusion that time had fallen away, that he was still living in his native land, a young man with the whole of life ahead of him. Not true; he was forty-four and about to face the mid-life crisis.

The red flags were up today. There was a moment when he thought he'd risk it anyway. What did it matter? Petra was leaving home, what had he got to live for?

He shook himself. His parents adored his visits, waited for him to come and tell them about his London life. He never had much to say, though he tried to be with them as often as he could. His own eyes misted up as he remembered theirs, proud with the knowledge that a slate miner's son had made good.

'Manager, is it, Dewi?'

'Only a small department,' he always told them. 'Jorncy's a multinational company, you know.'

'Well-known, though,' his mother always said, her innocent face wide with smiles.

He was the only one of their five children who'd got away from Wales, the only one who managed to help them out financially. All thanks to Jack, of course. He'd never have thought of leaving without Jack.

His closest bond was with Gwyneth. Their shared defect drew them together, kept them friends even at a distance. Her cleft palate was much worse than his. And the burden of living with it was heavier for a woman who, like it or not, had to rely on her looks as much as her brain. He'd invited her up to London when he'd first left home, tried to involve her in his social life, done his best to find someone better than Ian

68

for her. It hadn't worked out. Gwyneth's questing eyes, pert nose, dark mobcap of hair and neat little body had not been enough to compensate for the deep scar between nose and mouth. The men had taken one look, listened impatiently to her nasal speech – and fled. That's why she'd settled for Ian. That, and her guilt about the business with the cottages.

His mother never rang his home, always wrote. Her phone call had come out of the blue, had shocked him.

'Your mother, David. Something seems to be wrong,' Louise had said, holding the receiver as far away from her as she could. In case his Welsh mother contaminated her through the telephone lines, he'd thought bitterly.

His mother had told him that Ian had split Gwyneth's upper lip right open, all the way back to the palate, and knocked out her front teeth for good measure. It couldn't be worse. 'You'll come home, won't you, *cariad*? And you'll visit her in hospital?'

He'd decided right away that he'd do more than that. He'd contact the doctors, tell them not to stint on costs, that he'd pay for her to have the very best in comfort. Money was not an issue; he could afford to help his sister.

He'd even tried to involve his wife. 'Perhaps you should come with me, Louise. Gwyneth's having a terrible time.'

'It's the last thing she'd want, David. Trust me on that. We've never got on, and never will. Too much of a difference in our backgrounds.'

He'd had no idea what the hell Louise had been talking about. Her background wasn't anything special; her father had been a minor civil servant. Big deal. But he'd learned not to argue. What was the point? She'd only be unpleasant when what he wanted was an amiable family life. That's why he'd always gone back to see his family on his own, apart from that one time before their wedding.

Petra was at Exeter now, and over eighteen. He thought

about suggesting to her that she come to Wales with him. Another time; this wasn't the right occasion.

He turned back on to the main road, drove past the turn-off to Llandrindod Wells; best to go straight on to Aberystwyth. Gwyneth had to come first. The traffic had thinned out, the roads were clear, he no longer noticed the magnificent countryside he was speeding through. His mind was on his sister, on the hard life she'd led.

He parked the car, walked to Reception and through to the room they'd allocated her, knocked on the door.

Nothing.

He knocked again.

An indistinct murmur that sounded like: 'Come in.'

He could feel his heart pound as he went inside. His little sister, the one who'd always got him out of scrapes, the jolly girl who'd played goalie for their football team, who'd covered for him when he was kept in at school, who'd bathed his wounds, who'd hidden his boyish misdeeds from his father...

'Hello, Gwyn.' He held the bunch of flowers across his vision of her face.

He saw her hands clutching a pad and paper, waving it at him. *It's hard for me to speak*, she wrote. *The doctors don't want me to move my mouth.* Her left arm was attached to a drip. Her right hand caressed his as he laid the flowers down on the bedcover. She pointed towards a vase standing on the windowsill.

He bent over her head and kissed the top of it. Some strands of white among the black, but not too many. He placed the flowers in the vase. Her eyes slid towards a door; her bathroom. He went in and ran the tap, gulping cold water down, playing for time. Her face was a mass of bandages, the blood seeping through the area above her top lip. He could hardly bring himself to look at her.

He filled the vase, came back into the room, a determined smile fixed on his face. 'So you're quite the big business-woman now,' he said. 'Expanding.'

She'd done marvels with the garden centre. To think she'd started out selling some cuttings she'd got to root in their own little back garden. She'd always had green fingers; if it could be got to grow, Gwyneth could do it.

Her eyes smiled, then veiled.

'We've got to find a way for me to help you out, Gwyn. Get away from Ian; Mam says he beat you up because of the fifteen hundred quid. That right?'

She began to scribble. *He thought I had a lover.*

'You mean he thought you were on the game?'

She shook her head. *Every time a young English chap comes into the shop he thinks he's after me.*

He didn't want to upset her; but the idea of Gwyneth being sought out by handsome strangers was so incongruous, his eyes gave it away. It wasn't that she wasn't good-looking. Though forty-two, a couple of years younger than he was, she still looked youthful, even sexy. Her dark hair, cut in a gamine style, sat like a close-fitting cap above tiny ears. She'd kept her short figure a trim size ten, her arms and legs had the glow of flesh toned up by physical exertions. He guessed it wasn't difficult for her to keep in shape; working in the garden centre meant she got plenty of exercise. Only the deep lines on either side of her mouth and under her eyes gave a hint that she was no longer young.

She wrote: *Money from you was what did it.*

'Still thinks it's my fault he went to prison?'

Yes. But it was JACK'S! she wrote. *Always Jack's.*

He pulled a chair up and sat down beside her. 'That isn't fair, Gwyn, and you know it. Of course Jack was in it as well; I'm not saying he wasn't. But he never set fire to anything, never took paraffin to a target, never stole ... all he did was talk.'

Her eyes were cold. She'd never liked Jack Oliver. She thought he'd been responsible for inciting the others. Never committed any crimes himself, much too clever for that. It was true that, somehow, Jack had turned Ian against Dewi. Odd, really, as he'd been the one to stick by Ian, to try to help him out. For his sister's sake.

'Dewi, is it. You came straight here?'

His youngest sister Angharad knocked and came in without waiting for an answer. He was shattered at how much she'd changed since the last time he'd seen her. She was twenty years younger than he, and so he thought of her as a child. But she wasn't a girl any more; she was a young woman.

'Angie! I'm not sure I'd have recognised you, you're so glamorous. What have you been up to?' David asked, planting a kiss on her cheek.

'London's not on the other side of the world. You could come and see us more often – or invite us to visit you,' she said, her eyes friendly but her voice with an edge to it. Ashamed, he realised he hadn't been to Wales for a whole year.

She bent over Gwyneth, kissed her, put a bottle of Lucozade on her bedside table. 'Want something stronger next time?'

Gwyneth shook her head.

'You coming home with me, Dewi? You can give me a lift. I took the bus.'

'Of course I will. How're Mam and Dad?'

'They're all right – getting older, but all right. Mam's happy cooking for the family. Longing for me to marry and produce another grandchild.' She gave him a sidelong glance. 'What she really wants is that you bring Petra along.'

His mother always clamoured for him to bring Petra, longed to see the granddaughter he talked so much about. The truth was that Louise wouldn't allow him to.

'You know, I thought I might. She's at Exeter now; not too far. Next time I come I'll let her know; see if she'd like to join me.'

Angharad's face lit up. 'That would be good, Dewi. Now, see if you can persuade Gwyn to leave Ian. She says she can't do it.'

He took Gwyneth's hand and held it. 'Not easy after all these years. And he always was in love with Gwyn.'

'Funny way of showing it!'

'Wasn't always like that, you know. He was wonderful, looking after her when she was a little girl. She relied on him. Jack was too small, and I had the same problem as her, see.'

'Didn't stop you fighting, did it?'

He could see the scorn in his young sister's face, but it was so unfair. 'Didn't stop me, no, but Mam got upset. It meant going to the hospital each time they hit my lip. Always split open again. That's when Ian came into his own.'

Angharad looked at her sister. She nodded her agreement.

'He was the only one who didn't care about the hare lip. He really was in love with her.'

Gwyneth tapped her pad. *He was the one who went to prison.*

'It *was* unfair,' he explained to Angharad. 'Ian was sent down because of the arson – they wouldn't have jailed him for the burglary. It was bad luck; he'd just turned seventeen and I was still a juvenile. That's why I only got a caution.'

'What about Jack and Gwyneth?'

'Jack wasn't physically involved; he never took part in the arson. And Ian covered for Gwyneth, wasn't prepared to let them know she had anything to do with it. Denied it out of hand.'

'You mean he took the blame for her part?'

'That's right. So that was noble, in its way. He wasn't really interested in the arson; we stirred him up to that.'

'But he's a criminal! Always stealing.'

He sat down on the bed, while Angharad sat in the only chair the room provided. 'D'you think you can get rid of him, *fach*? He's really gone too far this time.'

Gwyneth's eyes flashed. She grabbed the pad. *You can talk! Louise bullies you – just uses words instead of fists.*

He flicked his eyes across what she'd written and looked out of the window. It was true; he knew it was true. But he was not a man to make trouble. 'That's different; she doesn't put me in hospital.'

Angharad took up the cause on Gwyneth's behalf. 'A different kind of bullying, Dewi. You happy with that woman?'

'She's a good wife ...'

'You *happy* with her? Now that Petra's gone, why don't you leave her – come back and live near us?'

It was something he'd toyed with. 'Petra's only gone to university. She'll be back in the holidays for three years – more if she goes on to do research. At London University, maybe. That's what she's planning.'

'If you came back, Gwyneth and you could live together. That really would keep Ian away.'

'And what would I do for a living?'

'You seem to spend far too many hours at that job of yours. Why not go for quality of life? You don't need much money for that. Why not go partners with Gwyn?'

He turned to his sister. 'Would you like that?'

She shrugged. *Nice idea; take some thinking about,* she wrote down.

He hadn't thought of it before, but coming back to live in Wales was a tempting proposition.

9

The air in the Mardon room Sally and Petra shared was hot
and stuffy. Or Sally thought it must be, she was having so
much trouble concentrating on the video. She was watching
the tape Petra had taken of Phil's last game – not for the
first time; more like the twentieth. Petra owned a portable
TV which she'd said Sally could borrow. But she'd had to
buy a VCR, one which could freeze the tape frame by
frame. If she was to work out what had really happened to
Phil, she had to concentrate all her attention on that
miscarried jump shot.

She rewound the last few inches of tape and pressed
the play button. She sighed, sitting cross-legged on the
floor, Yoga style. Her head ached, her eyes felt as
though pins were being stuck into them, the hand which
held the remote control was hot and had begun to sweat.
In spite of all her work she hadn't isolated anything
remotely out of the ordinary. 'Help me, Phil,' she whispered to herself. 'Help me find out who did this to you,
and how.'

Each time she played the video Sally marvelled at Petra's
innate talent. The images themselves were fascinating. The
concentration on detail, the angle of the shots, were
enviable. But she couldn't see anything, anything at all,
which could help her theory of foul play. She clenched
her teeth, narrowed her eyes to points, and pushed

the pause button. Phil's large, Reebok-clad feet stopped dead; not a good image. She clicked the still/advance button; the feet moved a fraction of a millimetre. Another click, another. After pressing the same button twenty times a different player's feet came into view. It wasn't possible to tell which one, but she knew what was to come from watching the tape so many times already. The feet belonged to Joss Black; he sported high-cut shoes, with a thick sole. She stared at the leg also just coming into view, squinted at it to improve the focus of her tired eyes.

A current of cold air stabbed at her. At first she welcomed it, then she frowned. She looked up at the sash window opened as far as it would go, saw no sign of increasing wind outside. Her head froze into immobility as she felt an icy draught across the back of her neck. Had someone opened the door behind her? She shook her shoulders, managed to twist her head round, caught the billowing of the light material of her shell-suit thrown across a chair, the upward movement of the door-handle. Someone must have opened, then shut, the door and she'd been too preoccupied to notice.

Not a fellow student, or a friend; they would have shouted out a greeting. Perhaps someone who'd hoped to find an empty room ... She shuddered as she realised it was worse than that. Someone had stood behind the door, hidden, watching her.

The sweat on her body grew cold. Whoever it was would have seen part of the tape whose very existence she'd tried so hard to keep secret. She couldn't have got it wrong. She'd caught the lift of the handle in the swivelling corner of her eye. Why would anyone want to watch her viewing a tape? There could be only one reason: to see what footage she was spending so many hours scrutinising. Only she, and

Petra and Ed, knew of this tape. Neither of them would ever have given her away. Someone had cottoned on.

Her mind went back to Bruce Traggard. Was he, or more likely one of his minions, spying on her? One thing was sure; the tape was no longer safe in this room.

She went over to the door and clicked home the latch, locking herself in. Secure now, she pressed play and waited until Joss Black's strapped leg came into view. The leather thongs, above and below the knee, were connected with some knobbly bits which covered frayed bandaging. Part of the bandage was spilling threads above the lower piece of leather. All of it a mess, but hardly threatening. One thong-end had worked loose, jutting out and weaving about *near* Phil's leg, but not touching it. Not, at any rate, in the moments before Phil's collapse. She pressed slow motion, forced herself to focus, stared again. Why was she drawn to the leather strapping? She shook herself impatiently: because the leg itself belonged to Joss Black, Phil's main rival. The leather served to trigger her imagination.

She settled back on the floor. Her whole body ached from sitting as she aimed the remote control again. She had to press hard; it was sluggish because the battery was running out. And she'd frozen those last few frames, moved back and forth, so many times that the tape was worn thin. Tomorrow she'd ask her tutor to let her use the department's equipment to make a copy. Slowly, pushing herself, she edged the pictures along again, trying to ignore the headache which throbbed so hard she thought it was about to split her skull.

She wished she'd kept that first tape. She'd asked, time and again, but the Thompsons hadn't honoured their promise to send it, or a copy, to her. Tears of frustration blurred her vision. All she could see now was Phil's brilliant forethought as he set up the play for the jump shot. If the American selectors needed convincing, it was all there for them. If – *when*, she screamed at herself – Phil recovered, she'd get a copy to them. But there was nothing there for her. She needed that first tape as well.

The Americans – the bastards – hadn't stayed around. Edward had told her that they'd asked to replace Phil with Joss. They'd shown some interest in Edward as well, but told Jack Oliver they'd wait to see how he developed in the coming year. What they'd been looking for was the determination to win. Joss Black had plenty of that; Edward had shown more interest in his friend's collapse than in the game. Even so, Sally could see he would be there within months. Not quite as good as Phil, but still outstanding.

As for Joss Black, he wasn't even in the same league. But Jack Oliver had spelt it out to Phil often enough: once the selectors had taken all the trouble to come over, they wanted someone to sign. Sally assumed that Joss had been better than nothing.

She unwound her legs and squatted on her heels. She was exhausted. Just one more scene she had to view again. She forced herself to look carefully at the shots of Phil's face, the way his eyes seemed to lose life, then stared. She couldn't detect any sign that he knew what was happening; just an instant freezing of his large body, a rigidity the doctors hadn't been able to account for. There *had* to be an explanation, something so unusual that it would not occur to the medical team. They weren't detectives; they simply ran through the possibilities as far as health was concerned. What if Phil had been drugged before the game?

Desperate to prove her theory of foul play, she'd gone to the police.

'Collapsed during a match?' the sergeant who had eventually agreed to talk to her had asked. 'That's not unheard of.'

'There was no reason for it,' she'd insisted. 'I know something's really wrong.'

'Aren't you a bit young—'

'I'm twenty-one!' she'd cried out, exasperated. 'It's just that I'm short.' And she'd shown them the driving licence she always carried. Even at the time she'd thought it ironic; she must be one of a tiny handful of women who would welcome the signs of ageing to quash that reaction.

'Sorry, miss. Unless the doctors give us cause for concern, we can't get involved. No evidence, you see.'

The door-handle behind her jiggled up and down as someone tried to get into the room. Sally froze in her seat. Was she in physical danger? Should she move one of the beds to block the door?

'Sally! You in there?' Petra's voice. She couldn't remember when she'd been so glad to hear it.

'Just a minute, Pet.' She unlatched the door.

'Why on earth did you lock yourself in?'

She'd turned so that Petra couldn't read her expression. 'Just wanted to concentrate.'

'For goodness sake, Sal. You're not watching that tape again, are you?'

The note of sadness hit her like a well-aimed punch to the solar plexus. She pressed stop and rewind as her friend bounced to the right side of the small space they shared.

In the ten days since Phil had first fallen into the coma, Petra had tried hard to be supportive. But she and Edward had fallen deeply, almost drunkenly, in love. They tried not to exclude her. Instead, they did their best to persuade her to join them on their outings to the cinema. She found it too heartbreaking to watch their ecstasy. It wasn't jealousy; she was only too happy that her best friend and Phil's should have got together. How wonderful it would have been...

Petra's determined voice broke across her thoughts. 'You're coming out with me tonight.'

As soon as she'd stopped looking at the video Sally realised that not only was her headache too violent to ignore, she could feel her stomach churn. Had she forgotten to eat today? She did remember wolfing some biscuits down for lunch. She checked her watch: nearly six. She really ought to eat something else.

'A film, d'you mean? What about Ed? Been confined to barracks by Bloody Bruce?'

Petra put her hands on her friend's shoulders. 'Now don't say no, Sally, please. You've got to stop this. I'm not being catty, but just look at you. Your hair's a mess, your eyes are black sockets the size of saucers, your face is chalky and thin because you don't eat properly, and your clothes suck.'

'Thanks – you're one hell of a friend.'

'This isn't helping Phil.'

Sally pushed Petra's hands away. 'I'm doing the best I can.' Petra was right; she had to take a break, otherwise she'd become completely stale. 'Where are you off to?'

'Don't get cross. It'll do you good.'

'Spit it out, Petra!' Her voice crescendoed high. She was becoming a virago; it wouldn't do. She forced herself into a softened tone. 'Sorry, I didn't mean to yell at you. You've got something particular in mind, I take it?'

'Come to the game with me.'

Her head jerked up and a shooting pain daggered through it. She rubbed her temples. 'Game? What game?'

'Ed's playing in one of the Education Department sports halls. Just a friendly game against Loughborough U.' She smiled, but it was obvious she was nervous. 'You need to be taken out of yourself.'

'And you think going to a basketball game will do that, do you?' Had Petra lost her reason as well as her heart?

'You've got to lay the ghosts some time, Sal. Phil isn't getting any better. I wouldn't be your friend if I wasn't prepared to tell you that. It's only because his mother won't let go that he's still on that machine.'

Sally rounded on her. 'You'd turn it off, would you? You'd just say, "Hey, this guy's never going to be what he was. Let's get him out of our way; let's go back to our life, forget him." That what you mean?'

Petra didn't back off. 'No, Sally, you know very well I don't mean anything like that. You've done everything you can. You've punished yourself because, in some way I can't understand, you feel guilty about Phil. You know he's as good as dead; the doctors have told you so time and again. And so have Bruce and Uncle Jack.'

'Don't give me buggering Bruce! He's never been able to stand me being near Phil, not at any price—'

'Face it, Sally! It isn't just Bruce who thinks Phil's dying.'

Sally pushed the eject button and retrieved her tape. 'There's something wrong about the way it happened. I can't prove it yet, but I just know.'

'All right, all right. You think someone's got at Phil, so you have to try and show it. OK, I accept that. Doesn't mean you have to encourage his mother to prolong that dreadful limbo between living and dying. I'm sure Phil can sense your desperation, how much you love him, that you can't bear to lose him. That's why he hasn't died.'

Sally's hands shook as she put the tape back in its well-worn cover, then placed that between two paperbacks, and the whole package inside a plastic bag with the logo EASTSIDE BOOK STORE printed in white capitals. She took the little parcel and put it behind her shoes at the bottom of her clothes cupboard. Someone had seen her watching that tape; they would be after it.

'Oh, Sally.' Petra's face betrayed her pity. 'Still think it's going to get stolen?'

'You never believe me!' she wailed, building a stockade of shoes in front of the plastic bag. She turned, her eyes flashing. 'Actually, someone was trying to break in just now.'

'What d'you mean, break in? Maybe someone wanted a chat . . .'

'Who'd want to talk to me? They all run when they see me coming.'

'It's my room too, you know. They might just have been coming to see me, I suppose.'

'So why didn't they knock? Why just open the door, then close it as soon as I turn round?'

Petra's eyes refused to meet hers. 'There are petty thieves about; we all know that. We keep the door locked when we're out. What d'you suggest – a burglar alarm?' She held Sally's coat out for her. 'Come on, Sal. It'll be worth your while. Ed promised to drive us over to the hospital after the game.'

Sally retrieved the tape from behind her shoes. It would be safer to take it with them. 'This can go in the Dolly. Ed's got so much rubbish in there I'll be lucky to find it again myself.'

Sally's tense fingers twisted in and out of hair she'd allowed to grow straggly. Petra was right. She wasn't helping Phil by wishing the past were still the present. It wasn't; she had to come to terms with that.

She tried to watch the players. Edward was coming along really well, almost as though he were taking over Phil's role to keep his memory alive. She saw Bruce Traggard, blond and tall like so many of his team, nodding at Edward the way he used to nod at Phil, giving Edward the little pat he always reserved for players he thought were working well. In spite of her personal antipathy to him, she had to admit he was an outstanding coach. He looked positively paternal.

'Getting good, isn't he?' Petra was on the edge of her seat. Edward had reserved two in the front row for them.

'No question.'

'Come *on*, Sally. You like the game. Enjoy it, for goodness sake!'

She still felt a tightness in the pit of her stomach. She hadn't been able to shake it off since Phil had gone into the coma. She leaned back in her seat, closed her eyes. The noise around her melted time away, turned the clock back to before that dreadful night. She kept her eyes shut, reliving the pleasure of watching Phil play, remembering how he waved at her, ran up to her after the game, oozing with life, with energy, with enthusiasm. 'Let's go for a meal,' he always shouted to her as he ran past on his way to shower and change. 'I'm starving!'

The roar of the spectators brought her back.

Petra was cheering, standing up. 'Ed's just running away with it! They'll have to find some competition for him somewhere.' Her voice, full of love and pride, cut Sally to the heart. 'Didn't you even look?' Petra sat down beside her. 'Well, it's all over now.'

'He's great.'

The home team, faces flushed with victory, filed past them. 'See you in ten minutes,' Edward said, stopping in

front of them. 'Glad to see you made it, Sal.' He nodded at
her.

'I don't believe she saw a thing. Are we going to grab
some food first, or go straight to the dependency unit—'

'What are *you* doing here?' Bruce Traggard had stormed
over to them and was towering above the still-seated girls,
his face a study in menace as his eyes fixed on Sally.
'Haven't you done enough damage? I thought I'd made it
clear: I don't want you anywhere near my players!'

She was too worn out even to think of a reply. Before she
could ease herself out of the seat and slink away, an
oppressive feeling of sadness making her faint, Edward had
swivelled towards Bruce.

'You got a problem, Coach?' The gentle voice had
turned into cold fury.

Bruce was big by ordinary standards; six foot four, a
massive pair of shoulders, the thickening of middle age
giving him weight. He was dwarfed by Edward. 'This is
nothing to do with you, Dunstan. I have to look out for my
boys. She's—'

'She's my best friend's girl,' Edward interrupted, the
normally modulated voice harsh. 'What's more, she's a
very good friend of mine. Now we've had enough of this
nonsense. You got something against her, let's hear it, we
want to know. If not, leave her alone!'

Bruce's face changed from anger into rage, a mottled red
spreading down his neck. The hand holding the score
sheets clenched white. Then he must have noticed the
coach from the Loughborough team passing, staring at
them. He eased up, his voice low. 'You have to admit it,
Ed. She's carped and made no end of trouble since that
night. She snoops around, makes appalling accusations,
upsets everyone. I've got nothing against you personally,
Sally. Just keep away from my team!'

'*Something* happened that night, Coach. We both know Phil didn't keel over for no reason. Sally has every right to try to find out what it was.'

'She hasn't got the right to make crazy allegations!' The controlled voice had lost its cool again. Bruce's eyes flashed as he turned to face Edward. 'And don't you think it's a bit off for her to switch to you before the poor boy's even gone?'

'Switch to me?' At first Edward clearly didn't follow Bruce's meaning, then he seemed to grow two inches. 'You saying you think we're going together?'

The threat in the blue eyes was so unlike Edward's customary amiable look that Sally gasped.

'Why else would she be here tonight?'

'*This* is my girlfriend, Coach. Petra Penn Jones; she's also a very good friend of Sally's. That's how we met.'

It seemed that Bruce Traggard had only become aware of Petra at that moment. He frowned down at her, a question in his eyes. 'Petra Penn Jones?'

'Thought I'd find you all here,' a familiar voice broke in on them. Jack Oliver waved round a genial greeting. 'Haven't you met my goddaughter, Bruce?' He laughed. 'Surprised you didn't recognise her! Louise Penn's daughter. You must remember Louise?'

Sally had been far too upset to notice Jack's arrival. She saw the mixture of surprise and annoyance on Petra's face. 'Uncle Jack!' So he wasn't expected.

'Hello there, Pet.' He was standing beside the coach, forced to look up at him. 'Well, Bruce – see it now?'

His face had turned from dark pink to puce. 'I'm sorry, must have been blind.' He tried to cover his unease with a smile which turned into a sort of grimace. 'Of course I remember Louise. Married David Jones, didn't she? So you're their daughter?'

Petra's nostrils flared their disapproval. She simply shrugged.

The man's whole tone had changed to syrup. 'I used to know your mother very well. Must have been all of twenty years ago. Quite a basketball fan herself, you know – that's how I met her.' He gazed at Petra. 'Always came to the games I played in. Then Jack here gave a party and invited both of us.' The grimace turned into a smirk. 'Great little dancer.'

Petra looked sullen. 'You must be thinking of someone else. Mummy isn't interested in basketball. She never comes to games with Daddy and me.'

Jack laughed. 'Even mothers were young once, Pet. Of course he hasn't got it wrong. Your mother was quite a raver in her day.' He grinned at Petra. 'She even had her share of boyfriends, would you believe.'

'I've met your father, too,' Bruce told Petra. Sally realised he was doing his best to salvage something from his misplaced attack on her. 'Same party. He and Jack were always inseparable.'

Petra just stared at him, but the charged atmosphere had lightened somewhat.

'I happened to be on my way to Bath,' Jack said, leaning over and pecking at Petra's cheek. 'Thought I'd call in and see how Exeter was treating you.' He turned to Sally. 'But you're the one I've really come to see. How are you, my dear? Bearing up?'

'I'm fine, Mr Oliver.'

'Perhaps this will help. I've managed to get a copy of your tape.' His eyes flashed at her. 'But you didn't get the last bit, I'm afraid.'

'Last bit?'

'When Phil went for the jump shot . . . and didn't make it. The tape ran out.'

Her heart thudded so loud in her chest she thought he must be able to hear it. She forced herself to sit quite still, then looked slowly up at Jack Oliver. His eyes were on her, intent.

She tried a watery smile, gulped, held her hand out. 'That's really sweet of you, Mr Oliver. Thank you very much.' She couldn't raise more than a whisper.

'Hope it doesn't bring back too many sad memories.' He patted her shoulder. 'So what about supper, then?' Jack, impeccable in a blue suit and white shirt, included them all in an expansive wave of his arms. 'You look half-starved, Sal. Come on, it's on me. I'll buy us all a slap-up meal.'

Edward coughed. 'There isn't time, Jack. I promised Sally I'd drive her over to the Bath Clinic right after the game. Phil's transfer there has made it harder for Sally and me to visit. We haven't been round to see him for two days.'

Jack wasn't so easily put off. 'All the more reason to get something inside you.'

'The thing is, Uncle Jack...'

'No good?' He smiled, his blue eyes brilliant. 'Tell you what – I'll take Sal over, and meet you two there. OK?'

It seemed to Sally as though she were walking in a dream. Jack Oliver ushered her out to his Mercedes, helped her into the passenger seat. She leaned her aching head against the soft leather upholstery. It felt blissfully cool.

'When did you last eat, Sally?' he asked her, his voice gentle.

'I'm not exactly sure...'

'You'll do yourself real damage, my dear.' The car moved smoothly out of Exeter. 'But I've got just the thing for you. Egg mayonnaise sandwich in the glove compartment.' He leaned over her, pulled it open and rummaged inside. 'Here we go, fresh from Fortnum and Mason's this afternoon. You have some of that. Do you the world of good.'

She ought to make herself eat, otherwise she might just faint. Would something left in a glove compartment be OK? She took out the package, saw that it was wrapped in an insulating bag, and that the sandwich itself was still in its sealed container.

'Thanks, Mr Oliver. That looks really good.'

'Phil Thompson?' The girl at Reception looked at them in surprise. 'We only put the alert out ten minutes ago. You got here very quickly. Yes, go straight to the nurses' station by the dependency unit. They'll tell you what to do.'

'Something's happened.' Sally's tight face broke into a beatific smile. 'Maybe he's come round at last. Maybe he's asked for me!'

She began to sprint along the corridor, leaving Jack behind.

'I'm Sally Wheeler,' she announced, breathless, at the dependency-unit counter.

'Yes? How can I help you?'

'Phil Thompson; they said at Reception that you'd called.' The tears weren't far away.

The nurse looked at Sally. 'We did call his mother at her hotel; she's on her way.' Her eyes took in Sally's height. She could see her trying to make an estimate of her age. 'Well, you're certainly not his mother. Are you his sister, by any chance?'

Jack had caught up with her. 'She's his fiancée,' his authoritative voice announced. 'Has he been asking for her?'

'We can't entirely make out what he's saying.' The woman's face softened a little, the tight lips loosened into compassion. 'But he was making a kind of S-sound. Your name is Sally, you said?'

'Yes. He calls me Sal.'

'That must be it.' Jack nudged Sally further along the desk. 'He'll want her with him.' He grasped hold of Sally's arm as he looked at the nurse. 'You'll let her go in right away?'

There were the beginnings of a frown. 'All right, I suppose so. But I do have to warn you: this isn't a good sign.' She came out from behind the counter and put her arm around the small figure. 'Would you like a cup of tea?'

It was true that she felt unusually thirsty. She clutched the bottle of Evian Jack had given her and waved it at the nurse. She'd already drunk half of it in the car on the way over. 'I just want to see him.'

'I must explain. When a patient gets as excited as this after coming out of a deep coma, it *can* mean he's recovering...'

'Or?'

'Or it can also mean it's near the end. And in his case...'

'We're wasting time!' Sally cried out.

The nurse turned to Jack. 'You'll have to stay here; we can only allow one visitor at a time.' She led Sally into one of the two little rooms reserved for very ill patients.

There was no window, no daylight. Just a small box of a room with the familiar tubes, the ventilator, the monitor screens. Her darling Phil was lying helpless in this inhuman box, surrounded by machinery. Tears blurred her eyes, but she kept them in check. She had to be there for him. She looked at the bed, saw Phil's massive head shaking from side to side. She knew at once that the nurse was right. He wasn't getting better; these were his death throes.

She bent over the bed, by his ear. 'It's Sally, Phil. I'm here, my darling.'

'... ant ... Sal ... portant...'

'It's me, Phil; Sally. I'm right here beside you.' She took his hand, almost twice the size of hers, and squeezed it.

His eyelids moved upwards, the intense blue of his irises focused on her. 'Sal! My Sal!'

'I'll always be here for you, Phil. Don't leave me, get better for me. I'll look after you. I'll always look after you.' Her lips brushed his hair, his forehead.

'... stake, Sal. Wrong ... know wrong ... can't ...'

'A mistake? You're saying there's been a mistake?' He was trying to tell her something, something terribly important.

'Ss ... got it wrong ... istake ... mustn't ...'

'Who got it wrong, Phil?'

'... said ss ... *can't* ... siss ... be wrong...' His head came forward as he tried to get up. '... stake...'

'I'll try to guess what you're saying, Phil. Squeeze my hand if I'm right. Someone made a mistake?'

She could feel nothing at first, but his eyes told her he was trying to communicate. Then she understood; she wasn't with the man she'd known, the strong giant of a man who'd had to hold himself in check every time he touched her. He was so weak now; if he was trying to press her hand, he'd only be able to manage a tiny signal.

'Was that someone Bruce – Bruce Traggard?'

She waited, but there was no squeeze. Heavy lids had covered his eyes again, and Phil lay still. Her heart thumped as she worried in case he'd gone back into his coma. But one thing she'd been right about. Something was wrong, and Phil knew what it was. He could help her find out, help her avenge him.

'Who was it, Phil? Who made the mistake?'

'Can't ... siss ... wrong...' His eyes had opened again, he stared at her. 'Sal; love Sal.'

She couldn't help herself, she clasped the big hand in hers and kissed it, held it against her cheek. Would she be able to bear the emptiness of never feeling his flesh on hers again? The tears were falling now, she gasped for breath, steeled herself. She only had minutes to find out! An S-sound. Apart from Bruce, whose name had S in it?

'Joss? Are you talking about Joss Black, Phil? Did Joss do this to you?'

The large blue eyes were open, rolled back, too much white already showing. There was no response to the word Joss.

He turned his head to her. 'Mummm ... wrong ... can't ... siss ... wrong...'

'Your mother? Your mother got it wrong?'

A small, slight squeeze.

'Love Sal ... love ... Sal ...' His eyelids were fluttering.

'I love you too, Phil; I love you so very much.'

She tried to think; she *had* to think. What could his *mother* have got wrong? Something to do with going to the United States? Was he saying US? Is that what 'siss' meant?

She felt a draught stir her hair as the door behind her opened wide. 'It's Mummy, darling! I came as quickly as I could.' Helen Thompson swept into the room, moved to the other side of the bed. 'How is he?' she mouthed at Sally. 'Did he speak?'

Even through her anger that his mother had interrupted them, Sally could sense Phil leaving her. He lay quite still, without even the tiniest movement.

She pressed his hand to her lips one last time, then gave up. She walked, unsteadily, out of the room and allowed herself to be led away. She didn't even look back. But she thought back. She *knew* now, knew she'd been right all along. Phil had told her that someone had done something to him. And that it had been a mistake.

10

Ethel Dunstan always made sure she was the one to collect the post as soon as it arrived, just in case *he* got in touch. Not that her husband or the boys would ever read a letter addressed to her, but she didn't want any awkward questions. She shuffled through the day's post and breathed a sigh of relief; it was OK.

The circular with the bland blue printing on the white envelope was right on top of the other mail. She gave the window envelope a cursory glance and was about to throw it out when her eye was caught by the large lettering on the envelope:

PERSONAL

PRIZE WIN NOTIFICATION

This is NOT a Circular – Urgent Reply Required from:
Mrs Ethel Margaret Dunstan
Gates End
Collington Gardens
Exeter, Devonshire

She gasped, a frisson of anticipatory pleasure running down her spine. Had she really won a prize, or was this just the usual junk-mail rubbish? She scanned the envelope again. It was addressed to her, and it spelled out, without any doubt, that it was a prize *win* notification – whoever had sent it was breaking the law unless she really *had* won something.

'Post come already?' she heard her husband ask as he shuffled down the stairs in his slippers. She wondered whether he put the shuffle on as part of playing out his persona of absent-minded professor. It was becoming quite irritating.

She made the effort to stop herself getting riled. He always dressed before breakfast, but he didn't change into his shoes until just before he left the house. It was a sort of fetish of his; he made the boys keep to it as well. 'Anything interesting, or just the usual assortment of bills we can't keep up with?'

She didn't trust herself to speak. If she had won anything she wanted to keep it to herself, at least for the time being. Instead of answering, she laughed. It sounded false to her, but it was the best she could manage.

'I take it that means no. Breakfast ready?'

'Just going to put the kettle on,' she called, escaping to the kitchen and slipping the envelope into the drawer in which she kept her recipe slips. She cleared her throat and turned to face Nathaniel. 'Quite right – bills, a pre-Christmas sale brochure from High and Mighty for Edward, a calendar from your garage.'

'Nothing from Dorling Kindersley?'

'Who?'

'The publishers who were interested in a multimedia text. First in the field, you know. They wined and dined me last week. They're after a CD-ROM in psychology for sixth-form students...'

'A school book, d'you mean? I thought you were head of a university department!'

Nathaniel Dunstan was a tall, gaunt man whose hair had turned a dull grey at thirty-five and was now sliding into a slow decline towards white. It seemed to Ethel that everything he wore looked grey, even when he chose blue or light-brown for the corduroys he favoured. His eyes, too, reflected grey instead of the blue colour they must once have been. He clicked false teeth into his mouth and sat down at the kitchen table, spreading *The Times* in front of himself. One leg was crossed over the other; it swung up and down in rhythm to the buzzing of the fifties' vintage refrigerator.

'An academic salary doesn't stretch that far. At any rate we're always short, and we do have to think about retirement.'

She looked away. He was accusing her of spending too much money again. 'You mean you can still be promoted?'

'What? Nothing to do with the university. I'm talking about providing material. The field is just beginning. If you hit the jackpot on one of those educational CD-ROMs for schools, you can make a fortune. And I know just how to do it for my field – psychology, in case you'd forgotten.'

One of his silly jokes. Was he becoming suspicious about the money? She'd taken enormous trouble to work the figures out just right but, in spite of his vague air, Nathaniel could be quite sharp. 'That sounds very nice, dear.'

'Nice? Not exactly the right adjective. A contract like that would be sensational! But the work itself would be very demanding, take up a great deal of time.'

Did he mean time away from home? That wouldn't worry her in the slightest. It would be all to the good to keep him occupied.

'Not that that would worry you,' he said, apparently well aware of her thoughts. 'Give you more time for the damned good works, I suppose.' He chuckled, good-humoured. 'Charity doesn't begin at home in this house.'

'I hope you're not saying I neglect you.'

He looked up from the paper. 'Something wrong, dear? Trouble with the boys?'

'Everything's fine; just eat your breakfast.' She plonked some cereal in front of him and poured his coffee. She had to humour him, sound amiable. He'd be off soon, and Edward and Harold had already left. They got their own early breakfast; Edward was always out at the crack of dawn to practise basketball, and Harold had to make an early start for his job as a motorcycle courier. They left home long before the post arrived. She'd have the place to herself as soon as Nathaniel went off for his first class.

The moment the front door closed Ethel pulled out the printed letter and began to read.

Dear Mrs Dunstan,
This letter is our official confirmation that you have won a TAX-FREE CASH *Prize with Draw Number: 2986937 that our recent Postcard advised was selected especially for you in the* NEW £250,000.00 CASH MATCH *Prize Draw.*

Could she really have won some money? The heavy weight of the secret she'd been shouldering for so many years began to ease, even at the idea of some lessening of the burden. She hadn't realised how much it had been taking out of her. £150 a month was a lot of money when you had to find it from a housekeeping allowance which was already fairly modest. Not Nathaniel's fault; he was as generous as he could be. But a professor at a provincial university, even a head of department, didn't earn an enormous salary.

She read on eagerly.

To get your Cash Prize simply complete the enclosed Prize Claim. You will be sent the full winning amount your Lucky Number has won within 5 days of the Prize Claim Expiry Date – 21st November 1993. YES, YOUR WINNER'S NUMBER: 2986937 has DEFINITELY WON a CASH PRIZE.

She couldn't think when she had entered a prize draw. What did it matter? Apparently she'd won something. The smallest amount, it seemed, was one of ten prizes of £500; there were also five of £1,000, and one each of £5,000, £10,000 and £30,000. And if she sent the claim form back right away she would double whatever she'd won!

She took the form letter through to the living room and sat down on her sofa. She poured herself a Scotch; this called for a celebration. Thank God Nathaniel wasn't the curious type. She'd keep her win very quiet; open a bank account at another bank, be able to pay that £150 as a cheque without worrying herself sick about transferring cash every single month.

Tears came into her eyes. Even £500 – and she could make that £1,000 by answering right away – would get her off the hook at Oxfam. She hadn't liked the way that new Mrs Hopkins had implied her collection funds had been on the low side.

'Your area is in one of the best parts of Exeter, isn't it, Mrs Dunstan?' she'd asked. That remark had sounded very snide to Ethel.

'That doesn't mean I can get together more,' she'd defended herself. 'Very often the poorer areas are the ones that come up with the biggest donations.'

True, as a matter of fact; but not quite the reason her

funds were so low. She'd had to top up from her collections for some time now. If only that awful woman knew how much she longed not to do that!

Tears of self-pity mingled with relief were spilling on to the piece of paper now. She took another gulp of whisky, blinked. Suddenly the figures of the date stood out and winked at her: *Reply by 21st November 1993*. It was October 1994.

There was no prize, small or large. Was it a hoax, a cruel, horrible hoax? Who would do such a thing?

And then she knew. Without even pulling out the other sheet, the one she knew she'd find in the reply-paid envelope. What was worse was that she was only too aware that the lurid words and figures cut from colour magazines would spell out an increased demand. She felt a numbing cold in her fingers. How was she going to pay more?

The paper slid out of her hand and to the floor. Nausea choked her, her breathing became laboured, she thought she was about to retch. She lay back on the sofa, the only comfort being that Nathaniel wasn't there to witness this. Deep groans of pain, of anguish, heaved through her body. It was half an hour before she could bring herself to read the blackmail demand.

She poured herself another large whisky – she'd have to find the cash for another bottle, but she could not do without it. She slipped her shaking hands into the envelope which had only so recently delighted her, removed the return envelope and fished out the piece of paper she knew would be inside.

She unfolded it; paste-ups from magazines, just as she'd guessed. She scanned them anxiously to find the new amount. There were no numerals on the sheet. The hideous words were there, as always before, but they were just words:

STOP IT

the first line screamed at her.

STOP THE RELATIONSHIP
BETWEEN YOUR DARLING EDWARD
AND FRESHMAN PETRA JONES
NOW – ON PAIN OF YOU-KNOW-WHAT

She frowned, reading it over and over again. What could it mean? Who was this Petra Jones, and why shouldn't she be seeing Edward?

It didn't make sense. Perhaps it wasn't meant for her after all. Was someone mixing up her husband and her son? Could Nathaniel be having an affair with a new student?

There was no mistake; the grinning cartoon face at the side, her blackmailer's hallmark, was leering at her.

She poured herself another Scotch, and then another one. With trembling fingers she punched in Nora Hopkins' number.

'I'm shorry Mrs Hop-kins. I jusht can't come in today. Terrible headache...'

Even she could hear the slurred sounds she was breathing into the telephone. She made an enormous effort to control herself, belatedly put her handkerchief in front of her nose.

'...Some short of cold, I think. A temperature. Sho sorry.'

It was too late. 'That's perfectly all right, Mrs Dunstan. I've been meaning to get in touch with you for some time now. I don't think we shall be requiring your help in the future. Mrs MacMillan is happy to take over.'

The phone clicked off. 'Bloody bitch!' Ethel gulped down another helping of undiluted whisky and stared at the note in her hand. What was she going to do? What the hell was she going to do? Even bumbling Nathaniel would begin to smell a rat if she took the whole of £150 out of her allowance every month.

What did the blackmailing bastard want now? Wasn't she paying him his bloody pound of flesh? She couldn't pay it any more; she had no means of making money. And how the hell was she supposed to control her son's love life? She didn't even know he had one!

11

It was as though Edward and Petra were drawn to each other by some sort of spell. They couldn't believe how much they had in common. Not just their looks, though they were both tall, fair-haired and light-skinned. Edward's eyes were the deepest sapphire blue, matched by one of Petra's in a lighter shade, while the other was a tawny-owl brown. The unusual feature gave her a look of artless innocence which Edward could not help but tell her he found enchanting.

'What d'you do in your spare time?' she asked him, smiling up at him in spite of wearing heels.

He laughed. 'I don't have spare time, but I fit in two hobbies: one is training my dog Bradley. Would you believe it? He helps me practise basketball. He and I have at least one session a day.'

'How clever of you.'

'Clever of Brad as well. He's a collie. That's a working breed – the sort they use for helping with rounding up sheep. D'you watch *One Man and His Dog*, by any chance?' He'd always felt that he and Bradley matched that image.

'Occasionally. It's not what you'd call my favourite programme.'

'My other love is listening to music. I find time for that by having it on when I'm studying.' He sighed. 'A sort of blasphemy, I suppose.'

She looked sideways at him. 'Pop?'

A beat as he tried to hide his disappointment. 'Well, sort of. Good for dancing, I suppose. Not really for listening.' He saw no point in pretending; if there were areas on which they didn't agree, they'd have to face them. 'My passion is Baroque – Vivaldi, Bach, Handel. That sort of thing. I don't suppose...'

Her eyes had begun to shine. 'What about Albinoni? That's the one I really go for. Corelli, too.' She almost stumbled over the names in her eagerness.

He put his arm around her waist, pulling her to him. 'And Pachelbel – that marvellous Gigue.'

'Not forgetting Monteverdi!'

'There's a concert at the Great Hall. Like to go?'

'Monteverdi, you mean?'

'The very one.'

'I'd love to, Ed.' He could sense the hesitation. 'It's just that I feel terrible about leaving Sally to it. She's been even worse since Phil died.'

He frowned. He was finding Sally's behaviour a strain. He also missed his friend.

'She sits in our room replaying those last two tapes of Phil, time and again. It's kind of crazy; I'm getting really worried about her.' Concerned eyes looked at him. 'Could I possibly ask her to come along?'

The reason for Phil's death had remained a mystery. The doctors had not been interested in seeing video-tapes. The sports-injury consultant Jack retained for his players – the foremost man in the country – had ordered a whole battery of tests. None of them had resulted in any conclusive diagnosis. In the end, the doctors hadn't been able to come up with a better reason than the one they'd mentioned in the first place: toxic shock syndrome.

'But she keeps telling you she can't find anything remotely suspicious on the tapes. Why's she so convinced there was something fishy?'

'I've given up trying to work it out.' Petra's sigh was a mixture of understanding and resignation. 'We don't even discuss it any more. As soon as I walk into the room she turns the recorder off and pretends to be doing some work.'

'Poor little thing. The grief, I suppose. Must have affected her brain.'

'Permanently, d'you think?'

'I'm sure she'll be better soon.' They walked along in silence for a few moments. 'If anyone can get her round, it's you. She's lucky to have you as a friend.' He stopped, bent down and kissed her full on the lips, ignoring the fact that they were walking towards the library, in full view of students and staff alike. 'I think we *should* ask her to join us. I'll get three tickets.'

Petra unlinked herself from Edward as they approached the library building. 'Sally is absolutely convinced someone got at him.'

He frowned. 'But there was no motive. It just doesn't make any sense. That theory about Joss Black won't do. We may be competitive, but if we killed off our opponents, there just wouldn't be any players left!'

'I said that – she insists the stakes were high enough in this particular case.'

He shook his head. 'Won't wash. And what about the inquest? Their findings were quite clear. Phil scraped his leg the week before; that's when the bacterium must have got into his bloodstream. *Staphylococcus areus* is very common; Phil wasn't infected by anything deadly or unusual.'

'So Phil was particularly susceptible?'

His eyes had gone empty. He didn't like to think too much about the fact that Phil had, for the many years he'd known him, shrugged off all kinds of abrasions, bumps and sprains. 'Must have been to that particular bug, I suppose. Bad luck when most people who carry the thing around are quite immune.'

'Apart from that, I suppose Sally thinks Bruce should have spotted something was wrong and stopped Phil playing. He did have that odd redness all over his face and neck. Even I noticed that, and I'd only just met him.'

Edward's shoulders sagged; the memory of his friend's death always made him feel almost ashamed to be alive. 'We didn't exactly need degrees in medicine to know he had a temperature. Classic signs of a bad cold, or even flu. As you know, Bruce didn't ignore it, he took all the right precautions. Phil's pulse rate was within normal limits, so Bruce thought he was OK, in spite of the rash and the conjunctivitis. Sally was lucky he didn't kiss her.'

She stopped abruptly, took his hand. 'You noticed that, did you? For God's sake don't mention it to her, will you? She thinks that was because someone got at Phil, told him something ghastly about her.'

'That's absurd. What on earth did she think that could possibly have been?'

Petra shrugged. 'No specifics.'

'Let's face it, Pet. She's paranoid about it. He'd have told me if there'd been anything.'

'I know that, Ed. I keep telling her that. But she insists it's more than negligence. The inquest quashed even that.'

'They did everything possible. They started out with an ECG, and the results ruled out a heart attack. Then they suspected toxic shock syndrome. They started in on antibiotics and rehydrating fluids. They even crashed huge amounts of immunoglobulin into him in hopes. What else could they have done?'

'It's the shock as well as the grief, I suppose. He was such a giant of a man, he must have seemed invincible. I've been wondering whether she needs to go and see someone.'

'A therapist, you mean?'

'Therapist, counsellor, yes. I'm getting really worried about her.'

They agreed on that, as they agreed on everything else – food, clothes, holiday destinations, the type of house they'd like to live in. It seemed as though they'd been cast in the same mould. A perfect match.

'You know,' Petra said, as they were walking down The Queen's Drive, 'I hardly like to mention I specially enjoy Thai food. I might find out you don't!'

He twirled her round in delight. 'This is getting ridiculous. I adore it. But perhaps we shouldn't jump to conclusions about some special bond between us. Jack Oliver introduced me to Thai cooking; it's one of his big enthusiasms.'

Petra smiled. 'Fair enough. He's taken my family out a couple of times as well. Drove us all the way to an inn in Stedham. Supposed to be one of the first places to start serving Thai food in this country, and one of the best.'

'Well,' he laughed, 'at least I haven't been there.'

It seemed only natural that Edward should invite Petra to meet his family even though he'd only met her three weeks before. They felt they'd known each other for years, had grown into a comfortable relationship. It wasn't simply that they were in love – although their emotions were deep enough – it was also that they became convinced that their marriage was inevitable.

'I mentioned my taking you home to Dad last night,'

Edward said nonchalantly the next day, when they met for lunch in the canteen. 'He sounded pleased; said he already knows you quite well.'

His father had commented, even before Edward told him he knew Petra, about a particularly beautiful freshman in one of his classes. His attention had been drawn to her because she was so demure. 'Girls with her looks are often arrogant and cynical. What saves Petra from either of these shortcomings is her differently coloured irises, I think. Given her a bit of an inferiority complex, I suppose.' He'd smiled at his son. 'I brought it out into the open in class. She responded very well indeed.'

'You're lucky to have such a good teacher for a father. I think he's got quite an unusual method of getting his points across.'

'You think he's good?'

Petra nodded. 'What I particularly like is the way he involves us, gets us to give our opinions. Not just a dull lecture. It's the participation which makes it work for me.'

'He does maintain that's the way to do it. Apparently he thinks you ask intelligent questions. Anyway, he said he'd be delighted if I brought you to Sunday lunch.'

'What about your mother?'

'You'll love Mum. You and she have a lot in common. For a start, she's very good-looking, just like you.'

'Is she quite tall?'

'You mean, did I get my height from her? Not really. She's about your height, her hair's darker, but that's because she's older. I think it was your sort of colour when she was young. That's what the photos show. And she has this marvellous flair for clothes, and knows just how to wear them. She's even been mistaken for a fashion model.'

'What does she do?'

106

'Works for Oxfam. Indefatigable; collects money, goes and picks up clothes and bric-à-brac from people's houses. Dad always says we don't see as much of her as the lowliest charity case! She's wonderfully caring.'

Edward drove Petra to his parents' house in the Citroën Dolly. Parking was always difficult, but he squeezed the little car expertly into a space no BMW or Rover could get into. Professor Dunstan must have been looking out for them because, before Edward could get his key into the lock, his father had opened the door. He smiled at them genially, and waved them in. Wisps of grey hair haloed a round of pink scalp, faded blue eyes skimmed over them, benign. His corduroy trousers had taken on the shape of his body, and the worn tweed jacket had leather patches on the elbows. He didn't smoke a pipe; he'd given that up some years before at his wife's request, Edward had told Petra. But he still chewed on an empty Meerschaum in the right side of his mouth. He was the image of the absent-minded professor.

Ethel Dunstan was standing by the marble mantelpiece in her gracious living room. Late autumn had brought a cold east wind. An open log fire was crackling in the fireplace, a magnificent fireguard assuring safety. Petra saw a dog spreadeagled on a sheepskin hearth rug, camouflaged by the colouring. The beloved Bradley, she guessed, then saw Ethel move, her heel catching on the dog's tail. Bradley jumped up, producing a flurry of barking after an initial squeal.

'What's that animal doing indoors?' a shrill voice yelled, entirely at odds with the image Edward's mother presented. Her tall figure was as slim as Petra's, discreetly dressed in a slate-blue Jean Muir which showed her delicate features and sapphire-blue eyes off to perfection. Petra realised with a shock that it was quite obvious that Edward was this woman's son. Whatever made her and Edward look alike did not preclude his taking after his mother. Was this the Oedipus complex at work, the son marrying a girl just like his mother?

Ethel stared down at the dog with distaste, then up at Edward. 'You know he isn't allowed in here.'

'Sorry, Mum. He must have slipped in while I wasn't looking.' Edward whistled to his dog, opened the french windows into the garden and shooed him out. Then he came back to stand protectively beside Petra.

Exquisitely manicured hands were stretched out in greeting. 'Sorry about that.' Ethel's voice had changed to a careful timbre, though Petra could hear the irritation just behind it. 'Bradley's a working dog; he has no business in my living room.'

'Edward's told me about him. He looked sweet.'

'Sweet?' She gave a kind of neighing laugh. 'I suppose. So glad you could come. Edward's talked of nothing else since Phil's girlfriend introduced you to each other.' The voice was now gentle and melodious, the perfect hostess.

'It's lovely to meet you.'

Ethel had come closer. By the way she inclined her head and peered Petra could see that she was somewhat short-sighted. She was within a yard now, looking intent. A moment later her nostrils had dilated, her eyes grown hard.

'You have one eye blue and one brown!' The soft tone had returned to a shrill inflection, the languid movements to a frozen stillness as she stared at Petra.

For the first time since knowing Edward she felt at a loss. Her normal response to this remark was that she'd noticed. She restrained herself, and merely smiled. What was she supposed to do? Wear two different contacts, coloured to make her eyes look the same?

'Really, Mother. You make it sound like a defect. It's one of Petra's special charms. Wouldn't you say so, Dad?'

'I would indeed. Delightful, quite enchanting. Never been lucky enough to come across it before I met Petra.'

'It's a genetic defect.' Ethel's voice sounded harsh now, as though she'd found Petra out in some criminal activity.

'My dear...'

'It isn't hereditary,' Petra managed to say, a mixture of shyness and anger making her sound hesitant. 'Just something that happens now and again. And it doesn't affect vision.'

'There's no need to defend yourself, Petra,' Nathaniel broke in. 'Even if your vision *were* affected, I know some other people who have a problem in that line.' He looked pointedly at his wife. 'Can't see more than three feet ahead, and even that is blurred!'

'Myopia is a common condition; everyone knows about it.' Ethel's voice was cold. 'You just said you'd never come across two differently coloured eyes before.'

Petra could see Nathaniel's body stiffen as he moved the pipe-stem in his mouth in and out in agitation. 'Not that uncommon; the French even have an adjective for it.' He took the empty pipe out of his mouth and banged it against the side of the grate. He took at least half a minute to do so; a trick she'd noticed him use in class, perhaps to cover up his search for a forgotten word. By the time he'd finished, his face had taken on a determined expression. '*Vairon*, they call it. And I can vouch for Petra's ability to see. Not only physically; she has considerable psychological insight. No problems at all.'

Ethel moved away from her husband, fumbling uneasily with a window which she tried to open. Nathaniel walked over to help her. 'Well, of course, you always know best,' she muttered, pushing him out of the way. 'I wouldn't have thought being a professor of psychology qualified you to pronounce on faulty genes.'

Nathaniel Dunstan drew himself up to his full height which, though nothing like as impressive as his son's, amounted to a respectable six foot. 'I think too much is made of differences. That is the whole point of natural selection. Without discrepancies we cannot progress.'

The look of withering dismissal Ethel directed at him stopped him short. He coughed, opened his mouth, inserted the pipe-stem again, moved it to a more comfortable position and smiled at Petra. 'How about a sherry, my dear? Medium or dry?'

She felt near tears, reminded of what Sally had always said about Phil's mother's attitude to her. Ethel's hostility would force Edward into a choice. Petra's eyes were on him, wondering whether he was affected, whether he'd lose interest in her.

Apparently not. He put his arm around her, hugged her to himself and glared at his mother. 'If you carry on like that, Petra will just want to leave before she's even sat down. What on earth does the colour of her irises matter? I didn't bring her here to be treated like a brood mare.'

'She's the first girl you've brought to meet us. I would have thought it was significant.'

His face was white, his eyes darkened with unaccustomed anger, glinting with something that suggested his devastation. 'Have we got any tomato juice?'

'You mean she wants a Bloody Mary?'

'I'm sure Petra can answer for herself, Mother. I shall be driving her back; I thought I'd stick to non-alcoholic drinks.'

'That's a new one.' The bitterness in the tone shocked Petra. Edward had never mentioned having any problems with his mother.

He stared at her. 'You know I never drink and drive.'

'You've only just been given that car. You did when you rode your bike.' She turned to Petra. 'Well?'

'If you have some Perrier...' Her voice was husky as she struggled to steady it.

'No problem, my dear. I'll go and get it.' Nathaniel put his hand on Petra's shoulder and squeezed it. 'You'd like a slice of lemon in it, and some ice?'

'If it's no trouble.'

'Nothing is too much trouble for such a lovely girl.'

As soon as he left the room Ethel's eyes seemed to disappear in a thin line, her lips drawn up into a snarl. 'I don't know whether you're aware that once a person has a genetic mutation, their offspring are also at risk.'

Petra's head pulled back sharply. 'There's absolutely no evidence for that. Mutation is the way new characteristics come into being. We all have them.'

'Precisely. And they aren't always benign ones.' The eyes now darted fury. 'Mutation suggests weakness in the whole organism. You can't deny it's there in your case, it's only too obvious. Who knows what changes could take place in your children?'

The noise of a high-octane motorbike drowned out whatever retort Petra might have made. Another young man, shorter than Edward but unquestionably his brother, burst into the room.

'Hello all,' a voice strikingly similar to Edward's boomed out. He engulfed his mother in a hug. 'Hi, Mum.' Then he turned and saw Petra, and winked.

'This is my kid brother Harold, Petra.'

Petra held out her hand, trying to hide her eyes with a smile she did not feel.

'Well, well, it's a real pleasure to meet the perfect Petra at last. I must say, my brother's showing unusual taste.'

His mother pushed him away from her. 'You might show some taste yourself, Harold. For goodness sake change into something decent before you join us for lunch.'

'Did I do something to upset your mother?'

Edward was driving the Dolly with grave intensity. He put his hand over Petra's. 'Nothing that I could see. I don't know what came over her.'

'It was obviously hate at first sight.' The beginning of a sob was in her voice; she cleared her throat and went on, 'I don't want to be the cause of any friction between you and your parents, Edward. Perhaps we should cool it for a bit.'

The car surged forward as Edward's large foot pushed down on the accelerator. 'I just don't know what's got into everybody. Bruce Traggard came over to see me the other day; he's never done anything like that before. More or less ordered me not to have a girlfriend. He didn't mention your name or anything, but presumably that's what he had in mind.' He pulled his hand away as they were coming towards a crowded roundabout and put his foot on the brake as a car swerved in front of him.

Petra said nothing. It seemed quite clear that the people round Edward did not approve of her. What had she done? Or was it that her background, like Sally's, wasn't good enough? Her father was only a small cog at Jorncy's, in a well-paid job, but a very mundane one. The Joneses lived in a pleasant house in Hampstead which, though not a period gem like the Dunstans' place, was larger. Petra never wanted for anything and her mother didn't need to have a job. She'd often mentioned how running a big house, with only a daily to do the rough, was quite enough to keep anyone occupied.

'Perhaps your mother thinks I wouldn't quite fit in socially.'

112

'Socially? You mean she thinks you aren't good enough for me?' He laughed. 'That can't be it. She may be bad tempered, but she isn't a snob.'

'Your father's a professor; mine's got a very ordinary job.'

'I hope you know nothing like that makes any kind of difference to me,' Edward said, putting back his hand and pressing down on hers. 'And I told Bruce what he could do with his suggestions. He said in that case I can say goodbye to any real prospects in basketball.'

'Oh, Ed! You mustn't get on the wrong side of him just because of me. You do enjoy the game.'

'Not all that much. Not nearly as much as your company. And I'm not keen enough to spend my whole time on it. I'm rather interested in my work, in fact.'

'So how did you leave it with Bruce in the end?'

'I said he could count me out.'

She felt a thrill, felt love for Edward well up in her. 'And?'

'He backpedalled. Said maybe I could see a little less of you, I wasn't practising nearly as much as I should, all that kind of stuff. I stuck to my guns, said take it or leave it. Apparently he was still taking it. Same applies to my mother, in my view.'

12

'I can smell roast beef,' Jack Oliver said, breathing deep, as soon as Louise opened her front door to him. He knew his smile would melt her, even though she was probably resentful that he hadn't warned her he was turning up for lunch. This was deliberate; he could easily have phoned through on his mobile. But he wanted his visit to be a surprise. He wanted to check what he already suspected was true. David, he knew, would be spending the morning at the Youthco Sports Hall, North London's latest answer to keeping the years at bay.

'Jack! Lovely to see you.' Her large mouth broadened into a genuine smile, then the corners tucked themselves in and turned it into a severe line as she remembered. 'We weren't expecting you today. Why didn't you ring?'

'I know, I know. Last-minute decision; I've got so much paperwork I should be doing. Anyway, it does stop you making a fuss on my behalf. You know I like to take pot luck.' He stepped quickly into the hall, avoiding a kiss. 'I've brought you a small offering.' He flourished a huge bunch of red roses from behind his back, then winked. 'And this is our little secret. Dewi'll never guess – he never did have much of a sense of smell.' He handed her a bottle of Dior's Poison. 'I know it's the right scent for you.' The snake-green presentation box matched Louise's alligator heels. He thought the name of the perfume suited her as well. He often wondered how David not only stood her, but seemed to enjoy living with her. As far as Jack was concerned, she was a calculating, money-grubbing bitch.

Louise's tall, somewhat angular figure was exquisitely wrapped in a cream silk Caroline Charles number. Her hair was carefully styled, her somewhat plain face made up to bring out its best points. His eyes swept over her without emotion. Credit where credit was due; she did her best with what she'd got.

She gave him a radiant smile, indicating a gracious forgiveness. It didn't reach her eyes, so he knew she wasn't fooled. But the muddy brown irises, normally so cold, had softened at the large bouquet, had taken in the roses were the colour of love. Her thin lips relaxed as she accepted the gifts. 'Oh Jack, they're lovely. You really are a one.'

The size of the bunch of roses was deliberate. Hot-house roses had no thorns, but the prickly leaves, provided there were enough of them, would have the desired effect of thwarting an embrace. He couldn't handle that. He knew she thought of herself as still in love with him, realised she'd only agreed to marry David for the chance it afforded her to be near Jack at times. She'd understood, right from the start, that the two friends would spend a good deal of their leisure time together. In fact, David was a discerning assessor of the basketball hopefuls Jack scoured the country for. Jack and David spent many hours watching videotapes of potential clients for Jack. They viewed them in David's study which was fitted up with state-of-the-art equipment.

'I hope I'm not imposing. You know I'll take you out if you prefer that.' He smiled. 'All you have to do is turn the oven off.' He displayed small, sharp teeth. The last thing he wanted to do was eat a restaurant meal. Louise's cooking, though not as good as the meals he'd so often enjoyed in Megan Jones' house, was reasonably satisfying.

'Of course not. It's my only way of paying you back,' Louise simpered. 'You do so love home cooking. I'll never know why you haven't settled down.' The unspoken implication was always that he regretted losing her to David.

He played on it, repeating himself without a qualm. 'Not quick enough on the uptake, was I? You know Dewi beat me to it.'

It worked every time. She giggled happily, motioned him to follow her into the kitchen, and poured them both a glass of sherry. 'Let's have a slurp,' she said. She was a keen follower of Keith Floyd's gastronomic exuberances, though her interpretation of his flamboyance tended to end in disasters. Jack was grateful to the TV presenter as he sipped at his drink. It allowed him to outmanoeuvre Louise's attempt to edge too close to him.

'All your own fault.' Her voice was girlish, the coquettish fling of her arm unnerving. 'You only had to say the word, you know. I always did prefer fair men.' She tittered, arched her eyebrows, bared large, strong teeth. 'That's why it's such a blessing that Petra couldn't have got her colouring from David.' Louise's face gave nothing away except a sort of twinkle.

So he'd been right; that was the confirmation he'd been waiting for. Louise had always made a point of her preference for fair men, so now he had a shrewd idea where Petra's colouring had come from, and why she didn't look like David. 'Took after you,' he said, gallant. He knew it wasn't true, but it's what she'd want to hear. The china rose complexion and delicate blonde hair bore no resemblance at all to her mother's mouse bleached into synthetic yellow, nor the sallow skin no amount of rouge could give bloom.

She was telling him Petra's father was fair, actually admitting it. He'd always suspected that; anyone who had eyes could tell. There wasn't really any doubt about it. 'She's a lucky girl.'

'Luck had nothing to do with it,' Louise laughed at him. 'I just made sure she wouldn't be dark.' There was a pause as Louise busied herself with the lunch. 'And she's not even grateful for her looks. She'd make such a marvellous model. D'you think she'll ever change her mind?'

He knew it was a bitter disappointment to Louise that Petra refused to be part of his growing 'family' of young people. They seemed to have a lot in common, she'd told him more than once. And they were all high achievers. High earners, he substituted for himself. 'My offer's always open; you know that.'

She downed the glass of sherry and pouted. 'But you won't do anything for David. I know he isn't good-looking, and all that, but I'm suggesting something managerial. They think highly of him at Jorncy.' Heavy lids lowered over the muddy eyes, barely controlled irritation filtered through the penetrating tones. She was always pressing him to find David a place in the Jack Oliver Media Agency.

He overcame the impulse to snap at her. Where the hell did she think her little extras came from? He put as much David's way as he could. With the best will in the world he couldn't overtly employ someone with a speech defect and a cleft palate, even a patched-up one. His firm was, to all intents and purposes, a part of the entertainment industry. All his employees had to be judged in that light. That applied to the ones behind the scenes as well.

He shrugged his relief as he heard the front door crash shut, and Dewi's nasal: 'Hello, sweetheart. I'm back.' His friend walked through to the kitchen. 'Not late, am I?'

'*Shwmae*, Dewi.'

'Jack – it's you! Thought you'd given us a miss this weekend.' He pecked his wife's cheek. She bent away and opened the oven door. 'Bang on time for the roast, though. What a surprise!' He opened the door leading down to his cellar. 'We're almost out of sherry. Time for an order to Harvey's.' He disappeared and returned with a bottle of Amontillado. 'Just back from Bath?'

'How d'you work that out?' Jack's smile turned to a look of furtive speculation.

'That wrapping round the roses. Take it you brought them – shouts *Flower Power, Bath* all over it. In spite of the brilliant way they disguise the lettering by twining roses all round it, I've managed to figure it out. They trying to draw attention by being illegible?'

Dewi was sharp, there was no question about that. He sometimes wondered whether his friend resented Louise's obvious admiration of him. Why would he care? Dewi knew quite well his inclinations weren't sexual. The hormones which had stunted his growth had also stunted his sexual appetite. They hadn't had any adverse effect on his other drives.

'Don't suppose you've seen anything of our little Pet since that dreadful business with Phil Thompson?'

He knew David missed Petra, hungered after news of her. The Joneses had known all about his special interest in Phil, that he'd sponsored him to study at Exeter. It was one of the reasons they'd finally agreed to Petra's choice of university. They were aware that Jack would be a regular visitor to the campus and would keep an eye on her for them.

He brought to mind a picture of his goddaughter. Beautiful, clever, knowing her own mind, yes – but neither little nor pet was an apt description. 'Took her out to tea, as a matter of fact.'

'She jabbers on about how happy she is every time she rings. Not that we're honoured that often, as a matter of fact. You'd think she'd never enjoyed life until she got away from us.' Louise looked quite put out as she basted the roast, turned the potatoes, brought out the Yorkshire pudding pans sizzling with hot fat and poured the prepared mixture into them. She straightened up. 'Goes on about how great it is to share with Sally, but that doesn't sound right. Is there a serious boyfriend, by any chance?' Her voice quivered, perhaps fearful of what he would say.

'She's a very attractive girl . . .'

'I told her, over and over again, to concentrate on her studies. Plenty of time for all that later.'

He knew exactly what that meant. Louise was worried that Petra would not meet the kind of future husband she wanted for her daughter. She didn't think she'd find him among the students at Exeter. She'd never forgiven Petra for turning down the opportunity to go to Oxford.

Jack tossed back the rest of the sherry and laughed. 'She's such a stunner, you're not going to be able to stop her having dozens of boyfriends! Bet half the men at the university are planning how to get her to go out with them.'

'Only half?' David walked out into the hall, opened the living-room door and held it wide for Jack. 'What's wrong with the other half?'

'Didn't get a look in last night, at any rate. I took her out to dinner with one of my specials, the boy who's taking Phil Thompson's place. He's a year younger. He was at Millfield with him.'

Louise, bearing a vase with the roses displayed in it, had followed them into the room. 'You've got another top basketball player at Exeter?' She frowned, the deep-etched lines between her eyes giving her a forbidding air. 'Why do you pick that university?'

'Because they've got three sports halls with basketball courts,' he said promptly. 'So many halls are well-equipped, but not large enough. They have to be the length of four badminton courts; mostly they're only three.'

'*That's* why you're keen on Exeter?'

'Loughborough's even better.' He grinned, seeing the look of horror on her face. 'And I'm talking about Edward Dunstan. His father's a professor at Exeter, so it was the obvious place for him.'

'You mean you introduced him to Petra?' David wanted to know.

'No need. She already knows Edward; Sally took her to that fateful match. That's where they met.'

'Hmm.' Louise busied herself positioning the vase of roses. 'Is Edward very tall, by any chance?' She glanced at David, then away. 'She's always been keen on tall men.'

'Six foot six; three inches shorter than Phil.'

She gave an understanding nod.

'Really short,' David laughed. 'Since when has Petra been interested in basketball?' He refilled their glasses.

'Honestly, David. Not basketball – basketball *players*,' Louise barked. 'That's obvious.'

'Sally was Phil's girlfriend, you know.' Jack drank some sherry, his eyes dull. 'He was the most promising player in the UK.'

'And Petra's fallen for his friend, is that what you're trying to tell us?' Louise looked knowing.

He sipped at the drink and rehearsed what he was going to say. He had to get it right; it was why he'd come to lunch today. High time he told them. He cleared his throat. 'The thing is, Petra and Edward have been seeing quite a bit of each other.' He sipped daintily at his sherry, declining a nibble. He had to watch his weight. 'Bruce Traggard put

121

me wise. He noticed because Edward's missed ball practice a couple of times.'

'You mean they go out together?'

'Perhaps a little more than any of us would wish. They seemed to hit it off right from the start and they're inseparable now, except for lectures.'

'What's he studying?'

'What? Oh, something in the Engineering Department. As I said, his father's on the faculty, so Exeter's the obvious place for him to be. They're a devoted family. There's a younger brother as well, Harold. Motorcycle fanatic. He wanted me to represent him. Not my line, though.' He laughed. 'I think Edward's mother wants to make sure that he doesn't marry for a good few years, and when he does, it must be to the right sort of girl.'

'And Petra isn't? That what you're telling us?' David's face darkened as he tossed back the sherry.

'That's not what I meant.' From what he knew of Ethel Dunstan she could be trusted to oppose the match, but he was hardly likely to tell the Joneses that!

'Petra *has* mentioned a Professor Dunstan – head of the Psychology Department, she told us. She's in one of his classes. That the same one?' David's voice was deep.

'Must be, I suppose.' Jack fiddled with his glass, twirled the liquid in it around. 'Only one Dunstan on the faculty.'

Louise laughed. 'You mean you checked them out because their son is one of your specials?'

Jack's eyes narrowed. She had a habit of being a bit too shrewd. 'Anything wrong with that? It's my job. Now that Phil's gone, Edward could become my top basketball player, quite good enough for the England team.'

'The one you're planning to build from your own clients?'

'Exactly. Put the game on the map in this country.

Anyway, Edward has the talent for it. He just lacks the determination – what I call the killer instinct. It's what you need to win.'

'I think that's true of our Pet,' David said, his face strained. 'I meant to mention it before, Jack. I'd really rather you didn't try to persuade her into modelling against her wishes. She wants to be a research scientist; let her be. What's the good of being a model, anyway? Soon as you lose your looks you've had it.'

'Not at all. A top model's rich by then, so what's it matter? She can do anything she likes with the rest of her life.' Jack tossed back the sherry in his glass and held it out for more. 'Want her doing what you always dreamed about, that the idea?' He stared at David, his eyes cold.

David stepped backwards and knocked against the vase of flowers so that it scattered all over the Wilton.

His wife was outraged. 'You're such a clumsy oaf!' she screamed at him. 'What on earth's got into you?' She took off her apron and dabbed at the water with it.

Jack picked up the flowers. 'No harm done, Louise. It's only water, after all.' He retrieved the vase, and put the roses back into the glass which had not even cracked.

'If she turns out like her father she'll be in trouble,' Louise snapped as she stalked out to the kitchen. By the time she came back she'd recovered her poise.

'More sherry?'

Jack put his glass out. 'As I said, Edward's a fine young man...'

'I don't know how you do it,' she trilled, the flower vase in her hands. 'You always seem to pick the winners.'

David, pouring the sherry, spilled some of it on the highly polished antique coffee table.

'For goodness sake, David!' Louise rushed out of the room again, returning with polish and a cloth.

The last thing he wanted to do was give Louise the impression that Edward would be a good match for Petra. 'Potential winners,' he said, a languid smile around his lips, his eyelids drooping demurely. The thick lashes raised the right response in almost every female breast. And this one was predisposed right from the start. 'It's hard to say about Edward. The physiological tests were brilliant...'

'You mean he's clever academically?'

She had this habit of interrupting him. He covered his annoyance with a laugh. 'That would be IQ tests, I suppose. We don't run those. We've evolved our own physio tests, based on the work that's been carried out at the University of Brighton. Our tests are run every six months or so. That gives us a really good idea of athletic potential, so it helps us to make our selections when the players are still very young. From a purely physical point of view, I mean.'

'Are you talking about strength?'

'Explosive strength, and the way the body's built. Also tells us about jumping and sprinting ability, stamina, disposition of muscles, quite complicated stuff.'

'And Edward's good?'

'All the bodily functions are A1 at present. Will be, for his athletic life.' He put his glass down on the table, waited a few moments, then looked up. 'The thing is, we found something else.'

'You mean there's something wrong with him?'

Jack stood up and walked towards the fireplace, turned round to face them. 'It's strictly confidential. I wouldn't dream of telling anybody else, but I feel I have to let you know. Petra is my goddaughter. I want to stop her getting too involved.'

Louise stared. 'Sounds bad. What on earth's wrong with him?'

'Genetic defect; something which won't show up till middle age. A terrible condition. He's got the gene for Huntington's chorea. That means he'll develop it, and it's hereditary, I'm afraid.'

David was listening now. 'So what is Huntington's, exactly?'

Jack put his hands behind his back. 'Used to be called St Vitus' Dance because, on the physical side, patients develop uncontrolled, involuntary movements. On the mental side there's serious deterioration of the mind.'

'But that sounds terrible!' Louise's mouth had dropped open. 'You mean it's in his family?'

''Fraid so. And apart from the disease itself, there are two things about the condition which are particularly trying. One, it's a dominant gene. That means each child has a fifty-fifty chance of inheriting it from an affected parent.'

'Not good.' David frowned at Jack.

'Tragic, in a way. The disease doesn't usually show itself until middle age; five years either side of forty is normal. So people don't even know whether they've got it or not, and by the time they do they may already have married.'

'Which makes it even worse.' David's face was impassive, but Jack knew he was thinking that he, too, had an hereditary defect. Nothing like as clear-cut, but it was still there, still in his genes. 'So, how do *you* know about it?'

'Bruce Traggard. He was reading through Edward's files and pointed it out to me.'

'You got the file with you?' David asked.

Jack stared at his friend. 'Out in the car. You mean you want to see it?'

David nodded. 'If it's something that's going to concern Petra, I really would. Anyway, I thought we went through Edward Dunstan's file together. Odd we didn't pick it up ourselves. I'm sure I'd have noticed something as drastic as that.'

Jack brought his arms forward again, took another drink of sherry, and moved towards the door. 'That was a long time ago, Dewi. Just after he'd done the initial physiology tests, I expect.'

'I see. I certainly don't remember anything particularly unusual.'

'Didn't know you were that interested. I'll get it for you, if it means that much to you.'

He went out and returned, a thick folder under his arm, and spread it out. 'There we are: physiology reports, academic records, sports records, medical history, genetic testing. The works.'

David looked carefully at Jack. 'This is a new one on me. What made you have the genetic testing done?'

He realised he was on tricky ground; David had a huge chip on his shoulder about the bloody cleft palate. 'Well, you know ... Bruce's idea. He keeps a close eye on all the players. He fusses.'

'It's a separate report. And, by the looks of the paper, much more recent than the latest physiology test.' Jack saw his eyes grow cold. 'I'd have been interested to see this anyway.'

Jack held it up, took a pair of glasses out of his pocket, put them on ostentatiously. 'Getting middle-aged myself,' he laughed. 'Hadn't really examined it to that extent. As I said, Bruce put me on to it.' He held the paper against the physiological tests. 'Quite right – different, more recent. Now you mention it, I don't think we went in for DNA fingerprinting when we took Edward on for the team. That's why it's a later report.'

'So what made Bruce bring it to your attention at this particular time?' David was scrutinising the DNA analysis.

He shrugged. 'He's always very concerned about his players.' Jack held his hand out for the report. Allowing someone else to hold such sensitive material made him nervous. David gave it back.

Louise was sitting on the edge of her chintzy sofa. 'But what does this illness *do* to people?'

Jack sighed. 'It varies; pretty appalling stuff. Mental disturbances are often the first signs – loss of memory, that sort of thing. Many victims suffer from an early kind of senile dementia. And there's the loss of physical control over limbs. Horrific for anyone, but torture for an athlete.'

'But that's just dreadful,' Louise breathed, shock making her voice hoarse. 'Does he know?'

'I doubt it. Unless the disease has made itself felt, even the affected parent may not know.' He looked intently from one to the other. 'And, do remember: you mustn't tell *anyone* what you know. That would be highly unethical, and potentially very damaging to Edward.'

'But...'

'It's not up to me, or anyone else, to interfere in Edward's private life. But I am very concerned about Petra's future.' He stared into the glowing flames in the fireplace. 'I'm afraid Pet thinks she's in love with the boy. You have to stop her marrying Edward Dunstan. It would ruin her life.'

13

It was a tiresome night. Excitement made it impossible for Petra to sleep, and consideration for Sally had stopped her from putting on the light and reading. Daddy had phoned two days before and asked if she'd like to go to Wales with him that weekend.

'I could pick you up first thing Saturday – around seven. The roads will be clear and we'll get there mid-morning. It will give us most of Saturday and Sunday.'

She'd found it hard to speak.

'Pet, *cariad*, are you there?'

When her voice did come it was breathless. 'Yes, Daddy, I'm here. Visit your family, you mean?'

'If you'd like that.' He'd sounded diffident, as though he could hardly believe anyone would be interested in such an idea.

'You know I've always wanted to, Daddy! I'll be waiting for you outside Mardon. No problems about parking or waking anyone.'

She folded her pillow into a sausage shape and pushed it under her neck. Pictures of the village of Pengwyn, with its six slate-roofed cottages hugging the steep hillside road to Llandrindod Wells, came into her mind. She imagined a bustling family of seven sitting around their kitchen table, eating porridge and Welsh rarebit. They were as her father had painted them in stories he'd told her over and over again, as soon as she was able to understand them. And yet he'd never taken her. In spite of that she was sure she'd find a warm, voluble, hard-working family who'd welcome her.

At least she had the genealogy off pat. She recited it to herself, she didn't want to get it wrong when she got there. Her grandparents were Megan and Dylan Jones. They'd brought their family down from further north, from somewhere in Snowdonia. The slate mine in which Dylan, and his father and grandfather before him, had worked all their lives had closed down.

That's when the family had moved to mid-Wales, a few miles south of the Victorian spa of Llandrindod Wells. There were just the two children at the time: David and Gwyneth.

'Why did they go there?' she'd asked her father. Her mother was the one who read her fairy tales; her father told her stories of Wales instead. She'd always assumed that if the wicked mine owner had taken her grandfather's livelihood, her father would see to it that there'd be a happy ending.

'They wanted somewhere with a good hospital for Gwyneth and me. To help repair our lips, you see. Gwyneth's was very bad; she had to have a lot of plastic surgery done on it.'

The frog would turn into a prince, the ugly duckling into a swan. 'Is Llandrindod Wells a big town?'

He'd smiled. 'Tiny, compared to London. But there was a good oral surgeon there. So much better than sending the poor girl away all the time. And Lland'od High School – we always shorten Llandrindod to Lland'od – had very high standards. They couldn't have done better for us.'

Her father David was the eldest. Then there were two girls, Gwyneth and Bronwen. Such lovely names; she rolled them round her tongue. The second boy, Huw, was twelve years younger than David and then there was Angharad, only in her early twenties now and still at home. More like a sister than an aunt, Petra had thought to herself, a thrill at the thought making her shiver.

The first, grey streaks of dawn showed lines of light around the curtained window. She could dress in the dark – she'd packed her overnight bag the evening before – and wait downstairs.

'Off already?' Sally asked, her dark head turned. 'Might as well turn on the light.' She pushed her covers off and sat on the side of her bed.

'Sorry. I did try not to wake you.'

'I wasn't asleep.' Her voice sounded weary. 'I can't get rid of these stomach cramps. I was afraid *I'd* wake *you* with all that rumbling.'

'Oh, Sally. You'll make yourself ill, worrying about what happened to Phil.'

'It's just some sort of stomach bug. I'll see you Sunday night, then.' The voice which had once been so eager, so full of life, was strained, the words punctuated by deep breathing. She lay back on her bed.

'Will you be all right on your own, Sal? Shall I ask Daddy if you can come along?'

A hand floated in the air. 'The last thing I need is a long car trip. I'll get some rest. Be fine by the time you get back.'

Petra pulled the covers over her friend and turned out the light. 'See you,' she said as she closed the door behind her.

'You've made good time, Daddy. I've only just come down.'

'All ready, then?' her father greeted her. 'Don't forget,

now. I've booked us into The Country House Hotel; thought we might have a bit of a holiday, take the family out to dinner. Did you bring a dress?'

'Yes.' She tried not to show her disappointment. 'Can't we stay in the cottage?'

'Don't think so, Pet. You'd have to share with your Aunt Angharad. Only two up, two down, you know.'

'That would be such fun, Daddy!'

'Not for her, maybe. Nor me, come to that. I'd have to bed down in the front room.'

Petra's face fell. She hadn't thought of it from their angle. Perhaps her father was also thinking of the stories her mother had always told her, the ones she'd never believed. Louise had talked about Gwyneth's first visit to London, over and over again, harking back to the time when she and David had just met. And Gwyneth had been horrible to Louise, just because she was English.

'They're Welsh Nationalists, you know,' Louise had said, her nostrils widening, her eyes hard. 'Real fanatics. Went in for burning down incomers' cottages – and worse.'

'Daddy as well?'

Louise had hesitated about that. 'Well ... he was just a child, sixteen at the outside. It was the chap his sister married, mainly. Ian something-or-other.'

She knew; she knew because David had told her about Gwyneth marrying Ian Davies, one of his best friends. They were a trio, he and Ian and Uncle Jack. 'Davies. Aunt Gwyneth married Ian Davies.'

Her mother had looked at her with suspicion. 'Know all about it, do you? Your father's been telling you all kinds of fairy tales, I suppose.'

'He's told me about what he did when he was young.' She'd wondered whether to go on, but she badly wanted to

know. 'You said "and worse". What's worse than arson,
Mummy? That puts people's lives in danger.'

'He burgled the places first, then set fire to them to hide
what he'd been up to. Not just political, you see. A
common or garden criminal.'

'Are you saying Daddy's family are crooks, Mummy?'

Louise had looked worried at that. 'Well, not all of them,
I don't suppose. Not his family exactly, anyway. Ian Davies
is the real black sheep. He's been to prison, you know.
Several times.'

All that didn't fit the visions she had of Gwyneth and Ian,
living next door to her grandparents, a snug cottage with a
kitchen range and the heady smells of home-baked bread.
'Daddy said Uncle Ian took the blame for some of the
things Aunt Gwyneth did, like setting the fire. Can't be all
bad.'

'Your father's very romantic.'

She'd decided to challenge her mother, though she'd
kept her tone light. 'Did you ever go to Wales, Mummy?'

Her mother had sighed. 'Just the once; just after we got
engaged. We took the train. There's a service to Llandrindod
Wells. Convenient, but it was a rather exhausting five-
hour trip.'

'Was it really beautiful?' She'd seen pictures of the old
Victorian town, the Rock Park Spa, the Lake.

'The place itself, you mean? I didn't notice; things
didn't work out. Best thing to do was to forget about it
all.'

Petra had pouted. 'Just because you don't want to know
doesn't mean I don't. They're my family, my flesh and
blood.'

Her mother had looked sidelong at her but hadn't
pursued the subject. 'Nothing to stop you going when
you're older,' was all she'd said. 'You can do what you like

when you leave home.' A cold, calculating look. 'Not that you'll ask my advice, in any case. But don't say I didn't warn you.'

She'd been fifteen then, resentful, biding her time. It had come today. David hadn't told Louise he was taking her to Wales; it would be their little secret, he'd said. No point in stirring things up. He'd smiled conspiratorially, explained that now she was in Exeter it wasn't all that much of a drive.

'How long did you say it was going to take us?' she asked her father now.

'Three hours or so. Up the M5, turn on to the M4, take the A roads through the Brecon Beacons and on into the Canolbarth – the very heart of Wales.'

'You don't have to sell it to me, Daddy. I've been longing to go for years.'

'We'll have a wonderful time of it. The scenery's breathtaking. I'll show you the drovers' ways and monks' trails on the hills right above Llandrindod Wells. And there's the lakes, and...'

'What I'm really looking forward to is meeting your family.'

He turned and smiled at her. 'Of course you are. I'm sorry, I should have taken you before.'

'We're going now.' She turned to look at him, saw the profile, remote, staring ahead out of the windscreen. A handsome man, except for the scar on his top lip which, though he tried to disguise it with a moustache, still showed slightly through the eyebrow pencil he used to colour the skin.

It was a golden autumn day. The Somerset Levels sped by as the Toyota Camry purred along the motorway. They crossed the suspension bridge into Wales. Flat English pastures gave way to rolling Welsh hills. The colours were brighter here; autumn yellows interspersed with vivid reds, a contrast with the duller greens of the low-lying moors.

'It's beautiful,' she told her father, spellbound. 'I don't know how you could bear leaving it.'

'Hard, sometimes.' She could see him struggling with something. 'Don't forget, there's no need to bother Mummy with any of this. You know she doesn't like the Welsh.'

'Doesn't want me to get to know your family, you mean. Just because she hasn't got any.' Louise's parents had been killed in a car crash when she was only fifteen. She'd spent the rest of her childhood at boarding school, and been sent to a reluctant great-aunt during the holidays.

At first he looked as though he was about to tell her off, but when he spoke he sounded sad, not angry. 'Getting two families together is always difficult. You'll find that out yourself when you meet the man you want to marry.'

Now that he'd pointed it out, she could see that her meeting with Edward's mother had been just that.

Her father's brown eyes looked intently at her. 'That isn't yet, I hope?'

Had he heard about her and Edward? Who could have told him? Bloody Bruce might have told Uncle Jack that Ed had overslept – once! – and been late for practice. And blamed her, the way he'd always blamed Sally.

'Wouldn't you be pleased if I did meet someone special?' she stalled.

He put his hand on her knee. 'Nothing better, Pet – if he's the right one, that is.' He turned to look at her. 'You're sure you're not already involved with anyone?'

'You needn't worry about that, Daddy. I'm only going to marry someone really special. And I'll bring him to meet you and Mummy as soon as I'm sure. I can promise you that.'

* * *

135

'Oh, it is wonderful to meet you at last.' Megan Jones, a little dumpling of a woman with twinkling eyes smiling out of a round face, advanced towards Petra with arms outstretched. 'I've waited so long for this.'

Petra stooped politely to be hugged by the grandmother she'd never met, had only heard about when Louise wasn't there. Louise had always said the Welsh were so clannish, they couldn't stand it if one of them married someone from England.

'And this is your grandfather – *taid* in Welsh.'

'You never said, Dewi; you never let on what a pretty girl you've got.' An old gnome of a man with tightly curled white hair walked up to Petra, held her by the arms to look at her, then kissed her on both cheeks. '*Dewch i mewn* – come in, come in. *Croeso adref* – that's welcome to our home in Welsh. A beautiful language; part of your heritage, *mechan i*.'

The pretty stone cottage stood along the single, narrow street winding over a hill, exactly as she'd always pictured it. The door stood open and they went into the front room, stiff armchairs, hardly used, dismal on either side of the fireplace, some polished furniture of a dark and dingy kind Petra had never seen before, and a piano.

'Sit down, do. A cup of tea, is it?'

'That would be lovely.'

Megan bustled off to the kitchen as father and son settled into the chairs. Dylan pulled out a pipe from a well-worn pouch. 'Will this upset you?'

'Of course not.' Petra hated the smell of any tobacco smoke, but it was her grandfather's house.

'Why aren't we in the kitchen, *Tada*?'

'You know your mother, Dewi. The parlour's for company.'

'But we're not...'

'You've never brought Petra to see us before, Dewi. Until we get used to her she's company.'

Petra heard the sound of the front door, the chatter of voices as someone joined her grandmother in the kitchen, then the hush.

'I saw the car. Where are they?'

'They're in the front room with your dad. Go on through, I'll bring the tea.'

'Dewi! So you've brought Petra to meet us at last.'

A woman in her late thirties had come in, looking remarkably like Megan must have looked when she was younger. Her small, round figure oozed friendliness, and when her smiling face turned to Petra, her voice lilting in an indecipherable confusion with Dewi's, it still managed to convey pleasure at this meeting.

'This is your Aunt Bronwen, Pet.' She saw her father kiss his sister on both cheeks and twirl her round. 'Still wearing the highest of heels.' He embraced her. 'I see those roses in your cheeks haven't gone.'

'I didn't bring the family,' Bronwen told them when all the greetings were over. 'Thought it would be too much for the poor girl, see. You can come and visit my house.' She turned to Petra. 'We don't live far. Gwyneth's next door, and I'm on her other side.'

'How lovely for you all.'

'We like it.'

The door opened and shut again, and this time the visitor came straight into the room. 'And this is your Uncle Huw, Petra.'

The same smile as her father, but a taller man, his hair abundant, the same eyes watching Petra with interest.

'Quite a beauty, your girl,' he said, turning to his brother. 'Favours her mother, does she?' He smiled into Petra's eyes, hugged her to him. 'Good to meet you, girl.'

'Petra doesn't particularly look like either of us,' David explained. 'She just had the sense to pick the best from us both.'

'However she did it, she's great.'

Megan came in, bearing an enormous teapot which she set on the grate by the fire.

Bronwen went out into the kitchen and returned with two heaped plates. '*Blas ar Cymru* – a taste of Wales,' she said, as she set them on the small table in front of the fire.

Megan began to heap a plate with scones and butter. 'I hope you like *sconau gwenith* – wholemeal scones. We always have them for tea, but I thought you'd be hungry after your long journey. And there's some Welsh cakes – *picau' maen* we call them.'

Her dreams were coming true. The friendly Welsh grandmother, the heavenly smell of home baking. 'It all looks wonderful.' She reached out eagerly, buttered a scone. 'It's scrumptious!'

'And where's the *teisen arbennig mamgu*, then?' David asked, his mouth full of scone.

His mother laughed. 'That means my special cake, *fach* – Gran's special cake. Well, I'm in good practice with that one. I've got two growing grandsons living next door but one. They keep me busy. Don't be impatient now; you'll have it for tea.'

Dylan offered the plate of scones again. 'Hope you don't go round not eating because of your figure,' he said. 'You girls are always worrying about your weight.'

'Don't worry, *Tada*. She's got a healthy appetite.'

'Easy for some.' Bronwen winked at Petra. 'Doesn't show so much when you're tall.'

She hadn't heard the front door open and shut. Another member of the clan came into the room, much younger,

138

showing just how attractive her sister Bronwen must have been in her youth.

The figure, though small, was slender. Her black hair, wavy without being too curly, hung down to her shoulders. Her eyes, enlarged by skilfully applied eyeshadow, beamed a slightly deeper tawny brown than Petra's at the girl.

'I have to starve myself to stay like this,' she laughed, coming over to Petra now sitting on the floor in front of the fire. 'I'm Angharad. The one who almost ran away to America.'

'And now she's settled down at last,' her father smiled. 'Met Mr Right; that's what it's all about. When she's had a baby or two she'll be just like our Bronwen.'

'Angie!' David kissed his youngest sister. 'You see? I kept my promise to bring Petra over.'

She broke away from him, tossing her head. 'About time, too.'

'Now, now, Angharad. You're forgetting Dewi's always so busy. He hasn't got the time to come gallivanting to Wales every few weeks,' his mother came to the rescue. 'Let's just enjoy him while we can. And Petra, too.'

It was true that her father worked an enormous amount of overtime, particularly when she was younger. But even so her parents had managed to go on holidays. Good holidays, at that. To the Caribbean, the Seychelles, New Zealand, and California. None of those places were exactly next door to London.

Angharad turned to her newfound niece. 'Do they call you Pet?'

Petra smiled uneasily. ''Fraid so.'

'I wouldn't worry,' she said. 'It suits you.'

Petra looked round the room. 'Daddy told me loads of things about all of you. Only Aunt Gwyneth is missing. Will she be coming, too?'

It seemed to Petra that they all talked at once. What finally emerged was that Gwyneth had had an accident, and was in hospital. In Aberystwyth, at least an hour's drive away.

'So we could visit her there?'

The silence was as expressive as the hubbub had been. 'I think it would be better not,' Megan Jones said at last. 'She isn't looking her best, see. Very sensitive, is it. Maybe next time you come.'

The door burst open, and was left that way. A burly, heavy-shouldered man loped in.

'Quite the family gathering,' he said, his eyes small spots darting round.

'Now, Ian. Dewi's brought his little girl. This is your Uncle Ian, Petra. He's Gwyneth's husband.'

'Told you all about your Aunt Gwyneth, is it? Bet no one's mentioned me! Black sheep of the family, that's who I am. Try to keep me locked up, they do, but I get out now and again.'

'Daddy's told me about everyone,' Petra said, smiling to hide her nervousness. The wicked uncle had made an appearance.

He turned to Megan. 'Thought I wouldn't notice his bloody car? It's big enough!'

'Ian and Gwyneth live next door,' David reminded Petra, his eyes strained as he looked at Ian. 'Hope I'm not parked in your way, Ian.'

'*Does dim awyr iach yma,*' he roared at them. '*Mae lle 'ma'n drewi.*'

Huw Jones walked over to his brother-in-law. 'Come on now, Ian. Petra can't understand Welsh. And there's no need to get steamed up.'

'Welsh?' he roared. 'Of course she can't speak Welsh. She's English!'

'She can't help—'

'Don't think I haven't remembered you're a bloody traitor, David Jones!'

'It's years ago, Ian.'

'Nor likely to,' Ian muttered, eyes hooded, shoulders hunched. 'Some things you don't forget.'

'Why can't we just be friends, Ian?'

'Friends with a Welshman turned English? You're the one they should have put away.'

'You know it wasn't my fault...'

'You're a bloody deserter, David. Ran off like the rat you are.' He strode towards the door. 'But don't you worry. I'll see you get what's coming to you.'

Huw had gone over to him and tried to put his arm across him. 'Get off!' he shouted, moving massive shoulders in a gesture of disgust. *'Mi ga'i di nol am hynny! Paid a meddwl wna'i ddim.'* He rushed out, slammed the door shut, then opened it again. 'And you can tell that to little Jacko as well; giving himself airs.' He cackled. 'Jack Oliver Media Agency, is it. What's he do, promote midgets?'

'Ian! There's no call for any of that—'

'Or maybe harelips are in fashion, is it?' He scowled at David, then squinted at Petra. 'Yours, is she? Not much of a chip off the old block, then.' The stained teeth bared at Petra. 'Lucky for you!'

'Will you have a cup of tea, Ian?'

'Dial! Dyna be' ga'i!' he yelled at them. 'That's what I'll have! And don't any of you forget it.'

The weather had been perfect. They were driving back now, through the autumn mists hugging the hills, hovering over the lakes, winding along the rivers. The dark was falling fast as Petra tried to get a last glimpse of a golden weekend.

'Well, Pet. What did you think? Worth waiting for?'

'Oh, Daddy. I wish you'd taken me when I was a little girl as well. It's just so wonderful. I felt like Cinderella at the ball. When I get married I'm going to live in Wales – well, in Powys. It's just *so* beautiful.'

'You really liked it?'

'And your family. Aren't they friendly? Mummy always said...'

'Your mother's a city woman. She thinks Llandrindod Wells is in a time warp, still in the Victorian age.'

'Something wrong with that? It had its points.'

She heard the soft, guttural laugh which went with the lilting speech. 'Maybe you wouldn't have been too keen at the time, Pet. Any daughter of mine would have been in domestic service, doing what she was told.'

'What was all that to-do with Uncle Ian about?'

'Hmm?'

'All that stuff in Welsh. You know I can't understand it, but it was clear enough he wasn't being very nice. What did he say?'

'Well, you know. He's a Nationalist. He thinks Uncle Jack and I betrayed Wales by leaving to find work in England. He thinks it was our duty to stay.'

'Why didn't you?'

'There wasn't any work for us, Pet. Hard enough to make a go of it in London.'

'What was that word he kept shouting – *dial*?'

Her father said nothing.

'Daddy? What does it mean?'

'Revenge, that's what it means. He said he was going to get his revenge on your Uncle Jack and me.' The voice was sad. 'But don't give Ian a thought, Pet. He's all hot air and jealousy. You needn't worry about him.'

14

Ethel Dunstan sat at her desk in her living room, studying the statement which had arrived that morning from the bank. They were overdrawn again. What was she going to tell Nathaniel?

'Hi, Mum. All on your own?'

Who did he think would be with her during a weekday morning? 'Harold! I thought you'd be zooming round the town on your bike by now.' Had he lost the latest courier job? He wasn't reliable, that was his trouble.

He came into the room, his helmet under his arm, his black leather gear making him appear taller than he was. 'Just thought it might be good to have a chat.'

Had he noticed something? She shook herself; she was beginning to imagine things. What could Harold possibly know about her problems? He wasn't very bright; she didn't see how he could suspect anything at all, let alone know about what she'd hidden so successfully for years. Now if Edward had started questioning her...

'Is Dad all right?'

Worried about his father? That was a laugh. Nathaniel had no problems that she could think of. 'Your father? You mean you think there's reason to worry about him?'

'He's been kind of strange lately.'

Ludicrous. The man had an easy job which he adored, and

he was head of his department. What problems could *he* have? She stared, unable to take in what Harold could be thinking about. 'He's the way he's always been, isn't he?'

He didn't look at her directly. 'Well, you know. He seems to forget things. He promised he'd let me have a bit of extra cash.'

So that was it; he was after money again. He really ought to be earning a living for himself by now. He'd chosen not to continue with his education, and he was eighteen. High time he thought about a career instead of gallivanting around, pretending to be a courier. 'Cash? I thought you were getting plenty of that from your job.'

'Doesn't pay all that much.' He fidgeted with his helmet, turning it round and round. 'Anyway, it's just a temporary thing. What I really want to do is race, you know that. It's what I've always dreamed about.' His sullen face had been transformed into an eager hope. 'That pays well – once you get started and win a few races, that is. I need some capital to get me going.'

'Capital? What for?'

'Can't race without a decent bike. That's what Dad promised me. He said he could let me have around ten thousand pounds.'

She drew her breath in. 'Ten thousand? I'd no idea he had anything like that put away.'

'Not put away. Something he's hoping will come in. He mumbled about a new contract. I thought he meant another book.'

'Book?' Then she remembered what Nathaniel had said. 'The CD-ROM contract, I suppose.' Nathaniel hadn't mentioned the project to her recently, but he had said it would bring in a lot of money. If there was going to be enough to offer Harold £10,000 out of the proceeds, it would solve all their problems. 'That's come off, has it?'

'I thought it had. But when I asked him the other day he didn't even seem to remember talking to me about it. Anyway, he said there wasn't a contract, and he had no savings. So that was that. Just wondered whether you knew anything about it.'

She looked at her son. He wasn't as athletic as Edward, but he was quite robust. 'Have you tried to get Jack Oliver to represent you, Harold? If you're as good at this motor-cycling stuff as you say you are, he might be interested.'

'He turned me down.'

'That was for basketball, I know that. Some rubbish about the physiology testing, and your not being able to twist fast enough. Doesn't apply to motorcycling, presumably. What about that? Why not tell him that's what you're really interested in? He might be keen on that.' It would be a wonderful solution. Jack Oliver might do what he'd done for Edward for Harold – pay him a retainer while he was training, help him out with equipment.

She sighed. That would at least free some of the money from the housekeeping. Harold paid her a pittance for his board and keep, then ate more than anyone she'd ever known.

He came over to the desk and looked down at her. 'Sorry, Mum. I thought you knew. He turned me down for that as well.' He stared at the sheets she'd been reading. 'Guess you can't do much for me. Having enough problems of your own.'

What did he mean by that? Had he seen anything? Did he know? Presumably he'd seen the D on the statement.

'All I was suggesting was that you talk to Dad for me...'

The phone by her side began to trill. She picked it up. She wasn't expecting any calls. Perhaps it was Dorling Kindersley for Nathaniel. 'Professor Dunstan's residence.'

'Mrs Dunstan?' A very rough, deep voice she didn't recognise. Didn't sound much like a publisher. There was something oddly mechanical about it, almost distorted.

'Speaking,' she said, a doubtful tone giving her answer a suggestion of irritation.

'I – told – you – to – stop – it.'

The roughness was still there, but it had turned into much more than that. Ethel felt each enunciated word strike through her. There was a steely edge of menace to the syllables, as though each one could stab her, make her bleed. Her throat thickened into a choke.

'Who is that?' Her question sounded like a whisper.

'Stop – it.'

Louder than before, cold, unemotional, definite. 'Stop *what*?' she squeaked, panic building up, pounding the blood through her temples, making her feel hot. 'I don't even know who you are!'

'You – know – me.' There was a pause, and then a cackling sound.

It was *him*. He'd never contacted her by phone before. What was she going to do? 'What do you *want*?' she hissed, sounding much more in control, almost her normal self.

But it had no effect, because he'd put the receiver down. She could hear nothing but the long hum of a disconnected line.

'Whatever's wrong, Mum? A nuisance call?'

'Nuisance?' She stared at Harold, her face drained of all blood. 'I'm not quite sure. I couldn't make it out.'

'You wouldn't want to, if what I heard is right.'

She gulped. 'You heard?'

'Not what he said. I've heard people talk about calls like that. What did he do – breathe heavily at you?'

'He spoke. It sounded sort of metallic, as though it wasn't a human voice – sort of artificial, more like a computer.'

146

'You mean that sing-song stuff without expression?'

That wasn't what was missing; he'd expressed himself only too well. 'As though the voice was made of steel. I can't really explain it.'

'A computer freak. Well, that's a new one on me. Better get on to BT...'

She got up and walked towards the kitchen. 'Think I'll just put the kettle on,' she said. 'Like a coffee?' She walked up to the high cupboard, brought down a bottle and poured herself a stiff Scotch while she waited for the kettle to boil.

Harold had followed her. 'My God, Mum, as bad as that?'

'Did give me rather a turn. But let's forget that now. We were talking about you. Perhaps Ed could talk to Jack Oliver, put in a word for you.'

'I thought of that. D'you think he would?'

'Of course. He's one of the Jack Oliver specials now, you know. They're grooming him to take Phil Thompson's place. They're very pleased with him. I'd think they'd want to keep him happy...'

'He's really got everything, hasn't he?'

'In basketball, you mean?' She hadn't thought it through before, but it must be hard for Harold to cope with his brother's success.

'Yes, and he's got that smashing girl – Petra, isn't it? She's wicked!'

She'd forgotten about Petra Jones. So *that's* what the phone call had been about. How could she have put it out of her mind so completely? She'd assumed that because Edward no longer mentioned the girl he'd stopped seeing her. 'You mean they're still going out together?'

'Far as I know he's crazy about her. Whenever I go over to see him play basketball, she's with him. Anything wrong with that?'

'She's got a genetic defect, Hal.'

147

He stared at her. 'Has she? Poor girl. Ed never said a word. What's wrong with her?'

'He didn't have to. You must have noticed. She's got one eye blue and one brown.' She found the way he gaped at her intensely irritating.

'You can't be serious, Mum. That's what you call a genetic defect – because her irises are different colours?' He paused, trying to work it out. 'Not blind, or anything, is she?'

She poured hot water on to coffee granules. 'Not as far as I know. It's just that once there's a problem...'

'She's a lovely girl, Mum. Really stunning to look at, and so bright and friendly.' He frowned. 'I'd have thought you'd jump at a daughter-in-law like that. *And* she wants to have a big family. Not just a career girl.'

So Harold had fallen for her as well. 'You've seen something of her, have you?'

'Just that day she came to Sunday lunch. And a couple of hellos when I talked to Ed.'

A noise she had found irritating for some minutes penetrated her mind: Bradley barking in his fenced-in part of the garden. Her anger focused on the animal. 'That wretched dog's barking again. He really gets on my nerves.'

'He's heard our voices. Wants some company, I expect.'

She flounced over to the sink and looked out. 'I hate that grating noise. D'you think you could shut him up?'

'Why don't you let him come into the kitchen, Mum? He's lonely while Ed's out. That's all it is.'

Sentimentality about some bloody dog. Just like her sons to think more about Bradley than they did about their own mother. She turned her fury on Harold. 'You know I can't stand animals in the house. He makes a mess of everything with those long hairs of his. And he's always trying to get at me!'

Why did Edward have to make trouble for her? Wasn't it

enough that Harold was nothing but a liability? Somehow she had to make Edward see sense. She had to make sure that he had no option but to give up that girl.

15

Sally woke to pitch dark. She listened for the regular rise and fall of Petra's breath and heard only the ticking of her clock. A wave of panic flooded through her veins, the blood making her hot enough to fling off her covers. Had they got at Petra now? She turned on her bedside light. Her roommate's bed hadn't been slept in. She fell back on her pillow, exhausted. How could she have forgotten that Petra had gone to Wales for the weekend? She sighed as relief allowed her to relax. She switched on the main light and the TV. Three in the morning brought snow to the screen of BBC1, but a blast of static filled the room. She lunged at the set and turned off the volume. At this rate she'd wake the other students.

She switched to the video channel, put in Petra's tape of Phil's last match and was about to settle into the lotus position to watch it yet again when she was caught by a cramp in her guts which was stronger than anything she'd felt before. She gasped; she needed something to settle her stomach. What could she eat or drink that wouldn't make her worse? She'd heard that even tapwater could be dangerous. 'Bacteriological deterioration', the Devonshire authorities had warned on national TV only a couple of days ago. They'd advised people to boil all drinking water.

There wasn't much to choose from. Petra had several tins

of Diet Coke stacked on the windowsill by her desk, and there was a rather old bottle of squash. Then she remembered the partly finished bottle of Evian water. She took a sip of that, found it soothing, drank a little more. It cooled her throat, calmed her stomach to start with. Then, within minutes, she began to retch. She felt the peristaltic waves of muscles contracting without something to work on. In spite of Petra's valiant efforts to get her to do so, she hadn't been able to eat very much. She'd been losing weight steadily; her clothes were hanging loose.

She'd tried to do something constructive about it. After Petra had left for Wales she'd made the effort to see the nurse at the medical department.

She remembered the consultation vividly. 'Just a bug, I expect.' The woman dismissed her as though she couldn't have worked that out for herself. What did she think she'd come for?

But she persisted, in spite of the nurse's bored look and the air of martyred resignation. Why choose the job if you were unwilling to care for people? She pulled what energy she could together and tried another approach.

'Whatever it is, it's making me feel really ill. And the symptoms do seem to have been around rather a long time. Could it be food poisoning?'

A tight, dismissive smile. 'You'd know about food poisoning.'

That goaded her into a less submissive attitude. 'If there wasn't something wrong I wouldn't be here!'

A grudging nod. 'So when did you first notice anything?'

She had no trouble pinpointing the time. Just after Phil died. In fact, it was right after those last few words he'd managed to say to her, a few minutes after she'd run out of the dependency unit. The very last food she could remember enjoying, she thought with a certain irony, was that

152

sandwich Jack Oliver had produced for her. Even as she remembered eating it she began to retch again. That's when it had first started; right after Phil died.

'It was when I got back from Bath one Saturday night. Almost exactly two weeks ago.'

'You were in Bath? Did you go out for a meal?'

She hesitated. If she told the nurse what she'd been doing there, she'd get the same old diagnosis. She could do without the amateur psychology, but she hadn't the energy to lie. 'I went to visit a friend at the Bath Clinic.'

'Ah – a hospital. Places like that are hotbeds of *staphylococcus*, I'm afraid. Can't be avoided. Eat anything there, by any chance?'

'Nothing at all. Someone gave me a bottle of spring water – an unopened one. And I had a sandwich before we got there.'

'You were with friends?'

'Yes.'

'And the sandwich; where did that come from?'

'A friend had it in the glove compartment of his car.'

The nurse's head jerked up. 'You mean you ate something that had been lying around...'

'It was fresh from London that afternoon, and still sealed. From Fortnum and Mason; can't have been anything wrong with it.'

'Glove compartments can get warm. That's the best environment to hasten the multiplication of bacteria.'

'It was in a cooler bag.'

'I see. Did anyone else exhibit any symptoms?'

'No, just me. But I was the only one who had a sandwich.'

The nurse looked at her with that mixture of arrogance and disdain which Sally had come to dread. 'Was it anyone close?'

The woman had sussed it out already. Her mother always said that she made life harder for herself than it already was. 'In the car with me, d'you mean?' she prevaricated.

'Were you visiting a close relative at the Clinic?' The nurse's biro was poised for making more notes. She'd already written volumes. 'Hysterical symptoms', Sally assumed.

She fiddled with the friendship ring Phil had given her, then clasped her belly as another spasm went through her.

'You're obviously in pain.' The starchiness had been replaced with wariness, an alert eye. 'Well? Were you visiting a relative?'

She concentrated on not spilling tears. 'My boyfriend; he'd had an accident. He was in one of the private rooms in the high dependency unit. I'd just been with him; he'd been in a coma for ten days and had finally come out of it. He spoke to me.'

The biro moved again. 'So it was good news?'

'He died.'

The pulled-in breath sounded almost like a whistle. If nurses weren't used to the facts of death, who was? 'That must have been terrible for you. Were you very involved?'

'We were going to get married.'

She had the grace to stop writing and look at her. 'I'm so sorry, my dear. How dreadful for you.'

'Everyone says I feel like this because of Phil dying. Of course that was the worst thing that's ever happened to me.' She gulped as she fought back tears. 'But this seems more of a physical reaction to something my body can't tolerate.'

'Grief comes in all sorts of guises.' The silken oiliness of the professional. 'We all have to give it a chance to work through.' The tone was brisk, dismissive. 'Now then; have you been ill all the time, or off and on?'

'At first I thought it had gone away. Then it came back again.'

The biro moved through another two lines as the nurse looked across. 'If it had been food poisoning, you'd have felt ill all the time.' She smiled – a strained, palliative grimace which wouldn't have fooled a toddler. 'What sort of sandwich was it?'

'Egg mayonnaise.'

'I see; that can be dangerous. So we can't entirely rule out salmonella poisoning. Sometimes it hangs about. But in this case I think we can assume your symptoms are psychological; a form of grief. I'll give you something for your stomach, but I'd like you to take a mild sedative as well. If there's no improvement by this time next week we'll have to send you to the Royal for tests. OK?'

She'd left, clutching the pills the nurse had given her. But she wasn't intending to go into the Royal. All they'd do there was send round some shrink and waste her time. She was sure it was a physical problem. And yet she'd been so careful about what she'd eaten! Paranoid, Petra had called her.

She shook off the frustration the memories provoked, took the cap off the bottle of Evian water, drained it. Time to get herself a new one. At least bottled water would be safe.

The vomiting subsided. Memories flooded back to her as she went over Phil's last words time and again. It wasn't just the words, it was the fact that he'd spent his last ounce of strength trying to alert her to something he'd found out. He'd *told* her there'd been a mistake. He'd been the only one who'd known for sure that something wasn't right.

She heaved again, brought up the water she'd just drunk, her body wet with sweat.

She really was unwell, and she could feel herself getting worse. What if she died before she could find out what was happening? She knew, instinctively, that something horrific was going on. She needed help, someone she could confide in, trust. When Petra came back from Wales she'd go through the whole thing with her, tell her everything she'd gleaned so far.

Sally blinked as the light hit her eyelids.

'You're in bed early. Still feeling ill?' Petra's voice held worry interlaced with excitement.

'Sorry. Thought you wouldn't be back for a couple of hours yet. I meant to have a hot drink ready for you.'

'I'm fine. We left my grandparents just after tea. Daddy's still got the drive to London, so we stopped at a service station and had fish and chips.'

'How was it?'

Petra sat down on her friend's bed, her eyes soft, a smile curving her mouth. 'Just wonderful. They were all so friendly, Sal. I don't know what my mother was going on about all these years.'

'Every single one?'

'Of the family, yes. Unless you count Ian Davies, my Aunt Gwyneth's husband.' She laughed. 'He ranted on a bit in Welsh. Sounded really fed up, but I never found out why.' A small dimple of dismissal appeared on either side of Petra's mouth.

Sally sat up in bed, her arms around her drawn-up knees. 'He doesn't count, I gather.'

'And the countryside's so beautiful, you've no idea...'

Without warning the vomiting began again. Sally grabbed the bowl she kept by the side of her bed just in time.

Petra soaked a flannel in water, wrung it out and brought it over. She helped her wipe her mouth. 'This is getting serious, Sal. I've got to get the doctor. This isn't good enough.'

Sally shook her head. 'No need, I'm all right now. I went to see the nurse after you left. She said to wait a week; insisted it was almost certainly psychological. Gave me a tranquilliser.'

'But there's blood—'

'All she did was say it was a form of grief. Forget the medics; they weren't up to it with Phil and they aren't up to this.' Her eyes glittered. 'There are things I've got to tell you.'

Petra refreshed the flannel and offered it to Sally. 'You've found something on the tape?'

'No. I've looked and looked, but I haven't been able to find anything suspicious.' She was about to get up when Petra pushed her back. 'But I know there's something!'

'Don't you think you ought to rest now, get some sleep?'

'You tired?'

'Well, no. I'm too excited. It was a wonderful weekend.' Her face turned dreamy. 'I think I'm going to live in rural Wales when I settle down. Have a large family, just like the Joneses.'

'I need your help, Pet.'

She felt Petra's arms around her, hugging her, holding her tight. 'I always said, Sal. Any time. What would you like me to do?'

'Please don't think I'm crazy. Whoever was behind Phil's death is after me as well.'

'Oh, Sally! Why on earth . . .'

'Because I know there's something wrong.' Petra's face betrayed the feeling of helplessness Sally had seen there several times before. Petra didn't believe her, but she still had to tell her. One day she would remember, and it would all make sense to her. 'If they start to suspect you, they'll be after you as well. So promise me; don't tell a soul what I'm going to tell you. Not even Ed. Not yet, anyway.'

Petra looked startled, but nodded her head. 'Whatever you say. But who is this person who's after you? And what am I not telling Ed? You're not making sense, Sally.'

'I know I don't know *what*'s going on, but I know something is.' She pushed back the short hair from her forehead, kneaded her temples. 'Someone is hiding something, some really dreadful secret. Phil's dead, and he shouldn't be. He was killed to shut him up.'

Petra held her by the shoulders. 'You have to face it sometime, Sally. The doctors spelled it out: toxic shock syndrome. It's rare, which is why neither Bruce nor the team doctor spotted it in time, but it does happen. And the effects are only reversible before a certain point. Phil had gone beyond that. It wasn't anybody's fault.'

She shook Petra off. 'That's not all. The most telling part is Phil. He was dying, Petra, and he spent his last breath on warnings to me.'

Petra could not keep the look of pity out of her eyes. 'Warnings? I thought the last few words were what he felt for you, just between you and him.'

'The very last ones, yes. But there was something else – something special he wanted me to know. He'd even hinted at it before the game, something he'd just found out, something terribly important he *had* to tell me about.' Her eyes were dry, her throat hoarse. 'He wasn't himself. Not just the temperature and all that; his attitude. You must have noticed, too – he didn't even kiss me, he was so upset.'

Petra couldn't meet her eyes.

'I knew you'd spotted it. Whatever it was, he said it was devastating, had made him terribly unhappy. And he said it again at the Clinic, kept on about it being important. Kept repeating that word.' She gulped as she thought back. 'He was so anxious to tell me, Pet. So distressed it even got him out of the coma for a short time.'

She could see that Petra was all attention now. 'Anything else?'

'He reckoned there'd been a mistake. I suppose it could have meant that he'd been killed in someone else's place.'

'Any more?'

'A double *ss* sound. At first I thought it meant Joss – you know, the player who was marking him – and then I thought he was trying to say "Bruce". I asked him to squeeze my hand if I'd got it right.'

'And did he?'

'I think he was too weak. But it *had* to be Bruce...'

'Hold on, Sal. What did he say – *exactly*?'

'I don't know that I can reproduce it word for word, but I'll have a go.' She summoned every ounce of energy she had. 'It sounded like: "Not ss ... *can't* ... siss ... be wrong..." His head even came off the pillow an inch or so, he was so worked up! Just think what that meant at a time like that. It just *has* to be significant.' She put her palms in front of her face, shook herself backwards and forwards. 'He tried to get up, Pet – in the state he was in. I know he meant *something* by it!'

'He said "can't ... *siss*"? Perhaps he was telling you that Joss or Bruce wasn't to blame. Had you thought of that?'

'He said there'd been a mistake! Somehow his mother came into it as well...'

Petra went on holding her, patting her. Sally could tell she didn't believe a word of what she was trying to tell her. 'You think I've flipped, don't you? Round the bend.'

Petra stood up. 'Have we got any milk? I could make you a hot drink.'

'You think Helen Thompson's attitude to me was all right, just because she behaved at the Royal that time. You think Phil was going to tell me it wasn't going to work out, that he'd gone off me. That's what you think, isn't it?'

'I wouldn't know about that. I don't suppose that's what it was at all.' She began to unpack. 'The dependency-unit nurse said people get all worked up just before they die. It's normal.'

'His last words were "Love Sal ... love ... Sal ..."' She wept, her shoulders shaking, her belly cramped, until there was nothing but the moan of exhaustion.

'You really will do some damage to yourself, Sally. You can't go on like this.'

'What you don't seem to understand is that the same thing's happening to you and Ed! Can't you see what I mean? Just think for a moment, Pet. Ethel Dunstan took against you on some trumped-up rubbish because she can't stand the idea of your seeing Ed. Helen Thompson took against me. Bruce Traggard goes spare at the thought of Ed having a girlfriend and warns him off, just like he did with Phil and me. And didn't you tell me that even Mr Oliver mumbled about your being too young to commit yourself?'

'Well, I am only eighteen. From his point of view that's young.'

'Ed's in practically the same position as Phil was: very tall, educated at Millfield, highly gifted at playing basketball, falls in love early. And he's represented by the Jack Oliver Media Agency!'

'And he has the same coach, and plays in the same team. That's hardly surprising. Be reasonable, Sally. The only substantial point you've got so far is the way Ed's mother acted towards me.'

'And you don't believe my version of Helen Thompson, do you?'

'She seemed OK to me.' Petra's voice was low, embarrassed. 'She *was* worried about her son.'

160

'So that excuses anything she did. And what about Phil's last words? You're saying because he was dying they're of no account?'

'Of course not, Sally! But—'

'But you think I misunderstood him, I've got it all completely wrong.' She turned on the video and fast forwarded the tape. 'I know you've seen this tape several times; I just want to show you that it has to have happened just before Phil collapses. That's the important bit. I can't find anything wrong, but I can feel it in my bones.'

'But what on earth do you think is going on, Sally? Have you at least got a theory?'

'Traggard has a whole team of brilliant players. He wants to train them up to go to the States. There's millions in it for the top players, and thousands in it for him. So he wants to keep his players from getting serious with a girl. Well, an English girl, that is. He thinks she'd get in the way.'

'So he'd hardly *kill* one of his players, now would he?'

She intended to go on, whatever Petra thought. 'Joss Black was signed up by Jack Oliver before the game. The only thing that was stopping him from getting a chance at the States was Phil. So he got rid of him.' She stared at Petra. 'It worked, as well. They took him on instead.'

'You're suggesting a double sort of conspiracy. Traggard and the boys' mothers against you and me, Joss Black against Phil. That right?'

'No,' Sally wailed. 'No, that doesn't sound right. It sounds bloody stupid. But there *is* something going on, I know there is.' She sat for a moment, her head in her hands, trying to think it through. She couldn't do it. 'Just one more thing. Why am I ill like this? Why can't I get better? It's not something I've eaten; I've been really careful. And I've only drunk Evian water.'

'It *could* be grief, Sally. You do seem to get better and then worse again.'

There was nothing more she could do. It was hopeless. Petra was determined not to understand. 'I've got to go home, Petra – get out of here before they kill me. I'll be safe with my mum.'

Petra switched off the video and TV. 'You're right, I think you should go home, Sal. Give yourself a chance to get over Phil.'

'I've made a copy of the tape and hidden it the way I showed you. Between two books, inside a plastic bag, in the back of my locker.'

'Shall I ring your mother and ask her to pick you up?'

'Do you think Ed would drive me back?' Her voice had lost its strength. She merely whispered. 'My poor old mum hasn't got a car, or any money.'

'Tomorrow after practice,' Petra said. 'I'll catch him as he comes off the court. We'll get you home, Sal. You've got to get out of here.'

16

'Your dribbling's coming along really well, Edward. Looks like you've been doing something special. You want to share it with the rest of us?'

Edward laughed as he walked along with Bruce Traggard, their long strides covering twice as much ground as shorter men's. Even with Petra he had to remember to adjust his gait. 'It's an idea I had. I've trained my dog to get the ball from me. He's quicker than any human.'

Bruce was looking expectant, but at the word 'dog' his eyebrows bushed up in disbelief. 'Your *dog*? How does a dog manage a basketball?'

'He can't. At first I just let him jump at the ball. That kept me moving all right. Then I had an idea. I covered it with that nylon netting they use for protecting soft fruit against birds. Meant he could get a hold of it. Slows down the ball a bit, but it does work.'

The coach slapped him on the shoulder. 'Sounds crazy to me, but it obviously does the trick. Keep it up.'

So Bradley's clever playing with the ball had improved his own reflexes enough for Bruce to notice. It made Edward think about his pet. He'd been late leaving for practice that morning, and the collie had seemed unusually quiet. He'd struggled to his feet when Edward had come into the kennel to feed him, then stood, unmoving, his tail hanging limp between his legs. At first he'd thought his dog must be worn out, but there was an odd look about him, as though he were moping. He'd have to go back and check on him.

'Not that you listen to advice.' The light bantering tone had changed to a rasping snarl as Bruce's eyes focused, then narrowed.

Edward followed his gaze and was surprised to see Petra standing outside the Sports Hall. He slowed; it had to be something important for her to run the risk of trouble with Bruce.

'Just remember one thing.' Bruce was striding out, slightly ahead of him. 'We're playing at Loughborough this Friday; you're on the team.'

As though he didn't know. He tried not to let his nervousness show in his face as he came nearer Petra. They'd agreed not to meet in public to avoid confrontations with both Bruce and Ethel. Petra's presence meant she had good reason; she wasn't the clinging type. The constant interference in his private life was getting to him. 'You noticed any shortfall in my play, Coach?' he shouted after Bruce.

The man turned his head, stopped short, fished a notebook out of his pocket and began to write. 'It's not just a question of the game, Dunstan. You have a choice: take basketball seriously, or play around. It's up to you. My job's to report on your progress in every field. You know all that.'

'We've hardly seen each other. She was away at the weekend—'

The notebook was slammed shut as Bruce Traggard stalked rapidly away. Edward was torn between his pleasure at seeing Petra and his wish to fulfil the promise he'd made Jack Oliver when he accepted the sponsorship. At the time he'd made light of the fact that he shouldn't commit himself emotionally. He hadn't expected to fall in love.

'Hello, Pet. Something wrong?' She was standing, her shoulders rounded, her eyes strained, watching his reactions. 'I thought we'd agreed not to be seen together on campus.'

He hadn't realised she was so near to tears. 'Sally's really ill.' Her voice shook, but he could see her force herself to carry on. 'She won't let me get a doctor, or take her to the Royal. She can't carry on like this; I've managed to persuade her to go home.'

'Yes?' He was beginning to find Sally a strain. Every time he came across her she looked miserable, harped back to Phil's death, related her latest paranoia. He'd had enough of it.

Petra made a desperate effort at a smile and ended up with a grimace. 'I can't just put her on the train; she isn't fit to travel on her own.' She avoided tears, but her voice quivered. 'She isn't up to travelling on public transport.'

He wasn't sure what she was getting at. Was he supposed to offer to escort Sally back? 'Didn't your father stay the night? Why not ask him to give her a lift? I'm sure he wouldn't mind.'

'He dropped me off and went straight on; wanted to be in time for work this morning.' She stopped, her eyes large. 'I know it'll get you into all kinds of trouble, but I don't know what else to do. I haven't got a driving licence, otherwise I'd ask if I could borrow the car.'

'You want me to drive her home.' Even if Petra hadn't asked him, he knew it was the only thing to do. Mrs Wheeler didn't drive and, anyway, hadn't got the money to run a car. Phil had been his best friend; he had to do what he could for the girl he'd left behind. 'Coach'll go spare. Come on, I'll walk you back to Hall. We'll sort it out.'

'You mean you will?'

He wanted to take her in his arms, to hold her until she relaxed, to kiss her tears away. All he could do was smile. 'Sounds as though you ought to come as well.'

He could tell she wasn't even thinking of the consequences – for either of them. 'You're right; she keeps being sick. I'll ring her mother and pack her things. Can you bring the car round here?'

She was about to dash away as he caught her arm. 'Hold on a minute. I've got to go home first.'

'To change?'

'Check on Bradley – you know, my dog. He looked under the weather when I left. I'll be back in an hour.'

'Edward? Is that you?'

He'd hoped his mother would have gone out shopping. He wasn't in the mood for her innuendoes. Since Petra's visit she'd bombarded him with reasons why he shouldn't go out with her. Instead of calming down, the whole thing had got worse recently. She'd attacked him with a barrage of arguments about why he shouldn't marry, and why Petra, in particular, was quite the wrong choice.

'Does she have tall parents?' she'd suddenly asked him. Out of the blue, it seemed to him.

'Not really; she's taller than both of them.'

'So she's *abnormally* tall for her family?'

'You could much more easily say that of me,' he'd tried to reason with her. 'I'm six inches taller than Dad.'

'If Petra is taller than her parents, and you're definitely taller than yours, your children would, in all likelihood, be taller still. Had you thought of that?'

'I haven't lost any sleep about it, no.'

'Perhaps you should,' she'd said, a triumphant look in her eyes. 'At least think about it.'

None of it made sense; he'd given up trying to understand. In the end he'd had to tell her to stop, or he'd leave home. After that she'd taken to veiled, barbed remarks he found almost as tiresome.

He had to go through the house to get to the garden. The collie had been in glowing form yesterday morning. He'd even taught him a new trick, and Bradley had caught on within half an hour. He smiled to himself as he remembered his dog's exceptional intelligence. Last night Bradley had seemed tired, but it was this morning that he'd been so unlike the pet he knew and loved. He'd hardly been able to get him out of his mind during practice.

He popped his head round the living-room door.

'I wasn't expecting you back until this evening.' His mother's voice was oddly low-key.

'Just wanted to check on Bradley. He seemed unwell when I went out.'

'That's what I wanted to talk to you about.'

His mother talk about Bradley? That had to be bad news. She didn't like animals, particularly dogs. And where she could tolerate some dogs, she could not stand Bradley. Far too dynamic, with his lively interest in chasing anything that moved and barking his joy at finding it. The certainty of disaster made him march into the room and tower over his mother sitting at her desk. 'Didn't get out of the garden and into the road, did he? Hasn't been run over or anything?'

She didn't look up at him, but kept her eyes fixed on a letter she was reading. Private, apparently. She'd put her arm over the sheet of paper. 'Run over? Nothing like that.'

'So he's all right?' Was she about to tell him he couldn't keep the dog any more? He wouldn't know what to do without Bradley. He was much more than a pet; he was as much a working dog as any sheepdog. Bradley had become a brilliant team-mate!

'I'm afraid not. I had to take him to the vet.'

'*You* took him? When?'

She scraped the hard-backed chair back from the desk, turned the sheet of paper she'd been reading over, and stood. There was something unusual about that letter, different in some way. He couldn't really see it because he'd moved out of range. He wasn't comfortable with physical endearments from his mother since the time she'd been so impossible with Petra.

'Just after you left. He seemed unusually quiet.'

He frowned. What had possessed her to go out and look at his dog? Bradley spent the day in his kennel, or a fenced-in part of their garden, waiting for Edward to return from college. As far as he knew his mother never gave him a thought, or noticed him.

The unasked question must have been obvious. 'You mentioned he was off-colour last night. I just pottered out to see how he was.'

'Really?'

'You're away all day. I thought something might have to be done. He looked all in. So I rang the vet; they said to bring him round.'

'You mean you took him to a vet yourself?'

'In his basket.'

He'd no idea his mother knew he had a special basket for transporting the dog. 'Thanks, Mum. That was sweet of you. Where did you take him?'

She was still avoiding his eye. 'Oh, you know. Johnston and Lever, isn't it? The one you always go to.'

He didn't even know his mother knew which vet he used. There was something odd about her attitude. Her voice was flat, the strident tones restrained. It was as though she felt guilty about the dog. What could it have to do with her?

'What did they say?'

Ethel's head swivelled up to meet his eyes at last. 'They? What d'you mean, they?' Her eyes showed fear.

'At the vet's, Mum. What did they say?'

Her head bent down again. 'I see what you mean.' Her hands spread out in a gesture of helplessness. 'Well, you know. I don't know about animals. I just left him there. They said they'd see to him.'

'But what made you take him, Mum? What was wrong with him?'

There were tears in her eyes as she looked at her son. 'He was lying on his side, and sort of gasping. When I went up to him he didn't even lift his head. I knew something was terribly wrong.'

'D'you mind if I give Fred Lever a ring?'

She pulled a handkerchief out of her pocket. 'You know you don't have to ask.' She was sitting on her sofa now, weeping openly.

He sat down next to her. 'Whatever's wrong, Mum?'

'I didn't wish him any harm, Edward.'

He put his arm around her shoulders. 'Thanks for doing as much as you did, Mum. It was wonderful of you.' He could feel her shoulders stiffen, could sense her wanting to get away.

She wiped her eyes and nose again, took his arm from around her shoulders and held his hand. 'Don't you think it might be a kind of warning?'

She'd surprised him already, but this was way out. Was she going through the change? He'd heard that women behaved in a peculiar way at that time. The end of the reproductive years; surely she wasn't confusing the dog with a baby? 'You all right, Mum? You're not usually so tearful.' He didn't like to say it was out of character, that she couldn't have cared less about the dog.

'About you and that girl, Edward: I know something terrible's going to happen if you go on seeing her. I can just feel it!'

What on earth was she talking about? It was the weirdest thing he'd ever come across.

The tears began to gather again. 'Can't you just take my word for it, Ed? A mother feels these things, you know.'

He picked up the phone, tapped the vet's number in and heard the engaged tone. He put the receiver down, waited a moment, pressed redial.

'Johnston and Lever.'

'Hello, Trish. It's Edward Dunstan here. Could I—'

He heard the intake of breath. 'I'm sorry about Bradley, Ed. I know what he meant to you.'

'You mean—?'

'I'll get Fred to have a word. Hold on, I think he's just finished with a client.'

Fred Lever's ebullient voice explained that the dog had died within minutes of being brought to the surgery. There had been no time to do anything for him, although he'd dropped everything else to take a look. Trish had seen right away that it was an emergency. 'I'm so very sorry. He was a great little chap.'

'Thanks, Fred. Any idea what happened?'

A pause, a clearing of the throat. 'What did you give him last night?'

'Give him? Feed him, you mean?'

The vet sounded embarrassed. 'Had to be something he ate. D'you leave food where vermin or flies can get at it?'

'He gets a small tin of dog food I open at the time.'

'What about the biscuits?'

'Food poisoning – is that what you're saying?' He saw his

mother's head jerk up, the blood rush to her face. Why was she so concerned?

There was a pause. 'We'll have to establish what kind of organism caused the trouble. You say you're careful about opened tins. Maybe an infected batch from the supermarket? Should we alert them?'

There was an echo here from something else ... Sally was suffering from food poisoning. Was there a source of contamination in Exeter? 'There was one thing. It wasn't just supermarket tins. I gave him a marrow bone from the butcher, fresh the day before.'

'If there's anything left, bring it down. We'll check it out.' Another clearing of the throat. 'Shall we, er, deal with him or will you come and pick him up?'

'If you could hold him for the moment, Fred. I'll come round tomorrow.' He replaced the receiver, missing the cradle because his eyes were streaming tears.

'Is he all right?' he heard his mother ask, her voice shaky.

He stared at her. 'Brad's dead,' he choked. 'Poor little chap.'

'Oh God, Ed. That's terrible. I didn't think he'd *die* ...'

He put his arm around his mother, surprised at the strength of her feelings – it was as if she felt responsible for his death. He shook the thought off. How could she be? He was being absurd. 'It wasn't your fault, Mum. You did everything you could.'

If Bradley was dead, there was no point in not keeping his promise to drive Sally to her home in Battersea. At least she'd be taken care of for a while. He'd bury his little pet tomorrow. Why did everything seem to be going wrong?

17

'Well now, *fach*. There's nice to see you again – and so soon too, isn't it.'

'Hi, Gran Megan.' Petra stood at the wide open door of her grandmother's cottage and basked in the warm smile, the welcoming arms, the strong Welsh lilt which her father's long stay in London had softened in his case.

'I'd have made more fuss with Dewi about bringing you to meet us if I'd known you'd like it here so much.' She hugged Petra to the mohair cardigan which covered her cushion of a bosom. 'Never thought you'd come and visit your old gran again so soon, mind, never even crossed my mind. Thought you'd be much too grand for us.'

Petra stooped down to the small figure and kissed both cheeks. Though crossed with a myriad small lines, they had the soft feel of crumpled silk. Megan Jones' hair was a speckled grey, the deep black of youth still shining at the neckline. Tawny brown eyes twinkled with life, and the arms she flung around her granddaughter were strong and impetuous.

'All on your own, is it?'

'For the moment.'

Dark eyebrows arched in surprise. 'Your *Tada*'s coming on later? Well, there's a thing, then. Spoiled I am.'

'Not Daddy; my boyfriend's driving down from Lough-borough later.' Perhaps she should have phoned. It might

173

have been tactful to mention that Edward was coming to join her. She decided to launch into the safe territory of a description of him instead. 'He's a basketball player, you see. He's got a match up there today. He'll be driving down after that.' She and Edward had worked out that one way they could spend some time together would be by meeting in Wales. No one here to tell tales on them to Edward's family or to his coach.

The small figure beamed. 'That's what I like to hear. A boyfriend – steady, is he? Going to get married soon?'

Petra extricated herself from the firm embrace. Her grandmother bustled ahead of her while she stood, a little uncertain, inside the kitchen door.

'Come in, come in. We don't stand on ceremony here. Just sit you down while I get the tea. Your *tad-cu* will be home in half an hour; the light goes early now, and he's on an outside job. Angharad's at one of those classes she's so fond of. Why she wants to learn French I'll never know. Not so keen on the Welsh as she should be. Language enough for her, I would have thought.' She turned with a wide smile. 'They teach it at all the schools now. When we first came down from the North they didn't have that.'

'Aunt Angharad is thinking of qualifications, I suppose. That's what Edward and I still have to get – our degrees. We can't be married before that.'

'All this learning. Will it get you a better life, that's what I want to know?' Megan uncovered a bowl which had been sitting on her range, sprinkled some flour on the kitchen table, plonked what looked like a large, grey-brown mass on the light fawn wooden top and began to push her fists into it. 'I like to bake the bread. You ever kneaded yeast dough, *fach*?'

'I'm afraid not.'

'So have a go then. Good for you.' She grinned. 'Makes

174

your hands white. The yeast, you see.' She took a tea towel
and tied it round Petra's waist. 'Wash your hands first, then
dust them with flour.'

Petra dutifully held her hands under the single, cold-
water tap and began to dry them.

'Hold them by the warm, or the flour'll stick to you. Then
rub about a fistful round them.' Petra watched closely as
Megan rolled the dough into a rugby ball, moved it back
and forth, placed the heel of her palm into it, and bent it
over. She handed it to Petra. 'That's right. Use the lower
part of your palm, see. Then double the dough over on
itself, turn it around and do the same thing again. You go
on doing it until it's shiny; elastic, like. Then it's divided up
and put into the tins to rise. That's when you bake it. Easy
when you know how.'

Petra began to knead the squelchy mass. At first it
seemed difficult, but as she got into the rhythm of it,
listening to her grandmother ramble happily on about
when her father was a boy and they were still in North
Wales, she felt the dough mould to her hand, felt the
roughness disappear and become smooth, felt the satisfaction of physical exertion.

The movement soon became tiring. 'Is it ready now?'

Strong, expert hands took over. 'Almost. Another
couple of turns, just to get the real smoothness into it. And
now we divide it up.'

'Shall I fetch the scale?'

At first Megan didn't seem to understand what she was
talking about, then she smiled. 'I don't need that, *fach*.
This makes three loaves, see. No problem there.' And she
divided the dough into three equal pieces, bullied them into
loaf shapes and placed them into the pans. Well-used,
black pans. Megan caught her looking at them. 'They're
quite clean; non-stick with use, they are.' She laughed. 'I

hardly need to oil them.' She lined them up on her hearth, placed a tea towel over them, and stood back. 'Another three-quarters of an hour, and we can bake them. Ready for our meal.'

'I thought you weren't supposed to eat freshly baked bread?'

The small, globular muscles of her grandmother's upper cheek had been kept in good trim. They rose, two tight rounds underneath crinkled eyes, and grinned with mischief. 'Not supposed to, is it? Tastes very good; you'll see.'

The kitchen door opened and a cold draught surprised Petra.

'Shut the door, Gwyneth! The dough's proving.'

'Sorry.' A slim, female version of her father walked into the room and peered at Petra. 'So you're Dewi's girl,' she said, appraising eyes moving slowly, deliberately, from the blonde hair to the shapely ankles. 'Not much resemblance to him that I can see.'

'Now, Gwyneth! Is that the best you can do when you meet your niece for the first time?' Megan wiped her hands on her apron and hugged her granddaughter again. 'You know her mother's tall.' The brown eyes looked steadily at Gwyneth. 'And you can see it on the photograph.' She pointed to an old picture of David, Louise and Petra. 'You can see she's the same colouring as her mother.'

It wasn't only Gwyneth who was staring. Petra was devastated by the sight of her aunt's upper lip and the area below her nostrils. The whole skin seemed to have turned a deep purple-blue, interspersed with some yellowing at the edges.

'I had an accident,' she said, following Petra's horrified look. 'Didn't they tell you I was in hospital when you came with your father?'

176

Petra forced her lips into a smile. 'Sorry, Aunt Gwyneth. I didn't know it was so bad.'

'Needed a considerable amount of plastic surgery. Still more to come. Means I can't say some letters very easily. Especially this.' She drew a large M shape into the flour on the table. 'You'll have to imagine them.'

'Of course.'

'I don't remember your mother being all that tall.' The brown eyes seemed to look through Petra, beyond her.

She moved further away and nearer her grandmother, lowering herself on to a stool. 'Not specially tall, no. She's just about Daddy's height; tall for a woman of her generation.'

Gwyneth laughed. 'You're much taller than she is. Good four inches, I'd say.'

She could not help herself; she flushed to the roots of her hair. 'Many daughters are taller than their mothers,' she said. 'You're taller than yours.'

'Only an inch or so.'

Megan had begun to clean vegetables, to peel potatoes and onions. 'We're having *pasteiod cennin*; we like our leeks. And *tatws popty* – potato pot. I expect your mother makes that.'

'Mummy worries about her weight. We don't often have potatoes.'

'No sign of *you* having to worry about that,' Gwyneth said. 'Not anorexic, are you?'

'I've got a high metabolism.'

'Even three pounds shows when you're short.'

Petra looked at her aunt, avoiding the upper lip. 'You're very slim yourself, Aunt Gwyneth.'

'Hard work, running a garden centre. Lugging great crates of plants about.' The sharp eyes still lingered over Petra. 'Here all on your own, is it?'

It wasn't going to be easy to sidestep the issue with Gwyneth, but she wasn't up to explaining the whole thing as yet. 'I thought it would be lovely if I could meet you this time.'

Megan began to skin onions in the sink, running the water from the tap. 'Cold water stops them making you cry, like,' she said. 'Maybe you know that.'

Petra went over to the sink. 'Really? I'll have to tell Mummy. She likes to cook.'

'And she's bringing her young man, Gwyneth. Isn't that wonderful?'

The dark head swivelled. 'You're not engaged already, are you? You're so young...'

So it was all going to start again, even here. Petra stiffened. She could feel a look of mulish antagonism knotting her brow into a furrow of anger, and tried to relax her muscles. 'We've only recently been introduced by friends. We met at the beginning of term. So we're going out together, to get to know each other better. Edward's never been to Wales; I thought it would be wonderful to explore the area. He's got a car, you see. His sponsor let him have it.'

Gwyneth had stood, listening to the long speech, the expression in her eyes suggesting she knew exactly what it was all about. 'What does he do?'

'He's a basketball player. He's very tall, you see.'

A flicker as the eyes registered understanding.

'I think you know his sponsor.' Petra smiled at them. 'He comes from round here originally. Jack Oliver, of the Jack Oliver Media Agency.'

She stopped, aware that mother and daughter were exchanging looks. 'Oh, yes. We know all about him, *fach*,' Megan said. 'Jack and his mother lived only four doors along the road. Came down from North Wales same time as

178

us, almost thirty years ago.' Her eyes searched Petra's. 'Your father and he were always best friends; right from early on.'

'They still are. Uncle Jack's my godfather, you see. He's always at our house.'

'Is he, now. Done very well for himself, and such a little boy when we first knew him. His mother was very worried about him. It's what made them come down here. The hospital, you see. We have a very good hospital.'

There had never been any suggestion from her father, or Uncle Jack, that he'd been unwell as a child. 'You mean he was ill?'

The grey head shook a no. 'Not ill, exactly. He was just so small. Very sad, really. His father couldn't take having such a tiny son, and he was the only one. His only child, see. So his mother came down to Llandrindod with us. We'd found the hospital for Dewi and Gwyn. And they were really good to Jack and his mother. The programme was just starting.'

'You'll have to explain a bit more, Mother. Jack wasn't just small, Petra. He had trouble with his growth pattern. Something to do with his 'ituitary gland.'

'His what?'

'Pituitary gland.' Megan was not to be interrupted. 'They injected growth hormones into him. Like a miracle, it was. You could see him grow before your eyes, almost. Four inches that first year. Wonderful, it was.'

Of course she knew her godfather was small; he was only five foot. Presumably he would have been even smaller if he hadn't had treatment. 'You mean he would have been a dwarf if he hadn't been helped?'

'No question at all; pituitary dwarfism, they call it. Not cured completely, of course. But not too bad a height for Wales. We're shorter, on average, than the English. His mother was over the moon. And so was he, poor little thing.' Megan sighed and lifted the tea towel to inspect the dough.

'Not so much of the poor.' Gwyneth had pulled out a stool and perched on it, her feet off the ground as though to prove the point of height in Wales. 'What he lacked in height, he made up for in cheek. Always plotting, he was. Too small to do things, he said. Directing others to do his dirty work for him, keeping his fingers clean.'

'Gwyn always thought he should stay in touch. When his father ran off, his mother had to go out to work, see. He often came to us for his meals.' She opened the oven and put the loaves inside. 'That's done, then. So, Jack's the one who sponsors your boyfriend, is it?'

'Yes, he does. It's quite a coincidence, really.'

'Small world, I always say.' Megan piled layers of potatoes and onions into a pie dish, sprinkling them with salt and pepper, and a green leaf she had chopped up.

'What's that, Gran Megan?'

'We like to use sage. Gives the *tatws popty* a good flavour.' She put dollops of butter on the top and placed the whole thing low in her oven.

'Your *god*father, is it? So he goes to church, does he?' Gwyneth's expression had the look of a snake about to strike. 'That makes a change from what he used to be.'

'Oh, it's nothing to do with religion. None of us are exactly active churchgoers. I think it's because Uncle Jack and Daddy get together all the time. They watch basketball, and he comes to lunch most Sundays. He likes Mummy's cooking, and he takes a special interest in me. He isn't married, you see.' She smiled. 'I expect you knew that.'

Gwyneth's eyes were still slit. 'One of the effects of his condition. Not much of a sex drive.'

'Gwyneth!' her mother shouted out, upset. 'You've no right to say such things in front of a young girl.' She turned to Petra, her face red. 'We don't know anything about that, Petra. We knew he hadn't married. Well, we hadn't heard any different.'

'So he hasn't got any children of his own,' Petra hurried to explain. 'He and Daddy look at videos of his favourite basketball players – his "specials", they call them. They've got very expensive equipment set up in Daddy's study, so they can monitor every move in the games. He's much more than just the usual agent. He takes a real personal interest in all his clients.'

'Saint Jack; very fetching.' Gwyneth's cold tone cut through the fug of the kitchen.

'Now, Gwyneth.' Megan turned to Petra. 'It's the pain talking. Jack was always a bit of a boy. Had to be, really. It was hard for his mother to make ends meet.'

'What Mam isn't telling you is she looked after him like her own. Had his tea with us after school every day.'

Petra could picture it all as she looked round the kitchen. Nothing had changed since her father's childhood, she felt sure; a wooden table in the middle, a china sink with a single cold-water tap, a Welsh dresser to hold the crockery. Megan and Dylan, her father and his brother Huw, Gwyneth, Bronwen and Angharad, and then Jack, all round the kitchen table. Hungry after school, eating laver bread and bacon, pease pudding and *pwdin afal cymreig* – the Welsh apple pudding her father was always going on about. 'No one can make it like my mother,' he always said, turning his nose up at Louise's apple pie.

'Uncle Jack told me about your cooking, Gran Megan. Said you were the best cook in the whole of Wales.'

'Remembered me, is it?'

'Didn't remember you fed him every day!' Gwyneth

exploded. 'But then, Dewi didn't remember to bring his only daughter to see us.'

'Don't listen to her, *fach*. She's upset ...'

Gwyneth whirled round to her mother. 'I'm not upset! I just think she ought to know what he's really like. I'm not saying Dewi's any better.'

Megan shot her daughter a look which told her to keep quiet. 'Dewi and Ian – that's Gwyn's husband, you met him last time you came – always looked after Jack, stopped the other children getting at him. And Gwyn, come to that. And Jack gave something back; he did the thinking for them. It's because of him that Dewi moved to London.'

'And left Ian to rot in prison.' Gwyneth's defiant stare silenced her mother. 'Jack never came back for a visit, not even for his mother's funeral.'

Megan took a huge yellow bowl from her dresser, put flour into it and added pieces of lard. She used her fingertips to pinch and rub the fat into the flour. 'Shortcrust pastry for the *pasteiod*,' she said. 'Know how to make it?'

'Mummy buys it frozen, I'm afraid.'

'Much better when you make your own.' She dribbled the mixture through her fingers, fluttering, feathering. 'Not too much working it, mind. Ready to have the water now.' She added it and turned to her granddaughter again. 'You'll be staying with us here, won't you, Petra?' Her voice was soft, but there was no question about a negative reply. 'Not right to stay with a boyfriend.'

Petra was delighted. This was what she'd wanted when she'd visited with her father. 'If you can find the room.' The dimples in her cheeks deepened. 'I thought, maybe, that I could share with Aunt Angharad. Edward can find a B & B ...'

'No need to bother with that. He can come and stay next

door with us. Ian and I don't mind; we've got the spare room.'

'I'm sure that's too much bother...'

'No bother. When are you expecting him?'

'Any time now. If he can find you in the dark. I gave him a local map.'

'Before you go,' Gwyneth said, grasping Petra's arm and pushing her into one of the easy chairs in her front room, 'I'm sure you and Ed would like to see a few family photographs.'

'Have you got some of Daddy?'

'Just one or two.' She went to the cupboard in the corner, drew out an album and brought it over. 'This is me when I left school.' Gwyneth pointed at a picture of a very pretty young girl with an unfortunate shadow under her nose. 'And this is the whole family.'

'Let me guess which is which.' Petra took the album and peered, intent, at the similar-looking faces. All bearing the imprint of the crop of dark hair, deeply set eyes, and the small, triangular face of their mother. 'This one's Angharad.'

'Very hard to tell.' Gwyneth's eyes mocked her. 'She's still a child in that.'

She'd only met her once, but she was sure. 'And this is Bronwen,' she said. 'Have I got it right?' Neither of them referred to the reason she'd know who her father and Gwyneth were.

'Quite right.' The eyes resumed their lynx-like expression. 'And this is how your mother looked when I first met her.' She picked out two photographs. One of a group, and another of a young woman standing between two young men.

'She came down here? I always thought...'

'She only came here once. But these were taken when

Jack gave a big party in London – business. Dewi asked me to come up. That's when he met your mother. That very night.'

'That's Mummy between Daddy and Uncle Jack, isn't it?'

'That's right. Dewi hasn't changed much.'

'Mummy was really pretty in those days.'

'We were all pretty then.'

She saw Ed glance at her and look away again; also saw that Gwyneth had noticed.

'She had a boyfriend then, only sixteen, and almost as tall as Edward.'

'Can I see that?' Edward asked, leaning across, taking the picture of the group and peering at it.

'Someone you recognise?'

'I think that's Bruce Traggard – yes, that's him!'

'You know him, do you?' Gwyneth looked surprised. 'I didn't realise.'

'He's my coach. We'd heard he knew Petra's mum before she married. It is him, isn't it?'

Petra looked at her aunt. There was a sort of triumph in the brown eyes. She was trying to get something across to her; something which wasn't too pleasant.

'That's right. He was crazy about her.'

'But my mother was eighteen when she met my father; she's always told me that. She said she'd been foolish to marry so young.'

'She was older than Bruce. That was the point. She dropped him like hot cakes as soon as she saw Jack.'

Louise had never made a secret of her admiration for Jack. But there had never been anything between them, Petra was convinced.

Gwyneth smirked suggestively. 'Jack didn't want to know, of course. I told you why already.' Her eyes checked to see whether Petra had remembered her snide remark, and understood.

She refused to look at her aunt. Instead, she bent over the photographs again.

'So she went for Dewi instead,' Gwyneth went on. 'He fell head over heels in love with her, see. And her no better than she ought to be.'

Petra drew back. 'What's that supposed to mean?'

Gwyneth shrugged. 'All I'm saying is that you don't show any resemblance to any of us. Except for your one brown eye; that's the only thing.'

Petra stood up. 'I think it really is time Edward and I were leaving, Aunt Gwyneth. It was very nice of you to put him up; we do appreciate it.' She looked coolly at her aunt. 'I hope your lip heals soon. You never said how it happened, exactly.'

The lynx eyes retreated. 'In the garden centre. I have all these crates piled up. One of them fell on me.' She held her hand in front of her mouth as she was speaking. 'It'll be OK soon.'

'We'll just nip next door and say goodbye to Gran Megan.'

It was with some relief that Petra and Edward got into the Dolly. The car was facing uphill, and Edward had trouble starting it. He pulled on the handbrake, revved up the engine and tried to put her into first gear. The car jolted, almost hitting the one parked in front of it.

'Careful, Ed. You'll crash into Aunt Gwyneth's car.'

'I'm doing my best not to,' he said, getting the Dolly into gear and grinding up the hill.

The noise of the engine revving up had brought onlookers out to wave them off.

'We'll be the talk of Pengwyn for months,' he said, grinning at Petra. 'Fame at last!'

18

The post had started arriving earlier again. There'd been a period of about six months, two or three years ago, when the first post hadn't turned up until after he'd left for work. It wasn't that he didn't trust Louise – well, not exactly that. As far as he was aware she'd never opened a letter addressed to him. But she did scrutinise the envelopes for clues to their contents. What was unnerving was how much she could glean from such an exercise. She had a native intelligence which used to surprise him, until he started taking it for granted. What a waste that she'd never bothered to train her mind and use it.

David picked up the bundle of letters and flipped through them. He'd finally trained his solicitor to send anything urgent care of Jorncy, and the bank to send statements care of the solicitor. Years of uneasy frustration had convinced him to change to a new bank, one Louise knew nothing about, refusing even to give them his home address. It was the only way to prevent what were referred to as computer errors, but which he knew very well had to be the computer operator's. That meant the bank couldn't be trusted to send his private statements only to him.

He glanced at the envelopes. The monthly Access statement, several mail order catalogues which Louise liked to browse through, a flyer for an investment letter. He frowned; where had they found his address? He didn't like unsolicited mail. Christmas cards from the Mouth & Foot Painting Artists. He lingered over the envelope; he liked the way these people had overcome their handicaps yet did not whinge. They offered their cards and calendars for sale, but didn't try to use moral blackmail to influence their customers. Instead, they had pride in their work. He made a mental note to order several sets.

The chocolate-box colours of a picture postcard he instantly recognised as a view of fishing on the lake at Llandrindod Wells caught his attention. He sighed; a postcard from his mother. Thankfully she'd written the short message in Welsh, but that wouldn't have stopped Louise deciphering the meaning. *Don't wait too long before you come and see us again,* it said. *We miss you, Dewi. Lovely, it was, your little Petra coming to see us; I think she must have taken to us!*

He looked towards the hall stairs. Louise hadn't stirred yet; she was waiting for him to put the coffee machine on. He pushed the card deep into his dressing-gown pocket. Though she had no interest in his Welsh family, Louise's curiosity would see to it that she read his mother's spidery hand. She'd only have to see the word *Petra* to know exactly what had happened. He shuddered as he pictured her examining every item of mail which came into the house, using her powers of observation to extract its significance. She made a kind of fetish of it.

The last letter was addressed to her. A plain, white envelope in neat, laser printing. He put it with the pile of catalogues and bills on Louise's side of the kitchen table, and switched the kettle on.

'Soft-boiled or scrambled?' he called up the stairs.

He could hear her running the water to brush her teeth. 'Soft-boiled. Only two and a half minutes, don't forget!'

She came down wearing an expensive satin dressing gown over the satin nightdress with its bodice of little pearls sewn into lace. Louise spent a great deal of time and money on her body and her wardrobe. In spite of that the years had taken an unusual toll. Her mouse-coloured hair would have been better without the lavish amount of henna her latest hairdresser had persuaded her to use. The dye had coarsened it even more; it hung, limp and lifeless, around a sallow face. Even the much-lauded Ralph could not coax it into a springy form for more than two hours after her weekly visits to his salon. A complete waste. It was as well they could afford it.

Louise came in and sat on the side of the table away from the cooker. She looked at him expectantly. It had been agreed, right from the beginning of their marriage, that he would make breakfast on Saturdays and Sundays. At the time he'd been only too keen. Those heady days when he couldn't do enough to please her.

'Otherwise I never get a break,' she'd always insisted. 'It's all right for you. You have the stimulation of your colleagues at the office. All I ever do is slave away in the kitchen.'

'I do work fairly hard myself.' He'd never bothered to point out that his office at Jorncy wasn't exactly a hub of social activity. Most of the day he spent alone, or working in the isolated area to which only he and his assistant had direct access.

To his wife's astonishment he'd been made head of his department almost ten years before. It hadn't surprised him. He was devoted to his work, came in at least an hour early and often left two hours after everyone else. Jorncy weren't stupid; they'd agreed a modest salary and were happy to pay him overtime so that they didn't have to increase his basic pay.

'Running to keep up, I suppose,' Louise always dismissed his efforts. In her imagination he was in charge of a team of dedicated young assistants who tried to take over his job. One of them would, she was sure, soon succeed.

This morning she seemed content to demand a perfect soft-boiled egg. 'Did you put the timer on?'

He turned to the eggs, hiding the guilt she'd notice on his face. 'Just ready,' he murmured. 'I'll run them under the cold tap.'

He placed the cooled eggs on egg cups, sliced off their tops, and handed them over to his wife. The coffee had filtered through, and the toast was popping up. He poured boiled water over a tea bag for himself.

'Planning anything special today, dear?'

'Hmm?' She held the pile of mail in her left hand and scanned it. 'Selfridges always does a good catalogue.' The colourful packages were quickly placed into a pile beside her plate. She stopped at the white envelope and frowned. 'It's from Wales,' she said.

Extraordinary how quickly she'd worked it out. He hadn't even noticed that. 'Really?'

'Didn't you see the Welsh stamp?' She eyed him with disdain. As far as she was concerned he was a slow-witted bungler.

He never bothered to point out that their living standard was higher than many managers'. Why would he invite her scepticism? He preferred the scorn; he smiled as he realised it was the one area which held her back. She'd shown such promise, such life when he first met her. Never beautiful, she was alert, a brilliant dancer, good at tennis and an outstanding hostess. He'd been bowled over by her, had loved her slavishly for years in spite of her increasing irritation with him. Now she was so convinced of his uselessness that she never even questioned it.

'Must be from that tiresome sister of yours.'

'Really?' Would Gwyneth write to Louise? Out of the question. If Gwyneth did write, it could only be bad news. One meeting with Louise was all it had taken to antagonise her for ever. Not surprising; Louise had drawn attention to the harelip within minutes of meeting her. 'What makes you say that?' He kept his tone neutral.

'Windowless white envelope means it isn't a bill, the address is printed by a bottom-of-the-range laser, a stamp instead of a franking machine means it has to be a very small business, and it comes from Wales.' She frowned at it. 'My glasses are on the shelf behind you. Could you pass them to me?'

'Why don't you just open it?'

She put her glasses on and peered at the stamp. 'The postmark's very faint, but it isn't Llandrindod Wells. I get it – it's Aberystwyth.' She grinned at him. 'Isn't that where your sister goes for her plastic surgery?'

'Very impressive,' he said. 'Now open it and see if you're right.'

'What'll you bet?'

This was becoming tiresome. 'Five pounds,' he said. Worth it to get her to open it. For some reason he couldn't understand, the whole performance was making him nervous.

The crimson California nail on her right index finger was always the first to chip. She used it like a tool; she grasped the envelope and tore along the seal with it as though it were a letter-opener.

Two crimson nails were clamped on either side of a folded white sheet. 'That's odd. It isn't laser-printed or written. It seems to be some sort of brochure.' Her brows were pulled into a tight knot, with a deep vertical cut, as though made by a knife, dividing them. She spread the paper out and stared at it.

Her features turned from puzzlement to fury, then froze. 'My God, it's worse than I thought. A disgusting, cowardly anonymous letter.' Her voice had all the venom of a cobra about to strike.

A feeling of despair he couldn't quite understand spread through his chest. 'Anonymous letter? Why would anyone send you something like that?'

She looked over at him, the muddy eyes shot with sparks of gold. 'Accusing me of being a whore.' She laughed; a sudden, thin bark of a laugh. 'Last thing to accuse me of. I've no idea what that can be about.' She had already scrunched the paper up into a ball and was about to throw it into the pedalbin when she swivelled back to her husband. 'But it *is* that sister of yours.'

'What is?'

'She's sent it; I know perfectly well it's her. She never could stand me, and now she's decided to stir things up. Nothing else to do in hospital, I suppose.' She looked at him, her mouth open, her teeth exposed.

'You've got that wrong,' he said triumphantly. 'It can't be her, she's out of hospital.'

She brushed it aside. 'I *told* you not to have anything to do with her. But you know better; you're the brilliant one!'

'What are you talking about, Louise?' He took a drink of tea to steady himself. There had to be a meaning behind the letter; something far more significant than Gwyneth being spiteful. 'It's just some sort of nut writing anonymous letters...' He'd never persuade her, but he had to try.

She took the piece of paper, began to flatten it on the table. 'Not a nut; someone who knows something about me. Just look at this disgusting rubbish. See that?' She handed him the piece of paper.

WHORE! WE ALL KNOW YOUR DAUGHTER ISN'T DAVID'S.
THE COACH COACHED YOU IN MORE THAN DANCING.
CHEAT! LIAR! SLUT!
THOUGHT YOU'D GET AWAY WITH IT.
WRONG!

The words had been cut out of newspapers and pasted on. Their meaning began to trickle through to his mind. Coach? The letter was accusing Louise of having some sort of involvement with a coach. That had to mean Bruce Traggard. He knew, of course, that she'd had an affair with him before they met. Which she had, in fact, finished that very night. To be precise, the night she met Jack and Jack had introduced her to him. But he'd been so sure she'd never seen the man again.

He folded the piece of paper to hide its grotesque message. 'It has to be someone we know.'

'I just told you that!'

'Talking about Bruce Traggard, I suppose?'

Her lips had curled up into a snarl. 'I don't exactly make a habit of sleeping around with basketball coaches. Or anyone else, for that matter. He's the only one I've ever known.'

'So you did sleep with him?'

'For God's sake, David! I never pretended anything else. I had a fling with him, before I met you. I was young; barely eighteen, Petra's age! So bloody what?'

'So this, I suppose. Petra was born within ten months of our getting married. *Is* she his? Or don't you even know?'

She banged her fist on the table. 'No, she is not!'

'You're sure? You're sure you didn't cheat on me?' He

grabbed her hands across the table, shattering crockery, ignoring it. 'I know I said you could—' He choked, recovered his breath. 'But I didn't agree to this!'

She tried to twist her hands free. 'Let go, will you? You're hurting me.'

'*Did* you cheat on me?'

'You can't believe this rubbish!' He'd freed her hands and she was rubbing her wrists. 'I told you not to go to Wales, you'd stir everything up.'

He gulped, took a handkerchief out of his pocket and the postcard from his mother dropped out.

She grabbed it. 'Llandrindod Wells – your mother.' She stared at him across the table, then back at the card. A few moments of concentration and she'd worked it out. 'You took Petra, didn't you?'

'She wanted to go. She wants to know her roots...'

She tore the card into little shreds. 'Know her roots? Wherever they are, they're not in Wales. You know that just as well as I do!'

'You want me to tell her that? We always said there was no point in it.'

'My God, David, you don't have to be a complete moron. The reason I wanted you to stay away from your family is just this. She spotted it right away, didn't she, that sister of yours?'

'She wasn't there; she was still in hospital.' His heart missed several beats as the wording of his mother's card came back to him. Did it mean that Petra had gone back on her own? Had she met Gwyneth this time?

For a moment Louise was stumped. 'She must have been told about her, then. Your other sisters, I suppose.' The frownline deepened again. 'I know Gwyneth sent this. I can feel it in my bones.'

'It doesn't matter who sent it, Louise. What matters is

what you did.' He remembered Ian's face at his last visit, the way he'd screamed he'd take revenge. This was just the sort of thing he'd do. And post it in Aberystwyth; just his style.

He stood, walked over to his wife, placed his hands on her shoulders and twisted her torso round. 'Petra is unusually tall.' He stared into her eyes, a sullen expression on his face. 'And fair. You said you'd stick to our bargain.' His voice was a croak, he dug hard fingers into her shoulders.

She tried to twist back and found herself unable to do so. 'For God's sake, David!'

He let go, walked to the sink, turned on the cold tap and bent to drink some water straight from it. 'You did trick me, didn't you?' he said, turning, water dripping down his chin. 'I knew it was odd she's so fair. Just that one brown eye...' He slumped back into his chair and put his head in his hands. 'And all the time you were pregnant with his child. You're right; I'm a bloody fool.'

'She isn't Traggard's, David. I don't know what the big deal is even if she were,' she said, her voice hissing through her nose. 'What difference would it make?'

'This difference,' he said, pointing at the word COACH. 'If Bruce Traggard is Petra's father it would explain why she looks so like him. She's supposed to look like me!'

'Good trick,' she yelled back at him. Then her voice lowered. 'Look, David, we made a pact when we got married. You agreed to it; I asked you often enough if it was OK with you.'

'I didn't agree to Traggard!'

'And Petra isn't Traggard's daughter. I give you my word on that.'

'Your word? I'm supposed to be impressed by that?'

'I've never lied to you.'

As far as he knew that was true; she'd never found it worth her while. 'But you did cheat?' She hadn't kept to their bargain. The implications were beginning to sink in.

'Not really cheat, David.' Her voice had taken on a persuasive tone. She even smiled at him. 'I did make a slightly different choice. You know I like fair men...'

Tears had come into David's eyes. 'You mean you opted for a fair one.' He put his head into his hands again, pushed back the black curls peppered with white.

'It doesn't make any difference, David. I wish you'd understand that.'

'I should have guessed. How could I have been such a bloody idiot? It's crystal clear for anyone to see!' The face which emerged from his hands was drained of all blood; he could feel it, like a physical emptiness. 'You don't understand, Louise. You promised me, and I trusted you.' His voice was hoarse and thick with the horror of what had happened. 'You're a stupid, headstrong woman; you don't know what you've done!'

19

Petra was nervous about finding herself in a department she'd never been in before. She stared at the serried ranks of lockers. At first she couldn't see any numerals at all, as though her nervousness had made her blind. After a few moments she calmed down and her eyes adjusted to the dark. She focused on the numbering engraved into the key: 231.

'You come for the audition?' A fruity male voice erupted behind her.

She startled round as though she were a rabbit. A rotund, middle-aged man stepped in front of her, looked her up and down and smiled in invitation.

'I'm sorry, nothing like that. I'm here for a friend.'

'Anyone in particular?' His voice had taken on a mistrustful twang, and his eyes had lost their friendliness. 'We don't encourage people outside the department to come in.'

'Sally Wheeler,' Petra breathed, hoping that whoever this man was he'd heard of Sally. 'She asked me to pick up her gear. You wouldn't know where I can find Locker 231, would you?'

He looked her up and down, his eyes now blatantly suspicious. 'You're the second person in as many days. I know Sally hasn't been well, but this is getting out of hand.

She seems to have a genius for asking other people to do her chores for her.'

'You mean someone's already been?'

'Been and gone. I didn't believe their story, so I didn't let them take anything.' He sized her up again. 'I suppose you're here instead?'

Petra showed him the duffle bag she'd brought to put the equipment in. 'No. I'm her room-mate; I've come to clear the whole locker out. She's got some sort of virus, you see. She's quite ill – had to go home for the rest of the term. If you could just show me...'

'You've got the key, have you?' He sounded oddly concerned about Sally's belongings. 'And proper identification? Our students keep all kinds of expensive equipment in there, you know. Cameras, lenses, all very costly.'

She realised that he was wearing a uniform. A caretaker, perhaps. 'I've got the key,' she said. 'And my name is Petra Jones. You can check that on the student register, if you want. You'll see Sally and I share a room in Mardon.'

He shrugged. 'I'd better make sure. Come into the office, and I'll bring it up on the computer.' He led the way through a labyrinth of corridors. 'Won't take long.' He sat down in a swivel chair, and turned. 'What department are you in?'

'Biology.' The computer monitor showed a list of students. A quick flick at the keyboard and she could see another entry, listing students with the name of Jones, then Petra Jones, Department of Biology, Mardon Hall.

'Can you prove who you are?'

'Here's my student card.' She showed him the card, sporting the picture she'd taken in a photo booth while Sally waited for her outside.

He grinned at her. 'Keep that away if you do go for an audition,' he said. 'Don't know how you managed a mug shot with looks like yours.' But he led the way and found the locker for her.

'Thanks.'

'Bring the key back to me if she's going to be away for the rest of the term. We'll issue her with a new locker when she comes back.'

Her fingers fumbled the lock. It seemed to have stuck. She was reluctant to find the man again and ask his help. She pushed the key in, slipped it fully home, and couldn't turn it. She held it halfway, jiggled it about and found it needed an odd twist to pull back the spring. Sally hadn't mentioned any problems, but then she'd been too ill to do more than whisper goodbye.

The lock gave way at last and Petra opened the door. The muddled jumble which greeted her was a surprise. Sally was neat; why was everything in such a mess? She picked out an ancient 16mm movie camera, various reels of film in metal cases, several enormous outdated reference books, filters, a tripod, strobe lights, white sheets, black sheets, a grey card, four video tapes. There was no separate bag with a videotape slotted between two paperbacks.

She placed the whole lot inside the duffle bag and slung it over her shoulder. It was heavy, and she wasn't looking forward to carting it up to London. However small Sally might be, she must also be strong. She'd carried all this gear around herself. Before she was ill, that was. There was no way she could have coped with it now.

'Why couldn't I bring Edward?' Petra demanded, leaning back in the front passenger seat of her father's Toyota. He'd insisted on picking her up from Paddington, and she was glad of that because of the heavy duffle bag she'd brought for Sally. It also gave her the chance to talk to her father on his own. Besides, there was something about being alone together in a car which invited confidences. 'I thought you'd be pleased I wanted to introduce him to you.'

'Your mother didn't think it would be a good idea, Petra.' His voice was listless, almost apathetic.

Petra sat silent, and stared out of the windscreen. This was a new side to her father. So often, in the past, the two of them had formed a gentle alliance against her mother. Affectionate teases, slight jokes had helped them cajole a sullen Louise into laughter, had released the tension which so often threatened their enjoyment as a family group. Louise's growing irritations with her life spilled out in anger at her husband and her daughter. Petra had been glad to escape to Exeter. She was impressed by her father's continuing devotion to such a selfish, demanding woman.

'I thought she'd like the chance to meet a really tall man. She's always going on about height.' She thought back to what Gwyneth had told her, and was tempted to tell her father how often Louise had downgraded him because of his lack of stature. But her own love for him kept her quiet.

'It's nothing to do with how tall he is, or anything else about his looks, Petra. It's simply that we both feel you're much too young to marry. You've hardly started out in life.'

'You and Mummy married young.' She knew she wasn't on good ground there. Louise had often complained that she'd married too young, and look where it had got her. It seemed to Petra that it had got her a cushy life in a comfortable house, with a husband who was willing to put up with all kinds of moods. And it had also got her a reasonably dutiful daughter.

'Things were different then.' The monotonous voice, deprived of its lilting enthusiasm, sounded flat and pedantic. 'She's worried about losing you too soon. Just like me.'

A small, almost perfunctory smile touched his lips but saddened his eyes still more. 'We thought we had years of your company yet.'

Her father always defended her against her mother, whatever she did. It was an unwritten rule of their family life. She couldn't remember a time when he hadn't taken her part. Something was wrong.

She glanced at the impassive profile beside her. The smiling, joky man she'd grown up with had disappeared. Instead, she was with someone who spoke in platitudes and sounded depressed. What was the matter with him? There had to be a reason other than that she had a boyfriend.

'I only wanted you to meet him, Daddy. Both of us know we need to get our degrees before we even begin to think of settling down. I just wanted you to see what he was like.'

'It might have given him the wrong impression, Petra.'

'I suppose Mummy thinks I ought to marry someone rich, someone with an important job. Or at least someone involved with celebrities, even if he isn't one himself. She's a snob, a social climber. And I'm supposed to help her up in the world.'

In the past her father would have laughed and suggested Prince Charles, once he was divorced, or perhaps an invitation to the Palace. This time she could see he'd taken her seriously. 'Really, Petra! What a way to speak about your mother.'

What if she was exaggerating a bit? There was a germ of truth in what she'd said. 'You know it's true, Daddy.' She stared straight ahead, unsmiling in her turn. 'Either that, or become famous in my own right. That's why she's so keen for me to go in for fashion modelling. Instant success, or meeting a tycoon.'

He sighed. 'That isn't true, Pet. We're both delighted if you do what makes you happy.'

'You've got a very funny way of showing it.' Why was he trotting out a series of banalities? 'I suppose it may be true of you, Daddy,' she said, her voice shaking with the love she felt for him, aware that her love for Edward was nudging her into more adult feelings. She turned to face him; he kept his eyes on the road ahead. Perhaps he'd already guessed what she was about to ask. 'But what about you? You married for love; do you think I should just give him up?' Her voice rose to an infuriating high. There was no need to be defensive about her feelings for Edward; there was nothing to be ashamed of.

'He's stopping you from going out with other boys.'

'But he's just right for me, Daddy!'

'He sounds a very nice young man. I keep telling you that's not the point.'

The resignation in his voice made her look at him again. She saw him grip the steering wheel as though he expected to lose his contact with sanity if he did not.

'You can't mean that. It's not that easy to meet the right person. Why are you so against him when you haven't even met him?'

'You haven't known each other long enough to make any sort of long-term commitment.' His voice sounded tight and very nasal, as though he was reciting a prepared speech. The knuckles showed even whiter as he breathed in.

'That's what we're trying to do: get to know each other!'

He cleared his throat. 'And I suppose I do agree with your mother that a professional basketball player isn't quite the sort of husband we had in mind for you.'

She couldn't believe what she was hearing. He and Jack spent all their spare time going to basketball matches together, reading the sports sections of the newspapers. 'But I thought you liked basketball?'

'I like it as a sport to follow. I like opera, too – doesn't mean I'd want you to become a diva.'

What *was* up with him? 'I don't think he specially wants to be involved in basketball for the rest of his life, Daddy. But Uncle Jack footed the bill for Edward's schooling, so he feels he can't let him down now, just when it's beginning to pay off.'

Her father nodded. 'If he's any good he'll get sent off to the States next season. There's no real future in this country yet.'

'I know.' She put her hand on his arm. 'But he'll earn pots of money over there, and he can save it. It would only be for a few years.'

'You can hardly blame us for not wanting to see our only child dragged abroad.'

She tried again. 'As it happens, Edward is interested in the hardware side of computers. There are some very good career prospects for that.'

'Computers?' He frowned, as though it was a subject he found distasteful. 'A very competitive business. He'd have to be really good. You've just met him, Pet. He's a second-year student, he can't know anything about the commercial world. Neither of you have any idea what's ahead for you. He isn't my concern. But you, Pet, you really ought to give yourself the chance to meet other young men.' The corners of his mouth had dropped in an uncharacteristic curve of dejection. His eyes looked vague, uncertain, as he tamely steered the car behind the other traffic in his lane. He made no effort to nip ahead the way he usually did, slipping through amber lights, boasting about his driving. 'I think you should have a long talk with your mother.'

'Oh come *on*, Daddy. What's all this about? You sound just like an echo of Mummy, and I know perfectly well you're not!'

They had stopped at a light, but he kept his eyes straight ahead. 'Your mother really does have your best interests at heart. You should talk to her, listen to what she says.' He turned to look at her for the first time since she'd got into the car. 'I mean it, Pet. She'll explain it better than I can.'

'*She* married young. Are you telling me she made a big mistake, and she's trying to stop me doing the same? Is that it?'

'Perhaps I'm not the right husband for her; perhaps I held her back. I've often thought she should have used her brain. She does have a good one, you know.'

'Modern marriage doesn't mean the end of a woman's education. What's to stop her, even now? She lives in London; she can go to courses, or even university, any time she wants to.'

He put his hand out and patted her knee. 'Let's not go into all that now. The three of us are going to have a wonderful weekend, just like we used to do.'

That brought a tingle of pleasure as the memory of the glorious autumn days in Wales came back to her. 'I loved the time we spent in Powys together, Daddy. I don't mean just because we were with your family, though I loved that. Maybe we could take Mummy some time. Show her that marvellous scenery.'

He sighed. 'Not such a good idea. I took you on your own because your mother and Gwyneth never got along.'

Nothing she said worked. He was determined to reject everything she suggested and to take Louise's part against her. 'We wouldn't have to stay in Pengwyn. It's such a beautiful country. How can you bear not to go back quite often?' She thought about how she and Edward had walked the hills, driven down to the Elan Valley, explored the walks there. 'Why have you never thought of going back, Daddy?' Strange that she'd never thought to ask him that

204

before. Perhaps it was because she'd always seen Wales as some sort of fairy tale, not a real place at all.

'What would I do? You've seen my family, you've talked to them, heard how hard it is to make a living there. The last state-owned coal mine closed in 1994. That's why Jack and I went to London to seek our fortunes in the first place; and we haven't done too badly.'

'*He's* done brilliantly.'

'And I've done very much better than I could have hoped, Pet. A great deal better than if I'd stayed in Wales, or gone back. Haven't I always given you everything you wanted?'

She put her hand on his. 'Of course you have, Daddy. I wasn't suggesting you hadn't. But you do have to work such long hours, all that overtime to make money.'

'It's the penalty for not going to college, Pet. That's why I'm so keen that you should get as many qualifications as you need for whatever you want to do.'

'You know I want to do research.'

'And I hope you'll go right to the top of your profession, my dear. As I'm sure you will.'

Petra was in her mother's 'farm kitchen'. It bore no resemblance at all to Gran Megan's. That was a real country kitchen, with an old-fashioned country cook to bring it alive. Here a range of smoothly finished cupboards, carefully jointed together and covered with a seamless top, edged two walls. The double sink, and the dishwasher beneath, were under the window. A round table stood off towards the fourth corner of the room. Louise was preparing the ingredients for French onion soup.

'Have you ever heard of letting the cold water run while peeling onions?' Petra asked. 'Then your eyes won't water.'

Louise stopped taking the skins off and looked up. 'Really? Where did you learn that? Sally's mother?'

It was too late to pull out now. She'd forgotten that this was one of her grandmother's handy hints. 'Gran Megan told me. She made leek pasties when I was there, and she had no trouble at all.'

At first there was no answer. Louise did, however, put on the cold tap. 'Brilliant if it works,' she said at last. She busied herself with more vegetables. 'Got on well with them, did you?'

'They *are* my family.'

The expected outburst against the Joneses didn't come. Louise's eyes held a hint of compassion. 'You miss having an extended family, do you, Pet?'

She fidgeted with some fragments of the cheese she was grating. 'I know you couldn't help becoming an orphan, Mummy. And it wasn't your fault your great-aunt died.'

'But you can't understand why we didn't take you to see Daddy's family. Is that what you're thinking?'

She shrugged. 'I did seem to click with them right away, at least with Gran Megan and the aunts.'

Petra looked at her mother and saw that her eyes were wet in spite of the cold water. Perhaps the tap had to be run before starting to peel the onions. 'So you think you have a lot in common?' Her voice was unusually husky, and low enough for Petra to have to strain to hear her.

'Half my genes are from them, Mummy.' She looked at her mother. It was hard to judge because of the onion tears, but she didn't think there was any reaction to her statement. Gwyneth must have been trying to stir things up. 'I know I don't much look like any of them; only my brown eye is exactly the same colour as Gran Megan's. But that's

206

not the important bit. What really matters to me is the Celtic heritage. It's hard to describe, but it felt as though I was coming home.'

'I see.'

'They're so genuine, Mummy, so warm. They live in these terrace cottages built on a steep hillside. They walk in and out as though they lived in one big house.' Her face couldn't hide the radiance she felt go through her. 'Why don't we all go together? Daddy can book us into a swish hotel so you'll be comfortable.'

'Not my sort of thing, Petra.' Her lips had the determined set which meant further discussion would only lead to a row.

Might as well be hung for a speckle-faced Welsh sheep, Petra thought to herself. 'Edward and I were there together one weekend. Aunt Gwyneth put him up. I stayed with Gran Megan. They thought he was wonderful.'

'*What?*' The familiar shrillness ricocheted round the kitchen, bouncing off hard surfaces. 'You took him to Wales? You're intending to go through with this nonsense?'

'It isn't nonsense, Mummy. I've reached the age of majority, I can do what I like.'

Louise clattered a Le Creuset saucepan on the stainless steel sink, making a grinding noise. 'You're young and ignorant, Petra. You've got no idea what you're talking about. Hasn't your father told you?'

'Daddy?' Was there something specific? Had her father been too cowardly to bring it up? 'He said you'd explain better than he could.'

The deep lines running from Louise's nostrils to the corners of her mouth increased the grim look in her angry eyes. 'Left me to do the dirty work, as usual.'

'You mean you've got some concrete reason against my marrying Edward?'

Petra noticed her mother's hands were trembling. 'This isn't going to be easy. Your father's given you the idea that you're a little princess, that you can have anything you want. Not this time. You can't marry Edward.'

'What do you mean, I can't marry Edward? Why not? What *have* you got against him?'

'Your godfather came specially to tell us.'

It wasn't at all what she was expecting to hear. 'Uncle Jack? What's he got to do with it?'

'You know he has files on all his clients. Each athlete is given a complete physiological test at regular intervals. And lots of other tests as well – DNA fingerprinting, for example.'

'So what? If Edward wasn't all right they wouldn't have taken him on in the first place. His brother Harold was turned down.'

'He's all right now; he may not be all right in the future.'

'You mean he has some sort of illness? Is that what all this is about?'

'It's rather difficult. It's highly confidential, and we shouldn't really be discussing it. But I can see you won't take any notice unless I tell you what I know. Edward suffers from an hereditary disease.'

She stared at her mother. 'Disease? What disease? Why haven't I noticed it?'

'It's called Huntington's chorea – a very serious illness, Petra. It doesn't show up till middle age, which is why you don't realise there's something wrong with Edward.'

It was a shock. She pulled out a chair from around the kitchen table and sat down on it. 'So how does Uncle Jack know?'

'He's only recently found out. Bruce Traggard spotted it, going through the files.'

'That awful man again!'

'It's his job, Petra. He's the team coach. It's why Phil
Thompson was always preferred to Edward. They know
the onset isn't till middle age – thirty-five or even ten years
later, if you're lucky. So it didn't stop them taking Edward
on for basketball. It won't show up until he's finished with
all that.'

The shockwaves were making Petra's heart beat at twice
its normal rate, producing runnels of sweat under her
armpits, making her shiver. 'They're absolutely sure he's
got it?'

'Jack brought the whole file round. He showed us the
special DNA report. There isn't any question about it.'

Her eyes brightened. 'There must be a mistake. His
parents are middle-aged, Mummy. I've met them – there's
nothing wrong with either of them. I'd have seen something
like that. They're both quite fit.'

'Really, Petra. You've met them once. How could you
possibly tell?'

'I'm in Professor Dunstan's class. I see him every week.'

She shrugged. 'So what. I don't suppose you even know
what the symptoms are!'

'So what are they?'

'Jack told us they're quite variable. Some people
become forgetful, others show physical signs, like jerky
movements. You can't just tell by coming across people
occasionally.'

'Does Edward know?' Professor Dunstan was undeniably
absent-minded. Was it the beginning of disease?

She shook her head. 'Only if his parents have told him. It
isn't Jack's business to tell his players; he and his coaches
are very strict about that.'

'It would stop them doing their best, you mean,' Petra
cried out. 'They wouldn't get a return on their investment!'

'What on earth do you expect, Petra? You want Jack to

tell Edward, ruin his chances of making money so he can retire when the time comes? No one knows how to cure Huntington's; what good does it do to know?'

'The reason he has to know, Mummy, is the reason you're telling me. It will affect his attitude to marriage. He has to be in a position to tell his future wife.'

At least this new information made sense of her parents' odd behaviour. Did it also explain Ethel Dunstan's hysterical manner? No wonder she'd talked about a genetic defect! How could she have blamed Petra's eyes instead of telling her the truth?

Petra knew she couldn't pretend that she wouldn't have to think about it, but Edward's parents had gone ahead and had children, so why shouldn't they?

'So now you know why you can't marry him, Pet. I'm sorry. I can see you're in love, and I do know how that feels.' She'd washed her hands and dried them. She pulled a chair out next to her daughter. 'We're your parents, we love you very much. That's why your father's so depressed; he just can't face the thought that you might have to cope with a tragedy like that.'

She stared at her mother. 'Because of his cleft palate, you mean. He's always been worried that he might pass that on.' Her eyes flashed anger. 'And so have you – that's why you only had one child.'

'A cleft palate isn't hereditary in the same way, as I'm sure I don't have to tell you. No one knows exactly how that comes about.'

'But I might be a carrier.' She saw her mother's eyes slide away. 'That's true, isn't it? Edward could take the line that one of our children might have a cleft palate.' She looked straight at her mother. 'That's the real reason you kept me away from Wales, isn't it? Because of Aunt Gwyneth. You didn't want me to know how bad it could be.'

Louise got up abruptly, walked over to the sink and began to peel the potatoes for the roast. 'You certainly have a high opinion of me.'

'We all have potentially defective genes,' Petra said, her voice shaking. 'I'm in love with Edward, and I want to marry him.' She was surprised to find that the feeling which triumphed, the feeling she was left with, was one of relief. At least she knew what she was fighting against. Instead of swimming through a sea of treacle, she could confront the enemy.

'Why don't you have a chat with Jack, Petra? Talk to someone who isn't as close to you as we are. You're terribly young, and so good-looking. You've no idea what the world could offer you.'

'No, Mummy. It's my life, and I'm going to decide for myself. I'm the one that has to live with my decision.'

Her father had come into the kitchen, and taken a chair beside her. 'Are you really going to put your children at such risk?' He shook his head at her. 'Why can't you give yourself the chance to meet someone else? You have your whole life ahead of you. Couldn't you wait a bit?'

'You and Mummy didn't wait. Mummy was the same age as me. You've forgotten what it feels like.'

He tried to take her hands, but she pulled back.

'I don't care about Edward's genes. I'm in love with him, and I want to marry him, for better or for worse.' She stood, a beautiful girl at the threshold of womanhood. 'And medicine has made great strides already. By the time he's middle-aged they'll have found a way to overcome his problem.'

'But what about your children, Petra! Do you really want to expose them to such a disease?'

Some of the recent work she'd been doing in biology came back to her; she remembered the age she was living

211

in. 'We have genetic fingerprinting now. You said that's what pointed up the disease in Edward. It would do the same for a foetus in the womb.'

'That helps?' David asked, watching her.

'Either the doctors will know how to alter the faulty gene, or there's abortion.' Her voice dropped at that; she wasn't at all sure she could go through with such a solution. 'I'm going to go into medical research myself. Perhaps I'll find the cure.'

David sat as though turned to stone. 'You mean you're going to go through with it? You're going to marry him in spite of what we've just told you?'

She stood, her whole body transformed by love. 'I think I'd better go back to Exeter right away. Whatever you both say, I'm going to marry Edward.'

20

Petra stood waiting outside the small terraced house which had been converted into three flats. Beatrice Wheeler lived right at the top, in a one-bedroom loft which was too cold in winter and too hot in summer. She wondered how she and Sally were managing through Sally's illness; it couldn't be easy to share such a small space most of the day.

No sign of anyone at home. Petra stepped back from the pavement and looked up at the top window. The curtains were drawn. Had she not pressed the bell hard enough? Should she ring again? She was about to push her finger back on the bell-tip when she heard someone inside, on the stairs. There were no carpets; the noise of heavy footsteps on bare wood could be heard through the front door. Didn't sound like Sally.

'Sorry you've been kept waiting, love,' Sally's mother wheezed as she opened the front door wide and pulled Petra through by her arm. 'Lovely to see you.' A paroxysm of coughing shook her, then she cleared her throat. 'It's my chest,' she gasped, straining to get her breath and making it worse. 'Dad was a bit of a smoker. They say it's got to me.'

Petra hid her surprise behind a large smile. 'Hello, Mrs Wheeler. How nice to see you.' Beatrice Wheeler was already walking ahead of her, grasping a frail-looking banister and hauling herself up the narrow stairs and tall treads. 'Sally does know I'm coming?' she called out.

The heavy figure stopped and turned. 'Counting the minutes since you rang, love. She thought you weren't coming till tomorrow. And she's longing for that stuff you said you'd bring. Just nipped out to get some milk and biscuits; we're a bit short.'

Petra heaved the duffle bag and its heavy load of films and camera over her shoulders and grasped the useless cut flowers she'd brought. She cursed herself for an idiot. What good would they be? She knew perfectly well that Sally and her mother had very little to live on. Joe Wheeler had died of lung cancer two years before, leaving his widow with a signalman's small pension and the consequences of passive smoking. Sally existed on a student grant.

'Come right in.' The second flight of steps was even steeper than the first. They led, round a sharp bend, to a small door. That, in turn, led up some further steps into a surprisingly cheerful little hall with a glass roof. The effect was bright even on a grey November day like this one. It was also cold. Mrs Wheeler's features fell into what Petra guessed to be a habitual pattern of resignation. She'd known more sorrow than joy in her life, and she lifted the corners of her mouth into a smile against defeat. Podgy hands waved Petra through into the room beyond.

'I've put the heating on.' She stood, ready to take Petra's anorak. 'You young people – not much of a coat, is it? Hardly weighs more than a feather.' November winds, straight from Siberia, were threatening a cold winter. 'Go on through to the lounge. I'll put the kettle on.'

The flat was comfortable for a single person, or a couple. There was one bedroom, the living room, a kitchen with a small table at the side for eating, and a bathroom. Sally had left home some years before, when she was eighteen. After her father's death her mother earned a little extra by cleaning for a couple of mornings a week.

Mrs Wheeler came into the room while she was waiting for the kettle to boil. 'See what I've got my latest great-niece?' She showed Petra a small teddy bear. 'Her christening's next week.'

'He's very sweet. I still remember my first teddy.'

'I always wanted a big family,' Mrs Wheeler confided to Petra. 'No good, though, just didn't work out.' Her face looked forlorn. 'Even Sally wasn't really ours, you know.'

'Sally did say ...'

Mrs Wheeler frowned, then hesitated. 'Adopted, she was. Not that Dad and I could have asked for a better daughter of our own, don't think that.' Her soft eyes glowed with pride and love. 'Fancy her being so clever, and all. Just goes to show.'

It wasn't clear to Petra what it showed exactly. A cleverness which came from the unknown parents, presumably. What was surprising was the resemblance between Sally and Mrs Wheeler. They had the same soft brown eyes and tightly curled black hair, the same snub nose. But Sally was even shorter.

'She's lucky to have such a wonderful mother.' She knew that Sally had tried to find out about her own background, who her parents were. What Petra couldn't understand was why. In her view nurturing was what really mattered to a child. She wished her own mother was more like Mrs Wheeler.

'You all right, dear?' The slow voice was right beside her. 'Penny for them.'

Petra brought herself back, arranged her features into a pleasant expression. 'Miles away. I expect Sally's told you I've got a boyfriend. Phil introduced us.'

'She did mention it. I'm ever so pleased for you.'

'Before she gets here, Mrs Wheeler, can I just say this. Sally tells me she's back to normal, but every time I talk to her on the phone she sounds, well, out of breath, as though she'd just run a marathon. How is she really?'

'She's ever so much better.' The plump body had difficulty moving between the heavy furniture in the tiny room. 'Let's get you something solid to put your cup on.' She pulled a small table out from under a larger one and began to polish it in an absent-minded sort of way. 'Truth is, I'm still worried about her, whatever those doctors say.'

'They say she's OK?'

'They've washed their hands of her. As much as told her not to bother them again.'

'But you don't think they're right?'

She lumbered down on to her sofa and leaned back. 'If they can't cure it with a quick dose of antibiotics, they don't want to know. I've got emphysema; they just say learn to live with it.'

Petra searched Mrs Wheeler's face for clues. 'What did they say was wrong with Sally? Salmonella poisoning can't go on for weeks, can it?'

'They say it's triggered irritable bowel syndrome in her – something they can't do anything about. Advised us to sue whoever was responsible for it, if we could pin them down.'

'How d'you mean, responsible?'

The brown eyes were vague, without hope. 'If we could prove that something she ate gave her the food poisoning in the first place – cold ham, egg mayonnaise, anything like that – and we could remember where it came from, we could take them to court.'

'You mean something she'd eaten in a restaurant?'

'Or a take-away, or from the supermarket. But she can't remember anything like that. Too late now, anyhow. They should have told us at the beginning.'

'But she'll get over it eventually?' Petra found the idea of lively, creative Sally being chronically ill because of someone's carelessness too horrible to contemplate. 'She's young; it's only coming on top of that business with Phil. How is she coping with that now?'

'Says she'll never find anyone like him again.' Mrs Wheeler's legs planted themselves firmly on her linoleum as she heard the kettle whistle; she levered herself up. 'I'll just have a cup with you. Then I've got to go out. Sally'll be back in a minute. You two won't mind being left to it, I know.'

'Pet! You're the best, lugging that stuff up for me. I feel deprived without it.' Sally put her head round the door of the room. 'I'll just put the shopping in the kitchen.'

'Hi, Sal! You're sounding much better. That's just great. I needn't have bothered to fetch your gear. You look as though you could come back to Exeter with me today.'

'I've thought about it, Pet, but it's better if I wait till I'm really over whatever it was before coming back. I'll hang on till next term; ease myself into work slowly.'

The telephone began to ring, an insistent buzz from the tiny hall outside the living room.

'You take it, love,' Mrs Wheeler said, walking past and waving goodbye to Petra. 'I'm just off.'

Sally picked up the receiver, subduing the brief flicker of hope that she'd hear Phil's voice at the other end. Phil was dead; she had to come to terms with that.

'Hello,' she said, hesitant.

'That you, Sally? Jack Oliver here.'

'Mr Oliver!' He was about the last person she'd expect to call her. Was he looking for Petra? 'How are you?'

'Fit as a fiddle, Sally. What I'd like to know is how you're coming along. You sound much more like your old self. So, tell me – how's it going?'

'I'm very nearly fit, thanks. How very nice of you . . .'

He laughed. 'It's not just a social call, my dear. I do have an ulterior motive. You may not be up to it; just say so if that's the case. I wouldn't want to rush you back to work before you're ready.' He paused.

Sally felt herself thrill at the thought of work for the first time since Phil's death. 'Work, Mr Oliver? You mean you'd like me to tape a game?'

'All in good time, Sally.' He cleared his throat. 'I know you don't think I take your work seriously, but I've been looking at some of those tapes you took of Phil's matches.'

At first she couldn't speak. Excitement brought a frog to her throat.

'Sally? You still there?'

'You mean you've found something? Someone did get at Phil?' she finally whispered.

'I'm sorry, my dear. I didn't mean to upset you. No, I haven't found anything like that. Nothing remotely suspicious. What I *have* found is talent. Sitting there, going through all that work you did, I realised just how gifted you are.' He chuckled. 'I hope you don't mind, but I got a copy of that little film Channel 4 transmitted – *The Changelings*. Really good stuff, Sal. My congratulations.'

She could hardly believe it. Was he telling her he was interested in her work? 'Thanks,' she breathed.

'So what I'm ringing about is to ask whether you'd be interested in showing me the rest of your work. Apart from that short film, I've only seen the tapes you took of Phil. Bruce tells me you did a whole lot of sports photography even before you met him.'

She could hardly breathe. 'That's right, I did.'

'I think you've got something, Sally.'

'Really?'

'Absolutely. What about bringing over all your work? We could have a chat.'

'You mean you're thinking of representing me?'

'Exactly. Bring along everything you ever did, right from the start. I always like to see how my artists develop.'

'I took some 16mm film with an old movie camera I bought in a junk shop.'

'Good, good. Bring the films as well. And all the latest tapes, of course. Right to the very end.' There was a slight pause. 'I know those memories are painful, Sally. For me as well as you, you know. But I do need to see them.'

'You mean including that copy you gave me?'

'Yes, indeed. Phil's parents have clung on to the original. And anything else you might have, anything at all.' There was another short pause. 'The end of that last game, for instance. Did you by any chance tape that?'

She hesitated; that was Petra's work. She'd have to think it through. 'I can get it all together for you, Mr Oliver. Petra's just brought round my gear from Exeter. You'd like me to send everything over to you?'

He laughed again. 'Now I know you wouldn't want to trust your precious work to the post. What about bringing it round here yourself? Then we can have a look at it together.'

'That would be wonderful, Mr Oliver! I'd much rather do it like that. When—'

'No time like the present, my dear. Shove it all in a bag and come right over. Expect you in a couple of hours. OK?'

Sally had allowed Petra to help her load all her films and tapes into the duffle bag. Once they'd taken out the cameras and lenses it wasn't too heavy.

'Does Mr Oliver have a projector for the 16mm films, Pet?'

'He's got every kind of equipment you can imagine. Don't worry about it.'

'You talked him into it, I suppose?'

Petra put her arms around her. 'I wanted to, but haven't really had a chance to. So it's all your own work, Sal. I'm so thrilled for you.'

It was a stroke of luck that Petra was there to help her carry the gear to the Underground. She even helped her on to the right platform, then went off to get her connection to Paddington.

Sally stood waiting for the train, thoughts racing through her head. It was a pity she couldn't show Mr Oliver the footage of the last tape of Phil, the one Petra had taken. Much as she'd have liked to take it, it wasn't her work. Petra had tried to persuade her to take it along, to tell Jack Oliver that she'd taught Petra how to take the shots, but Sally had turned that down. It wouldn't be right.

She saw the electronic lettering signal that the next train was hers. Not too many people on the platform; she hoped she'd get a seat. Though much better now, she still felt frail. She'd been relieved when Petra had pressed some money on her; it meant she could take a taxi at the other end.

'Ask Uncle Jack to send you back in a cab,' Petra had instructed her. 'He'll be happy to do that. He mightn't think of it himself, that's all.'

She saw him out of the corner of her eye as she bent down to pick up her duffle bag. A tall, black man whose round eyes were intent on her. She watched him come towards her as though in slow motion.

A feeling of terror spurted action into her limbs. Was he about to grab her precious bag? She squatted down, grabbed it with both her hands.

When she looked up again he was still coming for her, running now, his right arm held out to snatch the bag as he ran past her. She clutched it to herself; she wasn't going to let go. If he wanted that bag, he'd have to grab her with it!

She saw his eyes, the whites large, the pupils tight with determination. And then she knew; if he didn't get the bag, he'd get her. It was too late to move. She heard the roar of the train and saw the man's huge hands spread out to push her.

She leaned away from the gaping space the train was about to thunder through, flattened herself on to the platform, her body over the duffle bag.

The huge black body bent over her, grabbed it out from under her and kicked her in the belly. She tried not to let go. He kicked again, harder this time. She gasped, her hands flying to her groin. She felt him push her off the platform and on to the rails.

She heard the screams of the other passengers, felt the hard steel of the rails hit her head, her body. He'd taken her bag ... and then she knew that that wasn't the only thing he'd come for. She was in someone's way; he'd come to take her life.

21

'Thought we'd go to San Tarrantino's,' Jack Oliver said, smiling at Petra sitting next to him in the car. 'Exeter's restaurant for top people. The food's good, too.'

'It's very sweet of you, Uncle Jack.'

'Dewi would never forgive me if I didn't look after his little girl whenever I'm in Exeter.' His eyes swivelled over to her. 'It's been hard for you. Sally's death was a terrible shock to all of us.'

'I wish I'd waited to put her on the train,' she said, her voice quivering. It was only because Sally had been so ill, for so long, that she'd been able to come to terms with her death at all. At least that was some sort of preparation.

There was a question in Jack's eyes, but Petra couldn't work out what it was. He was being as kind and supportive as he knew how. He'd turned up at Exeter a couple of times since Sally's death, insisted on taking her out to dinner, asked questions about her work, skirted around the subject of Edward.

Petra found it difficult to tell lies. She had admitted that she and Edward still saw each other; what she'd refused to say was how they arranged it.

They met in Taunton; she took the train, Edward his car. Once there they drove out into the lovely countryside and enjoyed each other's company. There weren't many opportunities to meet, so the ones they did have they savoured. It seemed to strengthen their relationship. It didn't take a genius to work out what they were doing, and she was sure Jack had already done so. She suspected that this dinner wasn't just a godfather's treat; it was going to be a showdown.

'If you'd like to leave your coats, it's just round the corner.' The waiter who had come up to take them to their table looked at Petra's shabby black anorak, then at Jack's camel hair coat.

'Should I ask Dewi to increase your allowance, Pet? That thing really isn't warm enough.'

Her father's delight in paying for her education made her feel good. She didn't want more. And she was going to make sure she acquired a first, or at least a second-class degree, to make up for her father's lack. She was going to make him proud of her. She certainly didn't want Jack contributing. Whenever he did anything for her she got the feeling that he was trying to own her in some way.

'Daddy's giving me quite as much as I need.'

Jack took the offending garment and handed it, together with his own coat, to the girl behind the counter. While he was waiting for the tickets he examined Petra's dress. 'You look stunning, my dear. I can see you've done your best to dress down, but the effect is still sensational.'

She met his look square on. 'I've only got one cocktail dress.' It would have been more honest to say she only had one cocktail dress at college. She'd chosen to bring the black one back after the funeral because she was in mourning for Sally.

'And black's a colour you can keep for wearing when you're older,' he said, looking at her searchingly. 'Just don't make a habit of the sackcloth and ashes. Sally wouldn't want that for you. She'd want you to think of her, but not to brood about the way she died. I'm afraid it's the

224

times we live in, my dear.' He took her elbow and guided her towards the dining room. 'The witnesses said she hung on to that bag.'

'You mean she should just have let go? Let him have all her precious work?'

'Better than losing her life, Pet.' He sounded gentle, but she felt he'd simply swept Sally out of his mind. Was she getting as paranoid as Sally had been?

'And she'd want you to enjoy yourself, for goodness sake! No bread and water tonight; I'll order for both of us.' He picked up the menu and began to read, though she was sure he knew it by heart. The waiter had greeted him like a long lost friend. Naturally; Jack would bring all his West Country clients here. The feeding grounds for the golden boys and girls.

'And while I'm busy, you can take a look at this. It's your Christmas present. I won't be spending the actual day with you.' He caught the question in her eye. 'I have to be in New York. Business.' He laid a rectangular box beside her plate.

She sized it up; too big for jewellery, thank goodness. Perhaps a silk scarf, or blouse, though the package was small for that. Her mind began to work on what Jack had just said. She and her parents would be spending Christmas on their own. The thought was not immediately appealing. Could she and Edward go off together after Boxing Day? Now that Sally was ... no longer in London, she didn't want to spend the whole of her vacation there.

'Well, aren't you even going to open it?'

Why was he showering her with presents? 'I thought I'd look at the menu first, if that's all right.'

He grinned. She could see he knew he'd won the first round. 'What about the lobster mayonnaise?'

It was after she'd eaten the sandwich Jack had given her

that Sally had been taken ill, Petra remembered with a start. 'Is that made with real egg mayonnaise?' she asked the waiter.

'Of course, madam.'

'That's a good choice. We'll start with two lobster mayonnaise, then...'

Petra looked across at him. He didn't even remember Sally's illness. 'I'll have the calamari,' she said. 'Mayonnaise can be very dangerous. Sally was still weak from that salmonella poisoning weeks after she got it. I hadn't thought of it before, but she ate an egg mayonnaise sandwich. You remember – you gave it to her before we went to see Phil for the last time.'

When she looked up from the menu again she was startled to see his eyes had hardened into cold darts of steel. 'What are you getting at, Petra? I hope you're not implying I'd take you to a place that couldn't be trusted.' He stared across at her. 'And that sandwich came from Fortnum and Mason. I hardly think that could have been the problem.'

She was going too far, allowing her sorrow at Sally's death to get the better of her. She dropped her eyes. 'Of course not, Uncle Jack. It's just that I'm going to be careful.'

'I'll have the steak,' he told the waiter. 'Blue.'

'Certainly, sir. And you, madam?'

She'd wanted the steak as well, but she wasn't willing to follow Jack's lead. 'The tuna,' she said. 'And a large salad with French dressing.'

'A white wine, Pet?'

She shrugged. 'If you prefer red with your steak, carry on. I don't mind.'

'Champagne, then,' he said, a smile back on his face. 'Let's celebrate Christmas early.'

'You know something, Uncle Jack? If Sally had been

herself that day, that awful man would never have been able to push her like that. She was tough and streetwise; had to be.'

'Whatever you say, Pet. Now can we leave the subject?' She could see he was thinking that she was getting as bad as Sally had been. 'What about opening your present?'

She held it up and began to unwrap it slowly, precisely, pretending to undo the Sellotape while playing for time. What was wrong with her? She knew her godfather was just trying to be nice to her, yet for some reason she thought of the present as a sort of bribe. But for what?

The wrapping off at last, she saw it was a jewellery box after all. Curiosity overcame her reluctance to enjoy beautiful things when her friend was dead. She opened it: a matte gold choker lay inside, fine strands interwoven into a plait. It was beautiful.

She couldn't avoid the wetness in her eyes. Sally would have enjoyed seeing her wear something like that. 'That's lovely, Uncle Jack. Thanks very much.'

'Shall I help you put it on?'

She took off the small cross her father had given her before she went to college. Jack got up and went to stand behind her. He took the necklace and clicked it into place, then returned to his seat. 'You are a really lovely girl, Petra. It suits you. I've taken out insurance for it so you can wear it whenever you like.'

It startled her. 'Insurance?'

'All risks. It's fine gold, my dear. The design's a special French one. They make them by hand, of course, in the traditional way.'

'You mean it's valuable?'

She could see him trying to decide whether to tell her what it was actually worth. He shrugged. 'You could say that. Don't let it show when you're walking around. That's when you should remember what happened to poor little Sally. Be careful to hide it under a coat, or scarf, or something.'

'You really shouldn't...'

'Nothing is ever completely free. It gives me great pleasure to see you wearing it, and to do something for my goddaughter.'

She fingered the gold. 'If it's that expensive...'

'For goodness sake, Pet. Try to enjoy it. Make the most of what life offers you.' He fiddled with his cutlery, placing it more precisely, adjusting the wine glasses, the water tumbler. 'There's something I feel I have to raise with you.'

'You mean the necklace is a bribe?'

'Honestly, Petra. Sometimes you go too far.' Remarkably even teeth glinted at her. Were they his own, or had he had them capped? They looked natural – and a bit predatory. 'I hope you won't think I have anything other than your welfare at heart, Petra. Let me put my cards on the table right away. I'm not doing this because I think you'll get in the way of Edward's career.' He looked over at her to see how she was taking it. She stared back, making her face expressionless. 'It's you I'm thinking about.'

She'd been right – he had invited her to talk about her relationship with Edward. She'd wondered why her mother had given it a rest. A put-up job.

'You mean the business about Edward's gene for Huntington's.'

His eyes opened wide and he nodded agreement. 'Your father's worried sick about it, perhaps because he himself has a genetic defect. It isn't easy to live with, you know. Like it or not, it permeates your whole existence. Everything you do – everything – is tainted by it. Fact of life.'

'You think Daddy's more worried about Edward's inheritance than Mummy is?'

228

He pressed his lips together. 'Your mother has an unusual grasp of the problems people face. She's always been very sympathetic to Dewi's.'

'Sympathetic!' She couldn't help herself. The idea of her mother as a supportive and compassionate character had never occurred to her.

'She knows what he has to put up with. So do I; I saw him battling with that upper lip all through his childhood. He was very keen not to pass it on, and it's a relatively mild problem. A cleft palate can be repaired as far as function is concerned. Advances in plastic surgery mean people's looks aren't that much affected. But the mind, my dear; the sufferer's mind is terribly vulnerable. You really mustn't underestimate the effects of knowing about a hereditary disease.' He looked earnestly into her eyes. 'You can have no idea how pleased Dewi was that he didn't pass his defect on to you. Ecstatic when you were born. It's probably the reason your parents didn't have any more children.'

'He told you that?'

He shook his head. 'We've never discussed it. Even after so many years of friendship it's the one subject we never talk about.'

The waiter brought the first course and tried to give the lobster to Petra. 'The calamari,' she said.

'You're still thinking of marrying Edward?'

She speared a succulent piece of squid on to her fork. 'We'd prefer to graduate first.'

He was scooping up great forkfuls of lobster, filling his mouth. It didn't seem to stop him talking. 'Unless Edward goes to the States, I take it. Then you'd go with him?'

No point in denying it. 'Yes, that's what we agreed.'

The fork stabbed at several pieces of lobster, stacking them. 'Ed doesn't know about his faulty gene – at least, not unless you told him. I'm sure you wouldn't have been so irresponsible.'

'I haven't told him so far, no.'

'And I hope you won't.'

'I'm not a child, Uncle Jack.'

'Each one of your children would have a fifty-fifty chance of suffering from the same thing, you know. The odds don't get any better after you've had one child...'

'I do know that.' She couldn't help a small smile of triumph. 'But they don't get any worse, either.'

'Touché.' There was admiration in his look. 'But you're at a much greater disadvantage than Edward's parents were. Modern genetic fingerprinting makes it easy to test for the condition, right from the start. In other words, you're bound to know. I've no idea whether Edward's parents know about him; I suspect not. The chances are they're just putting their heads in the sand, and hoping.'

'You mean you think they've no idea?' That was appalling. Then she remembered Ethel's anxious face, her conviction that having one eye blue, one brown was some sort of horrific defect. Surely that was because she knew, and was afraid to tell her son? It even made emotional sense of her antagonism.

'The chances are Edward will be asked to go to the States. I don't want to deprive him of such a splendid opportunity. He'll make a lot of money and, wisely invested, he can be comfortable for the rest of his life.'

'Which you don't want me to share.'

'I think you're too young to make a final choice, Pet. You won't be able to leave him if it doesn't work out; you'll be tied in by guilt.'

'You're just assuming I can't handle the whole thing! I told Mummy and Daddy: modern medicine might find a cure, a foetus can be tested and, if it carried the gene, aborted. We could use in-vitro techniques and discard embryos which have the gene...' She pushed the almost-full plate of calamari to one side. 'It's nothing like as bad as you make out. And Daddy *did* have me. He took the gamble!'

Jack had stopped eating too. 'That was quite a different situation. A cleft palate isn't directly heritable, and the incidence is pretty low.'

'Daddy would have known all about that when he married. He'd have done his homework.'

Jack signalled to the waiter. 'You can take these away.' He was not smiling now, but his voice was still persuasive. 'It wouldn't be very kind to tell Edward about himself, you know. You've no idea how he'll take it. Suppose he decides never to have children?'

'That's between him and me,' she said, feeling her eyes flash anger she didn't even try to hide. 'I think his parents are completely irresponsible not to let him know.'

'I've told you I'm pretty sure they aren't aware he has it, Pet.'

'They must know it's a possibility! It's *his* choice whether he has children or not. How can he make that choice if he doesn't know something like that's in his family?'

'But once he knows he'll spend every waking minute of his life trying to work out whether the odd lapse of memory is the onset of the disease, whether a stumble is the first sign of the chorea. You want that for him?'

'Want it for him? How can you even say such a thing, Uncle Jack? I'm in love with Ed; the last thing I want to do is hurt him.' She drank some of the champagne he'd ordered, grateful for the liquid, hoping it would relax her. 'We're very alike, so I'm sure I know what he'd say. We're adults, perfectly capable of making our own decisions. And we can only do that if we know everything.'

'So you'll just go ahead?' She felt him trying to mesmerise her with his eyes, but she didn't even look at him.

'We can go for genetic counselling. Then we can weigh up the pros and cons. I don't believe it's a reason for us not to get married.'

22

'I'm beginning to develop a real phobia about this place.'
Edward was only half-kidding, his tall frame stooped, his
eyes shifting from the nurse at the reception desk to the
trolley bearing a patient. 'Last time we were here it was
very bad news.'

'I was rather hoping that this time around would be
better than expected.' Petra had thought long and hard
about whether she should tell Edward about his genetic
inheritance. The more she'd agonised, the more convinced
she'd become that he *had* to know – even if it meant he
turned his dismay on her.

To her surprise, the revelation had not been quite as
traumatic as she'd expected, though the reason for this was
sad. She'd run into Professor Dunstan when she was
researching genetic diseases in the library. He'd walked
straight past her, had shown no signs of recognition.

At first she'd thought it was because he was preoccupied.
'Good morning, Professor,' she'd greeted him.

The somewhat shuffling gait stopped after a few seconds.
He'd stood, swaying unsteadily until he'd grasped hold of a
bookshelf. It seemed to her that his stare, blank at first, had
turned furtive. 'Good morning, yes, indeed.' He'd smiled
back in his turn but she could see the emptiness in his eyes.

'It's Petra Jones, Professor – in your first-year psychology class.'

233

He'd obviously put his reading glasses on as a protective measure; they were for reading print, not faces. 'Of course – Petra. You'll have to forgive me, my dear. Getting absent-minded in my old age.'

She could guess what had happened. He hadn't prepared himself for the possibility of meeting any of his students and hadn't recognised her as Edward's girlfriend. She knew he'd taken to her, she wasn't being arrogant to realise that her looks made people – particularly men – remember her. She'd looked at him carefully. He wasn't just unsteady on his feet; his hands were trembling, his head nodding. He added a travesty of a smile to pretend he knew who she was. She'd noticed this tendency to shakiness before, in class. And he always asked his students to take over any motor functions on the basis of class participation.

At least it proved that Jack's information was correct. She was positive that Professor Dunstan was the Huntington carrier, and that he was beginning to show the early symptoms of the disease. But she'd been very careful not to mention anything about his father to Edward.

'I knew *something* was up with Dad.' His handsome face had lost colour, looked drained of life. 'He has the weirdest memory lapses. And I'm terrified to pass him anything at the dinner table because he's liable to spill it. My mother just yells at him.'

'I'm sorry, Ed.'

'Don't be; I'm glad you told me. I'm guessing that the strain of keeping it a secret is getting to him. I don't think my mother has the faintest idea.'

Her voice had almost forsaken her at the enormity of that. 'Really, Ed? Are you sure?'

'For all we know he doesn't know himself, Pet.'

That hadn't occurred to her. They'd driven out to walk in Stoke Woods. Edward was striding through, oblivious of the beauty surrounding them. Petra had trouble keeping up with him, but as she explained how she knew about the Huntington's he stopped for a moment to consider the implications. 'You mean my parents might actually know I've inherited it?'

'That's what I assumed, but Uncle Jack is right – not necessarily. They could only know about you if they've looked into it. The reason Uncle Jack knows is because Bruce Traggard spotted it in your file.'

'Traggard? You're telling me Traggard has access to information about me which I don't?'

'You know they do all those tests, Ed. Right at the beginning, when they first approached you at your school, before they even took you on.'

'The physiology tests, you mean? How would that show up anything like Huntington's?'

'You're right; I don't think it would. It's the latest technology which would do that – DNA analysis, genetic fingerprinting.' She took his hand in hers, but he wanted to use his physical energy – to prove he still had it, she imagined. He shook her off and strode ahead. She sprinted after him. 'I would guess the agency runs the most up-to-date tests at regular intervals. You have to understand that you're a commercial investment, Ed. Jack Oliver is a businessman, not a philanthropist.'

He frowned. 'And Traggard's gunning for me.'

'Trying to protect his investment, that's all. That must be at the bottom of all that nonsense about your going out with me. They thought that if you wanted to get married, they'd have to tell you. And telling you is going to have consequences on what you decide to do with your life.'

'You're getting very cynical, Pet.'

'Because of Sally, I suppose. The way she ended up; I can't get it out of my mind.'

'I find it all a bit hard to understand. If Jack knows about this business, why did he invest in me in the first place?'

'Because I don't think he had any idea then. He spotted you at primary school, didn't you say? All this genetic testing is very recent. It's quite a rare condition, and not one they'd look for unless they knew about the family history. I read it up; they've only isolated the gene responsible in the last little while.'

'After Millfield, you mean?'

'Probably. And now that you've turned out to be such a good player...'

'And Jack's invested so much cash...'

'It's in their interests to carry on in hopes that you won't develop symptoms until much later. You might not notice anything until you're getting on for fifty. How old is your father?'

'Forty-eight. Now I think back, I must have spotted it ages ago. He finds it hard to carry things for Mother, and every now and again his arm starts twitching in an odd sort of way.' Edward's whole body showed the dejection he was feeling. 'I told myself he was getting older, that his lapses of memory were because he was the proverbial absent-minded professor.' A small spark of hope shone in his eyes as he turned to Petra. 'Some people do age before others. He's always looked a bit frail.' A slow, embarrassed smile. 'Well, compared to Harold and me; particularly me.'

She'd noticed from the start that Edward hadn't inherited his father's bone structure. 'He does have a very slight body build compared to yours.'

Edward had seemed more upset about his father than himself. Petra guessed that a defence mechanism protected him from facing the consequences of the defective gene in his own case. He'd agreed to the genetic-counselling session, and now they were at the hospital, about to face the counsellor and what she had to say.

'Edward Dunstan and Petra Jones,' the nurse called out. They looked at each other and moved quietly, as though the public announcement of their names was the equivalent of telling the world why they were there.

Dr Sheila Cressing didn't look the part of the stereotypical consultant. Petra assessed her age as early thirties, her manner as concerned, her looks outstandingly beautiful and her racial heritage as a mixture of Mongolian, Negroid and Caucasian. Petra thought that might give her a deeper understanding of her patients' problems.

'Do sit down, make yourselves comfortable.' A dazzling smile showed perfect teeth.

Edward walked awkwardly towards a chair and stumbled. She noticed, and smiled at him. 'Whatever problems we may discover, we have all kinds of ways of minimising them. Medicine has made enormous strides in the last few years.'

Petra could sense Edward relaxing. She looked over at him and wondered whether to let him do the talking, or whether she should be their spokesperson. Dr Cressing resolved that by focusing on Edward, assessing his height.

'You're thinking of getting married, I understand? That must mean you're both very happy.'

'We're very much in love,' Edward agreed, his deep voice reverberating round the room, his eyes on Petra. 'But we hope we're not irresponsible.'

The Mongolian eyelids made it hard for Petra to read the doctor's expression but it looked benign. 'What I would like to do is to ask questions; find out what brought you here before your wedding rather than after it. That is rather exceptional.' She turned to Edward. 'You're unusually tall. Would you mind standing up for me?'

He stood, a splendid example of a trained, athletic male in the full vigour of his youth. 'You want to do a physical examination?'

'Nothing like that. But the first thing that crosses my mind – and you have to remember that that's what I'm trained to do – is to assess whether an exceptionally tall man is simply tall, or suffers from gigantism.'

'Gigantism?' The horror in his voice exploded round the room.

'I'm so sorry, don't be alarmed. I brought it up because it's relevant. Let me explain: height is regulated by hereditary factors, in other words genes. Tall parents are more likely to have tall children, but by some odd quirk of nature very tall parents usually have children not quite as tall as themselves. A return to the average.'

The young couple looked at each other, smiled dutifully. They knew all that.

'I'm sure you've thought about that already. But you must be around six foot six, Edward. Is that right?'

'Give or take a millimetre or two. My coach tends to bash the bar hard on my head.'

'You're an athlete?'

'Basketball player.'

'A very suitable sport.' Her face had taken on the soft gentleness of a doe's. 'Six foot six is at the extreme end of the normal height curve. If the pituitary gland over-secretes growth hormone, and if this happens during childhood, people can grow to anything between six and a half to eight feet.'

'So Edward might have a problem?'

'I don't think so. The most common reason for pathologically accelerated growth is a tumour in the pituitary gland.

If you had that you would have noticed by now. You would have headaches, there might be pressure on the nerves to the eyes and vision would be impaired, and there is usually a failure of sexual function. I'm pretty sure all these are ruled out – right?'

They grinned at each other. 'Right,' Edward said. 'Nothing like that at all.'

'You'd also notice distorted growth in peripheral body parts: hands, feet, even the head.' She looked at Edward's shoes. 'Your feet are large to support your frame, but they aren't disproportionately large.' She cleared her throat. 'What I don't want to hide from you is that some forms of excessive height are familial. It is possible that some of your children will be as tall, or taller, than you, Edward.'

'And what about me?'

The consultant looked surprised. 'You?' She looked down at her notes. 'Petra, isn't it? Well, you're well within the norm. No problem there.'

'Ed's mother insists that because we're both taller than our parents our children would be taller still.'

The dark head shook from side to side. The doctor's hair was cut in a pageboy, the ends permed to give the effect of a helmet. 'I'd say that was completely wrong. If anything, what I first mentioned would have a double effect. If you're both the tallest in your family, your children are likely to be shorter than you.' She smiled again. 'But height isn't what you've come about, is it?' She looked from one to the other.

'Maybe we could get the easy things out of the way. Edward's mother is worried because one of my eyes is blue, the other brown. She thinks that's an inherited genetic defect, and could lead to much worse things in my children.'

This time the doctor looked completely taken aback.

'That's quite some theory; completely false. It is an exceptional feature, but it is not directly heritable, nor does it affect vision. It will have no bearing on your children, except for their noticing it in you.' She looked at them with a level gaze. 'We are all affected by people's perceived attitude to our looks, I'm afraid. If you're honest with yourselves, you will find a prejudice against me because of my obvious racial heritage. You'll think it makes me less likely to be a first-rate medical adviser.' The double eyelid lowered a little further as she looked at Petra. 'Isn't that so?'

'It does affect me, I can't deny that. What I thought was that it might make you more aware of people's problems.'

The laugh was much louder than the consultant's delicate bone structure would have led Petra to expect. 'I must remember to put that on my CV! Now then; what's really troubling you?'

Petra looked at Edward, but he was not about to speak. 'We've found out that Edward has Huntington's chorea,' she said. 'We know that it's a dominant gene, and that each of his children will have a fifty-fifty chance of inheriting the faulty gene.'

'Correct.'

'We understand the time of onset is variable. It can be as early as the twenties, or as late as fifty.'

'Right again.'

'And that there isn't any cure.'

'Perfectly correct. You've done your homework well. Now, before we go any further, how do you know Edward is affected?'

They explained the circumstances, and the doctor made a note. 'I'll assume that is correct, though I think you would be wise to have your own tests done. There's always the chance of human error.'

They nodded.

'But, now you're here, you'd like me to go into the pros and cons of having children, knowing that one of the partners is affected.'

'Yes,' Edward boomed at her. 'It's one thing to inflict looking after an invalid on a future wife – she knowingly takes it on. It's quite another to bring afflicted children into the world.'

'I'm not sure that I agree with you, but it isn't my job to discuss that. We have made enormous strides, as I mentioned to you. There is now a test – a reliable test – which can be carried out on the foetal cells. This can tell you whether that foetus has Huntington's or not.'

'And we can decide to have a termination if the child is found to have it, is that right?'

'A very difficult choice; I wouldn't like to pretend anything else. When you become pregnant you can arrange for a test to be done at around ten weeks. The obstetrician will insert a needle into your abdomen, into the placenta, and draw out some fluid. That will carry the child's genetic fingerprinting, and the diagnosis can be made from that. It takes a couple of weeks. The waiting time can be quite unpleasant.'

Petra could feel her eyes prick with tears.

'I don't want to let you go away with the idea that there are easy solutions, but at least there *are* solutions. You can always decide not to have the test. In that case you will not know whether your child has the disease or not. We do not, at present, consider it right to test children. That is a decision for them when they come of age.'

'You'd hide it from them?'

'That would be up to you. Personally I would prepare my child for the possibility, if only because one of the parents will eventually develop the disease.' She hesitated. 'You have some difficult thinking ahead of you. Let me just say that I think true love is worth more than any disease; it is a precious gift.'

Petra smiled through her tears. 'I'm afraid there's still one other problem we would like to ask you about.'

The doctor drew out another sheet of paper. 'Something in *your* family?'

'My father has a cleft palate; so does my aunt.'

She must have known that Petra did not suffer from the condition, but her eyes went towards Petra's nostrils. 'That is quite different from Huntington's. I'm sure you've already worked that out.'

Petra smiled. 'I did read it up.'

'There are two distinct conditions: cleft lip and cleft palate. When the foetus is being formed in the womb it sometimes happens that the two sides of the upper lip don't grow together properly. That's called a cleft lip, and modern surgical techniques can be used to repair it. It isn't really a problem.'

'You mean it wouldn't show?'

'Not quite. The first operation is performed right away, immediately after birth, provided the child is considered able to cope with it. It's a functional measure, necessary because there could well be feeding problems if it isn't done. Plastic surgery is left till later; that's usually done at around the age of two, to improve the looks. Modern techniques are very successful.'

'And a cleft palate? That's more serious, I take it.' This time Edward was asking the questions. It was interesting that Petra felt she would much rather leave it to him.

'It affects the roof of the mouth, so that there's a gap – a sort of slit – between the two sides. The statistics are that forty-five per cent of cases involve both lip *and* palate.'

'And the repair for cleft palate?'

'Generally involves more extensive surgery. The initial surgery is, as with the cleft lip, done as soon as possible. Again, the primary problem is feeding, because infants with cleft palates often find it difficult to suck. In some cases they even find it difficult to swallow.' She looked at the young couple, clearly not enjoying this second litany of problems. 'Having a cleft palate can mean a lot of visits to various specialists. Children often show a history of ear infections and speech problems, so that the services of paediatricians, oral surgeons, plastic surgeons, orthodontists, otolaryngologists and...'

'What's that?'

She smiled. 'Sorry, they are better known as ENT – ear, nose and throat specialists. And the other professional who can be useful is a speech therapist. Otherwise speech can be very nasal.'

Exactly how it had affected Gwyneth, Petra remembered, and her father, but to a much lesser extent.

'But what you really want to know is whether it's hereditary or not, isn't that right?'

'Yes.'

'The good news is that some cases are caused by a defect in the intra-uterine environment in early pregnancy. That was much more common in the past than it is now, and you could certainly be shown how to avoid that possibility.'

'My father's family come from North Wales. I think they had a rather hard time just before he and his sister were born. Could that account for it?'

The consultant shrugged. 'I can only make an informed guess on very little evidence; it's possible. There's also the possibility of an hereditary factor. That, I'm sorry to tell you, is on the increase. Probably because modern surgical techniques have helped many more children not only to survive, but to have excellent plastic repairs done.'

She smiled. 'Which, of course, leads to affected people marrying.'

'So what are the statistics? Not the same as for Huntington's?'

'Not remotely. One birth in around seven hundred has some degree of cleft palate. I've tried to explain that there are several types, ranging from the mild to the very severe.'

'That's for the hereditary factor? One in seven hundred?' Edward sounded surprised.

'Sorry, I'm giving you the wrong impression. One in seven hundred of normal births. If one parent is affected, the risk goes up to around one in eighty. That becomes a higher risk still if an affected mother has an affected daughter; then the chances of another daughter inheriting the condition is one in seven. That won't, of course, apply to you. I think we can safely say your chances are not very different from the rest of the population.'

'So that shouldn't really influence our decision to get married?'

'I would say not.'

23

It was a very large tree – an oak, Petra felt sure, though she couldn't identify it. It had no leaves, but the vast, short bole and the three thick branches spreading out into a network of smaller ones had the rounded shape of an oak. It must be a woodpecker which was making that insistent tapping noise. Tap, tap, tap. Instead of being soothed, she found it irritating. All the same, she looked to see whether it was a black and white one, or the more exotic green variety.

She couldn't see anything at all; just hear that persistent rat-a-tat, rat-a-tat. She was staring at the dark outline of the tree, imagining the bird's beak beating a rhythm on the bark, making a hole, when there was a crash and the huge tree fell over, its branches quivering as it hit the ground.

The whole world shook, she felt her body being rocked.

'Petra! I'm sorry to wake you.'

She opened her eyes and stared at one of the younger members of staff living in Mardon, Brenda Gordon, a laboratory assistant in the Biology Department. 'What's wrong?' she said, sitting up in her bed, dazed. 'Have I overslept?'

Exams were starting today and she'd been revising long into the night. She looked at the window; the light in the room wasn't on and she could see faint daylight outlining the drawn curtains. 'What time is it?'

'Getting on for eight. I'm sorry to wake you, but the Warden sent me. She wants you to come and see her right away.'

Petra sat up in bed, trying to wake up and make herself aware of her surroundings.

'I knocked for ages; thought I'd wake up the whole corridor.'

'So how did you get in?' Surely she'd locked the door? Had Brenda actually broken it down? Was that why the oak in her dream had crashed?

'The Warden has a duplicate key. In the end I used that.'

Petra stared at her, the mists of sleep still fogging her brain. She found it hard to function first thing in the morning.

'I'll just draw the curtains, then leave you to get dressed. If you could come over to Mrs Bellray's office right away.'

A summons from the Warden was serious. It usually meant that a grave crime against Hall rules had been committed. But she and Edward had been so careful; she didn't think anyone had noticed that he'd spent the Sunday night here. She'd waited for him to leave the dressing rooms behind the Sports Hall, then they'd crept in under cover of darkness and he'd left at the crack of dawn. Going to practice, as he always did.

'You all right?'

'Of course. I'll get dressed right away.' Anyway, staying overnight with a girlfriend was such a common occurrence it hardly rated as a serious crime. 'What's wrong?' She looked intently at the girl pulling back the curtains and standing, awkward, in front of the light. Brenda's long, kinky hair was usually held back with a loose hairband. Now it was billowing round her narrow face and over her forehead. She hadn't combed it yet, Petra realised. Brenda wasn't all that much older than herself; perhaps in her mid-twenties. Her normally large, steady grey eyes were shifting busily around the room, avoiding Petra. Full, fleshy lips covered protruding teeth and made her look as though she were pouting. A smile which didn't reach her eyes made the teeth look like weapons.

'I was just asked to fetch you, Petra. The Warden will tell you what it's all about.'

She knew. She knew and wasn't going to say a word. Did it mean she would be thrown out of Hall – thrown out of University, perhaps? She shuddered as the repercussions of such a possibility began to seep through. Her father would be so disappointed. And her mother would be triumphant, telling her she only had herself to blame...

'I'll leave you to dress. Come over as soon as you're ready.' Brenda was by the door, making her escape. Petra could see now that she wasn't properly dressed herself. Her jeans were covered by a pyjama top which was, in turn, covered by a large sweater. Her feet were bare in moc-casins. 'All right?'

'I won't be long.' Whatever it was, she was going to face it herself, like an adult. No hiding behind lies.

Her knock on the Warden's office door was firm.

'Come in.' She hadn't seen much of Mrs Bellray after the welcoming talk on the first day. Her ramrod figure, dressed in the sort of suits Petra had seen in old movies of the fifties – tweeds in muted heather colours, slim skirts with a box pleat at the front, tailored jackets – were matched with carefully chosen accessories. Iron-grey hair was permed into a neat wave softening the thin face with its spiderwebs of lines. The Warden's plucked eyebrows gave an innocent, almost childlike, expression to the deep-set hazel eyes which looked up at Petra from the desk with its single folder.

'There you are. Brenda said you were fast asleep; I'm sorry she had to wake you.'

Petra smiled, a veiled smile of exploration. 'My alarm would have gone off in a couple of minutes anyway. I've got a psychology exam today.'

The eyes were too deeply set in shadow for Petra to read. Mrs Bellray turned away from the window at her left and stared at the wall behind Petra. She seemed to be trying to decide what to say. 'Exams, of course.' A vague smile as her eyes focused on Petra's face. 'I hope you've settled down after that terrible business with poor Sally Wheeler. That must have been devastating for you.'

It didn't sound like the beginning of dismissal. Something was wrong, but the woman behind the social mask was sorry for her, not angry.

'People have rallied round. It's a very friendly campus.'

Mrs Bellray had picked up a letter opener and was twiddling it in her hands, her eyes looking down at it. 'Do sit, my dear.' She waited for Petra to settle into one of the two chairs opposite her desk. 'There's been a phone call.'

Had her mother rung to say not to bother to come home for the Christmas holidays? Were they so angry with her that they refused to get in touch themselves? Then she shrugged that aside. Sally! Had the police found the man—

'You mean it's about Sally?' The blank eyes across the desk told her Mrs Bellray had no idea what she was talking about. 'Have the police found out who pushed her?'

'I'd forgotten there's an investigation going on.' She stood, the letter opener still in her hand, twisting it as though it were a key to what she was about to say. She walked a few paces, then perched uneasily on the desk in

248

front of Petra. 'It's nothing to do with Sally, Petra. The phone call was from a Jack Oliver. He said he's your godfather.'

'Uncle Jack?' She frowned. Was he about to get at her again? Is that what her mother had arranged, that Jack should put the pressure on? 'What did he want?' She sounded irritable, in spite of trying to control her voice.

Mrs Bellray picked up the tone right away. 'You're not too keen? He's driving up from London. I'm sorry, my dear. I . . . he said he was very close to the family.'

'Well, yes, he is. He's always at our house.' The figure on the desk was too near for comfort. She found it hard to think with the intense eyes scrutinising her, watching for reactions to news she had not yet been given. 'Did he say what it was about?' Her voice was high, but under control.

'Yes, my dear, he did. That's why he's driving down. I'm so very sorry. Something quite dreadful has happened.'

'If it's not about Sally . . .' She stopped. How could she be so stupid? That was old news. Something terrible had happened recently. A lump came into her throat as Edward's tall frame filled her mind. Her eyes began to fill with tears. Not Edward! Please God, not Edward struck down by the same thing that had happened to Phil. Why hadn't she listened to Sally? How could she have been so idiotic as to believe all those other people, when Sally was her friend? 'You mean something's happened to . . .' The tears were pouring down her cheeks. She put her hands up to her face and gratefully took several tissues from the box Mrs Bellray offered her.

'I suppose you guessed there was a problem,' she said, standing and walking behind Petra's chair, putting her arms around her shoulders. 'When you went home for Sally's funeral. I suppose you knew then that something was wrong.'

She tried to focus on what the Warden was telling her, tried to get the picture of Edward lying prostrate on the court out of her mind. 'I'm sorry, Mrs Bellray. Something's wrong at home?'

The older woman pulled the second chair closer to Petra and sat down on it, facing her, taking her hands in hers. 'It's your father, my dear. I am so very sorry.'

'Daddy?' It took her a few seconds to acclimatise to that. 'There's been an accident at work?'

'I'm terribly sorry; your godfather will be here quite soon. He'll explain it all.'

'Is Daddy in hospital?'

The hands clasped hers even more tightly. 'There's no good way to do this. I'll just have to tell you straight out. Your father is dead, my poor dear. Your mother found him, early this morning.'

She jumped up from her chair, snatching her hands away, backing towards the window. 'What d'you mean, he's dead? He can't be! I saw him when I went home to be at Sally's funeral, and he wasn't even ill!'

'There are all kinds of illnesses, my dear.'

Then she remembered that her father had been different ever since that difficult visit, when her parents hadn't allowed her to bring Edward. That, it turned out, was also the day Sally had been killed. Had she been so wrapped up in her grief about her friend that she hadn't even noticed that her father was ill? Was that why he and her mother had been trying to persuade her not to marry so young, because they knew he was dying? Why hadn't they *said*?

'What's happened to him?' she whispered. 'How could he be dead? He sounded all right when I rang on Sunday.'

Mrs Bellray had come up to her again. 'I know your best friend has gone as well, Petra. As I said, your godfather . . .'

'But *why* did he die?'

Surprisingly strong arms steered her back into the chair. 'I think you should sit down, my dear. This is a terrible shock for you. Worse, coming so soon after the other one.'

'I want to know *why*!'

She found her hands clasped again. 'You must remember that illness can take many forms. Your father wasn't physically ill, not as far as I know.'

Mentally ill – her father? That was ridiculous. What was the woman talking about? 'You're saying he went mad? That they injected some sort of tranquilliser and he died? Is that what you're telling me?' She tore her hands away and pushed them through her hair, pulling at the strands, welcoming the pain. 'I don't believe you! My father is as sane as anyone I've ever known.' Daddy, her loving father – she was his special reason for living. Had she driven him mad by saying she was in love with Edward?

'There isn't any doubt, my dear; you have to believe me. I am so very sorry, but your father took an overdose. No one knows why, I understand. Pressures at work, perhaps. Your godfather...'

'An overdose? You mean he committed *suicide*?' Her voice came out in rasps of horror as she stood, about to head for the door. Would he really have reacted in that way because she said she was going to marry Edward, whatever he or her mother felt about it? How could she have been so cruel, so determined to do what *she* wanted that she hadn't even thought about her father. How could she have been so selfish!

Mrs Bellray was at the door before her. 'Just sit down, Petra; come along. You've had the most appalling shock. I'd like you to stay here, with me, until your godfather arrives to pick you up.'

'Really?' she whispered. 'He took his own life? They're sure?'

'I'm afraid so.' Mrs Bellray switched on the intercom to her secretary. 'Rose? Are you there?'

'Yes, Mrs Bellray.'

'A pot of tea, please. Lots of sugar.'

'Oh, Petra! How could he have done such a thing? What on earth could have possessed him?'

'Uncle Jack told me he was worried about Jorncy making him redundant.'

Louise looked at her daughter carefully. 'There were a couple of problems at work, I think.'

'Problems? He never mentioned anything like that to me.'

A dart of a smile, and then her face took on a mask. 'He wouldn't have wanted to worry you. They were talking of changing their policy; having to let some of their staff go. They were going to start with people who had no qualifications. Early retirement.' Louise frowned. 'How anyone could have done more than your father, I'll never know. Those multinationals are revoltingly ungrateful. He's always been so reliable...'

Petra vaguely remembered her father talking to her about Jorncy. A long time ago, when she was still quite young. He'd said they'd always been pleased with him because he'd been the reason for some sort of breakthrough. Not his highly qualified colleagues, but David Jones, the one without even an A-level to his name. 'He told me he'd invented something.'

'That was years ago, Pet. Anyway, he was working for them.'

'You mean they didn't have to pay him for it?'

'No, not even acknowledge it. Legally, it was their property.'

Perhaps Louise had tried to help him. Her father said

she'd always supported him. 'Did you suggest that he should do something about that?'

'Ask them to pay him, you mean? Jack suggested something along those lines. Eventually they offered him a few thousand on an ad hoc basis. Ex-gratia payment.' She looked at Petra with an odd stare. 'He was always on maximum salary. I'll give Jorncy that.'

Money wasn't everything, Petra thought bitterly. He must have worked at least half as much again in hours as anyone else at the place. He was *always* doing overtime.

Louise's face seemed to have lost what life it had. The lines cut deeper, the eyes had sunk back, the cheeks hollowed out. 'Suicide! And to leave me to find the body. What have I ever done to him except stand by him?'

'Is he here?'

'They took him off to hospital, still trying to save him. I told them he was beyond that. They never listen.'

'Tell me what happened.'

Puffy eyelids swerved towards her daughter, the glint of irritation subdued by the enormity of it all. 'Well, you know our routine. He often brings me a cup of coffee before he leaves for work. Not on the really early days, but I look forward to it when he leaves around seven. I woke up, saw he'd gone, then looked at the clock. It said seven-thirty.'

Petra could imagine that her mother had thrown back the bedclothes, ready to snarl.

'I thought he'd forgotten, as a matter of fact. So I went down and into the kitchen, to put the coffee machine on.'

'And?'

'There was no sign of anyone having been in there. The water was cold, the milk not in yet.' She sat, a grey pallor covering the sallow complexion. Her eyes stared through Petra. 'So I went to his study. I knew he often worked there before he left for the office. His computer was on, those stupid coloured stars shooting all over the screen. I knew he had to be nearby. He never leaves it on during the day. And then I saw him, lying on that leather couch he keeps in there. He and Jack always watch the videos from that.'

'You thought he was asleep, I suppose.'

'It seemed odd, but yes, I did. He had been sort of tired lately.'

'You noticed he hadn't been himself?'

Her eyes were glazed. 'I suppose now that I think back on it, I did.' She avoided Petra's eyes, and paused. Then she turned, suddenly animated. 'It was when he took you to Wales; that's what started it off. Somehow he never seemed the same after that.'

'But we had a lovely time! Everyone was really nice to us . . .'

'Even Gwyneth?' Louise's vague look had become alert. 'She didn't get at him?'

'She wasn't there, Mummy.' But there had been some sort of trouble with Gwyneth's husband Ian. 'Uncle Ian crashed in, right at the end, and shouted at Daddy. It was all in Welsh, so I couldn't understand it. But he kept shouting one word, sounded like *Dalai Lama* to me. I asked Daddy later; he said he was saying he'd get his revenge. When I asked what for, he kind of didn't go into it.'

'That man's a criminal, you know, a menace. He always blamed your father for leaving Wales and finding a good job. Ridiculous.'

'D'you think that worried Daddy?'

She shrugged. 'People who leave and make good always feel guilty, I suppose.'

She wrung her hands, caught herself on her engagement ring, twisted it round and polished it on her dress. 'At first I thought your father was asleep. I shook and shook him. When his mouth fell open I suddenly knew what had happened.'

'Poor Mummy.' She held her mother tight.

'I rang 999 right away; then I tried the kiss of life but I knew it was hopeless. He must have been dead about an hour already. They dragged him off and everything.' She turned, her face grey again. 'I didn't bother to go with him. I called Jack.'

Even in her grief she'd called Jack because he was the man she was interested in, Petra realised. How could she have allowed her husband's body to be taken away without going with it?

'Uncle Jack said there was a note addressed to me.'

Her mother's head flicked back. 'Not a note, exactly. He found something on the computer.'

'Uncle Jack did?'

'Yes. You know I don't know how they work.' She stared beyond Petra at the study door. 'Jack printed it out. It didn't make any sense to me; I chucked it into the fire.' Her chin stuck out at Petra, but her eyes looked anxious.

'It was addressed to me and you just burnt it?' That sounded a monstrous thing to do.

'I thought it would be best.'

Tears began to form. 'I'd have liked to have that. I'll see if I can retrieve a copy.'

'I *burnt* it, Petra. There are only ashes . . .'

She was desperate to see that last message. Why had her mother destroyed it? 'I don't mean the copy you burned. The data might still be in the printer memory. I'll go and get another print-out.'

'You young people all know how to work these machines,' she heard her mother say as she walked into her father's study. The printer was still on. She set it off line and pressed

Form Feed. She hoped Jack hadn't printed out anything since then.

The machine whirred into action.

I hope my darling Petra will understand one day. I had no idea that the arrangements I agreed to were changed. I'd give anything to undo what I allowed to happen, anything at all. It's too late; there's nothing anyone can do.

Forgive me, Pet; I can't live with that. Remember that I've always loved you, always will.

You've always been a clever girl; you'll sort it out.

David Jones, the man who was proud to call himself your father.

She read the words, but couldn't understand the meaning behind them. None of it really added up. The strangest thing was the phrase 'proud to call himself your father'. Had Gwyneth been right when she'd hinted that Louise had had a lover?

She clutched the print-out in her hand and walked back into the living room. 'What are the "arrangements", Mummy?' she began. The phone started its insistent trill. 'I'll get it,' she said, picking up the receiver. 'Hello?'

'Hello, yes. That's Petra, is it? Hello, *fach*. It's your Aunt Gwyneth here. I am so sorry, Pet, so sorry for what happened.'

'Oh, Aunt Gwyneth.' She began to cry. Was it really true what Gwyneth had said? Had her mother taken a lover? Was she really not Daddy's daughter? Is that what 'arrangements' meant and the reason he'd committed suicide? 'D'you know why he did it? Did he talk to you?' Surely he wouldn't have *agreed* to a lover?

'No, *fach*, he did not. But it's got nothing to do with you,

I'm sure of that. He thought the world of you, and was proud to be your father.' That phrase again; he must have meant it. 'I'm sorry. I shouldn't have talked to you the way I did. It was all wrong; nothing to it at all. Just the pain in my lip, you know. You mustn't think...'

'I'll hand you over to Mummy,' she breathed into the phone. That had to be the reason her father had taken his life. Gwyneth must have put the thought into his mind, and once he'd heard it voiced, he'd seen that it could be true.

As soon as her mother put down the receiver she looked her straight in the eye. 'Am I Daddy's daughter, Mummy? Aunt Gwyneth hinted that you'd had a lover, when you were first married. Is that true, and did Daddy find out? Is that why he couldn't bear to live any more?'

Louise's face contorted into a gargoyle of fury, the blood rose deep and purple. 'I did *not* have a lover, Petra. You have no right to ask your own mother such a terrible question, but I swear to that. Swear it on your father's memory.'

She drew herself up, and looked straight at her daughter. 'Your aunt is a lying, jealous bitch who always tried to stop your father marrying me. Now – who are you going to believe, her or me?'

24

The heavy, good-quality envelope was impressive, the return address unknown to Petra. Had she filled in some sort of form and asked for information? She couldn't remember. Already late for the first psychology lecture of the new spring term, she stuffed the envelope into her briefcase. She didn't find it again until a week later, while she was waiting for another lecture to begin.

She drew out a single white sheet. The top left-hand corner was filled with a word in large letters – FOTHERINGTONS – underlined in a discreet blue. The right-hand corner had a small illustration which, to Petra's unpractised eye, looked rather like a wreath. It encircled the word SOLICITORS, also in blue, picked out in small capitals. Under the logo she found the address: Fotherington House, Aldermanbury Square, London EC2. There was a letter, short and to the point.

Dear Miss Penn Jones,
Re: Mr David Jones, deceased
We have recently been notified of the death of your father, Mr David Jones. Please allow us to send you our sincere condolences.

You may be aware that Mr Jones was a valued client. He left instructions that, in the event of his death, we should contact you.

Your late father advised us that you are residing at Mardon Hall, Exeter. May I suggest a meeting at your convenience, either in Exeter or in London.

I would be grateful if you would write to the above address, and suggest a time and place.

Yours sincerely,

R. E. Broughton

A formal letter from a firm of solicitors she'd never heard her father mention? Not that she could remember him talking about solicitors at all. Was she about to learn something which might throw some light on his death? Had he left her a proper letter, to explain why he'd killed himself?

She examined the rest of the paper for clues. The message was followed by several inches of text in small print: a set of headings, also in blue, followed by names. There was a substantial number of listed Partners, and two rather smaller lists of Consultants and Associates. The firm had offices in London, Douglas (IOM), Hong Kong, Sydney, Paris, Vienna, and a half-dozen small towns in England. 'Members of European Law Group' was printed in blue again, telling Petra that the firm was regulated by the Law Society in the conduct of investment business. What could all this possibly have to do with her?

She examined the list of partners, bending the paper to catch the light so that she could read the small print. R. E. Broughton was among them. So the letter had come from an important member of the firm.

'You're looking very grave, Petra. The law caught up with you at last, has it?'

'What d'you mean by that?'

Her sharp tone surprised the student sitting next to her

into glancing at the paper in her hand. He retreated hastily. 'Joketime, that's all. I should mind my own business.'

She brought herself back to the lecture hall. 'Sorry, Pete. It's a letter from a solicitor I've never heard of. No idea what it's about.'

'There you are; always suspected you of being a hardened criminal.'

It must have been the way both Edward's and her parents had behaved which had planted such an idiotic idea in her subconscious, allowed her to feel guilty when there was nothing to feel guilty about. She and Edward couldn't go on like this; they'd have to come to some sort of decision. She looked up to see the lecturer walk into the room. She wouldn't be able to concentrate; she edged her way out and looked for the nearest phone box.

'Could I speak to Mr Broughton?'

The bored tones of a girl on the switchboard. 'Mr Robert Broughton or Mr Richard Broughton?'

The choice unnerved Petra. 'I don't know,' she faltered, hating the way her voice shook. She took a breath and made herself sound in charge. 'I've had a letter from an R. E. Broughton...'

The girl had clearly had this problem before. 'That'll be Mr Robert Broughton,' brusque tones informed Petra, implying she had no time for such ignorance. 'Who shall I say is calling?'

'Petra Penn Jones.'

The voice disappeared, leaving Petra with the strains of a Strauss waltz as she watched the telephone machine debiting precious digits of change. She fumbled through her purse, found a pound coin and put it in. 'Hello?' she tried for some sort of contact. 'Could I just leave a message?'

The waltz had changed to a polka.

'Are you there, Miss Jones? Mr Broughton is in a meeting. Can I get him to call you back?'

'I live in a Hall of Residence. Perhaps you could give me a time to call him.'

'I'll put you through to his secretary.'

Another precious half-minute went by while an internal phone began to ring. There wasn't time for all this nonsense...

'Mr Robert Broughton's office.'

'This is Petra Penn Jones; I had a letter from Mr Broughton.'

A pause. 'Could you give me the reference on the letter?'

'Look, this is a pay phone, and the money's running out...'

'I need the reference.'

'REB/LTS 060195.'

'What can I do for you, Miss Jones?'

'Perhaps you could tell me what it's all about.'

'You'll have to speak to Mr Broughton. If you give me your number, I'll arrange for him to call you back.'

'I'm a student; I live in a Hall of Residence. When can I call Mr Broughton to talk to him?'

'I'll check his diary.' Three, two, one ... 'Tomorrow at ten fif—' The phone went dead. She'd ring at ten-fifteen the next morning. If the secretary had meant ten-fifty she'd just have to ring again.

'You know, I've never been to Exeter before.' The short, rotund figure of R. E. Broughton – Mr *Robert* Broughton, Petra remembered – was dressed in a grey pin-stripe complete with waistcoat, white shirt and a bowler he'd doffed and put back on his head. He was also carrying a furled umbrella. Petra wondered whether she'd been propelled back into Dickensian times. 'A quite delightful town.'

City. Exeter was a city because it had a cathedral, but she forbore from mentioning it. She'd suggested tea at a small restaurant in the Cathedral Close. A good choice; the building looked as though the twentieth century hadn't made much of an impact.

Mr Broughton had sent a confirmatory letter insisting that she bring proof of identity, preferably her birth certificate. She couldn't get a copy from St Catherine's House at such short notice, and she didn't want to alert her mother, so she'd brought along her current passport.

'Cream tea for two?' The waitress glanced at them with some interest. Petra supposed they did appear an odd pair. They consented and waited for the order to come as though, somehow, it would clarify what Mr Broughton had to say.

'Shall I pour?'

Mr Broughton agreed by nodding his head several times and clearing his throat. They sipped tea and crumbled the stale-looking scones which had been served with it. Petra was too nervous to eat, and Mr Broughton was, quite probably, watching his weight. He had confined himself to a few remarks about Devon and its famous clotted cream, with the eager air of a dachshund about to be fed a delicacy. Petra was sure that under the veneer of amiability there was a snappy nature which would erupt as soon as Mr Broughton was annoyed. For the moment the round face, oozing perspiration, was beaming at her. Small, brown-stained teeth glinted through thin lips. He had a high forehead which looked immense because his hair had receded into a small semi-circle around the back of his skull.

Petra took a further sip of tea, then decided to allow her eyes to bring the man sitting opposite her to the point. He, however, went on drinking tea and gazing through the small, leaded windows overlooking the Close. He was clearly waiting for *her* to make the first move.

'You were my father's solicitor, Mr Broughton?' Her eyes looked straight into his. 'He never mentioned you to me.'

An even broader smile. 'You're a very fortunate young lady.'

Because her father had never mentioned Fotheringtons? He couldn't mean that. 'If you could just explain...' She'd been waiting, as patiently as possible, for two weeks now.

'To have such a generous father.'

What was he getting at? 'Generous?'

He frowned. 'You have no idea? There is a substantial trust fund, set up in your name.'

It was the last thing she'd expected. A letter, some documents, even a diary. Was he talking about *money*? 'A trust fund?'

'In a bank on the Isle of Man – a common location for trusts of this kind. Your father arranged it some years ago, with instructions that we should get in touch with you in the event of his death. We were so sorry to hear about...'

'Yes.' She frowned again, trying to understand what her father had had in mind. 'Was there a letter for me?'

'Letter? Lodged with us, you mean?' He gave her a quizzical look. 'Nothing like that. Were you expecting one?'

'You heard that my father had died. Were you told anything about the circumstances?'

The smile had left the round face as he sensed a difficulty. 'Nothing about the circumstances, no. Was there a problem?'

There was no point in beating about the bush. It was possible that the trust, whatever that meant, could be affected. 'My father committed suicide. I thought perhaps there might have been a note...'

Mr Broughton pushed his chair back several inches as though, somehow, connection with a suicide, however remote, might be contagious. 'I do apologise, Miss Jones. I had no idea...'

She looked directly at him. 'You only acted for him for this trust?'

'Indeed. You will understand that it was not part of his estate. *You* are the sole beneficial owner.'

She had no real idea what this meant. 'I see,' she said, her face set in a suitably grave expression. Why had her father left a trust fund for her? To allow her to be independent of her mother? A couple of thousand or so would make it easier if she wanted to join Edward in the States. 'And how much is in the fund?' She took a biscuit, found it completely stale and put it on her plate.

The beam was widening his face again. 'It's very hard to put an exact figure on it,' he said, back on solid financial ground. 'But the original capital figure, when the fund was set up, was half a million pounds. Sterling,' he explained, watching her face with small, probing eyes.

She didn't drop the tea cup, but it shook and the liquid spilled into the saucer and on to the surrounding table. 'Half a million pounds?' She stared at the man's grinning face. 'My father set up a trust fund containing half a million pounds? There must be some mistake.' She took her passport out of her handbag and gave it to him. 'I can see why you asked for identification. You're mixing me up with some other Petra Jones, aren't you?' For no particular reason she studied the top of Broughton's head and noticed it was so shiny it was reflecting light. 'My father couldn't have had that sort of money.'

He took the passport and flicked it open at the page

---

giving her date and place of birth. 'No mistake, I do assure you, Miss Jones. Though, as I said, we will have to see your birth certificate. Just a formality; I'm sure you understand.' He saw her difficulty with the tea and summoned the waitress. 'A new cup, please.'

While she was waiting Petra fumbled in her bag for a Kleenex. 'You're absolutely sure? Where could he have got such a sum?'

'That information, Miss Jones, is not something to which I am privy. Your father was not a communicative man. He simply approached us to set up the funds, I dealt with that side of his affairs and Fotheringtons have followed his instructions.'

'Funds?' He'd actually let something slip. 'There are others?'

The small eyes became pinpoints as he searched his mind for an out. 'A matter of expression.' His pupils widened again as he looked at her triumphantly. 'Of course the funds will, in fact, have increased considerably.' She looked vague; the amounts of money were too large to assimilate. 'Interest will naturally have been added and compounded with the original. My firm will let you have a proper financial statement as soon as possible.' A small, tight smile. 'Though, as I mentioned, proof of identity is crucial.'

'I'll arrange it.'

'Good. May I congratulate you?'

Congratulate? What was he talking about?

'It is a lot of money. Anything we can do to help, please don't hesitate. We are entirely at your disposal.'

She understood at last; she was rich, a potential client. 'That's very kind of you.' She looked directly at him again. 'What about other money? Did he leave something for my mother?'

A veil covered his eyes as his features took on a practised look. 'I can't comment on that.'

'I'm only asking to make sure she's all right.'

He relented a little. 'What I can tell you is that the fund isn't part of a will. Furthermore, it has no bearing on your father's estate. There's no need to wait for probate; the fund has been yours from the day he set it up. You need not worry about depriving your mother of anything.'

'Good,' she said. 'That's a relief.'

'You could have made use of it at any time.'

'If I'd known about it,' she said, a small, vague smile flitting around her lips as she caught on. 'Which I didn't.'

'So I understand.' The small eyes had disappeared behind a ridge of flesh as he impersonated another smile. 'I didn't deal with your father's will, but if he left his estate to your mother, she won't be liable for estate duty. Spouses are exempt.'

She already knew that the will had named Louise as sole heir. 'So my mother is well provided for?'

He shrugged. 'I can't possibly say.'

She turned her full charm on him. 'Of course. I just wanted to make sure she's all right. I'm not sure she understands about money.'

The small sigh of relief allowed another lapse. 'The house is probably held as a joint tenancy; that would mean it's hers now, whatever else was in the will.'

If her father had put £500,000 in a trust fund for her, she guessed he had no need of a mortgage. 'And there's no mortgage on it,' she tried out.

He smiled. 'You know I can't comment.'

So Louise was sitting pretty. She had the pension from Jorncy and the house, together with the endowment insurance plus the money in the building society Louise had already told her about. No need to worry on that score.

'And you've no idea how my father came to have all this money?'

He looked shocked, as though she had made an improper suggestion. 'I've told you everything I know. Why worry about it? It's yours. Properly invested it will give you the freedom to do whatever you wish for the rest of your life.' The face across the table from her was grave. 'I urge you to take reputable financial advice, Miss Jones. It can be very difficult to manage funds of this size. Please believe me when I say you need some help.'

'I have noted your comments.' She didn't like this round little man with his button eyes and his shiny scalp.

His eyes might be small, but they were able to assess her accurately. 'There is one other thing I should mention.'

'You have an idea why my father committed suicide?' She could not help herself, it was what she was most concerned about.

'What?' A momentary frown was almost instantly replaced by a composed look of understanding. 'I can't help you with that. No, what I was about to say was that your father specifically asked us not to allow the existence of the fund to be made known to anyone until his death, and then only to you.'

'You mean, it's a secret?'

'A matter of confidentiality which we extend to all our clients, even if they don't specifically ask for it. In fact, he made it a condition of his being our client that we kept his secret, even after his death. You can be sure it will go no further.'

Was there something wrong with this money? Had he committed some sort of criminal act? She put it out of her mind for the moment. 'I see.'

'Just one more piece of advice before I leave, Miss Jones.'

Her head jerked up. 'Yes?'

'Don't be in a hurry to tell anyone about your father's gift. Allow yourself time to think about it, assimilate it. It is a lot of money: it will change your life.' He stood, and paused as he looked down on her. 'You are young and, if I may say so, unusually good-looking. Your father's gift can make or mar your future. Try to be aware of that.'

She could see that this was a genuine attempt to help her. 'I hear what you're saying, Mr Broughton.'

'I'll leave you to it, now. Let me have that birth certificate, and I'll arrange for the IOM bank to contact you.'

She frowned. 'Contact me?'

'So that you can manage the money.' He stood, held out his hand. 'And do remember – I shall be happy to advise you if you should wish it.'

And he was gone, leaving Petra staring at the tea stains on the table. She got up and went outside, basking in the January sunshine, walking towards the Cathedral. The time had come to go inside for a short prayer.

Petra gave herself the rest of that week to think through what had happened without talking to anyone. Mr Broughton had been right. Inheriting such a large sum of money was going to change her life – and Edward's, too. And, though it was a pleasant shock, it was still a shock.

She was now financially independent. She could pay her own way through university without being indebted to either her mother or her godfather. She was surprised at the relief she felt at that.

A visit to her mother was clearly the next step. Their relationship had deteriorated further since her father's suicide, and Petra felt it was important to leave home as soon as practicable. She rang Louise and arranged to arrive late that Saturday and to stay for the weekend.

'Hello, Mummy.' Petra let herself into her mother's house and smiled at her.

'Where have *you* been,' Louise's tone was angry, 'all tarted up like that? Edward's come up to London as well, has he? Been skulking around in secret?'

Tarted up was hardly a realistic description of a casual anorak over a plain T-shirt teamed with a black skirt. 'I don't go in for skulking, Mummy.' Now that her father was dead Petra felt no compunction about seeing Edward. She hadn't bothered to hide her continuing interest from her mother. 'And I haven't come up with Edward. You know he plays in matches during the season. I've come straight from the station.'

To Petra's disgust her mother had grown younger, more attractive, since her husband's death. During the Christmas holidays she'd complained about the loss of the term insurance her husband had taken out, but she'd been satisfied enough with the endowment policy which she could hold to maturity, and the thirty thousand pounds he'd kept in a building society account.

'A deep one, your father,' she'd said to Petra, the muddy eyes glinting with flecks of gold brought out by the bold highlights in her hair. 'When he told me that Jorncy had paid him a few thousand for his inventions, I never thought he meant real money.'

She'd bought a whole new wardrobe, joined a ladies' bridge club, begun to canvass for the Conservatives. Her attitude to Jack Oliver had been that of the little girl who needs looking after. He'd countered that by offering to let his accountant see to her finances.

Her mother shrugged. 'Miss Butter-wouldn't-melt-in-her-mouth.' The habitual look of irritation, replaced by a more benign expression for a short time after her husband's death, had returned to her face. As far as Petra was concerned, that could only mean one thing: she didn't enjoy her daughter visiting any more than she'd enjoyed her husband's company.

She'd felt guilty about leaving her mother on her own when she went back to Exeter after her father's funeral, but clearly she needn't have worried. Louise appeared perfectly content.

She slipped off her anorak and was about to hang it in the hall cupboard when she noticed her mother's intense stare. Her eyes were riveted on her collarbone.

'Where did you get that from?' There was a curious mixture of anger and admiration in her eyes. 'Did someone give you that?'

It took a few seconds before Petra remembered the necklace her godfather had given her. She glanced down and saw it displayed above the boat neckline of her T-shirt. It was beautiful; an understated work of art. She'd kept a childish attitude to Jack, hadn't understood the sort of man he was. He had good taste, no denying it. It dawned on her at last that that was how he picked his winners.

'A present,' she said, her eyes cool. 'From a friend. Pretty, isn't it?'

'Pretty? It's exquisite.' Louise had come up closer and put a finger out to touch it. She frowned, a question in her eyes. 'It looks like gold – fine gold. Have I got that right?'

Her mother had a gift for picking out elegant clothes, jewellery and accessories. It was almost a passion with her. Petra had always felt she should be doing something with such a gift: running a shop, selling, designing. It wouldn't matter what. Why did she waste her time trying to find a man to latch on to?

'He did call it that. Why? Is that unusual?'

Louise shrugged. 'Definitely not Edward. That little lot must have set your "friend" back about ten thousand pounds. So, who is he, this new friend?' Respect was mixed with a less pleasant emotion; the muddy eyes had taken on a tinge of green.

This was ridiculous. Louise was treating her like a rival. To tell her the necklace was from her godfather would lead to the most outrageous accusations. She'd made it clear from the moment she'd found her husband dead that she considered she had first claim on Jack Oliver. 'Just an old friend, Mummy. Someone I met through Daddy.'

'Don't be ridiculous, Petra. Your father had no friends, or even acquaintances. Met him through Jack, did you?'

Was she being utterly naive? She saw Jack's blue eyes look at her, their glance admiring her, almost caressing her. Was he making a play for her, by any chance? Was that what it was all about? She shuddered at the idea. 'If you don't mind, I'm really tired. It was a long trip up, so I'll say goodnight.' She began to climb the stairs, then turned back. This was her *mother* she was talking to. 'See you in the morning.' She tried to put some affection into the phrase.

In her heart of hearts she knew she couldn't go on living a lie; she'd have to leave. There was no longer a place for her in her father's house. His widow wanted to make merry rather than grieve. She wanted no part of that.

She went into her room, sat on her bed, and drew out the print-out of her father's last message. She reread it for the umpteenth time, reminded of Sally's obsession with the tape of Phil's last match. This note held the secret to her father's suicide.

I hope my darling Petra will understand one day. I had no idea that the arrangements I agreed to were changed.

272

*I'd give anything to undo what I allowed to happen,
anything at all. It's too late; there's nothing anyone can
do.*

*Forgive me, Pet; I can't live with that. Remember that
I've always loved you, always will.*

You've always been a clever girl; you'll sort it out.

*David Jones, the man who was proud to call himself
your father.*

The arrangements – did that refer to money? Had she been
quite wrong to think that, somehow, it had to do with her
paternity? Now that a little time had passed since her
father's death she felt less inclined to blame her mother, or
herself, for his suicide. She was prepared to consider other
options.

And now there was all this money. The first thing she had
to decide was when to tell Edward. Such a lot of money
would mean that he could chuck that stupid basketball, and
they could get married right away. They could even buy a
sheep farm in Wales!

PART 2

25

October mists were curling like candyfloss around the trees stretching away into the hills. Vivid flecks of red and gold danced towards Petra's kitchen window on bright shafts of sunlight. She could hardly bear to tear herself away from the beauty of the morning skies, the drama of the sun burning off small wisps of vapour to reveal fantastic spectacles of colour. How could Gwyneth have imagined that she and Edward would find living in the country a bore? Each day showed them a fresh delight in the glories of nature all around them, brought a new excitement in simply being alive. Watching great bands of yellow streak across grey and bring the dark hills into view was enough to keep Petra spellbound all day. Except when her daughters needed her.

'Mummum.'

'Jacintha, sweetheart.' Petra turned, startled to see her elder daughter crawling towards her. 'Climbed out of your cot, did you?' A new development. The one-year-old must have managed to clamber over the cot rail and creep down the stairs and on into the kitchen. Though she wasn't walking yet, she was remarkably agile, showing every sign of following in her father's footsteps and becoming an athlete. She would have to try to keep one jump ahead of her.

Petra scooped her little daughter off the floor, kissed the

fair locks still tangled damp from sleep, and lifted her into the highchair. 'How's my little Cinthy, then? Had a good sleep?'

''Leep,' the little girl mimicked her. ''Leep.'

She looked at the child and watched as her supple body leaned out of the highchair, her long arms reaching down to the struts. She *was* going to be tall, whatever anyone said.

Petra went back to her Rayburn, stirring the oatmeal which formed the first course of their second breakfast. Edward always got up at six and made them tea while she gave the baby her early feed. Then she went down to prepare the meal which would set her family up for a day of hard but satisfying work. Good, nourishing oatmeal, stone-ground, organically grown. Megan had taught her to make it in the traditional way, starting it the night before and leaving it to simmer on the slow hotplate of the multi-fuel cooker. Both Petra and Edward had come to love it; as for Jacintha, she knew nothing of the gaudy cereal packages which had filled the shelves of her grandparents' kitchen cupboards.

The sad fact was that Jacintha knew nothing of her grandparents either. But she did have the Jones clan within an hour's drive. Great-grandmother Megan doted on her first great-granddaughter in just the way Petra had always known she would, and Great-aunt Gwyneth had taken on the role of surrogate grandmother. More than that; to Petra's surprise she'd become a firm friend of hers.

'More, more!'

'Hungry already, are you?' Petra cut a piece of home-baked, wholemeal bread and gave it to her toddler.

The sound of barking brought a smile of anticipation to Jacintha's eyes. It wasn't hard for her to work out that it meant her father and his dog were in the little courtyard just outside the cosy kitchen. 'Dada, Dada,' she babbled.

Petra waved out of the window at Edward as he twisted and turned, dribbling the ball between him and Bradley Mark II.

'Daddy and Bradley are practising basketball,' she told her little girl as she gave the oatmeal another vigorous stir. 'You'll have fun playing with them, as soon as you can walk.'

As far as Petra was concerned her family was nothing short of a miracle. She had a loving husband and two children within a couple of years of marriage: a pair of lovely girls who took after their parents in terms of health and vigour. There were no signs of any of the terrible genetic defects the grandparents they'd left behind in England had prophesied. Could such luck last? Would she and Edward be able to have the six children they were planning? Or were they tempting fate by being greedy?

Petra had enjoyed looking after Jacintha when she was a baby, and now she had a second one. Corilla was two weeks old, and every bit as adorable as her sister. Petra thought of her daughters as her golden girls: fair-haired, blue-eyed, beautiful. She and Edward had had the tests for the Huntington gene done on both foetuses; to their immense relief they'd proved negative.

The crunch of boots on the gravel of the path leading up to the door told her and Cinthy that Edward had finished his game with his collie and was coming in.

'Dada,' Cinthy announced, standing on the footrest of her chair and nearly toppling out. Petra rushed over; she'd forgotten to strap her daughter in. A small prick of worry shortened her breath as she tried to stifle what she'd suspected from the moment Jacintha was born. She was much longer than other children of her age; had been, right from the start.

'You're fussing about nothing,' Edward had tried to

soothe her. 'We're living in Wales. You're comparing her to children from a different racial heritage. The average height in Wales is much shorter than in England. Besides, Cinthy has tall parents.'

'My father was Welsh,' she'd reminded Edward. 'And he was only five foot six. You'd think that would make a difference.' She wanted to believe Edward. She wanted to believe the staff at the hospital where Jacintha was born. In spite of reassurances by the doctor who'd delivered her, the midwife, the health visitor, Petra remained convinced that her baby was longer than normal.

When she'd got her home and was on her own with the baby, she'd taken the trouble to measure her. It wasn't easy, but she'd finally worked out a way. Jacintha was fifty-five centimetres long from the tip of her head to the heel of her foot. She couldn't find many statistics in the library baby books to compare that with, but she'd gleaned that the average length at birth for girls was nearer forty-five centimetres.

Concerned, she'd pestered her GP.

'You new mothers! Always worrying about your babies. There's nothing wrong with her, Mrs Dunstan. Children develop in all kinds of different ways.'

'The books I've read ...'

He'd laughed at her. 'Books! Well, babies do tend to break all the rules, you know.'

Eventually he'd referred her to a consultant paediatrician in Aberystwyth. More to get her off his back than because he thought she had a point.

She remembered taking Jacintha to the hospital. The consulting room was small and stuffy, and Jacintha, only three months old, had begun to fret. The consultant's well-fed body was straining his clothes. He had a large file open in front of him; it contained a single sheet of paper. 'Well, now. Jacintha is a very healthy little girl. Why do you think there's a problem, Mrs Dunstan?'

'She seems rather long to me. I can't even use the first-size baby clothes I bought her. I had to buy the one-year-old size. You can see she's already growing out of that, and she's only twelve weeks old.'

'Children don't all develop in the same way.' A frown was turned into a smile as he saw Petra trying to read his face. 'New mothers always worry when their children deviate, however slightly, from the norm.'

'I'm not talking about slightly.'

'At this stage we can't really say whether a child is going to be tall or not,' he interrupted her. He looked at her keenly. 'Is your husband shorter than you?'

'My husband is six foot six.'

A hearty laugh. 'Then I would say you should expect your little girl to be a little longer than average. Tallness is an hereditary trait, you know. But don't distress yourself. You'll find the baby will end up shorter than her father!'

She didn't think it funny. 'I wasn't doubting that. I was just anxious that she'd get too tall. Fifty-five centimetres is nearly ten centimetres longer than the average given in the books.'

That condescending smirk. 'Are you qualified in medicine, Mrs Dunstan?' Of course he must know she wasn't; she was only nineteen at the time and he had the notes, short as they were, right in front of him.

'I'm working on a degree in biochemistry.'

His eyelids flickered. 'Indeed. That must be difficult while you're busy producing a family.' He didn't say he didn't believe her, but that was the clear implication.

'I'm studying with the Open University.' When she and Edward had left Exeter, they'd decided to opt for the OU courses instead of trying to get a place in one of the nearby

Welsh ones. It meant that Petra could start a family, and Edward could run the sheep farm as well as study in the evenings.

'Ah, yes.' He didn't even bother to look at her this time.

She seethed inside. If everything was fine, why was all the equipment made for children on the short side for Jacintha? She'd practically grown out of the carry-cot the salesman had assured her would last for a year.

'Most Celts are short by Anglo-Saxon standards,' Edward had droned on each time she brought it up with him. 'It's only natural that they would stock the kind of baby equipment most suited to their needs.'

Whenever she was told that she was imagining something her common sense told her was a problem, she thought of Sally. Hadn't they all said she was imagining it when Phil was dying? And then he'd died. And when Sally had escaped to London, saying someone was going to kill her if she didn't get away, she'd ended up in front of a train, quite dead. And it had been Sally who'd insisted that someone was trying to steal that tape of Phil's last game. And the copy had disappeared from her locker.

Was it wrong the way she and Edward had run away from the past? Were Jacintha's excessive centimetres a kind of punishment for not staying to investigate what Sally had been so sure were signs of a deadly secret? Had she been right?

The back door was thrown open and Bradley Mark II bounded in, his paws making a mosaic of marks on the polished flagstone floor.

A short, sharp whistle from Edward and the dog slunk out again. Jacintha was straining towards him, her little hands held out. ''Alee!' she called.

Petra watched her daughter's long arms reaching further

than any child her age was meant to reach. 'Don't lean down so far, Cinthy. You'll topple the chair.' They'd have to buy a lowchair next time they were near a town large enough to stock one.

Edward shut the back door on his collie. 'He's a working dog, Cinthy. We only play with him outside.' He walked over to his wife and kissed her thoroughly. 'Hi, sweetheart.'

'Dada dada dada!'

'I'm getting round to you.' He undid his little daughter's straps, lifted her out of her chair and kissed her as well, then put her back, carefully strapping her in again. 'Waiting for me before we start breakfast, are you?'

''Eck'ast,' she said, her spoon ready in her hand, banging it against the tray.

'Let's put your bib on, then.'

''Ib. Dada, 'ib.'

'Daddy doesn't need a bib. At least, I hope not.'

It must have been the banging of Jacintha's spoon against her tray which had prevented them from noticing that Bradley's barks had changed from cheerful acceptance to a warning tone.

There were three loud knocks at the front door, followed by silence.

They stared at each other. Their farmhouse was remote; too far for casual visitors to come calling. Petra stood protectively by her child while Edward walked out into the hall, leaving the door to the kitchen wide open.

They were nervous about unexpected callers. When they'd decided to move to Wales they'd agreed it would be best to sever all links with both family and friends in England, and to make a new start. They'd been sick of being hounded, told what to do. So they'd settled into an old farmhouse, miles from the nearest town. The only people they trusted were the Jones clan.

'Someone must have driven up without our hearing them,' Edward said as he walked back into the kitchen. Petra saw him check the side window to see if a car had parked in their drive. 'There's a swish car outside – that new Jaguar E-type, no less!'

'We don't know anyone who drives a car like that.' Petra stroked Jacintha's hair and looked up at Edward, a worry of surprise at such early visitors catching at her throat.

A volley of rat-a-tatting spelled out its Welsh melody.

Da daa da da da daaa da da da
Da daa da da da daaa da daa

At first Petra couldn't place where she'd heard that sound before, then it all came flooding back. Her father had always rat-tatted out *There'll be a welcome in the hillsides, There'll be a welcome in the dales.* Instinctively she felt the familiar pleasure of her childhood, followed by a frisson of apprehension. Perhaps Huw Jones used the same signal, she tried to comfort herself. But she knew it couldn't be Huw, or any of the locals. None of them drove a Jaguar, let alone the latest model.

She saw Edward frown, his eyes sliding away from hers. Why was he looking guilty? The fleeting thought that he'd contacted a basketball promoter crossed her mind. She knew he'd been missing the game, the company of the other players, the thrill of the matches. She put the thought aside as unworthy. Why would he risk doing something like that? It would blow their cover.

'I'll answer it,' Edward's loud voice boomed out. 'Whoever it is must be lost, asking for directions.'

After two years of country life Edward looked even more magnificent than when he'd been a full-time athlete. The jeans and handknitted jumper he wore showed off his large frame, now filled out from youth to man, to perfection. He had the healthy complexion which was the bonus of an outdoor life in the rainsodden hills of Powys. His muscles rippled their prime condition, exercised from walking the hills looking after his sheep.

Petra was proud of her husband. He'd taken to the life of a sheep farmer with astonishing ease. True, they had arranged with the man they'd bought from, Gareth Evans, that he would stay nearby and help Edward learn the ropes. But it was Edward himself who trained Bradley Mark II for the sheep-dog trials. And it was Edward who'd picked out two more collie puppies and was bringing them along for entering the *One Man and his Dog* trials two years from now.

'Proverbial bad penny,' Petra heard a familiar, lilting voice ring out. 'Hope you aren't going to be too angry with me. Thought I'd arrive early in the day and catch the proverbial early worm.'

Could it really be true? Could he have found them? He was clever and persistent enough.

'You'd better come in.' Edward sounded subdued as he led the visitor through to the kitchen at the back. 'Look who's here, Petra. A ghost from the past.'

'Hello, Goddaughter. Surprise, surprise.' Jack Oliver, looking not a day older than the last time she'd seen him, walked into Petra's kitchen. 'I see motherhood becomes you.'

26

The young couple stared at Jack, momentarily speechless.

He walked up to Petra and put his arm around her waist, kissed her on both cheeks. 'Thought I'd better come at the crack of dawn, in case I missed Ed. Out with the sheep most of the time, I gather.'

Petra was the first to recover. 'Uncle Jack.' It could not be said that she sounded delighted; she was too shocked for that. But, of all the people they'd left behind, Jack was the one she was least uneasy about seeing again. 'How on earth did you find us?'

The same old attractive smile curled the corners of his mouth upwards, the same hint of a dimple creased his cheeks. Petra felt the same affection for the familiar, easy laugh, the lilting voice, the questioning eyes which managed to convey approval as they swept across first her face, then her body.

'That all you can say? No "how lovely to see you"?' His eyelids dropped halfway to indicate distress. 'And I'd promised myself my little goddaughter would be so glad to see me, she'd actually throw her arms around my neck and say so.'

Petra wiped her hands on a tea towel, then embraced him. 'I *am* glad to see you, Uncle Jack. But it's a bit of a shock, you know.'

His eyelids had swung up and there was a teasing look in

his eyes. He stood back from Petra and offered Edward his hand.

'Hello, Jack. Good to see you again.'

'It was a blow to get your letters,' Jack said. 'After all those years I thought I deserved better than that.'

Petra was determined not to be made to feel guilty. After all, it had been his own fault. He'd put moral pressure on her, and commercial pressure on Ed, not to marry one another. 'So how *did* you find us? I thought you never came back to Wales.'

'Not for myself, no.' He walked over to Jacintha and extended a finger which she promptly grasped. 'Didn't waste any time, did you?'

'Her name's Jacintha,' Edward said.

Jack was looking at her with interest. 'Chip off the old blocks, all right. Spitting image of you both, somehow. I don't know how she's managed that.' The glinting eyes and bright expression told Petra that he meant exactly the opposite. He thought he did know. Precisely what he thought that was she couldn't make out.

She watched as Jack engaged the child's attention, remembered how often he used to play with her when she was small. 'So you knew where we were, but you didn't know about Jacintha,' she started off.

Edward began to lay the kitchen table, setting a place for Jack as well as himself and Petra. 'Like oatmeal, do you, Jack?'

He made a face. 'I'll skip that, if you don't mind. Had my fill when I was a child. Do you go on to something tastier after it?'

'The works – sausage, bacon and eggs, mushrooms, laver bread, tea, toast and marmalade,' Edward recited. 'The mushrooms are from the fields, the eggs from our own chickens and Petra bakes the brown loaves you see there. If we happen to be near a beach she gathers seaweed to make some laver bread. We buy in the bacon and sausage, but we're working on that!'

'Traditional Welsh breakfast, eh? Doesn't seem to have affected your figures. Both as slim and youthful-looking as ever.'

'We work hard physically. We need a good breakfast to start the day.'

'So where do you practise, Ed? Where's the nearest court?'

'Practise? Edward doesn't play basketball any more, Uncle Jack. He just plays around with Bradley, that's his collie.'

'Doesn't practise, eh?' He grinned. 'Can't swallow that one. Even if he roams the hills for exercise, he still needs ball practice.'

Petra frowned. 'Only if he wants to play basketball to a high standard. He's given all that up.'

Edward was straightening the cutlery with exaggerated attention. 'There's a good court in the sports centre at Lland'od High School,' he said, turning his back to Petra and busying himself putting away the early-morning cups and saucers. 'Thought that was your old school.'

'Nothing as fancy as that in my time.'

'Ed's a sheep farmer, Uncle Jack. He doesn't have enough leisure time for basketball.'

Jack had taken Jacintha out of her highchair and was supporting her under her armpits, holding her out in front of him. She gurgled delightedly. He put her on her feet and held her up. 'She walk yet?' Petra could see him sizing up the child, his eyes thoughtful.

'She's younger than she looks,' Edward said. 'She's only just over a year.'

'I know that.'

'You know about small children, Uncle Jack?'

'I can work out how old she is. Last time I saw Petra was in January 1994. She wasn't pregnant then, I'm pretty sure. It's October 1995. Even an old bachelor like me knows it takes nine months to have a baby. So, assuming you got busy the moment you ran off to get married, the little one's a year or so old.'

Petra, the oatmeal pot in her hand, grinned down at him. 'You're always so sharp, Uncle Jack. You work everything out.'

He shrugged. 'I like children, always have taken a special interest. She's on the tall side – that's what you were saying, isn't it? She looks older because she's taller than most children of her age. She'll be late walking because she has to have strong muscles for those longer limbs. Lucky girl.'

So what she'd suspected, and what the doctors had denied, was obvious to Jack. And the new baby was even longer at birth than her sister had been. As soon as she'd got her home she'd measured her. Fifty-seven centimetres; both her girls were going to be tall. No surprise there, no worry about that. The real question was: how tall?

The wailing of an infant began to infiltrate the kitchen. Edward stood. 'I'll go,' he said. 'She's a bit early for her ten o'clock feed. I'll see if I can settle her.'

'You've got another one? Another little girl?'

Petra felt the pride of the new mother, knew her eyes were shining. 'Her name's Corilla; she's only two weeks old.'

Jack whistled. 'You really have been busy, haven't you?'

She began to fill Jacintha's bowl with oatmeal, blowing on it to make it cooler, then started feeding her little daughter. 'So, tell me. How *did* you find us, Uncle Jack?'

'It wasn't very difficult, my dear. When an athlete like Edward starts playing for a team, I'm always on the scene within a month or so; six months at the outside.'

The spoon stopped in mid-air, and Jacintha began to make eager noises, her little mouth wide open, like a nestling waiting to be fed. 'Player like Edward? What are you talking about? I told you, he's a sheep farmer now, not a basketball player.'

Jack was perched on the high, three-legged stool Edward had bought for himself. Petra was amused to see that Jack's legs were several inches off the floor so that he looked oddly boyish. 'Your husband likes a game every now and again. He pops up here and there and joins in. Rumours have been flying round basketball circles about a tall, fair-haired player from Wales. That's unusual in itself, so I pricked up my ears. My scouts are always out, searching all over the country.' He stared at her without a smile this time. 'England, Wales, Scotland, even Ireland. The whole of the UK's my patch. Edward signed up with a Swansea team this season. That's when I thought we could be back in business. Getting quite a name for himself, even if he does pretend it's Jones!'

'Jones? Edward plays basketball for a Swansea team and uses the name Jones?'

'Borrowed it from you, I dare say.' He grinned at her embarrassment and shrugged. 'There may be quite a few Joneses in Wales, but the number of Edwards is fairly limited. So it wasn't too hard to put two and two together when I heard about a player called Edward Jones.'

'And this team he plays with in Swansea; they told you where he lived?'

'He gave a false address.' An impish grin. 'But it made me think. I should have guessed about Wales before; you went on about it enough after your first visit. But somehow

I got the impression you'd gone abroad.' His nostrils widened as his eyes took on a sad look. 'Must have been something or other in that letter my goddaughter sent, saying she thought she'd leave England.'

She was putting oatmeal into Jacintha's mouth at a rapid rate. 'Perfectly true.'

'So it was. But Wales is part of the United Kingdom. You put me off the scent deliberately.' He stood and held his hands out. 'Can I have a go?'

She gave him the bowl and spoon.

'Dewi told me how you'd taken to his family. I should have guessed from that. Once I'd grasped that the player could be Ed it wasn't hard to work out that you might be living within easy reach of Lland'od. I went round to the Sports Hall, asking questions. Ed uses his real name there; the rest wasn't that difficult.'

'So that was it.' And she'd thought Edward spent all his time walking the hills, looking after his sheep, training his dogs.

'I've known for a couple of weeks now. I didn't look you up right away. Bit upset, really. First you don't invite me to your wedding, though I've known both of you for a good part of your lives, and specially you, Pet. Then Edward disappears from the team without a word...'

'He wrote to you.'

'Big deal. He wrote me a scrappy letter, announcing he was leaving. Mid-season, no explanations. He was under contract to me, you know.'

'Contract?'

'I sponsored him through Millfield, then through Exeter. Putting it bluntly, Pet – he owes me.'

She caught her breath. 'You mean you're going to prosecute him?'

The face she saw was not the Jack Oliver she was used to.

292

He had the cold, calculating look of the businessman. 'I certainly could.'

Without even thinking about it she put some bacon in a pan and began to fry it. 'Are you going to?'

'You both disappear without any forwarding address, so no one knows what's happened to you...'

'I've been in touch with my mother and told her I'm OK.'

'Very considerate of you.'

'And Ed's let his people know that they can contact him through Harold. He needs to find out how his father's getting on now and again.' She shook the pan holding the rashers. 'The Huntington's showing itself.'

'Ah, yes. So what about the children?'

'We had the amniocentesis testing done. They're both OK.'

Jack had returned to his perch and was swinging his legs. 'Neither of you had the courtesy to get in touch with me since you left, let alone think of taking me into your confidence.' He examined his manicured nails. 'Don't imagine I don't understand; I know we all gave you hassle. And I did the same thing at your age – left Wales and went to England. Just thought you might have given me the benefit of the doubt, Pet. I did my best to be a father to you after Dewi died.'

'You'd have told my mother and Edward's parents where we were.'

'No, as a matter of fact I wouldn't.' He watched her as she helped Jacintha drink from a trainer cup. 'I see your daughter isn't a fussy feeder.'

'Wouldn't get much food if she were.'

'So, tell me. You say you earn your living sheep farming. But how did you get the farm in the first place? And this *cruck frame* must have set you back a bob or two. Very nice.' His eyes travelled over the seventeenth-century farmhouse, with its timbered frame enclosing white-washed rendering, the stone surrounds, the flagstoned floors. 'It's a lovely old place.'

She saw he meant it. 'Thank you.'

'The gold necklace wouldn't have been enough to pay for it. So David set up a nice little trust fund for you, did he?'

She drew in her breath. Had Fotheringtons been persuaded to break the confidence? 'You know about that?'

'Not really. An informed guess.' He swung a foot backwards and forwards, examining it. 'I know he always put something by for you, whenever he had a bit over.'

Did Jack know where the money actually came from? She should have thought of that before. 'I was a bit surprised by the amount of money, Uncle Jack. Have you any idea where he got it?'

He didn't look at her, but continued to let his eyes roam around the room. 'Getting on for a hundred thou, I would say. Then it had to be done up, plus the farmland, and the stock on the farm. And then there's that Range Rover you've got sitting in the drive, as well as the little runaround. Couldn't be done on less than half a million.'

'You're very sure.'

He shrugged. 'I'm in business.'

'So how did he come by it all?'

Jack smiled. 'Well, even if I knew, I wouldn't tell on my old friend. One thing I can tell you, though; he didn't steal it.' His eyes took on a sly look. 'Bit of a dark horse, our Dewi. Something of a gambler.'

'You mean he won the money by going to the races?'

'Won it?' The smile was enigmatic. 'I suppose you could say that. He took an outside chance, and it came off.' This time he looked at her full face. 'So now I know how you managed it, but I still don't know *why*. What made you go off like that, bury yourselves in this godforsaken place?'

She stared at him. Could he really not see how fortunate they were? 'How can you say that? We have everything we've ever dreamed of. The most glorious views you can imagine – just look out of this window at the sun painting the greens on those hills.'

'It's the back of beyond.'

'Fresh air, no traffic, friendly neighbours, Daddy's relatives nearby...'

'Get on well with the Joneses, do you?'

'Gran Megan is a marvel.'

'I'll grant you that; she was always good to me.'

'And Gwyneth has turned into a terrific grandmother. I don't think either of the girls' real grandmothers could hold a candle to her.'

'The worthy Gwyneth.'

'Anyway, we got sick of being hounded.'

'No one could do anything about your getting married even if they'd known about it. You were both over eighteen. Didn't mean you had to run off and hide, did it?'

Petra shrugged. 'It seemed like a sort of jinx was following us around. First Phil dies, then Sally gets murdered. After that Daddy commits suicide. All within the space of a few weeks! Can you blame us for wanting to make a completely new start, for leaving it all behind when we had the chance?'

'And you've had no problems since you got away from us. Everything in the Welsh garden is lovely, is it?'

'Yes. As a matter of fact it's idyllic.'

Edward walked into the kitchen carrying an infant. 'She won't settle, I'm afraid. Here, let me finish feeding Jacintha while you take her over, Pet.'

'I gather you and Pet disappeared because you wanted to put the past behind you,' Jack said to Edward. 'I did

everything I could for Phil, you know. And for his parents.
I tried to help Sally's mother, too...'

'She told us.'

'I was willing to help the poor lady out. She wouldn't...'

'No.'

He changed the subject. 'So this is number two, is it?
What did you say you'd called her?'

'This is Corilla.'

He took the baby, held her wrapped up in her shawl,
looked up at Petra. 'Another long one, isn't she?'

'You seem to be an expert on small children, Uncle Jack.
You got a family stashed away somewhere?'

'It's what I do for a living, Pet. I've looked into it
carefully, and I've discovered a formula you can use to
extrapolate height from birth length. And I'm a good
judge of length.' He handed the infant back to her
mother.

'The consultant paediatrician at Aberystwyth said you
couldn't tell about height until after puberty. That's when
the growth spurt occurs.'

'Poppycock. If they're much taller than average before
the spurt, you can have a pretty shrewd idea. Doctors never
seem to have any plain common sense.'

'You think they're bound to be tall?'

'I'd say both your daughters will end up fashion model
heights.' He grinned. 'How about my signing them up?'

Petra felt a sort of sickness in her stomach. The pressure
was starting again, and within minutes of someone they'd
known before their move to Wales turning up.

'We're not going to sign them up to do anything, Uncle
Jack. We want them to be free to choose for themselves.'

He put his palms together and lifted them to his chin,
looking at Petra in mock resignation. 'I know, I know. But
it's wonderful for them to be tall. You two have no idea

296

what a bore it is to be as small as I am. People think you're
of no account; ignore you.'

'Sally was always going on about it.'

A shadow crossed his face. 'Ah, yes. Sally was on the
small side, too. Gave her a chip on her shoulder.'

And he hadn't got one? Petra wondered whether he
realised just how much his own short stature had influenced
the way he reacted to people around him.

He gave her a quizzical look. 'Aren't you glad your girls
will be spared that?'

'I suppose they could be *too* tall,' Petra murmured,
hardly daring to voice her real fears.

'I wouldn't worry about that,' he said. 'I've come across
children just as long as both of them. You had her
christened yet?'

'Corilla, you mean?'

'You got any more babies hidden away? She got a twin,
or something?'

Petra giggled. 'No. And we haven't had her christened
yet. You mean you'd like to be her godfather?'

He turned to the baby's father. 'Well, Edward? What do
you say?'

The sapphire eyes looked at his wife. 'If it's OK with
Petra.'

Was Jack offering them a way out of his pressing charges
against Edward? 'You were always a very good godfather
to me. Just one thing, Uncle Jack. We don't want you to tell
anyone where we are. If we want to do that, we'll do it
ourselves.'

'No problems there,' he agreed. 'And any time you want
to play in a decent team, Edward, I'll be happy to find you a
place. By all accounts you haven't lost any of your skills.'
He got off the stool and sat at the table, waiting for Edward
to serve the breakfast while Petra fed her baby.

'I'll have to discuss that with Petra.'

'You mean you *want* to go back to basketball?' She could hardly believe her ears. She wasn't going to go into it now, but Jack finding them was not what she would have wished. Problems had started surfacing as soon as Jack Oliver had come back on to the scene.

27

'I thought we said we'd discuss everything with each other, Ed?' Petra was in the kitchen, giving Corilla her two-o'clock feed while Jacintha was having her nap.

'Our discussions about basketball do tend to deteriorate into your saying you can't believe anyone would want to spend their life dribbling a ball around a court.'

Edward felt trapped. Disappearing into the blue couldn't have worked for ever. He knew he should have talked to Jack about breaking the contract he had with him. He also knew he'd never have managed to escape if he had. The man had a way of getting round him he found impossible to resist.

When he and Petra first moved to Wales, and the excitement of the new house and learning how to sheep farm had kept him too busy to think, he hadn't missed the game. But after Jacintha was born, and Petra spent so much time with her, he began to miss the companionship of the other players, the camaraderie, the drinks after the game.

He'd talked to Petra about going to the nearest sports hall to play with whatever locals he could persuade to let him join them.

Petra had even encouraged him in that, had understood it would be a good idea. 'I do see you'd miss it,' she'd agreed amiably, sitting in the rocker with the baby at her breast. 'And spending all your time away from other people isn't in your nature. I know you're much more gregarious than I am.'

He'd wondered how she coped with being on her own all day, with only Jacintha to keep her company. She didn't seem to notice; perhaps she even liked it. All she wanted was to have her baby with her all the time, and her husband's companionship at regular intervals. Occasional basketball games weren't going to get in the way of that.

What he hadn't bargained for was the enormous buzz he got when he started playing the game again. He'd trained Bradley Mark II to help him practise, right from the start, just as he'd trained Bradley Mark I. That had kept him in good shape. But there was nothing in those sessions which produced anything like the charge of adrenaline which playing with nine other men could produce. He'd found himself looking forward to lending a hand with even the least gifted players just to have another human he could measure himself against.

Inexperienced players found the level of his game hard to take. That's when he'd decided to drive around and investigate the position in some of the larger towns within a couple of hours' drive: Hereford, Aberystwyth, Swansea. He knew it was dangerous to go over to England, so he'd settled for Swansea as having the densest population. Not dense enough, of course. The basketball world was tiny. A player of his size and ability was bound to excite comment.

If he was honest with himself, perhaps he'd known what would happen, perhaps he'd hoped to draw attention to himself. And he'd managed to do it without, on the face of it, going against Petra's wishes.

'It's very hard to give up a team game after you've played

for as long as I have,' he tried to explain to her. 'Don't forget I started when I was eleven. That means I've been playing basketball for half my life.'

Her eyes shone at him, a tigress guarding her cubs. But she didn't speak.

'It's not that I don't find your company stimulating and all that, Pet. You know I do; I love being with you. And the kids. It's just that I need to use my body ...'

'I thought you did that. I thought you spent most of your time in the hills.' She bent over the small head lying in the snug round of her left arm and kissed it. 'But I was quite wrong. You'd driven miles away to Swansea to play basketball.' Her eyes had become moist. 'That's a kind of lie, Ed. You misled me.'

He couldn't really deny it. 'I do spend hours in the hills; you know I do. But walking and climbing aren't the exercise I'm used to. I've been trained to react quickly, to twist and turn with only seconds to do it in. And I've learned to dribble a ball as though it was an extension of my own body. Driving sheep just isn't the same.'

'And you miss the adulation of the crowd, I suppose.'

That, too. More than he cared to admit. He'd even taken out a map of the States and looked at it. Perhaps it would be possible to combine living in deep country with being a professional basketball player there. Georgia was a lovely state; good climate, lovely scenery, and had one of the top teams in basketball.

'Maybe we should think of moving to the States. Would that appeal to you at all?'

'You mean you'd want to turn professional?' She was so horrified her right arm jerked the nipple out of the baby's mouth.

His large feet shuffled as he tried to get it right. 'I don't like living off you, Pet.'

'Living off me? You run the farm!'

'But you bought it, with your money. It doesn't feel right; makes me feel like a sort of hanger-on. That's not my style. I want to be the breadwinner.'

He could see her struggling with something she wanted to say, but didn't feel was easy. 'And what about later, Edward? You know, when the Huntington's...?'

'I'm only twenty-one years old! If the illness surfaces early, it's still about fourteen years away. By then I'll be too old for professional basketball, so it won't apply. That's when we can farm the hills of Wales...'

She bent down to the child again. 'Now that Jack's found us all that's academic. If you don't play ball with him he'll probably sue you.'

'Jack's a businessman. He's not out for revenge; he'll come to some reasonable arrangement.'

'I know that. He's already spelt it out. The price is allowing him to be Corilla's godfather.'

He laughed. 'You make him sound like Don Corleone.'

She grinned at last. 'The Welsh instead of the Sicilian Mafia – that's one way of looking at it, I suppose.' She looked straight at him. 'You want to take over Phil's role, don't you, Ed? You want to be a star.'

'Phil wasn't just Jack's star player, Pet. He was the best this country's ever produced.' His eyes roamed outside the window as he felt the loss of his friend, the pain which would not go away. 'He was the only one who had no problem standing up against the Yanks. You never really saw what he could do. He was sensational.'

She looked towards him, her eyes soft with love. 'I know you miss him,' she said, her voice low. 'I know how it feels, Ed. It's the same for me with Sally. I miss her so much, sometimes I think I'll burst. None of the other women here can take her place. And I miss Daddy.'

'So what'll it be, Pet? Should I tell Jack to go to hell and see what happens?'

'Tell him you want to use this season to get back into the game without being tied to a top team. I'm worried about the girls; I want to sort that out.'

'The girls?' He tried to get his mind round that, but failed. She was becoming obsessive. 'The girls are fine, Petra. You've taken them for regular check-ups, haven't you? Did the clinic doctor find something wrong?'

'It's the one thing Jack's visit did for me. He confirmed what I've known all along, that everyone else says I imagine. They're too tall, Ed. We have to get them looked at by a specialist who really understands about height. I want to take them to Great Ormond Street, see the top man there.'

He sighed. It wasn't worth the hassle of arguing with her. He'd drive them all to London and get it settled, once and for all. 'And if he says not to worry, you'll take his word?'

She pressed the fore and middle fingers of her right hand together on either side of her nipple and wriggled it out of the baby's mouth. 'I'll take his word.'

She held the infant up to her shoulder, stroked her back, waited for the burp and stood to take her upstairs. Edward walked around the kitchen, clearing it, stacking the dishes in the sink.

She came down again and slipped her arm through his. 'Shall we go round the garden?' They walked out, their arms intertwined around each other.

'It is so beautiful, Ed. A sort of Eden.'

For Petra, maybe. He was an exile, waiting to get back to the Promised Land.

'Mr and Mrs Dunstan? I'm Adrian Planter. Do sit down, make yourselves comfortable.'

Edward saw Petra's face go white. She was so sure that the doctor would tell her there was a problem. He steered her to two chairs standing opposite a wide desk. When they had both sat down he held her hand.

Dr Planter had their file open in front of him. Reading glasses were suspended from a chain around his neck. He put them on, read for a moment or two, then took the glasses off and looked up. Keen eyes glanced rapidly from Edward to Petra and back again. 'Very interesting. I see you took the unusual step of visiting a genetic counsellor before you married. What made you do that?' His voice was soft, but there was an undercurrent of determination.

'We were told that I have the gene for Huntington's chorea.' Edward's strong voice was modulated, calm. He had had virtually two years to get used to the idea. Dwelling on future problems wasn't part of his temperament; he preferred to live in the present.

'Told? You mean someone ran the test without your permission, and gave you the result?'

Edward frowned. 'Well, yes.'

'The accepted procedure is to ask a patient whose family history shows the disease whether he or she would like to be tested. I've never heard of anyone being told, whether they want to know or not.'

'I didn't even know it was in my family.'

'I'm afraid I don't follow.'

Edward explained why Bruce Traggard and Jack Oliver would have knowledge he did not.

The consultant pursed his lips in disapproval. 'Some of the procedures used by sports promoters are, in my view, misguided. I'd say what you've just told me verges on the unethical.'

'People who sponsor sport feel they have to look after their investments.'

Adrian Planter shrugged, but made no further comment. 'And at genetic counselling, were you advised that tests would not be run on your children until they were old enough to decide whether or not to have such a test themselves?'

'It was mentioned. The point Dr Cressing stressed was that it was possible to test the foetal cells and that, if we wished, a pregnancy involving an affected foetus could be terminated.'

He checked the notes again. 'You've had two children since you married. There's nothing here about the tests. Do I gather you didn't bother with them?'

'We had the amnios done. We were lucky each time; they proved to be negative.'

'I'm delighted to hear it.' He cleared his throat. 'You are a tall man by any standards, Mr Dunstan. Did the question of your height, and the way it might affect your children, come up at the counselling session?'

'It came up, yes.'

'You were worried about it from the start? Is that why you're consulting me now?'

'My mother raised it with me before I married,' Edward explained. 'At the time I thought her remarks wildly exaggerated.'

Dr Planter put his reading glasses on again and read more of the notes. 'Yes, I see it was mentioned.' He looked over the top of his glasses, allowing them to slide down his nose and giving him the air of an inquisitor. He stared at Edward. 'And why did you make light of your mother's fears?'

He shrugged. 'I thought she was against my marrying Petra for some quite different reason.'

'The Huntington's?'

'No, I didn't know about that. I thought she didn't like her.'

'Actually,' Petra put in, 'Dr Cressing confirmed what I'd already researched. Tallness does run in families, but there is a tendency for very tall parents to have shorter children. Edward is much taller than his brother and his father; I'm taller than either of my parents.'

'You're a scientist, Mrs Dunstan?'

'I'm studying for a degree in biochemistry.'

'But you still felt it necessary to bring your children to see me.'

'Endocrinology is not my field.'

'Indeed. I'm sorry to tell you that, though what you say is true, there could also be a pathological tendency to increased height.' He steepled his hands, stared at his fingertips. 'Endocrine disturbance of some sort, genetically transmitted.'

'And you think...'

'I certainly feel you were right to be worried. We need to look into the whole thing further.'

Edward let go of Petra's hand and gripped the sides of his chair. Surely it was enough that he was a possible transmitter of the Huntington's? Was it too much to ask for normal children?

'The paediatrician at Aberystwyth said there was nothing to worry about! We're only here because my wife—'

Dr Planter held up his hand. 'And my colleague may well turn out to be right, but I have probably come across more cases than he has. A simple matter of distribution of population,' he added, challenging them to disagree with him. 'There is also the possibility that the projections of your daughters' heights may have been based on the male statistics. It is so easy to mix the tables up.' He waved that aside. 'Lengths of more than fifty-five centimetres at birth are a distinct warning sign. By my reckoning I would project adult heights of six foot six for Jacintha, and six foot eight for Corilla.'

Petra gasped, and Edward took both her hands in his.

'I'm sorry, Mrs Dunstan. I thought it best to give you the worst prognosis. It's impossible to tell what will really happen, since we cannot actually know until after puberty.'

'That's when the growth spurt is at its most critical point. Yes, we know.'

'And the environment – in particular the nutrients you feed your children – will also very much influence their final height.'

'You mean we could arrange a diet to keep them smaller?' Petra's forehead was creased in thought. 'Exactly the opposite to what we've been doing, I would think. We've been giving them what is considered an excellent diet.'

'Restricting excess protein in itself would not achieve what I'm sure you would prefer; a height below six foot at the outside.'

'So what can be done?' Petra whispered, then cleared her throat. When she spoke again it was in a normal voice. 'Can you offer any treatment?'

'It's possible. We have some compounds which can calm down the growth hormones. You'll appreciate this isn't a simple matter. What I would like to do is to arrange a full fingerprinting of the children's DNA, as well as yours and the four grandparents'. That would give us a proper genetic framework to base treatment on.'

Petra looked at Edward, then back at the doctor. 'My father is dead, I'm afraid.'

'Really?' He looked at the notes again, but didn't seem to find much there to help him. 'Was he much older than your mother?'

'A couple of years; he committed suicide.'

'Ah, yes – a different matter. I'm sorry to bring up unhappy memories.'

'Thank you. What would you like us to do?'

'The nurse will take the samples from the four of you. With your permission, of course.'

'No problems about that,' they both agreed.

'If you will try to arrange for the other samples to be available as soon as possible? I'd like to consider whether we need to start treatment before next year.'

28

Contacting her mother after not being in touch for nearly two years wasn't going to be easy, and Petra didn't look forward to the phone call she knew she had to make. However, her children needed a sample of their grandmother's DNA, and her permission to have it analysed. For that Petra was prepared to beard Louise.

'Is that you, Mother? It's Petra here.' The hospital phone box had the small, plastic hood which was supposed to keep out surrounding noise. It didn't; all Petra could establish was that the receiver had been picked up, and the connection made. The rest was silence.

'Mother?' She turned to wave at Edward sitting with the baby on his lap and trying to prevent Jacintha from climbing down from the plastic chair in the waiting room. He wouldn't be able to cope on his own for long. 'I'm in London,' she said, forcing her voice into a jolly, bright sound. 'I thought you might like me to come and say hello.'

'I take it you want something,' Louise's brisk voice came down the line. 'What is it?'

Her father must have been an angel to put up with this woman. She gurgled a laugh she did not feel. 'Well – sort of; not a big deal. But I do have a wonderful surprise for you. I think you'll be thrilled with what I have to show you.'

'That'll make a change.' A guarded, not entirely dismissive

tone, considerably lighter than the initial bark. 'Are the two of you in town, or are you on your own?' A sudden laugh. 'Or have you broken up already – is that what you mean?'

She couldn't help the frigidity in her voice. 'No, Mother, I do not. Edward and I are happily married, and hope to remain so for the rest of our lives. But I do have some news.'

'Yes?' Suspicion was mixed with curiosity.

'You're a grandmother now.'

Another laugh, a rather brittle one. 'Already? You're turning me into an old woman before my time.' She sounded out of breath, as though that really was a shock. 'I'm only just forty; I could have another child myself! Is that the wonderful surprise?'

'We've got two lovely little girls – Jacintha and Corilla.'

'*Two* little girls? You mean you've had twins?' At last there was genuine warmth in the voice.

Why couldn't her mother be like other mothers, thrilled at the simple thought of being a grandmother? Why did she want Petra to be some sort of circus act? 'Nothing as exciting as that. Jacintha's thirteen months, and Corilla was born last month.'

A long, drawn-out sigh. 'That's so exactly like you, Petra. Turning yourself into a brood animal.' The tones had regained their old sharpness, now mingled with disappointment. 'And you had fantastic opportunities to make something of your life.' An angry hissing tone, whether static on the line or her mother was hard to tell, made Petra put the receiver from her ear. When she returned it her mother was in full flow again. '...Even if you didn't want to take up Jack's offers, at least you could have trained your mind. I thought that's what you were always after?'

'I am studying for a degree. It is possible to be a mother and still use one's brain, you know.'

'I suppose you think I didn't.'

She'd forgotten the sudden twists and turns Louise took to score her points. 'Let's not quarrel, Mother. You have no living relatives except me and my children. Don't you even want to *meet* your granddaughters?'

'You mean you want to bring them round now?' The obvious horror at the idea of small children in her house was tempered with a certain curiosity.

Petra's immediate reaction was that it wasn't worth bothering. Then she remembered why she was ringing her mother in the first place. Not for Louise's sake, nor even for her own. She was in touch with her mother because she needed her help. 'We're leaving for Wales again this evening.' She tried to sound dispassionate, but her temper was getting the better of her. And it wasn't strictly true. They were intending to take a detour to Exeter, to try to pick up the samples from the two other grandparents. 'It's now or not for several months.'

'What on earth possessed you to choose such absurd names?' Louise greeted her daughter. Slatted eyes swept over Petra's perfect figure. 'Hasn't done your looks any harm, I will say that. If anything, you look even better.' She peeped at the baby in Petra's arms, and gasped. 'She's a real beauty!'

Why was her mother so obsessed with looks? Corilla was her granddaughter; what did her appearance matter?

Edward had followed Petra, Jacintha in his arms. He put her down on the hall parquet and straightened up to greet Louise.

'And this is Edward, Mother.'

Louise stared up at him. 'You told me he was tall.' Her voice held awe.

'Nice to meet you at last, Mrs Jones.'

'You really can't call me that; let's settle for Louise, shall we?'

He nodded.

'I'd no idea you were as tall as that.'

'It isn't catching,' Edward said, smiling at her.

There was no response to the bantering tone. Louise turned her gaze downwards. 'So that's Jacintha, is it?' She watched as her elder granddaughter crawled towards the stairs. 'Can't walk yet, I see.'

Edward was about to explain when a look from Petra stopped him. 'She's only just turned one; we like to let her develop at her own pace.'

Vague memories flitted across Louise's face. 'You'll have your hands full when she can. They get into everything.' A shrug. 'Can't say I envy you.'

That was exactly the memory Petra had of her childhood. A mother who tolerated her, a father who adored her.

'You seem to have been lucky with the children; they're both very pretty. But you won't know what's going to happen until they're almost middle-aged, will you?' She looked like a contented cat playing with a mouse which had no chance of escape. 'Perhaps that's the point.'

'If you're talking about the Huntington's, it's not a problem, Mother.'

'You think you can tell, do you?'

'I told you from the start; people have the option of genetic testing now. It's not what we're worried about.'

'So there is something?' She was quick to seize on that, almost delighted. 'You mean I was right?'

'Maybe we could go through to the kitchen and give

312

Jacintha something to eat? They've both been hanging round the hospital for several hours. And Corilla will want to be fed quite soon.'

'I don't know that I've got any food suitable for small children...'

'No problem. We've brought everything we need.'

Edward walked into Louise's kitchen and put a small picnic basket on the table. He took out a jar of applesauce and some home-baked Welsh cakes, then sat down. Jacintha settled demurely on his lap and began to eat.

Petra sat down beside them, unbuttoned her blouse and began to feed her baby. Her mother looked on in what appeared to be an attack of horror.

'*Breast*feeding, for goodness sake! You'll ruin your figure.' Neither Petra nor Edward rose to the bait. 'So, something is wrong. What is it?'

Petra turned the calm look of the practised mother on Louise. 'It seems there might be a question about the children's eventual height. We've only just found that out from Great Ormond Street – a Dr Adrian Planter who is a specialist in endocrinology.'

'You mean they're going to be giantesses?' Louise's immediate grasp of the situation was distinctly disconcerting. A fleeting look of concern was just visible in the muddy eyes.

'They could reach Edward's height or more,' Petra explained. 'Not something I would like to see. I find being five foot nine a bit of a handicap.'

'You're a perfect height, Petra. I don't know why you fuss so.'

'A matter of personal preference. Anyway, I'm sure you'll agree that anything over six foot for a woman is not desirable. If it can be avoided...'

'Are you saying that's where I come in?' She frowned,

the creases between her eyebrows deeper than Petra remembered. 'How, exactly?'

'If you could let the hospital have a small sample of tissue – blood, preferably. It's easy to work with.'

'For what, precisely?'

'So that Dr Planter can analyse your DNA and see if he can spot where the problem, if there is one, originated. I don't suppose for a single second it has anything to do with you, but the only way he can be sure is to have the DNA profiles of as many direct antecedents as he can get hold of.' She put on her best smile. 'For elimination purposes.'

'Rubbish!' Louise's voice was shrill, but she controlled herself. 'What I mean is: he can either cure them or he can't.'

'The results will be completely confidential, Mother. There's no way he would show your DNA analysis to us. He needs the data so that he can make an assessment...'

'I don't want my DNA analysed.'

'What possible harm can it do you, Mother?'

'I don't want anyone sniffing around the sort of genes I carry. It's none of their business.'

'But how could that affect you?'

'Knowledge is power. If it turns out that I have some sort of predisposition to some disease, it might affect my private medical insurance. That sort of thing.'

'No one's allowed...'

'So far. I'm not giving permission.'

Petra couldn't help herself. All her old antagonisms towards her mother came to the surface again. 'It's because you *did* have a lover, isn't it? You think it will all come out, that you had a tall lover, and now you're worried that the combination of him and Edward is what has made the children as they are. You tried to stop us marrying because Jack told you Edward was very tall, not because of the

Huntington's at all. *That's* why you made all the fuss in the first place, wasn't it?'

Edward put a restraining arm on Petra, and the baby, losing the nipple, began to whimper.

Louise stood up. 'I'm not sure how analysing *my* DNA could possibly tell you whether I had a lover or not, let alone his height. I've told you before, and I'm telling you again: I did *not* have a lover. If you persist in this accusation, you'll have to leave my house.'

It sounded so convincing that Petra paused. 'I'm sorry, Mother. If you say you didn't, I'll have to believe you.' In spite of herself, there were tears in her eyes. 'You are a mother, too. Can't you understand? I just want to do what I can for my little girls.'

'I told you not to marry Edward, that no good would come of it, and I've been proved right. You only have yourselves to blame.'

Perhaps Louise had adopted a baby, one Daddy hadn't approved? That would explain why she didn't look like either of them. *And* why Louise had refused to let her have her DNA. Because that would tell everyone that she wasn't her mother at all!

29

'Oh, Ed, *darling*! My little boy has come back to me.' Ethel stood on tiptoe and threw her arms around her son's neck. He had to bend for her to be able to do so, and felt both uncomfortable and embarrassed. Gently, he disengaged her hands. She looked at him reproachfully. 'How could you be so cruel, Edward? You haven't been to see us for years!'

It was the trauma of their visit to Louise which had convinced both him and Petra that he had to talk to his parents by himself. He'd settled his family back into their home in Wales and driven over on his own.

Nathaniel held out a hand but Edward walked up to him and embraced him. He was shocked at the fragility of a body which should still be in the prime of middle age, devastated by the trembling the poor man could obviously no longer control. Were his parents not even going to allude to the illness now so clearly taking hold?

'You don't look too good, Dad. Unsteady on your feet...'

He saw his mother look at Nathaniel, then back at him. 'You've noticed that, have you? I keep telling him to go to the doctor, but he won't hear of it.' She frowned. 'They brought him back from college the other day. He's getting very absent-minded. Couldn't find his own office, apparently.'

Didn't his mother know about the Huntington's? She wouldn't have seen it in her parents-in-law, whichever of them carried it, because they'd both died young. Was it possible that his father, too, didn't know about the dreadful disease he was suffering from?

No chance; his father was deliberately avoiding the medical profession. He knew.

'Would you like me to take you, Dad?' He realised it was a mistake as soon as he'd said it. Now he'd have to listen to several minutes of monologue as Ethel recited his sins of omission.

'And when you are here, you intend to spend all your time with your father,' she started.

He allowed the words to flow over his head, mentally doing the equivalent of turning off the volume control. His father's deteriorating health was clearly very worrying. Harold still lived at home, but was he really being fair, putting the whole burden on him? It was also up to Edward to see that Nathaniel was taken care of when the illness began to affect him in earnest.

'...the least you could do was come to visit me for my birthday, but of course not, all I got was a little card...'

'All right if I sit down, Mum?' His voice re-echoed round the room which seemed oddly empty. His eyes roamed the familiar walls and found them bare. 'What happened to the prints?'

That stopped the flow. Nathaniel, his lips clasped tightly round the Meerschaum, had collapsed into his chair and was, Edward could tell, doing his best to stop the pipe from nodding up and down.

'We got tired of looking at the same old things.' Ethel's voice, recovered from the interruption, was oddly high.

'You've stored them away?'

318

'There was this very nice man from Sotheby's; they were doing some sort of research in Exeter, and he came round, and made us a good offer. Too good to miss, really.'

He stared at her, too surprised to make a comment, and turned to see how his father was reacting. Nathaniel had changed so much since Edward had last seen him that it took time to take it all in. He'd lost at least a stone in weight, his hair had turned from grey to white and thinned to wisps across his scalp, and his eyes had sunk into their sockets.

'You didn't mind letting them go, Dad?' He knew the prints had come from his paternal grandfather; Nathaniel had always treasured them. It was then that Edward noticed that the rugs had gone as well. It explained why the room sounded so hollow.

'I'm sorry, Edward. What did you say?'

'You're looking a bit low, Dad. Are you OK?'

'Why shouldn't he be? Why do you criticise everything about us as soon as you turn up?' Ethel's voice was dangerously high.

'He's only being polite, my dear.' Nathaniel pulled his chin up and forced his lips into a smile which only accentuated the fact that his lips had thinned to a straight line. His eyes were steady, calm, but with a vagueness which seemed to come and go. 'We're fine, just fine.'

'Same as we've always been,' Ethel shrilled, plumping up cushions. 'Aren't we, Nathaniel?' She was lying. Her eyes refused to meet Edward's.

'Why don't we all sit down, Mum. I've got a lovely surprise for you. I think you'll both be thrilled by what I have to tell you.'

Their response to being told they were grandparents was definitely a notch up on Louise's, but there was a certain hesitancy he could not entirely understand. 'Aren't you

319

pleased? Wouldn't you like to meet the girls?' He beamed at them. 'Why don't you drive over to Wales? It's only about three hours if you pick a good time for traffic.'

'Your father isn't really up to driving at the moment.' Ethel's voice was no longer high, but so low he could hardly hear what she was saying. 'When he feels better...'

'You drive, Mum. Or get Harold to bring you over.' He looked around. 'Where is he, by the way?'

'He's got himself a job.'

'You mean you wouldn't be able to do the drive, Mum? We can put you up for the night; no need to drive there and back in the same day.' He couldn't understand the hunted look in her eyes. And she was a good driver. Was his father much worse than he seemed at this moment?

'Petrol is so expensive now, Edward. We've sold the car.' There was a gallant attempt at shrugging it off. 'And we live in Exeter; we don't really need one. Better for the environment, as well. All those petrol fumes.'

'You're short of money?' Surely his father's salary was more than adequate. They must have paid off their mortgage, their outgoings must be less now that both their sons were independent adults. 'Are you paying for Harold? Is that the problem? Perhaps I could...'

He could see the struggle on his mother's face. 'Let's not go into that,' she said, turning away. 'We're low on sherry. How about some orange juice?'

It took an hour's chitchat to ease his way into the subject he had come to raise. 'Our little girls are wonderful, you know. So pretty; both fair, like Petra and me. And both with deep blue eyes.' He smiled at his mother. 'You were always worried about Petra's eyes. Neither of them have that trait.' He pulled some snaps out of his wallet. 'See? Aren't they adorable?'

They studied the photos. When Nathaniel held them

they trembled so much both he and his mother found it impossible to watch. They busied themselves with pouring the orange juice, placing it on the coffee table.

'But we do have a little problem.'

For the first time since his visit Edward could see his father pull himself together. 'Problem?' The voice sounded almost like the one he could remember; he uncrossed his legs and placed them firmly on the floor. 'What kind of problem?' The eyes shone, brilliant, out of their deep sockets.

'The specialist thinks it's genetic.'

Quite suddenly Nathaniel's knees began to tremble, the liquid in his glass to shake. Edward stood up and took the glass from his hand.

'What on earth's the matter with you, Nathaniel? You've really got to see a doctor! This is ridiculous.'

It was crystal clear that his father knew about the Huntington's, but his mother did not. Had his father really allowed his wife to have children without warning her? He saw him tremble so much that his whole frame shook, and knew what he had to tell them would be good news for him.

'I expect he's just worried about the children, Mum. It's to do with height,' he rushed out. 'Petra measured them as soon as they were born because she thought they were unusually long.'

'Height? You mean I was right, they're going to be too tall?' Ethel gave a snort of cackling laughter. 'I told you, Ed. A mother always knows.' She put her hands up to her face and pushed back her hair, her eyes wet.

He tried to comfort her, going to stand behind her, his hands on her shoulders, awkward, not sure what to do. 'It'll be fine, Mum. Don't worry. It's all under control.'

'Height?' his father repeated. 'You're worried about a gene for height?'

'Really, Nathaniel. He just said that!'

'We consulted a specialist in London, an endocrinologist. The girls' lengths worry him. He's going to analyse the girls' and our DNA. He'd like to analyse the grandparents' as well to help him isolate what's been happening, and where it first occurred.'

The quivering had turned to trembling. 'A p-problem with the gene for height?'

'Yes, Dad. Everything else is fine.'

It was his mother's turn to show physical signs of stress. He could see the colour starting in her neck and spreading upwards, like a crimson tide which reached the roots of hair now faded to almost-grey. 'What do you mean?' she hissed. 'You want some doctor-or-other to have a sample of my DNA for testing? I don't want that!'

At first it was so similar to Louise's reaction that Edward completely missed the signs of loss of control rather than anger.

'I'm not having some fucking doctor messing about with me! You come here, after two years without any sort of contact, completely out of the blue, and then you want me to help you out...'

He went to sit beside her, putting his arms around her. 'But Mum...'

'Get your hands off me!' she screamed at him, throwing the glass of orange juice at him. 'Don't touch me!'

Edward's quick reflexes helped him move out of the way of the glass. It shattered on the bare boards, spraying him with juice. He brushed the liquid off with his handkerchief, his eyes puzzled, and tried again. 'It's nothing, Mum. All you need do is give a bit of blood.' He held her heaving shoulders but she twisted away.

'Don't you dare try to get that off me!'

He stood, putting his lips down to her hair, trying to calm

her. 'It's nothing, honestly. If you don't want to give blood, a scraping from inside your mouth—'

'Shut up!' she screamed, now grabbing his glass out of his hand and hurling it at him. 'It's disgusting! Get out of my house, you . . .'

Nathaniel had levered himself out of the chair. 'She gets overwrought. Too much on her mind. I haven't known what to do just lately.'

'You never bloody well know what to do, you slow-witted moron.' She gulped, then heaved a table over. 'Professor indeed! Who the hell d'you think you're kidding?' The sobs were noisy.

Edward began to collect pieces of glass, wondering just how he could leave his parents in their present state. He looked up to see his mother with a piece of broken glass in her hand, coming for him.

'I'll show you bloody blood,' she screamed at him. 'Your blood! Use your own fucking blood. Leave mine alone!'

He caught her wrist as she lunged for him and made her drop the piece of glass. She screamed, twisting and turning, trying to get away. As soon as she succeeded she began to hurl anything that came to hand.

He caught her again, pinned her arms behind her back. 'You'll have to ring the doctor, Dad. She needs a sedative.'

Shaking hands fumbled with the phone. Apparently he couldn't remember their GP's number; Edward saw him punch 999.

'What's going on, Dad?'

He shambled back to his chair, sat down. 'There's a bottle of Scotch on the top shelf in the kitchen, Edward. Do you think you could fetch it for me?'

'Hold on a sec.' He returned with a full bottle in his hands, and two tumblers. 'There isn't any soda. Water will have to do.'

'Neat for me,' his father said, his voice stronger at the sight of the whisky. 'Of course I know something's badly wrong. Not up to finding out what it is; I suppose I don't care.' He drank, allowed the liquid to seep into his system, his body more relaxed. 'There's never any money, and I give her plenty for the housekeeping. I've put by a small amount for later, but that's all. We haven't even got a mortgage any more.'

'For the future,' Edward said dryly. 'For when the disease gets worse.'

At first Nathaniel started, then he smiled. A sort of twisted smile with a rueful edge. 'I keep the Scotch on the top kitchen shelf. Now I can't even trust myself to get it down.'

'I'll sort something out for you.'

'For me?' The shrunken figure's shoulders hunched lower.

'The Huntington's, Dad. I'm not blind, you know.'

'How did you find out?' Edward recognised the same gleam in the eyes which he remembered from his boyhood, from the time when he and his father played games together. 'Could be all kinds of things. Can't be as obvious as all that.' Nathaniel looked reproachful.

'Only when you already know what's going on.'

'And you do.' He put his elbows on his knees, his hands over his face. 'I couldn't bring myself to tell your mother; I knew she wouldn't marry me if I did.'

'You mean she has no idea?'

'Not unless she's guessed. But she's too preoccupied with problems of her own. I irritate her, that's all.' He looked up through his fingers. 'She's been under such pressure lately.

324

I don't know what it's all about. Money, somehow. She keeps needing money.'

'Drugs?'

He shrugged. 'I haven't had the guts even to think about it. Too busy thinking about myself, as usual.'

'Something's got to be done. This isn't good enough.'

'I know it's unforgivable, Edward – not telling *you*, I mean.' He began to shake again. 'I thought there'd be time. Never thought you'd simply run out on us.'

Edward stood up and helped him drink more Scotch. 'I've told Harold. But you have to talk to him yourself, you know.'

'I will, Edward. Honestly I will.' Bleak eyes searched his face. 'How did you find out? The early symptoms could fit any number of diseases.'

The explanation of how Bruce Traggard had alerted Jack Oliver to Edward's problem because Petra was his god-daughter was a surprise to Nathaniel. 'You're telling me that Jack Oliver has all his clients' DNA fingerprinted?'

'Apparently.'

The whisky had done good work. Nathaniel seemed able to think. 'Bit dubious to do that without asking permission, isn't it? Unethical.'

'You mean, he didn't ask you and Mum?'

'All I remember is the initial physiology testing, at Brighton. Then he used his own experts. He explained he needed to repeat those tests at regular intervals. That seemed reasonable at the time.' There was a query in his eyes. 'Did you sign anything? After you were eighteen, I mean.'

A window opened in his mind. 'You know, Bruce did ask me to sign some sort of form. I didn't really take much notice; just assumed it was a legal requirement.'

'I take it that was it. Jack Oliver was always very careful

to spell everything out for us, just so.' He shrugged. 'So that's how you found out.'

'I'm sorry, Dad. I should have come and talked to you about it, but Mum and Louise Jones were so anti our getting married, we just decided to go ahead and do our own thing.'

'I can't altogether blame you.' He smiled. 'I'm so pleased for you, Edward. Two lovely little girls, and so quickly. Your mother and I had to wait quite a long time.'

'I thought that was planned.'

'Nothing happened for five years; we'd almost given up hope. Your mother went in for all kinds of tests. Very time-consuming and not very pleasant.' He cleared his throat. 'I thought that, somehow, I was managing to hold my sperm back. There was a sense in which I would have preferred not to have any children, as you can well imagine. I simply couldn't face telling your mother what might be in store. The longer I left it, the more impossible it got.'

He twiddled the whisky tumbler in his hands, keeping both sets of fingers wrapped round it. To prevent it spilling, Edward guessed, his heart contracting at his father's plight. 'In the end someone had the nous to suggest a sperm count. Ethel thought it would be terribly traumatic for me. Everyone fell over themselves to say it didn't prove anything about virility...'

'You mean you had a low one?'

He grinned, looking like his old self for the first time since Edward had arrived for the visit. 'I was overjoyed; I felt it meant we didn't have to worry any more. Then, suddenly, Ethel got pregnant with you. Even more surprising, she got pregnant with Harold only eighteen months later. Weird.'

'But nothing after that. Or did you take precautions?'

'You mean birth control?' He stared at Edward. 'No, I never even thought of it.'

'They always say if you relax it works.'

He laughed. 'Not for a low sperm count. I've never heard of that.'

'So you won't object to giving me a blood sample?'

'You're welcome to anything I can do for you. Which isn't much, of course.'

Edward sighed. 'Both grandmothers refuse to cooperate. We'll just have to hope the specialist can work with what he's got.'

'I'll see if I can persuade her when she's got over the shock, Ed. I think it was all too much for her.' The small, shrivelled figure looked forlorn and almost ready to give up on life. 'Better let me have your phone number and address. One thing you can be sure of; you won't get any unexpected visits from us.'

'You mean she's gone mad?' Edward could hear Petra draw in her breath as she stared at him over the oatmeal she was preparing for the following day.

They were in their kitchen after both children had been put to bed. It was their daily quiet time together, early enough so that they weren't too tired, yet after Jacintha's bedtime and before the baby's last feed. A time to be cherished.

'I don't think that word has any meaning now, medically speaking. What happened was that she lost control of herself; the paramedics gave her a sedative to calm her down. She seemed to be outside herself in some odd way, but not mad in the traditional sense.' Edward's genial features had lost the innocence of only two years before. The laugh-lines from nose to mouth had become grooves which showed even when his face was still, his cheeks had lost their squirrel chubbiness, his chin was more aggressively thrust out. 'They were brilliant in the way they handled her; just coaxed her. In the end they persuaded her to go to the Royal and see the psychiatric registrar.'

'She actually agreed to that?'

His eyes had lost some of the blue; there was a faraway gaze, almost a desire for escape. 'More accurate to say she was talked into it. Not by Dad or me; we both know she's trying to cover something up. We're not the types to interfere. And I doubt if merely talking about it to some doctor is going to solve any of her problems.' He shrugged in a helpless sort of way. 'We just didn't see what we could do. The paramedics seemed to think it was some sort of answer.'

'So you don't think she's mentally ill; you think she's in trouble.'

'I don't think my mother's insane, if that's what you mean. Far from it. She's very aware of what is going on around her. In my view what she needs is someone she can confide in. She doesn't seem able to do that with my father.' He turned to Petra, his eyes full of tears. 'It's not just that he didn't tell me. He didn't tell *her*! That was a terrible way to go about it.'

'I know you said his parents were already dead when they met. That's quite unusual; didn't she ask any questions?'

He pressed his lips together. 'I wouldn't know. Maybe not the right ones. Huntington's isn't a disease people know about unless it's in the family. And in the past such things used to be hushed up.'

'People were much more secretive. I suppose our society is more accepting.'

'Perhaps. She's always known there's something, I suspect. But I think she assumed it was a personality defect.

Many men leave the tough parts of family life to their wives. She often complained that Dad left her to cope with all the practicalities.'

'Easy enough to make that sort of assumption.'

He stood. 'You know, I need to get some exercise. Can we walk round the garden?'

'At this time of the day? It's pitch dark.'

'We can put the outside light on. I don't think you quite understand, Pet. I can't just do nothing but sit around. That's all I've done today – sat in the car and in my parents' living room. My body's used to enormous amounts of exercise. If I don't make sure I get some I get irritable.'

November winds had blown the leaves away and left dark criss-crosses of branches against the hills glistening with wet. Their light, helped by a full moon, picked out the path to their paddock. Edward pulled his skipping rope out of his pocket and began to skip. The regular swish of rope against the short grass was oddly comforting.

'You don't mind, do you? It'll calm me down.' He began to skip faster, accelerating the pace until the rope sounded like a whip, beating the ground.

'It can't be coincidence that both our mothers go bonkers as soon as we ask them for a sample for DNA analysis. There has to be a connection.'

The rope slowed, stopped. 'If they know each other, they're both superb at hiding it.'

'They haven't bothered to hide their displeasure at our marrying. We know they lose their tempers all too quickly. All I can think of is that they have something in common, but that it's not exactly personal.' Petra pushed a booted foot against a slush of leaves piled in a corner and kicked at it.

'Don't scatter those! I've piled them up for making leaf-mould.'

'This stuff about your father's sperm count. D'you think your mother could have taken a lover?'

He laughed; not the gay laugh he remembered from not so long ago, but a bitter, unhappy sound. He almost wished it were true. Petra was thinking that the connection between their mothers was that they'd both cheated on their husbands.

'I wish it was that simple, Pet. But it's my father who has the Huntington's. I think we're stretching things a bit if we imagine that my mother's theoretical lover also suffered from that.'

Nigma Rosen

30

Petra waited for Edward to leave the house with Bradley Mark II. Corilla was in her pram in the garden, and Jacintha was playing in the playpen. She tapped in Gwyneth Davies' number, her heart thudding in her chest.

'It's Petra, Gwyneth.'

'Pet! Lovely to hear from you. You bringing the babies over soon?' She sighed. 'It's such a joy to see them. I always feel like a real grandmother. It's just so wonderful.'

'Maybe next Sunday, if I can persuade Ed to take some time off from training the dogs.'

'Amazing the way he's taken to hill farming.'

She cleared her throat. 'Well, he was always good with dogs. He had a Bradley Mark I in Exeter. Trained him to help him practise ball skills. Those collies are good at all kinds of chores.'

Gwyneth laughed. 'You never mentioned that before.' There was a slight pause, then her voice came back with a question in it. 'You sound – well, different. Is something wrong?'

Petra explained about their visit to Great Ormond Street and what the specialist had said. Though she had mentioned her worries about the children's length to Gwyneth, neither she nor Megan had believed there could be a serious problem, though they admitted they'd noticed that the girls were very long. Like the paediatrician in

Aberystwyth, they'd been sure that children developed at different rates.

'Marvellous what they can do now, tracking down genes.' Another pause. 'So if you're getting the best medical help, what's the problem, Pet?'

'My mother refuses to let us have her DNA analysed.' She couldn't prevent a sob. 'And Daddy's dead!'

'Don't cry, *fach*. It's not as bad as that. You can ask Mam and Dad for samples of their blood; they won't mind. It'll help the doctors track down something. You can have mine, as well. Dewi and I both had the cleft palate; we were very alike in lots of ways. It'll give them something to work on.'

'That's really sweet of you, Gwyneth.' Both of them had agreed she should drop the title Aunt. Now that she was a mother, it seemed absurd.

'You know, it might be possible to get Dewi's DNA. Sometimes they keep blood samples with the medical records. Helps them with their research into particular diseases.'

'You mean I could ask for his records?'

'Take a bit of getting hold of, I dare say. Getting very touchy about records, they are. Hard enough to get hold of your own. But you can apply through your solicitor. You're next of kin and you can show you need them for your kids. Dare say you'll get them in the end.' Petra could hear her hesitate. 'You're thinking was he your father, is it?'

'Yes. That's why I rang you. I know you thought my mother had a lover.'

She could hear Gwyneth draw in her breath and tense, then exhale. 'I shouldn't have—'

'That's not what I mean. I thought you might be able to help me, Gwyneth. That you might know more than you liked to tell me.'

'There is one thing that might be useful.' She cleared her throat, and when she spoke again she sounded excited. 'I'm the same blood group as Dewi – a rare one. I told you that before. If you take some of my blood and check it out, it might get you a clearcut answer. Sometimes you can eliminate a father that way.'

Petra swallowed. When she spoke again her voice was thick. 'Sorry, Gwyneth. It hurts to think about Daddy, let alone that he might not have been my biological father.'

'It was wrong of me . . .'

'Better to know.' She took several deep breaths. 'It's easier to discuss it on the phone, somehow. Tell me what made you think my mother cheated on him.'

'You're sure you really want to know?'

'Yes, Gwyneth. More than that: I *have* to know. If David wasn't my father, I need to find the man who is so that I can ask him for a sample of his DNA.'

'The thing is, *fach*, I think you know him.'

'*Know* him?' A feeling of a destiny she couldn't shake off, a sense of fate, swept over her.

'Well, not so much you. Edward.' An embarrassed laugh. 'What I mean is, you're thinking about excessive height, aren't you? The man I suspect is very tall, and you do look a bit like him.'

'Who are you talking about?'

'Bruce Traggard; Edward's coach. He was the one your mother was going with when I met her.'

'I know that, Gwyneth. You showed us those photographs.'

'Well, very thick, they were. He was crazy about her.'

The idea that Bruce Traggard might really be her father left Petra feeling faint. She'd almost managed to convince herself that it couldn't possibly be him, whoever it might turn out to be.

Her heart sank at the thought. She hated Bruce Traggard. When Gwyneth had first implied that Louise had had a lover she'd kidded herself that Gwyneth had been jealous, and in pain. Not now; there was no way she would allow her antagonism to Louise to cloud her judgement at this point. 'Sorry, Gwyneth. Could you hold on a sec? I've got to get some water.' She took the portable over to her sink, put the cold tap on full blast and splashed her face, filled a glass. 'That's pretty horrific. It was supposed to be all over between them. He was only sixteen and all that. Are you sure?'

'Dewi and Jack were into basketball even then. I told you; Jack had a party. They asked a lot of people, players, coaches, everyone. Louise came with Bruce. That's when she and Dewi met.'

'You think she was already pregnant with me when she married Daddy?'

'I don't think that. They didn't marry right away, because she wanted Jack. She'd known him for a while, but he wasn't interested. Eventually she knew it wouldn't get her anywhere. He just hasn't got the same sex drive as other men.'

'He's still very attractive to women. They always seem to flock round him.'

'He didn't want Louise. The reason she hates me so much is I overheard him telling her. I didn't mean to; I was just there, and they came in and he started right in to tell her.'

'You think she married Daddy on the rebound?'

'*And* because he was Jack's best friend; it meant she'd be able to see something of Jack.'

'And you think she'd already got pregnant by Bruce?'

'No. You were born a full ten months after the wedding. I thought maybe she kept in touch with Bruce; kept him

334

hanging on, if you see what I mean. Didn't want to risk having Dewi's child.'

'The cleft palate, you mean?'

'That, and Dewi's dark looks. I saw her going for the blond types all evening.' There was a silence, then a cough. 'Just thought she might have used him as a stud. It wouldn't have been a problem; he was completely potty about her.'

'She swears she didn't have a lover, Gwyneth.'

There was an embarrassed laugh at the other end of the line. 'Well now, *fach* – think. What would you expect her to say?'

'I don't know; she really sounded so sure. Why shouldn't she admit it? She's not exactly tactful. Why hide it now that Daddy's dead?' Petra began to sob. 'After all, that's why he killed himself, isn't it? Because he found out that she'd had a lover.'

'I think he always knew that, *fach*. That's why he never brought you home. Maybe it was because he found out who the lover was. I think his problem was he never liked Bruce Traggard.'

31

'Does the christening robe fit?' Jack Oliver was standing just inside the Dunstans' farmhouse kitchen, waiting to drive the family to church. He'd sent Corilla an exquisite Victorian christening gown the week before. It was made of delicate linen lawn, embroidered in the finest white work. A myriad tiny pintucks had been stitched on either side of the central panel. As she'd lifted it, very gently, out of its tissue-layered box, Petra realised it must have taken months of painstaking handwork. Her eyes had taken in the tiny sleeves, the slender bodice. She'd known right away that it would never fit Corilla's robust frame. The child, though not particularly fat, was substantially larger than the average Victorian baby had been. More to the point, she was significantly larger than the average modern baby as well.

Jack was wearing Armani blue the colour of his eyes, with a dashing tie in shades of peacock and slate which managed to convey an air of understated conceit. He was holding a small package; another gift, Petra was sure, and found herself unaccountably annoyed.

'Well ... the more ornate the robe, the longer the length. So that part worked out fine. But I'm afraid she didn't fit into the bodice.'

'She's only six weeks old, Petra. Has she really grown that much?' Jack sounded quite shocked.

'Victorian children were tiny by our standards, Uncle Jack. And you know Corilla's above average size.' She found his look of disappointment mixed with pride extra- ordinary. What a strange man – but then, he wouldn't have been as successful as he had been, unless he was unusual.

'I had to improvise,' she went on. 'I undid the underarm and side seams, and left the sleeve open. Then I took off the neckband, let out half the pintucks, found a larger neck- band which I took off another garment, and had that stitched on by hand. I couldn't even have got her head through the original. Anyway, I'm rather proud of my efforts.'

She lifted the blanket from the baby sleeping in the pram. The rosy face was crowned by soft, downy curls of the lightest blonde. She looked adorable, but Petra was acutely, distressingly aware of the large hands and feet, the big head. She looked up at Jack, saw he had also seen. 'Like it?' Her voice was soft; it was almost as though she were asking him about the child lying in the cot.

The blue eyes met hers, a frost of disappointment almost immediately replaced by the habitual charm. 'You are a talented girl, Pet. I'd no idea you could sew.' There was genuine warmth and admiration in his voice. 'And I've brought my goddaughter her christening present, a string of pearls. I made it a long one.'

'You're so generous, Uncle Jack. I'll look after it for her.'

'Where did you learn to sew?'

'I worked out what to do. Gwyneth did the actual needlework.' She looked to see the effect the name would have on Jack. 'She's an expert, as you probably remember.'

'The commendable Gwyneth.' He always found some- thing derogatory to say about David's sister.

'Why are you so down on her, Uncle Jack? I thought you used to be such friends as children.'

'Down on her? You're imagining things.' The relaxation in the short figure changed to rigidity and Jack stood as high as he could manage. Petra noted the two-inch heels discreetly hidden under slightly long trousers. 'It's just that she has this habit of expecting things from me which I can't necessarily deliver.'

'Visiting your mother, for example.'

When he turned his eyes were hard. 'Not that it's any of your business, Petra, but my mother's dead.'

'Before she died, Uncle Jack, when you first went up to London. Gwyneth thinks she pined away because you were all she had and you never came back.'

'You've got very intimate, the two of you.' The pleasure had gone from his eyes. 'All that was before I really managed to find myself. Coming home meant criticism and what they called "taking down a peg or two". I always sent her money; she lacked for nothing.'

Strange how even someone as caring as Jack could manage to kid himself that his mother needed money more than she needed him. 'I suppose Gwyneth thought of herself as your sister.'

He snorted. 'Felt she could nag me, that what you mean? She certainly excelled at that.' He picked Jacintha up from the floor and put her, piggyback, across his shoulders. 'We need to get on with it. It's a good hour's drive to Lland'od.'

'If you could cope for a few minutes, Uncle Jack, I'll just slip on my suit. Edward's changing. Apparently he wanted to shave again.'

When Petra came downstairs the men were already settling the two little girls in the car seats at the back.

'You look marvellous,' Jack told her, his eyes sweeping

her trim figure. She could sense that the faint roundness of mature womanhood would finally stop him from suggesting she take up modelling.

'Thank you, kind sir.'

Edward came up to her and kissed her. 'No one would believe you're the mother of two children.'

'Well, I am,' she said. 'And proud of it.'

They began the journey through the lovely roads across the hills. 'We could take the scenic route along the Elan Reservoir. It's so lovely there.'

'It would take too long, Pet. We can't afford the time.' Edward cleared his throat. He was sitting in the front beside Jack, while Petra sat between the two little ones in the back. 'Have you told Uncle Jack about our visit to Great Ormond Street?'

'Not yet.'

The car swerved as Jack turned to look at Petra. Edward grabbed the steering wheel. 'Something's wrong with Corilla?'

'They both have a problem, Uncle Jack. You noticed it yourself; they're rather longer than average.'

'Oh, that. Supposed to be a problem, is it? I would have thought it was a big advantage.'

'A projected adult height of over six foot six is bad news for a woman. That's not the easiest height to live with for a man!'

'You mean they might get to Ed's height?' Petra could see his eyes looking in the rearview mirror towards the babies in the back. 'Who told you that?'

'An endocrinologist. Top London man.'

'I don't believe that; he's just being a busybody. You know yourself they can't predict height with any certainty until after puberty.'

'Of course he knows that, Uncle Jack. But when the birth

340

length is over fifty-five centimetres, there's real cause for
concern.'

'I see.'

'He's pretty sure he can give them something to stop the
overproduction of growth hormone.'

'*Over*production?'

Petra remembered that Jack had suffered from under-
production of the same thing.

'Petra was worried right from the start, Jack. I thought
she was fussing, but she was right. Lucky we had it
diagnosed so early on. That's given the doctors plenty of
time to stop them growing too tall.'

Jack drove along, the car gaining speed as he stared
straight ahead, clutching the steering wheel. 'What did this
chap say caused it?'

'He's trying to find out. He's having our DNAs analysed
to see if he can locate a reason.' Petra paused, giving
Jacintha the rattle she had dropped. 'He wanted the
grandparents' DNA, but so far we've only been able to get
hold of Nathaniel's.'

'The grandparents'?' The normally purring voice was in a
higher register. 'That's going over the top a bit, isn't it?'

'Not really; he needs to look at whatever evidence he can
locate. Anyway, Daddy's DNA isn't available – at least we
don't think so.'

The car swerved round a corner, almost running into a
sheep. 'Steady on, Jack!'

'Sorry, not used to country roads.' He cleared his throat.
'How could Dewi's DNA be available? He was cremated.'

'Gwyneth thinks they might have stored a sample of his
blood with his medical records.'

'What for?'

'They do that sometimes, to help research. We just
thought we ought to let you know what's going on.'

'Glad to hear it sounds like good news.'

'Daddy's DNA wouldn't be relevant, anyway. Gwyneth worked it out.'

'Gwyneth worked *what* out?' The irritation in Jack's voice was unmistakable.

'She always thought that I wasn't Daddy's daughter, that Mother had taken a lover. That's when she remembered that she and Daddy shared the same AB blood group. She realised it might show whether I could be his daughter or not.'

'I see. And you've gone into that, have you?' He sounded angry.

'I've told you before, Uncle Jack. I don't believe in hiding my head in the sand. Yes, and it turns out I'm blood group O. That means I'm extremely unlikely to be Daddy's ... David's daughter.'

'I see.' They drove without anyone saying a word for several minutes. 'I hope you're pleased with yourself, Petra. Thinking you've proved that Dewi wasn't your father must make you feel wonderful.' They locked eyes in the driving mirror, both steely, both determined. 'What does Louise say to all that? You have asked her, I take it, rather than relied on some tomfool medicos.'

'I haven't told her about the blood groups yet. She refused to let us have a sample to test her DNA. And she categorically denies that she had a lover.'

'You asked her that?'

'Before we even got married, when Gwyneth pointed out that I didn't look remotely like any of them.'

'Gwyneth scores again! So, do you believe your mother?'

'Sort of.'

'What on earth does that mean?'

'She was so positive, and yet I know Daddy wasn't my father. It's kind of bizarre. Of course there has to be a simple explanation. Perhaps you know something about it, do you, Uncle Jack?'

The short bark of a laugh was turned into a chuckle. 'So that's why you're telling me all this. Quite the little mystery.'

The car was going fast now, swerving the curves and gathering speed. 'Take it easy, Jack!' Ed put his hand over Jack's on the steering wheel. 'That's my whole family you're driving.'

'You know, Petra, I think you're making a mistake with all this business of digging into the past. Why not let sleeping dogs lie?'

'Because Daddy committed suicide because of it!'

'How can you possibly know that?'

'The letter, Uncle Jack. He left a note for me, remember? Mother said you were the one to spot it.'

He turned round again and Edward held the wheel. 'You want me to drive, Jack?'

'Sorry. I thought Louise chucked that into the fire, Petra.'

'She did.'

'And very proper, too. Some nonsense...'

'I found it in the printer memory and printed out a copy for myself.'

'A note written by a man who wasn't in his right mind. That was the finding at the inquest, in case it's slipped your mind. He was upset about Jorncy.'

'Well, Gwyneth agrees with my interpretation.'

'Oh, she does, does she?' He braked hard as a sheep looked as though it was going to leap across the road. 'And what pearls of wisdom has the blessed Gwyneth dropped from her blessed mouth about the identity of your father, then?'

'She thinks it was Bruce Traggard.'

Jack began to laugh. 'Bruce Traggard, eh? Well, Louise did go out with him for a while – I told you that myself. And you do look a bit like him; fair hair, tall, pink-and-white complexion. But if everyone talked paternity about a fleeting similarity of looks, we'd be in quite a pickle.'

'That's why I'm going to ask him for a sample.'

'Are you now? I think you'll find he won't be keen to give you one, my dear. Take my advice and forget it. David was a wonderful father to you, and I think you're making a big mistake ferreting around the past. Why go on about something which can't be changed? The doctors can cure your girls without all that; they're just asking for more data so that they can use it in their research. Typical of the medical profession; they're making use of you.'

32

'How nice to see you both again. Do come in.' Dr Adrian Planter had come out to the waiting room himself. 'I hope your little girls are being taken care of in our nursery.' He had clearly switched on his best bedside manner: affable smile, concerned expression.

'Yes, thank you. They're fine.' Edward was not interested in the niceties. 'Your secretary said you've had all the analyses done?'

'Indeed, quite right. Do come in and sit down.' Planter walked ahead, pointed them at the chairs they had sat in before, twirled himself into the leather armchair behind his desk and stared at two files lying there. He seemed abstracted.

Petra and Edward sat next to each other, tense and silent. Edward cleared his throat. 'My wife and I are quite anxious to hear the results, Dr Planter.'

He brought his eyes up to look into Edward's. 'I'm sorry; just collecting my thoughts.' He opened one of the files. 'Let's start with the two little girls.'

Edward wondered exactly what else they would have come all the way from Wales for, but decided not to voice that particular thought.

'What we have found is that your little girls, both of them, have a deficiency of somatostatin.' He looked at them, as though this would explain everything. 'It's a hormone which acts as a brake on body growth, counteracting the effects of both insulin and human growth hormone. When there is a deficiency, it results in abnormal growth, and the bone ends become enlarged. Clearly we should try to moderate this pattern. I'm happy to tell you we can offer treatment.'

He looked up, his eyes veiled, his gaze moving from Petra to Edward and back again. A small, tight smile lightened his eyes, but the way he clenched the biro in his hand showed he was nervous. That hesitant look again.

'Before I go into that in more detail, perhaps I should have explained at our first meeting that analyses of DNA can point to – unexpected findings.' His voice dropped to a sort of whisper; he was clearly finding it hard to talk to them. Then he braced himself by throwing his weight back into his chair, making it rock up and down. The effect was unnerving. 'What I'm trying to say is that the results of the tests aren't always entirely predictable. We are on very new ground here; the medical application of recent genetic discoveries is still in its infancy. I would like to emphasise that we cannot always be entirely sure—'

'You've found some problems, Dr Planter,' Edward said briskly, his firm voice under control. 'We expected that. That's why we're here.'

'Problems? Well, yes, there is a problem which will affect your children. Perhaps the best place to start is to confirm what I suggested the last time we met. We can definitely help your children. I think we can be confident that their adult height will not exceed six foot. We may do better than that; it's early days.' He sighed.

'You'd treat them with a hormone which inhibits the growth hormone?' Petra asked.

'Precisely.' He steepled his fingers in supplication.

Edward saw Petra's eyes challenge the consultant. 'And what about side effects? I don't need to tell you about the disasters that occurred when growth hormones were first used to help pituitary dwarfs. A significant proportion of those children ended up with Creutzfeldt-Jakob disease.'

'You're very well informed, Mrs Dunstan.'

'I'm very concerned for my children.'

'Let me put your mind at ease. That disease was transmitted by injection of contaminated human brain tissue. Since 1985 we have been able to manufacture somatotropin – growth hormone – in bacteria through genetic engineering. This bypasses the need to use products of the pituitary gland. Growth hormone is now completely safe, and we have learned our lesson.'

'But that's not the hormone you'll need to use for our children. Does that apply to somatostatin as well?' Edward stood up. 'Sorry – you don't mind if I stretch my legs?'

'Please carry on, Mr Dunstan. I do understand.' He waved his hand in agreement. 'In fact, somatostatin was the first human gene product to be produced in bacteria. It's a relatively small protein, which made it much easier to work with than growth hormone. So the treatment I'm going to suggest for your children is safe in the present state of our knowledge. I can assure you that I'm not withholding any information from you.'

'When do you suggest we start the treatment?'

'The sooner the better, I think. We can do the first injection while you're here. I'll get in touch with your GP for further treatment. You'll need to bring the children up to see me every six months.' He smiled. 'I do congratulate you on being such careful parents. Your girls are very lucky.'

Edward breathed out. 'And that's it? That's the outcome of all the tests?'

The chair swung harder. 'Well ... no. Not quite.'

'There's something else? Something you can't help us

with?' Petra's voice had lost its even tone; Edward was surprised to hear the quaver.

'No, no, I'd really like to put your mind at rest about that. What the tests have done is point up some unexpected findings.'

'So there *is* something you're still worried about?'

'Not for your little girls.' His fingers interlocked, then came apart as he took up a pencil and began to doodle. 'The material is a little – sensitive.'

'Just tell us, Dr Planter. We came to you because we were led to believe you always answer your patients' questions truthfully, don't hold anything back from them.'

'That is my policy.'

Petra looked at Edward. 'We do hope you're going to do that with us. Perhaps I should tell you that we already know about a potential consequence – well, I suppose I mean disclosure – from the tests.'

The relief was unmistakable. 'Indeed, I see. You knew about this when you first came to me?'

'No, we only found out last week. My ...' Petra hesitated, then went on '... father's sister shares his blood group.'

Edward could see the man was trying to absorb what she had in mind, but it didn't seem to be Petra's father he was thinking about. 'Blood groups can tell us very little.' He watched him slowly open the second file in front of him and draw out a single sheet. 'It isn't all bad news; some of it is very good. I think we should start with Mr Dunstan's side – Nathaniel Dunstan's DNA analysis.'

His father's DNA? It seemed the least important one to Edward. Of course, the consultant could not know that he had already found out that it was Nathaniel who carried the gene for Huntington's, rather than his mother.

'We already know my father's a Huntington carrier, Dr Planter. The disease has begun to show itself.'

The response was not what he was expecting. 'Quite true; we have identified the single gene responsible.' That look again. 'But there is also what might be called something of a ... *discrepancy*,' he murmured. Two pairs of eyes stared intently at him. 'There's really no easy way to tell you this, Mr Dunstan.'

Edward began to roam around the room again. 'Just spit it out, then!'

'Indeed, quite so. Nathaniel Dunstan is not your father.'

He realised his gasp was audible. He walked to the window and looked out. '*Not* my father? But that's impossible!' He turned on the doctor, towering above his chair. 'You don't know what you're talking about!'

'I'm very sorry. If I had realised—'

'Are you quite sure? He *has* to be my father. I've got the gene!'

'I can assure you that the DNA analyses show that you're not related in any way at all. I gather you had no inkling this might be so?'

'None at all.'

Petra stood up and walked over to Edward. 'I'm sorry, darling. It's all my fault...'

'Please, Petra and Edward – if I may call you that – I would like to make this clear, to emphasise it very strongly. None of this is in any way a fault of yours. You were quite right to try to help your little girls; it is your first duty. Let me stress again: you are innocent victims of new knowledge. You specifically asked me to treat you like responsible adults, and I respect that. But I feel it right to bring other conclusions from the DNA analyses to your attention.'

'In a way it's good news, isn't it?' Petra breathed.

He smiled. 'You're very quick. And quite right; it's very good news.'

'Good news!' Edward roared. 'I'm all for knowing, but to call it good news...'

Petra grasped Edward's face in her hands and kissed him, silencing what he was about to say. He saw her look at Planter, her face transformed by excitement. 'It means he doesn't have the gene for Huntington's! That's what you're telling us, isn't it?'

He smiled – a genuine, delighted smile. 'That's exactly what I'm telling you.'

Edward returned to his chair and sat down, his hands on his cheeks, then he pushed back his hair. He looked up through moist eyes. 'You're saying I won't develop this disease?'

'Yes, Edward. You have nothing to fear on that score.'

'And I can't pass it on to my children?'

'No.'

He felt his face relax into a big, broad smile. 'That's terrific.'

'It is. Now, please don't get too worked up about your paternity. You have no idea how common such cases are; it's not worth worrying about. Fatherhood depends on nurturing as much as on biological inheritance.'

Edward could feel tears streaming down his face, but he made no attempt to stop them. It was such a relief.

'What I simply cannot understand is why you were so sure you had inherited this disease,' the doctor continued. 'There's no sign of the gene in your DNA. I understood you'd had it analysed before. Some mix-up, perhaps? A technical error? That's always possible.' He looked from one to the other. 'I can assure you that our analyses have been checked and rechecked. You do not – and I repeat it because such news takes a while to sink in – you definitely do *not* carry the gene for Huntington's chorea, Edward. You will never develop that disease.'

350

He smiled at the consultant. 'It's miraculous news. I can hardly believe it.'

Dr Planter sat back in his chair and waited. Perhaps he was expecting one or the other of them to tell him how this mistake had come about. Edward had no idea, but he made a note to ask Jack the next time he saw him.

'You implied there were problems. Nathaniel Dunstan not being Edward's father is unexpected, but it's not a medical problem, is it?' Petra asked.

'Indeed.' The eyes had hooded again as he took out another sheet of paper. 'I am sorry to have to tell you that the rest of the news is – disturbing.' He smiled in a clear attempt to make what he was about to tell them more palatable. 'What the DNA shows, without any shadow of doubt, is that you are closely related. Are you aware of that?'

'Who is closely related, Dr Planter? My f— Nathaniel and me, d'you mean?'

'I'm sorry, I'm not making myself clear. You and Petra, Edward. I'm talking about a fairly close relationship. Are you first cousins, by any chance?'

The stirrings of a knowledge which had always been there, but which had only just found its voice, iced its way along Edward's spine.

'Not that we know of. You mean we have some common ancestors? Grandparents?' Edward's forehead was tightly set in two vertical straight lines. 'Now that you mention it, we've often thought how strangely similar we are.'

The doctor peered at him. 'Have you, indeed? In what way?'

'We like the same foods, we have the same taste in music...'

Dr Planter shrugged. 'Similar people are drawn to each other. Nothing more specific?'

Petra took over. 'That's what he's trying to tell you,

Doctor. Perhaps it's because we share some genes that we took to each other so immediately. We felt this incredibly strong bond as soon as we met.'

'You feel that, do you? There are studies which show that first-degree relatives, not raised together, find themselves overcome by an almost irresistible attraction to one another. It even has a name: "the sexual attraction of genes".' He brought himself forward in his chair. 'That could have happened in your case.'

'What have you actually found, Dr Planter?'

'As you know, I only have one of your parental DNAs. It's hard to say precisely, but my instincts tell me... Let me explain.'

'We both have some terrible disease?'

'Not exactly, although you do both have a distinctive mutation in the gene for height. The one you transmitted to your daughters.'

'*Both* of us?'

'Not just a mutation – the *same* mutation. It is virtually impossible for two unrelated individuals to carry precisely the same one. And you share a number of other genes, an unusually large number.' He looked at them again, as though looking would give him some sort of clue.

'So what are you saying?'

'What it boils down to is that I'm virtually certain that you have a joint biological parent.'

Edward's voice was just a whisper. 'You're saying we're half-brother and sister, is that right?'

'I'm afraid it is.'

He could see the tears gathering in Petra's eyes.

'It must be a most horrific shock, I know.' He stood, walked over to them, patted them on the back. 'I'll order something hot and sweet. Coffee or tea?'

'Coffee.' Edward had put his arm around Petra. 'There

may be a mistake, Pet darling. Jack – well, Bruce – got it wrong about the Huntington's.'

The silence hung between them as they looked at each other. Petra pulled away slightly, her face white.

Dr Planter returned to his desk and rang through to his secretary to bring some coffee. 'What I can also tell you is that you don't share the same mother. The reason I'm so sure is that the maternal genetic input is readily identified. Which means that you share the same biological father.'

'You're sure?'

'Absolutely positive.' He cleared his throat again, obviously nervous about the question he was about to ask. 'Can you think of anything that might throw some light on this?'

Petra's blonde head jerked up. 'As a matter of fact, I can. That's what I was trying to tell you earlier on. We've already established that my nurturing father was not my biological father.'

'Ah. Have you always known that?'

'I only found out a few days ago. My father – my nurturing father – and his sister are both blood group AB. I'm blood group O.'

He nodded. 'That ties in with what I've found out. Quite.'

'And I have a suspicion who my biological father is. My mother has denied it so far, but perhaps if I confront her...'

'Let me urge you to be very careful in how you deal with this, Petra. Think long and hard before you let anyone else know. All we need to ensure, from a medical point of view, is that affected people should be given the opportunity to know. Your siblings, for example. It's up to you, but you might feel it right to suggest that they make their own enquiries.'

'My brother Harold,' Edward said. 'Is that who you mean?'

'It would be a kindness in your family circumstances.' The

specialist paused. 'Perhaps you should think about your mother, Edward. Do you think it's possible that she could have had a child by the same man as Petra's mother?'

'She did refuse to let us have her DNA analysed, and she tried to stop my father giving his. That's a clue, I suppose.'

Dr Planter stood, took two cups from the tray his secretary had brought in and handed them to the young couple. 'I am so very sorry, Petra, Edward. What I would like to emphasise once more is that you have absolutely *nothing* to reproach yourselves for. And I would also like to add that there is a common misconception that brother/sister parenting leads to excessive genetic problems in their offspring. Statistically the chances are only fractionally greater than in ordinary unions. It's only a problem if the same faulty gene is carried by both parties. *That* is your problem. You really need not worry about anything else.'

'But what about the law, Doctor? Aren't we committing incest?'

'I strongly advise you to keep all this to yourselves. Clearly no one in your families knows . . .'

Edward saw him catch the look between them. What they did with the new information wasn't Planter's business; his responsibility was to tell them how the information affected them, and their children, from a strictly medical point of view. The ethics were up to him and Petra – and they wouldn't be easy to sort out. They were half-brother and sister; blood relatives. And they were married.

'It isn't up to me to tell you what to do. But I think it would be wrong not to try to trace this man and make him aware of the legacy he may be passing on, or may have passed on. But all that I leave to you.' He stood, signalling it was time for them to leave. 'I'm sorry to be the one to tell you such devastating news. It would have been completely unethical for me to keep this from you.'

33

As the memory of his father talking about his low sperm count came into Edward's mind, he realised that his mother's secret, the reason why she'd become hysterical at the idea of DNA testing, was that she had, indeed, taken a lover. And that she'd kept this knowledge secret from both her husband and her sons.

'It's possible,' Edward said slowly to Petra. They were on their way back to Wales, their little girls sleeping peacefully in the back of the car. He was negotiating the Hammersmith Roundabout, the Range Rover sturdy against yapping London drivers trying to edge in front of him. Confident in his greater size and strength, he didn't so much manoeuvre his car between them as simply ignore them. Sensing his mood, they kept out of his way.

'You swerved right in front of that blue Ford, Ed! Remember the girls are in the back. What's possible?'

He found it hard to assemble his shattered feelings. Nathaniel and he had thought of themselves as father and son through twenty years of living together. How did one adjust to knowing that that was a lie? 'I'd no idea, but now I see it's entirely possible. It wouldn't be the first time that a woman's taken a lover when her husband couldn't father children on her.'

'What are you talking about?'

He glanced at Petra sitting beside him. 'Planter told us

we have the same biological father.' His voice broke as he said it.

Petra put her hand over the big fist gripping the gear lever. 'I suppose he had to tell us that. He *could* just have told you there'd been a mistake reading your DNA, and you don't have Huntington's.'

'He couldn't have done that, Pet. He *had* to tell us everything. We're half-brother and sister, and we carry a mutated gene. It isn't right for us to go on having children.'

'He said...'

'I'm sorry.' His voice was hoarse. He swallowed, holding back tears. 'Perhaps it's the double shock. At least you already knew David wasn't your father. It's a bolt out of the blue for me.'

Petra linked her arm through his. 'Planter's going to be able to help our girls, Ed. They'll be all right.'

'Only up to a point.' He filtered the car into the motorway traffic. 'They carry the mutated gene for height they've inherited from us; their children will also be at risk.'

'You're being very gloomy. By the time they grow up the doctors will be able to use genetic engineering to change the mutation. And you've forgotten the really good news: you haven't got Huntington's!' She squeezed him tight. 'I don't think you've really taken that on board.'

He gave a sort of cackling laugh. 'Perhaps I never really believed I had it. For all I know, my unconscious was aware all along that Nathaniel wasn't my father.'

'You're very fond of him. That's what it is, isn't it?'

'He was a lovely father to me. It's so ironic; Mum did her stuff, but she never seemed to be that involved. He was. He doted – dotes – on us. Doesn't let on, pretends to be vague, but I know he cares.' The tears were streaming down his face. 'What I find so heartrending is that he's always trusted her, so he has no idea. I'm not going to tell him,' he breathed. 'And I'm going to make Harold promise me he won't, as well. I don't want Dad to know.'

'That's up to you, sweetheart, but what about your mother? She might blurt it out.'

Had his mother's constant attempts to put him off marrying Petra meant she *knew* about their blood relationship? No. If she had, she would have told him, because that would undoubtedly have stopped him marrying her! 'Not if I don't tell her, either.'

'Then you can't ask her who your father is.'

'Maybe we already know.' His voice had steadied again, a hint of aggression breaking through. 'Louise knew Bruce Traggard before she married; my mother *could* have known him before we were born. I can't think why I assumed she didn't. After all, my parents lived in London at the time. I was even born there. It's occurred to me that maybe Jack Oliver came to know about me in the first place because Bruce *told* him about me! I've always thought it extraordinary that Jack picked me out. I was just a schoolboy living in Exeter. Why would he have come across me?'

'You mean, Bruce knew about you, and told Jack that you and Harold were his sons?'

The powerful shoulders shrugged. 'Probably not. I'd guess he knew he'd got my mother pregnant. Then all he had to do was keep an eye on us, watch us in the school playground. Easy enough. And when he saw how I developed, that's when he got in touch with Jack.'

Petra stared straight ahead for a few moments as Edward moved into the outer lane. The traffic was light; they were going to make good time. 'My mother insisted she never had a lover.'

'But she must have done. You *know* she lied because you aren't David's daughter. Believe me, I understand exactly why you're resisting it, but you have to face it, Pet.'

'There's something else; I can feel it, sense it. I don't know what it's all about, but she sounded so sure of herself.'

'Well, I suppose there could be another explanation.'

'Meaning?'

'You could be like Sally – not David's child, or Louise's either. That's why she's so, well, detached. That's why you don't look much like either of them. In other words, you could have been adopted.'

'I've toyed with that, but I don't think so. I was born ten months after my parents married; they couldn't have adopted a baby as quickly as that. Anyway, it's not very likely, because I'm your half-sister. The coincidence would just be too great.' Suddenly Petra grabbed his arm with both her hands, and shook it. 'That's it! That's what we've forgotten about! Sally and Phil. Bruce Traggard was involved with them as well!'

'Don't pull my arm like that, Pet. We're on the motorway, going at over seventy.'

She let go. 'Sorry. But I've just realised how stupid we've been, Ed. Sally was right all along. Something sinister *is* going on, and when she tried to draw attention to that, we put it down to hysteria on her part.'

'You mean the way she was so convinced about Phil's death? That he was murdered?'

'Suppose – just suppose – she had a point. Let's try and figure out the motive for such a ghastly crime later. What she kept trying to tell us was that she had a tape with evidence on it, and that people were trying to get hold of it.'

'So Phil's parents asked for it — that's not at all unreasonable.'

'Forget Phil's parents; I don't think it's to do with them. Sally told me she was convinced someone had spied on her when she was viewing it in our room in Mardon. Stuck to that story even though I made fun of her. I thought she was being completely paranoid. Anyway, she'd made a copy and hidden it in her locker, but we took her home to her mother because she was so ill. That's when she asked me to bring her gear up to London, including the copy. I cleared out all her stuff, but there wasn't any sign of it.'

'That only proves she got it wrong, Petra. She was ill.'

'No, Ed. It wasn't there because someone had got at that locker before me. The caretaker told me someone had tried, and I noticed the lock was stiff. She had to be right, Ed. It's too much of a coincidence that the tape disappeared when all her other gear, some of it valuable, was still there.'

'I suppose it does need thinking through. But that's just the beginning, Pet. If someone *was* after that tape because it's incriminating, it means Sally was right about Phil's death.'

'Exactly. It wasn't an accident, and it wasn't some obscure disease no doctor had ever heard of. He was murdered.'

'But why, Pet? It makes no sense at all. OK, so Joss Black was jealous of him. Why would he *kill* him? He may have got to the States that particular year because Phil was dead, but he would have got there anyway. Bruce told us that Jack had already taken him on as a client, and was negotiating for him to play there.' He turned to Petra. 'I know about basketball. I can tell you Black's OK, but he isn't in the big league. He *couldn't* have thought he'd take Phil's place even if he was dead.'

Petra clutched the dashboard and gripped it. 'It wasn't just Phil, Ed. Sally died in a peculiar way as well.'

'She was *mugged*, Petra.'

'They never found the man who did it. And anyway, why would anyone want to steal that grotty bag?'

'People do.'

'And before that she was very ill.'

'Come on, Pet. The hospital was very clear Sally had food poisoning.'

'And that it made her paranoid. I know; I jumped to the same conclusion. But now I see that it could just as easily have been that she was right. She was ill because someone made her ill, *fed* her the salmonella for all I know. Wouldn't be that difficult, when you think about it.'

'You really are getting as bad as Sally.'

'Why was she attacked that particular day, Ed? Why would a mugger take videotapes?'

'He didn't; he grabbed a duffle bag.'

'Normally used for carrying casual clothes. An odd thing to mug for, don't you think?'

'You're suggesting the motive was that she was on to whoever killed Phil? That she was almost there, and they knew it?'

'Yes. And it had to be connected with basketball, because that was Phil's big thing. And it involves money, and that's always a powerful motive.'

'And Bruce Traggard is mixed up in it somehow. Even if we *are* letting our imaginations run away with us, you're right about that. Something is going on – something quite horrific.' He turned his head, momentarily forgetting he was on the motorway. The car swerved. 'Sorry, must concentrate.'

'OK, let's be really efficient about this. Got a piece of paper and a pencil?'

'In the glove compartment.'

'Let's make a list of what we know about Bruce Traggard. See how it goes.' Petra opened the compartment and took out a pad and pencil.

'Right,' Ed began. 'Let's start with what we're sure about. *Point 1*: Bruce gave Jack a document saying I had Huntington's. We now know that had to be a forgery. It was meant to put your parents against me, and to try and stop our marrying. *Point 2*: he put enormous pressure on me, saying he'd chuck me out of the team and that I'd lose Jack's sponsorship, if I went on seeing you.'

'You mean he tried to stop us marrying because we were both his children? In other words, he *knew* we were half-brother and sister!'

'Exactly. *Point 3*: my mother goes hysterical about you on some trumped-up rubbish. We could make an informed guess that Bruce told her he'd tell Nathaniel about me – and Harold, if he was his father, too – unless she stopped the marriage.' He gave a hollow laugh. '*Point 4*: he always hated Sally. He was furious with Phil for going out with her. It was after he talked to Phil's parents that Helen Thompson started being awful to Sally.'

'Why would he worry so much about Sally?' Petra asked, underlining the different points.

'Because she was always snooping around, and he reckoned that, sooner or later, she'd be on to him.

'*Point 5*: Phil was *very* upset about something before that last game. Something to do with his mother. Anyway, Bruce knew he was ill and in a state, and he still encouraged him to play.'

'You really think Bruce Traggard is behind all this?'

'It's possible. You're right; we shouldn't just have ignored what Sally tried to tell us.' He put his arm out and drew Petra to him. 'What we have to bear in mind is that we now know something that could be just as dangerous to us as Sally's tape was to her. I think we have to act, Pet, because we have no choice.'

She shuddered. 'He'll kill us, too?'

'He, or whoever it actually is.'

'What do we do next?'

'My mother's no use to us. She's completely hysterical. I think you've got to tackle yours, Petra. She must have some feelings for you. If you can get her to admit to Bruce Traggard fathering you, we can build on it.' He looked over his shoulder at the sleeping children. 'Should we turn back, do you think?'

'Let's get the kids home, Ed. If we're in danger, so are they. I'll take the train and go back to see my mother when I've settled you all in again at home. I'll express some milk to keep Corilla going. Anyway, I want to make sure the injections haven't caused side effects.'

34

Gwyneth locked up the office of her garden centre, then walked outside to check that her plants were stacked well away from the fencing which kept them from being stolen. Crime was increasing, even in Powys. Thieves had found it easy to steal any stock she left near the edges. They'd brought a dredger and used the mechanical shovel to scoop up pot plants and even trees. She'd had to increase the height of her fence at enormous cost.

The more exotic plants, the orchids she enjoyed growing in the special greenhouse she'd had built, had been expensive to insure. But it had been worthwhile. The extra business the exotics brought in had been substantial. Her most important customer was Korean. Mr Wong Lee was responsible for setting up a factory to manufacture a new make of Korean car. He liked to indulge his hobby for growing orchids and had become one of her best customers. To her relief Ian hadn't thought of him as a potential danger to Wales; he even seemed to approve of him.

Gwyneth got into her Vauxhall Cavalier and drove towards Lland'od. Takings on Saturdays were always above average, and today had been particularly good. She wanted to deposit the cash in the bank's night-till before she went home. Even Pengwyn was no longer safe from the odd burglary or two. Though her parents and Angharad

363

lived next door, and her sister Bronwen in the house beyond hers, her own house was empty during the day, and therefore vulnerable.

As she drove she sang. Ian had found work at last. Surprising – she'd never believed he would work again. He was now forty-seven; too old to be taken on as a casual builder if there were younger men around. But he'd found a proper job. Quite respectable, selling and installing calor-gas heaters and appliances.

'I'll need the car,' he'd told her.

'You mean you want to borrow it?'

'To get me to work. I've already said.' His eyes had gleamed with anger, and she'd retreated to a safe distance. 'I'm selling calor-gas cylinders. Got to get them to the customers somehow.' He'd turned, his face an ugly mixture of scorn and anger. 'Didn't think I'd get a decent job, did you? Think you're the only one who can earn money. I'll be off soon enough when I get what's rightly mine.'

His fury had been directed at her because of the long time it had taken him to find a job. He blamed her for not employing him at her garden centre. She couldn't do that; his truculent attitude would antagonise her customers, even the Welsh ones.

She'd thought of her almost-new car and shuddered at what Ian would do to it. Besides, she needed it herself.

'Why don't we go and find a nice van for you, Ian?' she'd cajoled him. 'That's what you need, *cariad*. A good van.'

'No need for you to buy me anything. I'll buy it myself.' He'd glowered at her. 'Drive me round to Evans, then.'

She'd sighed with relief. She knew she'd have to foot the bill, but it was a small price to pay for peace and harmony.

As she drove up to her house she noticed that the van wasn't parked outside it, or anywhere else on the narrow, steep lane the houses were built on. Pengwyn was a straggling village of a single street, hugging the steep incline up to a tiny chapel flanked by the village post office stores. 'Village' wasn't really a proper description of the huddle of houses clinging to the hillside. Only the very old and the very young used the stores now. The place smelt of damp and mice. Pity, really, how village life was being strangled by the new superstores which were drawing people to drive for miles, spending as much on petrol as they saved on the goods.

She was glad Ian wasn't home yet, but surprised. She shrugged; at least he wouldn't get at her for being late making his tea – unless he'd been and gone. She turned the key in the front door with some unease, and walked straight into her kitchen. No note; everything as she'd left it that morning. She breathed a sigh of relief, put the kettle on the Rayburn hob, began to peel the potatoes and put some bacon on to fry.

Still no sign of Ian. She put the potatoes in cold salt water, took the bacon off the heat, and went upstairs to change. The door to the spare room wasn't quite shut. She was about to pull it to when her eye was caught by the bedspread. It wasn't neat, the way she always left it. Someone had been in and left it rumpled. Did Ian have a woman?

She went up to the bed and began to pull the cover straight. Her foot was caught by something hard under the bedstead. She pulled the cover up, leaned down and pulled out a large cardboard box.

She hadn't put it there. Her heart lurched into her mouth and she slumped on to the bed. Not Ian thieving again! She couldn't bear it, she'd have to leave him this time. There was no way she could put up with the strain.

The shock was making her feel faint. She put her head between her knees and inhaled deeply. She stared at the strong, heavy box with HOSPITAL SUPPLIES printed on it in solid letters. Her breathing became easier – this was just a box Ian had used for storage. Perhaps he'd come across a hoard of the girlie magazines he loved to read.

The box sat in front of her, rigid, closed. The flaps had been stuck together with brown parcel tape she couldn't open without a knife. She pulled herself off the bed, went downstairs, looked out at the street. Still no van. She took the kettle off the hob, grabbed a small vegetable knife and walked upstairs, heart beating, nerves alert.

She slid the knife along the joins, pulled the flaps out and looked inside. A couple of brown folders were layered on one side; the other was filled with white styrofoam chippings covering small bottles and boxes. Adrenaline surged round her system and her armpits became wet. Her heart felt as though it were pumping through her mouth; she found it hard to breathe and began to pant. Drugs! Her eyes filled with tears as she tried to push the box away and haul herself out of the room. My God, he was into stealing drugs! The new job was just a cover. And she, of all people, had helped him find the transport to take the drugs around. Was he selling them to children?

As she kicked at the box one of the folders fell to the side and opened. Even through her tear-filled eyes she could see that it was a type of file she'd seen many times before: a medical record file. Curiosity got the better of anger and frustration. She bent down and pulled them both out.

The first one opened, showing handwritten notes. *Mutated gene for height*, she read. Where had she come across that phrase recently?

She flipped the pages back and found herself looking at the outside of another file. It seemed oddly familiar, as though she'd seen it before. Had Ian stolen *her* records? Was he going to beat her up again, and wanted to make it

366

harder for the doctors to treat her... She stared at the number code printed on the front. 3579 – the odd numbers after 1. Her brother David's file! Why would Ian take Dewi's medical records? What use were they to him? She knew that Petra had applied to the Powys Health Care Trust for them, to establish what she was already certain of: that David wasn't her biological father.

Who did the other record belong to? She flipped back to the other file again. *Rejected as a sperm donor on those grounds*, she read. She turned to the first page, looking for the name, when she heard the front door open. She froze, tried to stuff the files back into the box and found the styrofoam had slipped into the space. She looked round, frantic. Where could she hide them?

There was a bookcase in the room, below the window-sill. She grabbed the files, pushed them between it and the wall, shut the box flaps and kicked the box back under the bed.

She held her breath, trying to make out whether Ian was coming up the stairs. He usually went into the kitchen first. Gulping, she straightened the bedcover as quickly as she could and walked rapidly to her bedroom door and opened it. She was standing there when she saw the top of Ian's head advancing up the stairs.

She stood, paralysed. As he came nearer he looked at her, then towards the spare-room door. He knew she'd been in there.

She held on to the handle of the door behind her. What had she done with the knife she'd cut the tape with? Sweat began to trickle down her neck, her arms; she felt her palms moisten, felt the knife tight in her left hand.

'Just having a go at ripping your clothes to pieces, are you?'

'Hello, Ian, *cariad*.'

'You've done it this time,' he said, his voice unusually low. 'You've really done it this time. They'll find your fingerprints on it as well. So what are you going to tell them, eh, *ast*?'

She pushed herself away from him, backed into the bedroom. Could she be quick enough to close the door on him, then drag the bed across and stop him coming in? Would her mother hear her banging on the wall and come and rescue her?

'You bloody *hwran*.'

'*Cythral!*' she screamed at him. 'You devil! Don't you dare touch me!' She watched, unable to move, mesmerised like some bird by a snake, rooted to the spot, the knife now in both hands clutched out in front of her. 'Don't you come near me!'

He didn't move. '*Mi ga'i di. Mi dali di am 'ny,*' he snarled. 'You'll bloody pay for this. I'll kill you – see if I don't.'

'Easy now, Ian.' A voice she didn't know.

Two men in policemen's uniforms were behind Ian, followed by a man dressed in an ordinary suit. 'We've searched downstairs. Let's see what's up here, shall we?'

'What are you doing in my house?' she whispered, looking at the knife, at Ian, at the police. 'Why are you here?'

'Search warrant to search the premises,' the man in ordinary clothes told her. 'I'm Detective Sergeant Griffiths, Mrs Davies. We have reason to believe your husband stole some drugs from Llandrindod Wells Hospital.'

She stared at them. Ian was right; her fingerprints were on the box. Would they charge her as an accomplice?

'Know anything about it, do you?'

She held out the knife. 'I've just been in the spare bedroom,' she said, tears running down her face, unable to look at Ian. 'I used this to open the package. In there,' she said, pointing to the other door. 'Under the bed. I didn't know it was there.'

'What made you look, then?'

'The door was slightly open, and I saw the bedspread wasn't right; it was crooked. I went to straighten it and the box caught my foot. That's when I opened it.'

The two uniformed policemen went into the spare room, lifted up the bedspread and looked under the bed. They drew out two boxes. So there was another one she hadn't even noticed.

'You'll have to come with us,' Griffiths said, putting a hand on Ian's shoulders. 'We'll need you at the station to help with our enquiries.'

'Are you arresting him?'

'Not yet, love; this is evidence.' He pointed at the boxes. 'We'll need you, too. You'll have to tell us when this could have happened, what you know about it.'

'I've told you, I only just came across them.'

'Stealing drugs is a serious offence, love. You'll have to come and help us out.'

She breathed in hard, then calmed a little. They weren't going to think she had anything to do with it. What she really wanted to know was why Ian had stolen medical record files. And who did the second file she'd seen belong to?

'That you, Gwyneth? It's Petra here. I've been trying to get hold of you all evening! Are you OK?'

'I am now. Hell of a day it's been.'

'Ian again? Come and stay with us, Gwyneth. You can't let that man—'

'No, no, *fach*. He hasn't been beating me up – no chance of that. They've arrested him.'

Petra drew in her breath, horrified. 'Arrested?'

'Been thieving again. More serious, this time. He broke into the hospital and stole some drugs. One of the nurses saw him hanging around; the police got a search warrant.'

'And they found evidence?'

'In the guest room. Nothing special – the hospital doesn't keep much in the way of hard drugs. Too dangerous. All he got was some tranquillisers, painkillers, a bit of morphine. Not enough to set up in business.'

'Sounds as though he's getting really desperate, Gwyneth. Why on earth did he start burgling again when he's finally got a job? Thought he liked it, and everything?'

'I don't know. He doesn't usually manage to fool me, but he did this time.'

'There's something else, isn't there?' Petra could hear fear in Gwyneth's voice, and it was more than the fear of physical assault. 'What's wrong?'

'I've been trying to work it out. He's thrown out these hints that now he's got a way of making a living, he'll leave me. Too good to be true, I suppose I thought, and forgot about it. Then it got through to me that someone must have paid him to break into the hospital. I think stealing the drugs was a cover.'

'What else is there to take, Gwyneth? Hospital equipment isn't something one can flog like the odd VCR!'

She could sense Gwyneth thinking it through at the other end. 'Medical records, Petra. I only caught a glimpse, but he had at least two medical files.'

'Medical records?' A slow chill was spreading across her shoulders and down her arms. 'You mean, like the one I'm applying for?'

'That was one of them. I pulled out two, and I recognised Dewi's. Then I heard the front door, and shoved them

370

behind the bookcase. I've only this minute walked in; I haven't had a chance to look at them again.'

A lump had come into her throat, constricting it, making it hard to speak. 'Daddy's – David's file? Are you sure?'

'They're all numbered on the outside. I knew there was something familiar about those numbers, and then it came back to me.'

'You could have got that muddled, Gwyneth...'

'I recognised it, Pet. I've seen it often enough when we went to the hospital together.'

'What could anyone possibly want with Daddy's medical records?'

'That's exactly what I'd like to know. You applied for them yet?'

'I've instructed my solicitor. He's probably still swapping letters with Powys Health Care Trust. He warned me it would be difficult to get the records out of them, but he thought I had a good case. I haven't chased it up; pretty academic, now we know he wasn't my father anyway.'

'You're very upset about it.' She could hear the sympathy in Gwyneth's voice.

'I loved him as a father, Gwyn. I really did. I still mourn him.' She sighed. 'He'd have enjoyed the girls so much. He wouldn't have cared that he wasn't their real grandfather.'

'I don't care that I'm not their real great-aunt, Petra. They're lovely little girls, and you're a lovely young woman. We all wish you were Dewi's daughter, but you're as good as.'

'I'm sorry, Gwyn. I shouldn't be ringing up and bothering you. You've got enough troubles of your own.'

'You need some help? You only have to ask.'

'I wouldn't impose on you if it wasn't important. I've got to go up to London...'

'And you want me to help out, is it? Look after the girls?'

She laughed. 'I can make time. Ian's out of the way. He'll never get bail; they'll ask too much.'

'You think they'll keep him in?'

'I should bloody well hope so. We'll have to wait and see. Anyway, what were you thinking of?'

'I want to have a heart-to-heart with my mother. Once she knows I've got proof that David wasn't my father, she'll tell me who was. After all, she must know!'

There was a silence at the other end. 'She's your mother, Petra. I'm not going to say anything.'

'Oh, come on, Gwyn. I lived with her for eighteen years. I know she isn't a flighty woman! She must have some idea who it was even if there was more than one man involved. Ed and I are pretty sure you were right, and it *was* Bruce Traggard.'

'I should never have—'

'I'm glad you did, Gwyn. It's time I got to the bottom of it. I'd like to take the late train tonight. I've put the girls to bed. Can you come and cope until I get back? Corilla'll take a bottle for a couple of feeds. As long as it's milk, she'll guzzle anything. I'll be back as soon as I can – tomorrow night, I hope.'

'Be a pleasure.' She hesitated slightly. 'Ed will be around to help me out, won't he? In case I get into trouble.'

'Don't worry about that, Gwyn. He'll be around.'

35

'So you're all on your own this time, are you?' Louise greeted her daughter as she opened the door to her. Her sharp nose angled beyond Petra as though sniffing for evidence of uninvited guests.

'Hello, Mother. Yes, I told you on the phone.'

Her mother's arms reached out and twined themselves around her neck. 'It's good to see you.' She gave Petra a hug.

She hugged her back. 'And it's good to be welcomed.'

'I suppose I've been missing you. Last time Jack came to see me he told me about the christening, that he'd been to it. That hurt, you know. I wasn't even invited.' Reproach was in every syllable. 'After all, Corilla is *my* granddaughter.'

'You mean, you'd have liked to come?' Petra stood, uncertain and precarious on the step. 'It never crossed my mind that you'd want to be part of such a Jones' family event.'

'Well, are you coming in, or are you just going to stand there?'

Petra stepped through into the hall she knew so well. 'He asked to be Corilla's godfather.'

'He told me.' She led the way into the living room. 'Sherry?'

'Thank you.' Petra walked round the room she had so

373

often sat in with her parents. Strange how it all seemed years ago. Her mother had refurbished the whole house. Except for David's study; she'd left that as it was. Louise's choice of colours was bright and cheerful, and the house had a warm, lived-in air. 'He's been coming to see you, has he?'

Louise put two sherry glasses on the table and poured from the decanter Petra had saved so hard to buy for her parents two Christmases ago. It brought back the fact that her father was dead, and that it had ended up with her mother. Like everything else in the house.

Louise shrugged. 'I've always encouraged him to come the way he used to. He keeps away most of the time, but, yes, to my surprise he came to lunch last Sunday. I still haven't figured out why.'

'Maybe he has designs on you.'

She grinned at her daughter. 'I considered that. After all, I'm a good hostess, know how to keep my mouth shut, and he loves my cooking. And though I'm no beauty, I'm reasonably presentable. Not too tall, either.'

'So, did he ask you to marry him?'

'Nothing like that. Bit unlike his usual self, really. He can be so amusing, you know. But this time he just blathered on about how marvellous you and Ed are, what adorable children you've got, how they're going to be Jack's gift to the fashion industry when they grow up.'

'Over my dead body!'

Louise laughed. 'Well, I'd love to be around when that gets discussed. Perhaps your daughters will think differently from you, Pet. Perhaps they'll want the lime-light. I gather from Jack that you hide yourself away in a remote farmhouse and go in for being an earth mother.'

'You don't think that's worthwhile?'

'With your talents? You must be joking. Except I know you aren't.'

'You know I'm taking my degree through the Open University, Mother. And so is Edward. The rest of the time we enjoy our children, look after the sheep farm, grow our own vegetables, bake our own bread. I've even started making ewe's cheese. It's delicious.'

Her mother grimaced. 'They sell all kinds of exotic cheeses at Safeway's – assuming I feel a strong need for something other than ordinary Cheddar.'

'You like to cook, Mother. All I'm doing is carrying it a little further. I enjoy going back to basics. It gives me a feeling of oneness with the earth, with the elements we're all made of...'

'Spare me the details, Petra, please.' Louise grasped hold of her daughter's hands and turned them to look at the nails. 'Not as bad as I expected, but not that marvellous, either.' She put them down again. 'It could be worse.' She sat back in her chair and stared at Petra. 'There's one thing I've never managed to work out. How did you and Edward get the money together to buy a sheep farm? Even in Wales, farms aren't free.' She frowned. 'And they can't bring in much income.'

'Jack didn't tell you?'

'I didn't ask him. You mean *he* funded you?' Her eyes had grown hard.

'I wouldn't have accepted that. You never knew, did you?'

Louise put a well-manicured hand to a geometric hair cut which had taken five years off her face. 'Knew what?'

'Daddy left me some money. Actually, that's not right; Daddy put some money in a trust fund he set up for me. Quite a bit. After his death his solicitor got in touch and told me about it.'

'David? Put enough in a trust fund for you to buy a farm?'

'Yes.'

Her hands waved in dismissal. 'Something wrong there. He didn't *have* any spare money. He was just a manager working for Jorncy. Where on earth would he get real money?'

'You don't know anything about it?'

'No.' Suddenly she grinned. 'But I can work it out. How very stupid of me not to realise right away. Must have been Jack's way of getting it to you. He was always trying to get us to accept money on your behalf. He must have persuaded David to front it.'

'That doesn't make sense, Mother. Jack couldn't know that Daddy – David – was going to die...' She found it interesting that it was beginning to be hard for her to call David Jones by the name she'd called him all her life.

'If it was a trust fund in your name, Petra, all the solicitor had to do was tell you of its existence. How do you know it was anything to do with David?'

It wasn't an angle which would have occurred to her. But it wasn't the right reasoning. Mr Broughton had specifically said the money was from David, and she could swear Jack hadn't known that the trust existed until he'd seen their farm, and she'd confirmed his guess for him. If he'd known, he'd have worked out what she and Edward were planning to do. He'd have found them much sooner than he did.

'That would be typical of the two of them. Both crazy about doing the best for you, both petrified – if you'll excuse the pun – of letting you know what they wanted you to have.'

Petra laughed out loud. 'Every now and again I just love the way you're so – well, *blunt*, Mother.'

'You mean, because I don't prevaricate, hide behind

platitudes, pretend to feelings I haven't got? You find it refreshing that I tell the truth!' Louise said, her eyes challenging. 'Go on, admit it. You're sick to death of the mealy-mouthed, sentimental rubbish the Joneses dish out.' The gold began to fleck the muddy eyes. 'Have I got a point?'

'Gran Megan is sweet, Mother. There's no falseness in her. And Gwyneth is almost as forthright as you; in some ways more so.'

'Ah, Gwyneth. That's why you're here, isn't it? Because of her.' She frowned. 'Even Jack started going on about her. He doesn't take to her, I've always known that, but he can't stop going on about her, somehow. What I can't figure out is why.'

'Gwyneth is only part of it.' She glanced at the elegant woman sitting opposite her, dressed in Caroline Charles from top to toe, the short string of pearls replaced by two of a good length. 'Try not to get annoyed by what I'm going to ask you, Mother. There are some things I have to know.'

'*Have* to?'

'They affect my children.'

'So that's what it's all about! Jack mumbled something about blood tests – said Gwyneth had been on at you to find out what group you were and compare it to hers, because hers is the same as David's. She knows that because she and David always helped each other out with transfusions, when they had surgery done on their palates. That right?'

It was a relief that Jack had paved the way. But why exactly had he done that? Had he believed her when she said David wasn't her father? She put it to the back of her mind for the moment. 'Spot on. And it turns out the tests proved that Daddy couldn't be my father.' There was no visible reaction, and no response. 'Not exactly news to you, I know. But it was to me. Did Jack tell you I know?'

'He didn't go into it. Anyway, what business is it of his?'

'He takes an interest in me.'

Louise had stood, and turned her back to Petra, 'So, what did he have to say about it?'

'He told me to let sleeping dogs lie. I thought about doing just that – after all, what difference does it make? I loved Daddy; I think he was the best father any girl could have had.' She drank the rest of the sherry in the glass. 'But I can't just forget about it.'

Louise turned round to face her daughter. 'David was good to us, I know.' Her voice was low, and for the first time Petra realised that Louise might have missed her husband. 'I was a bit of an idiot about him, Petra. I know that now, and it's too late. He cared about me; no one else has ever cared about me in that way. And all I did was throw it back at him.'

Resentment was beginning to rise in her, but she choked it back. 'So you did take a lover, didn't you?' Her throat began to ache from the effort of keeping her voice under control. She wanted to yell.

Louise sighed. 'I've just told you, I don't bother with lies. Far too complicated. No, I never cheated on your father by taking a lover.'

The anger was spurting through her blood, rushing words to her mouth. 'How can you say that? You must have done!' She stared at the composed woman seated only a few feet away from her. 'He wasn't my father! So, unless you're going to tell me it was an immaculate conception, you must have had a lover!'

Louise began to laugh so much she drew out a paper tissue and held it to her eyes. 'You know, I've never thought of that before. It *is* the modern version of that story. I had a child, not by my husband, and I didn't take a lover. Come on now, Pet. You're supposed to be so bright. What's the answer? It's not exactly the Riddle of the Sphinx, you know!'

Petra stared at her as realisation slowly dawned. How could she and Edward have been so blind? 'You mean you wanted a child which wasn't David's, but you didn't want to take a lover?'

She nodded. 'You're getting there. A child that wasn't his because I was terrified it might end up with a cleft palate like Gwyneth's. Not the easiest thing to live with, is it? It doesn't just affect her looks, you know; it affects her speech, her breathing, her teeth. It's a serious disease, Pet. I couldn't cope with the thought of exposing a child of mine to that.'

Edward's father had had a low sperm count. His mother had wanted a family, and conceived at least one child who wasn't her husband's. There was, after all, a simple solution for both their mothers! 'Donor insemination techniques. You went to a sperm bank and chose a donor. That's what you did, isn't it?'

'You can buy sperm off the shelf, you know. Just like a supermarket, just another commodity.' Louise looked at the glass in her hand, her eyes bright. 'They wrap it all up in politically correct talk about helping women like me, say they'll match the donor to the husband's physique. All rot. When I told them what I wanted they just gave it to me.' Her eyes found Petra's, defied her. 'And please don't think that your father didn't know about it. He knew, and he approved; it was the agreement we made before we even married. There was nothing underhand or clandestine about it, and there was nothing to be jealous of. He was just as keen as I was to prevent our child having a genetic defect.'

'But why didn't you *tell* me?' Petra found it hard to sit still and started pacing up and down the room. 'Don't I have the right to know?'

'In those days we were advised to keep it to ourselves. We promised each other we'd never tell anyone.'

'You mean no one else knows?'

'No one.'

'Not even Uncle Jack?'

She hesitated. 'I've never specifically told him. I don't think David did either. Jack always knew I preferred fair men; he might have put two and two together and guessed, I suppose. It's not the same as knowing.' She looked up, her face without its sparkle. 'What good is it going to do you, Petra? Knowing, I mean.'

'I have to find the donor. That's the irony of it, you see – you didn't prevent a genetic defect. In fact, that's exactly what I have. And it could be said to be just as devastating as the cleft palate.'

'What on earth are you talking about?' The voice sounded cross rather than worried. 'They told me that they screened all donors very carefully. No way they'd let anything defective through.' She frowned. 'You always exaggerate.'

'Not this time.' The grim tone made Louise sit up straight. 'You know our little girls will be giantesses unless they're given the proper treatment; we told you that when we brought them to see you. It turns out it isn't a hormonal problem. It's something much more worrying.'

Louise stared at her, horrified. 'Whatever do you mean?'

'They have a mutated gene for height.' Her voice broke as she tried not to cry. 'They could end up being over six foot six.'

Louise gasped. 'But that's really appalling. You're sure?'

'There isn't any doubt. The peculiar thing is that it was

Ed's mother who mentioned such a possibility to him. That's what put the idea into my head.'

Louise frowned. 'That isn't so strange. After all, it's *Ed* who has that problem. Why on earth do you say it's you? You aren't that tall.'

'It's both of us, Mother.'

Louise listened without interruption as Petra explained what the consultation with Dr Planter had brought to light.

'There's some mistake. Ed's got to be Professor Dunstan's son. What about the Huntington's? They can't both carry it by chance – that's stretching coincidence too far!'

'Ed doesn't carry that gene, Mother. Dr Planter was absolutely certain; he checked and double-checked Ed's DNA. That's one of the reasons we know Nathaniel isn't his father.'

Louise stared at Petra, speechless. 'You mean you think you're half-brother and sister?'

'Dr Planter is sure of it. So now you know I'm not exaggerating, and I'm not being melodramatic.' She went up to her mother. 'And you'll also understand that all this is in the strictest confidence. I had to tell you, but you can see it would be drastic if anyone else knew Ed and I are blood relatives.'

'I'm sorry, Pet. You can rely on me.' Louise's eyes, too, had filled with tears. 'Anyway, who would I tell?'

'Jack, for example.'

'I've told you – I've never discussed it with him.' Her eyes flashed their annoyance. 'Least of all Jack! He's always trying to take over my family.'

'So tell me about the sperm. How did you choose it?'

Louise poured herself another glass of sherry. 'That's the only thing I did behind your father's – David's – back. He expected me to ask for a dark-haired, brown-eyed donor. I asked for a tall, fair-haired, blue-eyed one.'

Petra opened her bag and drew out the note she had read, and reread, so often that it was falling to pieces:

I hope my darling Petra will understand one day. I had no idea that the arrangements I agreed to were changed. I'd give anything to undo what I allowed to happen, anything at all. It's too late; there's nothing anyone can do.

Forgive me, Pet; I can't live with that. Remember that I've always loved you, always will.

You've always been a clever girl; you'll sort it out.

David Jones, the man who was proud to call himself your father.

She handed it to Louise. 'That's what he meant, wasn't it? He meant he trusted you to ask for sperm from a donor who had his physical characteristics?'

Louise read the note and handed it back. 'I suppose it could be interpreted in that way. But so what if I changed the donor characteristics? Hardly a reason for David's suicide, is it?'

'But that's what he means: *I had no idea that the arrangements I agreed to were changed ... I can't live with that.*'

'You're reading something into it that isn't there, Pet. He couldn't have known who the donor was any more than I, or anyone else, could. It's all kept highly confidential. They're identified by codes, not names.'

Petra put the note back in her handbag. 'Well, tall is what you got all right.' She looked at her mother curiously. 'Why did you stop at one?'

She shrugged. 'I'm not exactly the maternal type. David was quite happy. We decided to leave it at that.'

'Which sperm bank did you use?'

'Good heavens, Petra. All that was over twenty years ago! Some tiny place, rather a ramshackle affair somewhere near Harley Street – long gone, I'm sure.' She stared at her daughter. 'What on earth do you intend to do? Even if you do find the sperm bank, and get them to track down the donor, they won't tell you who it was.'

'Hi, Pet.'

Petra kissed her husband and children, and clambered gratefully into the car. Ed and the girls had come to pick her up from the station and take her back to their little refuge from the world.

'You don't know how wonderful it is to be with you all,' she breathed, her eyes shining. 'I hate everything about London.'

'Was Louise awful?'

'She was much easier to handle than I expected. And I felt an idiot not to have worked it out myself. The bottom line is that she didn't have a lover...'

'How could you fall for that one? She *must* have done!'

'No, Ed – there is another way. She went to a sperm bank; my father even knew about it. All very proper. But it's going to be hard to track the donor down.'

'A sperm bank, eh?' A long, low whistle. 'So Bruce Traggard's in the clear?'

'I certainly believe he wasn't her lover...'

'I don't think he was my mother's, either. That was always a long shot. So that could be what *my* mother did as well, Pet.' He put his hand on hers. 'So where would that leave us?'

'I thought about nothing else on the train. In a way it would account for everything – even your mother's unbelievable behaviour towards me that first day I met her.'

'That's it! *That's* what she's been hiding all these years! It would explain so much about her. She always seemed to be holding something back.'

'Well, somebody's on to a secret, there's no doubt about that. Maybe they're blackmailing her about going to an insemination centre. It used to be hushed up, my mother says.'

'That would fit. Dad's always talking about the amount of money she gets through. We were beginning to think it was drugs.' His voice sounded dejected, then he gasped. 'You know what? I think she killed Bradley.'

'Bradley? I thought he died of some sort of food poisoning.'

'Exactly! There was so much else going on, I didn't think it through. I knew it reminded me of something. It was just like Sally. Pet, I think she poisoned Brad deliberately.'

'Oh, Ed. Do you really think ... but why?'

'In an attempt to frighten me into not marrying you. She mumbled about his death being some kind of warning, that a mother always knows. That sort of rubbish.' He sighed. 'You know, Pet, this changes everything.'

'You're thinking that both our mothers were given the same donor by pure chance?'

'It must happen, but there has to be more to it than that.'

'And Bruce Traggard still has to be involved. He told that lie about the Huntington's.'

'Too true. So does it mean he's the sperm donor? Is that a possibility?'

She snuggled up to her husband and put her head on his shoulder. 'It isn't worth cheating on one's husband. My mother's got a point; lying is just *too* difficult.'

'My parents have been lying to each other for nearly thirty years,' he said, wonder in his voice. 'That's just incredible. I'm going to have to go and sort it out for them.

Then maybe my mother can concentrate on looking after
Dad. He needs her.'

'If you find out she used the same donor for Harold,
you'll have to tell him, too. Or get them to do it. If you can
trust them to, that is.'

'There's still one small problem, Pet.'

'I know. How could Bruce Traggard, or whoever it
actually was, possibly know who got his sperm? They have
all kinds of ways of making sure it's kept secret. No one
knows, not even the doctors or the technicians.'

He shrugged. 'Sufficient unto the day. Let's sleep on it.
You must be worn out.'

The Range Rover swung over the cattle grid guarding the
drive to their house. They parked the car, unloaded their
little girls, and walked into the kitchen. The warmth of the
Rayburn made them feel at home, and Bradley Mark II's
modulated barks rang out their greeting.

36

'It's Gwyneth, *fach*.'

The words came in a hoarse whisper at the other end of the line, and Petra would have had trouble identifying who it was if it weren't for the telltale pattern of speech. 'Hello, Gwyneth!' She wasn't sure, but she thought she'd caught a tiny hesitation. 'Is something wrong?'

'Can I come over? Something I've got to talk to you about. Something I've found out.'

Petra was very fond of Gwyneth. She understood why David had always cherished affectionate memories of his sister, and why it left a hole in his life when she'd refused to visit him in London. But she was tired out. 'Of course you can,' she said, trying hard not to let the ambivalence in her voice sound through. 'You know you're always welcome. But there's a howling gale and it's quite late...'

'It's intortant, *fach*,' the whisper, regressing to mispronunciation, urged down the line. 'It's those records. The second one's...' The voice dropped away.

'Gwyn? You still there?'

'Hold on a minute.' There was a silence, and then a sob. She could hear Gwyneth blow her nose as she came back on the line. '...Mutated gene for height...' Petra could hear her blow her nose again. 'You've got to know, Pet. It's...' There was a crackle which obscured the last word.

'I can't hear you, Gwyn,' Petra said, raising her voice in case Gwyneth couldn't hear her.

'...I should have known it was...'

A sudden lurch caught in Petra's throat. 'Known what was, Gwyn?' she hissed back as she looked nervously around her living room. Was someone getting at Gwyneth, or was it just the gales? Perhaps Ian was in the house... Then she remembered that Ian had been arrested and was being held, charged with burglary and possession of drugs. Bail had been set too high for him, or any of his friends, to be able to pay it. 'Try again, Gwyn. I think the line has cleared...'

Apparently she hadn't heard her. 'I can drive out to your place all right, don't worry,' she could hear between the static. 'I can't talk like this, *fach*.' The words were very hard to distinguish. 'With you in an hour or so, weather permitting.'

'All right, Gwyn. Take care.'

'I thought you said Gwyneth would be here by now?'

'I know – can't think why she hasn't turned up yet. I told her the weather was bad. Hope it doesn't mean she's had problems on the way. I heard a gale warning on the radio.'

Heavy storms had caused chaos for the last two days. Blustering gales had followed long periods of sheeting rain. The big sycamore outside the Dunstans' house had lost a chunk, and far too many slates had been torn off the roof. Edward, now an expert with the chainsaw, had made a good job of turning the fallen branch into firewood. He'd come in with his arms full of logs.

'They're pretty wet. I thought if we left them in the kitchen for a bit they'd dry out.'

Petra smiled at him, pain tugging at her. He did so love looking after his family. However innocent she and Ed had been, the fact had to be faced that they were half-brother and sister, and that they were married. Talking to Louise had highlighted what both she and Ed had managed to push out of the way, refused to confront. Some time, soon, they would have to consider the implications. Not now; not yet.

'I'll just get my boots off and wash my hands.' Edward came over to Petra sitting in her rocker, feeding Corilla. 'You look a picture. I really must get the video camera out before she grows out of this stage.'

He was trying to pretend that nothing had changed. But she knew; knew that their dream of a large family was over. Not just because of the mutated gene. Now that she and Edward were consciously aware of their blood relationship it was no longer possible for them to ignore its existence.

She smiled sadly, tears gathering in her eyes, as she felt her baby at her breast and rocked back and forth in the rhythm of maternity. She'd never be able to have another child.

'Put on the TV, will you, Ed? I always enjoy the local news.'

It had begun to rain again, the water lashing against the windows behind drawn curtains. The wind, caught in the window-frames Edward hadn't fixed yet, was singing and whistling loud enough to make Corilla let go of the nipple and stare at her mother.

'It's all right, darling. Only the wind.'

Petra wanted to feel radiant and safe, surrounded by the drawn curtains, the cheerful fire, the baby suckling at her breast, her loving husband by her side. Somehow the country winter was even better than the summer; the harvest in, the warmth of a snug nest. Louise had said 'knowledge is power'. But for them it was also devastation, the end of a dream. What were they going to do?

Edward tapped the grandfather clock, checked the time

on his watch. 'It's not like Gwyneth to put herself at risk, driving on a night like this. Couldn't whatever it was have kept till morning?'

'Apparently not. She sounded very excited, and sort of scared at the same time. Seemed to think she was on to something.'

'About Bruce, you mean? Couldn't she have said on the phone?'

Petra lifted Corilla up to her shoulder, and began to rub her back. 'Somehow I got the impression Ian was there. Silly, of course – he couldn't have been. Safely behind bars, thank goodness.'

'Afraid not, Pet. Someone came up with the bail this morning; the police let him go.'

'*What*? But that means she's in danger, Ed! How do you know?'

'It's all over Lland'od. I was in the Sports Centre at lunchtime and they talked about nothing else. I was going to tell you, suggest you ask her to come over. She can stay here for the time being.'

'You mean you wouldn't mind?'

He came and sat at her feet, leaned his head against her knees. 'She's at work all day; we'd hardly see her.'

'If Ian's there again she's got to leave. I didn't suggest it before because she's right next door to Megan, and it's a long drive to the garden centre from here. She starts work at seven – not very convenient.'

'There's nowhere else for her to go.'

'You're right, she can't stay there now. I suppose that's what the hurry was.' Petra paused, listening to the announcer's voice on the television.

'... *gale warnings in force. The police are asking drivers not to go out unless it is essential.*'

'She really ought to have more sense,' she fretted.

'Better to have slept on her mother's sofa than risk coming out in this.'

'... *serious road accident in the village of Pengwyn. The driver was fatally injured when the car ran out of control on Pengwyn Hill.*'

The well-known street came into view, the back of a blue Cavalier high in the air.

Petra's breathing seemed to stop. She gulped back air, then screamed: 'That's Gwyneth's car!'

'*Several more sheep have been found...*'

Edward switched off the TV, then came over and squatted in front of Petra, hugging her and the baby to him.

'They said fatal,' Petra whispered. 'That means she's dead.'

Without a word he went to the front door and engaged the bolts, then to the back door and did the same. 'I'm not taking any chances,' he said. 'It might have been the weather, or it might not. Ian's on the loose again. He's capable of anything.'

'Yes,' she wept. 'That's why Gwyneth was whispering on the phone. He must have been in the house.'

Edward came back, leaned over the back of the rocker and held her tight. 'Let's not jump to conclusions, Pet. We'll ring Megan, find out what really happened. That man is clearly out of his mind, and dangerous. It isn't just us we have to think about; our children could end up orphans.'

'I know.' Within seconds of hearing the news it seemed her breastmilk had dried up. She'd put the baby back to finish her feed, and Corilla was still suckling, but she wasn't getting anything. Her large eyes opened in reproach, her mouth a round of surprise. She began to whimper, and then to fret. 'I shall have to make up a bottle for Corilla,' Petra said.

'Give her to me. I'll hold her while I check on Cinthy.'

The feeling of warmth had fled, leaving the tug of fear, of grief, that she had felt when she'd heard about her father. She prepared Corilla's formula and tapped in Megan's number. Her fingers were cold and rigid; she got it wrong twice.

She perched on her kitchen stool, waiting as the phone rang and rang. Then she hung up and tapped at the phone again. Perhaps she'd got the wrong number. Eight rings; she was about to hang up again when the line came alive. 'Hello.' A faint voice, old, weak, full of tears.

'It's Petra, Gran Megan. I was just ringing—'

'My Gwyneth's dead!' she cried, a hoarse, grating sound. 'Oh Pet, I've lost my Gwyn. She called in just a few minutes before she went...' The voice petered out and Petra could hear nothing but wrenching sobs.

'That you, Petra? It's Angharad. How did you know?'

'The local news – we recognised the Cavalier. What happened? Was it the weather?'

'It's bad, Petra. She didn't have a chance.'

'How do you mean?'

'I was out there with her, trying to stop her going so late, saying she could have my bed.'

'Was it the weather?'

'The weather was all right. She was in such a hurry, said she had to get to you right away, she knew what it was all about.'

'She told me on the phone she wanted to tell me something important.'

'She was mumbling, you know...' Angharad told her. 'Sounded like "booze".'

Bruce; she was going to tell them about Bruce. The blood ran cold through Petra's veins.

'I couldn't quite make it out. Something about records.'

'Medical records?'

'I don't know. Some word which sounded like jeans; she said they were *your* jeans. Then she started the motor, put the car into gear and accelerated off. Next thing I knew I saw the brake-lights go on but she didn't slow or stop. Just gathered speed down the hill. I heard the crash.' Angharad began to weep. 'I'll never be able to forget it, Pet. That terrible, tearing noise! She hit the stone wall at the bottom of the hill head on.' Another bout of sobbing. 'She always kept her precious Cavalier in perfect condition. Why didn't it slow when she put on the brakes? Why did they fail?'

'It's you, Huw. Come on in.'

Petra opened the door and motioned Gwyneth's younger brother through into her kitchen. 'I'm so very sorry, Huw. You know how fond we were of her.'

'I know. She thought the world of you and the little ones. Made her feel she had something of David left.' He put his hand out to stroke Petra's arm. 'I know he wasn't your father, but he raised you. She thought that made all the difference, see.'

Petra's eyes were moist as she tried not to burst into tears. 'And she was right, he was a wonderful father.' She sighed. 'Come to see Edward? He'll be along in half an hour or so.'

'Thought I'd put you in the picture of what's going on. Best if you hear it from me.'

'Was Ian involved?'

'You've guessed.'

'Gwyn sounded odd on the phone – whispered, instead of speaking out loud. I thought he must be there, though I didn't know how he could be . . .' She swallowed her tears away. 'Then Ed told me about the bail, so we guessed Ian had been involved somehow.'

'We still don't know who came up with the money, and

we can't find out. Ian went round to Gwyneth's office as soon as he was set free. She said he could stay until he found somewhere to go.'

'Whyever did she do that? She knew...'

'Soft spot, I suppose. Always felt she owed him something.'

'So none of you knew he was out?'

'Came across him in the pub, about twelve-thirty. Already drunk by the time I got there. Came right over to me and started telling me how he knew Gwyneth was going off with an English lover; he had his sources.'

'What is this crazy idea he's got?'

'Always has had a bee in his bonnet about it, because she has these English customers. Well, I ask you – who else has got the money for special plants in a place like Lland'od?'

'But you didn't think he'd do her any actual harm?'

'He was out cold by the time I took him home at around three. We put him to bed in the spare room. She said something about ringing you and going over to see you. We thought she'd be safe until then.'

'That's right, she did – but not till around six that evening. She told us she wanted to tell us something important...'

'I suppose he must have come to and heard her on the phone. Imagined she was off with some lover when she was really coming to see you.'

'What happened, Huw?'

'The police discovered that the brakepipes had been cut so they didn't work at all. They came round to the house and found the tool Ian could have used to cut the pipes. They even found out it was my dad's; he'd lent it to Ian. So they arrested him on suspicion of murder. No chance of bail.'

'But if he was drunk...'

'He must have sobered up. Gwyn was on the phone – to you, Angie said. That's when he must have gone out and done it. My guess is he drove off in his van right afterwards, straight back to the pub. Drank himself silly again. Don't think he cared whether anyone found out or not. Maybe he's had enough.'

'Enough of what?'

Huw shrugged, his eyes staring out of the window. 'Poor Gwyn. She had such a rotten deal all her life.' He turned to Petra. 'You and Edward were wonderful to her. I can't tell you how much that means to me, to all of us.'

'We only did what we wanted to do. She was so – genuine.'

'You never had a prejudice against her because of her looks.'

Petra winced at the searing pain she had so often felt on her father's behalf. 'People don't know how cruel they can be.'

Huw embraced her, kissed her children, and insisted on leaving without even accepting tea. 'My old mam's very down. I've got to go and be with her.'

'It's just like what happened to Phil, Ed. Poor Sally was right. Why didn't we believe her? She tried so hard to convince us something terrible was going on.'

'You think it's part of all that, because Ian murdered Gwyneth? How can that have anything to do with it?'

'I don't know, sweetheart. All I know is that as soon as the outside world came into our lives again, everything turned sour.'

'Since the day Jack found us, you mean. You think it's all my fault.'

She put her arms around his neck. 'It never even occurred to me. All you did was play basketball. If he took the trouble to look for us, it was because he had a reason. Maybe it was rather more than just your brilliance at the game. We'll have to try and figure it out.'

'No way we can let it go now. Whoever it is thinks we know something. He'll kill us, too.'

'Let's write down what we know, Ed. Just like we did with the stuff about Bruce. Let's go back to square one.'

'OK, I'm all set. Shoot.'

'Shoot!' she remembered Sally shouting at her at that match, so long ago now. But that's when it had all started, at that basketball game when Phil collapsed. No, before that, actually. It was when Phil had behaved so strangely with Sally.

'I know it sounds odd, but I think it all started when Phil refused to kiss Sally. He was in love with her, and something stopped him.'

She saw Ed look at her, but he didn't argue.

'*Point 1*: Phil didn't kiss Sally. You think I'm being ridiculous?'

'I don't care; let's just write it all down. Actually I think that's *Point 2*. *Point 1* is Phil having some sort of bug no one could make head nor tail of. It may or may not have been flu.'

'*Point 3* is his collapsing and dying. When you look back on it, the doctors knew they couldn't save him. They just pretended.'

'*Point 4*: the tape Sally left in her locker was stolen.'

'Right. *Point 5*: Sally gets some sort of salmonella poisoning.'

'*Point 6*: Sally is mugged and killed.'

'*Point 7*: Gwyneth is killed.'

'*Point 7* is David Jones' suicide, Pet. And his medical records are stolen, which is *Point 8*. Gwyneth being killed is *Point 9*.'

'All right. *Point 10*: we find out you don't have the gene for Huntington's; someone told a deliberate lie.'

'*Point 11*: we share the same biological father, as yet unknown.'

'*Point 12*: Bruce Traggard is involved, as we've said before.' She turned to Edward. '*Point 13*: Bruce Traggard might think or know you are his son. That's how he knew to pick you out for basketball. Unlucky thirteen; let's make sure it isn't unlucky for us. Someone, probably Bruce, is trying to keep a deadly secret. We haven't anything but guesswork to go on, but we've got to find out.'

Edward put the pencil down and stared at his list. 'Never mind unlucky thirteen, you've forgotten *Point 14*: you were conceived as a result of a donated sperm. We're pretty sure I was as well. What all this leads up to is that, instead of being our mothers' lover, we think Bruce Traggard might be the donor for both of us. In fact, that's much more likely. We know our mothers were living in London at the relevant time, so the obvious places to begin researching are the London sperm banks. They're our way to find out and prove who our biological father was.'

'Brilliant. We can narrow it down a bit; we're only interested in those London sperm banks which were around in the seventies – well, twenty-two years ago.'

'How do you figure that out?'

'It must be at least twenty-two years, as you're twenty-one – that's when you were conceived.'

Edward grinned at Petra. 'London, here I come!'

'Not you, Ed – *me*. We're being stupid. My mother *knows* which sperm bank she used. I'll arrange to go and stay with her and worm the name out of her. Anyway, I'm the one with the scientific training.'

'What about the baby?'

'You know my milk never came back after the shock of

Gwyn's death.' She wiped away a tear. 'You can give Corilla her bottle as well as I can.'

'No, Pet. It's going to be dangerous; whoever is murdering people isn't going to stop. There's too much at stake. I can't let you do it.'

'I'm the one who has a good alibi; I'll just be staying with my mother. She's quite keen to help, now she doesn't have to keep that secret any more. And one thing I do know, Ed; she's not a part of whatever has been going on. It was David Jones who had all that money, and she didn't know about it. It's *Point 15*: someone was coining money from some racket or other. I have to face the fact that he was involved, somehow. Maybe I can find some clues in his study. My mother hasn't touched it since he died.'

'So I'll come with you.'

'And the girls? We can't just leave them. They could be in danger, if only as hostages. No, one of us has to stay and look after them. You go and stay with the Joneses; they'll help you. It's too dangerous to stay here on your own.'

'Ian's in prison, Gwyneth's dead. We could use their house, I suppose. Right next door to Gran Megan.'

37

'All right if I use Daddy's old study, Mother?'

The relationship between Petra and her mother had
become much warmer since Louise had finally admitted
how Petra had been conceived. They were closer now than
at any time since Petra had left for university. They'd even
arranged for Louise to come down to Wales for the Easter
holiday.

'Of course, Pet. That's fine with me.'

'You've still got the computer?'

'It's the only room I haven't touched. Everything's just
as David left it.'

Petra and Louise were having breakfast together. Louise
was in her dressing gown, about to go upstairs and get
ready to go out. She was an official at the bridge club
which had become an important part of her life. She was
also turning into an outstanding player, excited because
there was talk of her representing her club the following
year.

She smiled at Petra. 'If you'd find it useful, I'll shove all
that equipment in the car when I come to Wales. It's just
going to waste here.' An apologetic smile. 'I'll be glad to
get rid of it. I rather want to turn that study into a bridge
room. The club is looking for a new venue.'

'What about Jack? Didn't he want all the special VCR
equipment?'

'He said not.' Her eyes were vague. 'I was a bit surprised. He and David spent so many hours playing about with it.'

'He didn't even want the basketball tapes?'

She shrugged. 'I've no idea; he might have taken them. He was in there for several hours, going through the desk drawers, sorting out material.'

'One other thing, Mother. Don't get upset – I have to know.' Louise had stood, clearly longing to escape upstairs. Petra had wondered how she was going to get the information out of her. Now was a golden opportunity. She was in a hurry, she wouldn't have time to think about her answer.

She looked at Petra, frowned. 'I'm already late. Well?'

'Which sperm bank did you use?'

'Insemination centre, I suppose you mean.' Louise rolled her eyes towards the ceiling. 'Not harping on about all that again, are you? You know they won't tell you who your father is!'

'Of course I know that.'

'So what's the point?'

She stood, walked up to her and put her arms around her mother's shoulders. 'Trust me; there is a point.'

'The mutated gene, I suppose. All that was over twenty years ago, Pet.' She sighed. 'I'm not sure I can remember just like that. I'd have to think about it, dredge it up. "Sperm-something-or-other", somewhere near Harley Street. It was meant to be the best place in the country. That's all I can remember.'

While her mother was dressing Petra picked up a copy of the Yellow Pages and searched for sperm banks. There was no mention of any such facility. She turned to Family Planning clinics. The numbers she rang were not exactly helpful, but eventually one of them referred her to the Human Fertilisation and Embryology Authority. The

HFEA, she was told, were in a position to let her have a list of *existing* centres for donor insemination.

Petra rang the HFEA; it didn't take long to write down the names of three centres within reasonable reach of Harley Street. There was no guarantee that one of them was the one her mother had used, but she had to start somewhere.

All three had somewhat similar names: Spermease, Spermsure and Spermfreeze. Two had been in business for some twenty years; Spermfreeze was relatively new, but it was in a side street off Marylebone High Street. That was very near Harley Street.

'Was it called Spermease?' she asked Louise as soon as she came down, ready to leave.

'Was what ... oh, you're still on about the centre. Doesn't immediately ring a bell, but it was something like that.' She frowned, picking up her handbag and gloves. 'You know, I think it was Sperm Donors Ltd. Quite a small place. I took the tube to Baker Street and walked from there. Then, on the day I had my first insemination, I walked around in Regent's Park, the rose garden. I remember thinking it would be good for the child I might be carrying.'

'Thanks, Mother,' she said. 'That's great.'

'That tells you where to look?'

'Gives me three places to start with,' she said. 'Better than nothing.'

The first centre she visited – Spermsure – put several difficulties in her way. It took her half an hour to progress from the receptionist through to the secretary of the Managing Director.

'We *never* jeopardise the anonymity of the donor, Mrs Dunstan. I'm very sorry ...'

'You don't understand. I'm not interested in who the donor is for myself; I want to make *you* aware of his genetic make-up, the fact that—'

'I'm very sorry. All medical record lists, appointment lists, and any documents relating to our work are kept under the strictest security. It is now the law that we preserve the anonymity of the donor. Since the 1990 Act...'

'I have to see the Managing Director. If you refuse to make an appointment for me I shall report you to the HFEA. I can assure you they'll revoke your licence.'

'But I have *told* you, Mrs Dunstan...'

'I've done my homework. I know perfectly well that it is a requirement of the code governing treatment practice that you have to be able to trace the genetic identity of babies resulting from DI. I'm here for precisely that reason: to tell you about an inherited disease passed on by a particular donor.'

'You know of an actual disease?'

'I've brought along the DNA analyses of my husband, myself and our two daughters. You will see that we all have the same mutated gene for height. In our daughters' cases it has resulted in gigantism. Now, *when* can I see the man in charge?'

'I'll see if he's free now.'

Petra already knew that all modern centres used a code which identified the individual donor without revealing his social identity. She was ushered into an adjoining office and asked to sit down. The centre was relatively small; only the Managing Director's desk and chair were on a gigantic scale. The MD himself was brusque, and to the point.

'It is extremely unlikely that such a mutation could get through, Mrs Dunstan. You see, the sperm bank we use doesn't accept any donors at the extremes of height. Our particular stipulation is men between the heights of five foot nine and six foot two. We do not favour anyone shorter or taller. I cannot believe that such a donor would be on our past list. What you're suggesting is that we match each donor's DNA to the ones you have just shown us; an impossible task.'

'Not exactly impossible,' she argued. 'They could be traced. But, in any case, I think we could narrow down the numbers. There's only one year between my husband and myself. We could cut down the range to donors on your books in the years 1973 *and* 1974 – that's when we were conceived.'

The Director laughed. 'And have you any idea how many donors that would involve?'

'Not as many as all that,' Petra said calmly. 'Weren't you quite a small centre at the time? And we can whittle it down still further. We only need to look for donors with characteristics of fair hair, blue eyes, Caucasians, tall.'

'A very popular description. Anything else?'

'And I do have one name: Bruce Traggard. He couldn't have used a false name since you check the medical records, don't you?'

'Not the records, no; we check with the GP. That's to prevent unforeseen problems, and duplication with other insemination centres. Certainly we'll check out that name, but what we really need are the names of the *mothers* involved. That narrows down the donors to the ones who produced the successful pregnancies. Much simpler.'

Petra blushed to the roots of her hair. 'You must think me awfully stupid,' she said. 'I never even thought of that.'

'We have the advantage of you, my dear. It is our job. I can have the mothers' names checked out for you.'

He came back, smiling. 'We've never had a donor called Bruce Traggard,' he told her. 'And neither of the women you named are on our records. I think that clears our centre for you.'

Waiting for this result had taken up a good part of the day. Disappointed, Petra walked away and took a cab to the next centre. She picked on Spermfreeze. That was in exactly the right area, just a few streets away from Harley Street.

As she drew up at the address, she took in a deep breath. She had to carry on. It would be easier to get through the red tape this time, to get straight to the point. And all her instincts told her she was on the right track.

It was already three o'clock on a Friday afternoon and she was exhausted. Just one more push for that day; one more try. She was sorely tempted to relax by having tea, to think rather than act. Perhaps she could leave Spermfreeze until Monday.

A picture of her little girls came into her mind. She wanted to get back to them, let someone else take over this chore. But she was right there now, in a small sidestreet just off Marylebone High Street. Something stirred in her memory – because it was near Harley Street, she supposed. She found herself outside a modern building, all glass and chrome. She couldn't quite work out why it seemed so familiar. She walked in, looked at the directory in the impressive reception hall, saw that Spermfreeze was on the fifth floor, got into the lift and pressed the button.

'I'm afraid the Director isn't available without an appointment,' the receptionist insisted.

'It's urgent – from your point of view as much as mine.' Petra fished a photograph of her children out of her handbag. 'Look, I've left my two little girls at home in Wales. I can't leave them for long, and today's Friday. Couldn't you help me?'

'A mutated gene for height, you said?'

'Yes.'

She was ushered into another office, where a man was sitting in an enormous upholstered leather chair across an elephantine desk. The set-up was awe-inspiring, but Petra didn't find herself overawed. She had a job to do.

'Mrs Dunstan? Do come in. I'm Gerald Osborne, the Deputy Director. Mr Brentford has already left for the weekend. How can we help you?'

The by-now familiar recitation.

'A most interesting mystery. Of course we'll do what we can.' A sudden smile. 'We're not just an insemination centre, you know. We pride ourselves on having the most up-to-date sperm bank in the country. We have pioneered some quite sensational developments. Our name, for example.'

'You mean the freeze part of Spermfreeze?'

'Exactly. I'm sure you know that all sperm are kept, frozen, for six months. Donors are tested at the time of donation, and again six months later, to make sure their blood isn't HIV positive.'

'Yes, I had heard that.'

'And the techniques for freezing sperm are very delicate. It was one of our people who discovered the best medium, quite early on. As early as the seventies, in fact. It's still being used.' He laughed. 'That medium is one of our biggest assets. Competitors haven't been able to come near it. We have less trouble with unfreezing sperm than any other centre.'

Petra tried to take an interest in the pep talk he was giving her.

'And you're quite right to be concerned, Mrs Dunstan. But here, at Spermfreeze, we can assure you that if this donor was among our past donors, we will find him. We don't just have coded records, you know. We keep frozen samples of sperm from each donor. That means we can run DNA analyses on any of our donors, present or past, and check for genetic problems before we even contact them again.'

She was utterly exhausted now. She felt a sort of apathy; why didn't she just settle for Planter helping her little girls? Finding the rogue donor couldn't help *them*. 'So you're certain you'd be able to trace this man, assuming he'd been a donor here?'

'Absolutely.'

She had to try; it would be terrible if she didn't even try. She gave a small, wan smile. 'You're wonderfully efficient.'

He looked at his watch. 'I'm not trying to put you off, Mrs Dunstan, but—'

'You have to leave?'

'I have another appointment. And it is getting late, and a Friday afternoon. But I do have an idea. Why don't I introduce you to our Sperm Storage Manager? He's the one who would be able to solve your problem. Let me take you up a floor, and right through to his office.'

'Tom, you're still here. I knew you would be.'

'Yes, Mr Osborne?'

'I've got a young lady here with a most unusual request. I know you can solve it for her and also, if one of our past donors was involved, check it out for us.'

'Anything I can do, Mr Osborne.'

'This is Tom Dryson, Mrs Dunstan. He's been Manager of our storage centre for two years. Taken over from a real genius, and trained by him.'

The Deputy Director was already by the door, making a graceful exit.

Tom Dryson was standing behind his desk, looking at her in a more than usually searching way. He'd focused on her eyes, noticed her irises. She felt irritation rising up inside at this small man with a fuzz of mouse-coloured hair on a large head, wearing thick glasses perched on a thin, sharp nose. She had the impression he was trying to sniff out some secret. She thought longingly of home, her little girls. Should she just walk away? What chance was there she'd find what she was looking for? And this unprepossessing man didn't strike her as a useful ally.

The purpose of what she was trying to achieve came back to her. She swallowed her annoyance. 'You've been in the sperm-bank business a long time?'

'About twenty years.'

A glimmer of real interest. 'Really? The centre I'm actually trying to trace was called Sperm Donors Ltd ...'

'Then you have found it. That's what we were called when I first started work. We changed to Spermfreeze in 1977.'

She felt quite faint; she'd found the right place! 'May I sit down?'

'Do forgive me; how stupid of me.'

'I didn't think I'd find it,' she breathed. 'And now I have. It means you'll almost certainly be able to help me.' She looked up at him, knowing she had to allow the adrenaline to subside, to give her brain a chance to function. 'Why did they change the name?'

'In celebration. 1977 was the year we came up with the best medium for freezing sperm in the business. Still is, as a matter of fact. We're at the forefront now, and always have been. We pride ourselves on that, here at Jorncy.'

The tiredness left her, she pulled in her breath. '*Jorncy*? Did you say Jorncy? I thought you just said you were Spermfreeze?' She looked down at her list again. 'That's where I thought I was!'

'We're part of the Jorncy group.'

That's what her unconscious had remembered when she'd first taken in the address. That's where her father always came to work. In a big, modern building off Marylebone High Street!

'You know,' she said slowly, carefully, looking at the big head and the eyes hidden behind the pebble glasses, 'that's quite a coincidence. My father worked for Jorncy.'

'Your father?' He stared at her, apparently unembarrassed to do so.

She blinked. 'Well, actually, as I'm sure you've already guessed, my biological father was a sperm donor. I call the man who brought me up my father; my nurturing father.'

'Of course. He's retired now?' He looked at her again, his eyes intense.

'He's dead.'

'I'm sorry to hear that, Mrs Dunstan.' The eyes searched hers again, the mouth open as though about to ask a question.

Something compelled her to go on. 'His name was David Jones. You didn't come across him, by any chance, did you? In the canteen or something?'

Tom Dryson's frame crashed back into his chair and rocked it violently. He grasped the desk to stop it. She saw his hands were shaking. 'David Jones?' His voice was thick with something that sounded like emotion. 'Was your father a Welshman?'

'You did know him?'

'You're Petra, aren't you? Do forgive me; it's the different-coloured irises.' A nervous, hurried look. 'Please don't misunderstand me. It's a most attractive trait. I always thought so when I saw the photograph he kept on his desk.' He smiled. 'He worked such long, long hours. Staying after everyone else had gone home, here at least an hour early in the mornings. And he was so fond of you, always talking about you. He couldn't have been prouder of you if he'd been your real father.'

'That's what fatherhood's about – being with a child, bringing her up.'

'So what can we do for you, Petra – if I may call you that? My name is Tom.'

'So nice to meet you, Tom.'

'I was so very sorry to hear about his death. A deep one, was David. Always a little sad, never seemed to enjoy the incredible discoveries he made. Just shrugged them off.'

'Discoveries?'

'He must have told you, surely! He found the best freezing medium for sperm in the whole business. And he found an outstanding way to freeze sperm, *and* to unfreeze it. He also invented a wrapper for transporting small samples of sperm at body temperatures, and protecting them from sudden movements. He was a pioneer.'

'He didn't really tell us much about his work. I thought he was a manager, not a scientist.'

'He was. I worked as his assistant for nearly twenty years. He taught me all I know.' He leaned forward intently. 'Your father was Manager of this facility, Petra. It was his work which put Spermfreeze on the map. A most gifted man, with a remarkably inventive mind. We always thought it was such a pity he had no qualifications to his name. He would have gone right to the top.'

'I suppose that's why I'm taking a degree.'

'He was such a modest man. You probably haven't any idea what he contributed. Let me explain: freezing sperm is a difficult and complicated process. The specimens have to be cryopreserved.'

'I'm afraid I don't know what that means.'

'Frozen in a preserving mixture which may contain glycerol, egg yolk, fructose, citrate and any other useful ingredient, all mixed in distilled water. David devised just the right mixture, and it's still a Jorncy trade secret. No one has bettered it in all this time.' He laughed. 'You've no idea, have you? The "Jo" in Jorncy comes from Jones!'

She gasped. 'He never told us anything about that!' Was that where the money had come from? Why hadn't he *told* them?

'Then we cool the sperm gently in the vapour of liquid nitrogen and store it immersed at a temperature of around − 196°C. The unfreezing is the really tricky bit; David managed to do it without harming the sperm.'

'I see. And that's what you do, now?'

'I've added a little technique of my own.'

'Well done.' Dare she ask if that was well rewarded? 'I always wanted my father to let me look round the place he worked in. He said Jorncy wouldn't like it.'

'We are very secretive, I'm afraid. You know why. We can't allow the clients to know who the donors are, and it works the other way around as well. We can't allow the donors to know who conceived a child by them.'

'Forgive my asking, but does Jorncy pay you when you make an outstanding discovery?'

'A small bonus − nothing to get excited about. I always told David he could have made a fortune if he'd left and patented his ideas. But he would never even discuss such a possibility.'

'But in spite of all the secrecy, you can identify donors, can't you? You have a code.'

'In case of problems, yes. And also to make sure that we don't allow more than ten live births from a single donor. We think that's fairly safe. Anything else could lead to problems with half-brothers and sisters.'

She wasn't going to tell him how right he was. 'And I understand you have a sample of each donor's sperm − a frozen sample which can be used to identify the donor, and his DNA.'

'DNA? You've come across a problem which shows up in a DNA analysis?'

'Yes,' she said, her voice low, her eyes turned away. 'My little girls; they've both inherited a mutated gene for height. It leads to gigantism.'

'And you've pinpointed it's the grandpaternal input. So you want to trace the donor responsible, and make sure we alert all his children and destroy the whole stock of existing sperm. Have I got that right?'

'Exactly right. Do you think you can help? Mr Osborne said you had all the records.'

'In theory, of course we do.'

'What do you mean, in theory? Have some of them been destroyed?'

'We keep frozen sperm for ten years, Petra. That means we have to search the records for the ten years before the date in question, as well as the actual year of conception.'

Her heart sank. 'Which year did my father perfect the freezing technique?' she asked. 'Did you say 1977?'

He smiled. 'Quite right; I remember David said it was your second birthday that day. You've already worked out that we can forget frozen sperm. I can see you're your nurturing father's daughter.' His eyes twinkled. 'Quite a little triumph for the nurture versus nature debate, eh?'

She was too tense even to smile; all she was concentrating on was getting to the bottom of the mystery.

'Well now, if you'll just give me your mother's name. Then I'll have to get the Deputy Director's agreement to run through the programme.'

She could feel her face fall. 'He has to agree it?'

'He has the second part of the password to access the information. We really do try to keep both sides anonymous, you know.' He smiled reassuringly. 'Once we have the password, it doesn't take long. Now, what about your mother's christian names?' He handed her a pencil and a piece of paper.

'I'm afraid there's more than one woman involved. I have two names I'd like you to run.'

She wrote down Louise Penn Jones and Ethel Dunstan. That would, of course, make Tom Dryson aware that she was concerned about her husband's father as well as her own. She couldn't help that.

Tom Dryson looked at her quizzically, but made no comment. He rang through to Mr Osborne's office. 'It won't take more than a few minutes, Stella,' she could hear him urge the secretary. 'Can't you fit me in?'

At last he turned around. 'Sorry, but this may take some time. I've got to catch him between meetings. Would you like to go out and come back again? I'll be here till half past five.'

'If you don't object, I'd prefer to stay,' she said. 'It's taken a long time to get to this stage. Meanwhile I'll think the implications through.'

'Make yourself comfortable; have my chair. There's a coffee machine in the corridor.' He stood, and walked towards a steel cupboard. She saw compassionate eyes smile at her. 'No one ever came to claim the few things David left. I've kept them in a box. Maybe you'd like to look through them. I'm sure you'd like the picture of you, for a start.'

He unlocked the cupboard door. Behind it Petra saw a terrifying assembly of files.

'We're putting them all on disk, but it takes time. Right, here we are.' He handed her a shoe box. The lid had

DAVID JONES on it, spelled out in large capitals. Brown parcel tape secured it, tight, to the lower part.

Tom Dryson went out of the office and Petra was left to undo the box as best she could. She used the balls of her fingertips to find the end of the tape, then her right index fingernail to loosen a corner, and slowly, gently, she unravelled the sticky mass.

The first thing she saw was the framed photograph of herself – taken, she guessed, when she was sixteen. Underneath it was a double frame she remembered giving her father for a present; he'd used it for photographs of Dylan and Megan Jones the way they must have looked when David left home. There were several family pictures, one of Gwyneth on her own, and Gwyneth's wedding photograph.

The last picture was of four young people, their arms around each other, making faces. But she could recognise them all the same. David and Gwyneth Jones, Ian Davies and Jack Oliver. 'The gang of four', Gwyneth had called them. Something about Jack's face, the way he seemed to dominate the group, made her frown. This picture was telling her a story, but she couldn't understand the language.

There were only two more items in the box. A small key, and an envelope addressed to the IOM bank which held the trust funds. No address, and no stamp, but the envelope was sealed. Her fingers shook. She was about to open it when Tom Dryson came back into the room.

'I'm sure you'd like to have all those little mementoes.'

She sighed her relief. 'I would, thank you so much.' She opened her briefcase and put the contents of the shoebox inside. 'You've got the other half of the password?'

'All done. I've run the two names you gave me through the computer files.' He wasn't smiling.

'You've found the mothers?'

'Indeed; both present and correct.' He looked at her intently. 'And they had different sperm donors. However, Mrs Dunstan did have two children from the same donor. We always try to use the same donor when a client wants another child. We only refuse when the donor has exceeded the number of live offspring we allow for him.' He looked up at her. 'Actually, we now have a policy of keeping back some sperm for women who tell us they would like more than one baby.'

Petra stared into space. She'd found the sperm bank, she'd theoretically found her daughters' grandfathers. And yet she knew Tom's information was wrong. Dr Planter couldn't have made that sort of mistake. He'd been very careful to check his findings.

'That can't be right, Tom. I know these two donors have to be one and the same man. You see, my husband and I had our DNAs analysed by a top endocrinologist. He found that Edward and I have the same mutated gene for height. There's no doubt about it; the analyses prove we're half-brother and sister.' She held the DNA reports out to him. 'Here, have a look. You'll see what I mean.'

Tom Dryson took the sheets, but wouldn't meet her eyes.

'Could there be a mistake in the records?'

He looked up at last. 'I don't think so; we really are very careful.'

'There's always human error...'

He returned her reports and shuffled papers on his desk. 'I don't think that's what we're dealing with here. Not that sort of human error, anyway.'

'You mean you think you know what happened?'

He took his glasses off, polished them, put them on again. 'I think I shut my eyes to certain things, Petra.' His

414

voice was very low. 'I hero-worshipped your father, and it made me blind.'

A suspicion – a terrible theory – was beginning to form in her mind. Was it something other than modesty which had prevented her father from sharing his scientific triumphs with his family, with the world? Had David Jones been carrying on a more sinister, and more lucrative, trade?

Tom Dryson cleared his throat. 'The DNA analyses show that you and your husband share a biological father, so our records *must* be wrong. There's only one way that could have happened. Someone must have substituted sperm. That could have been done by someone working here. And, I'm sorry to tell you, David was in a position to do so.' He shrugged. 'With hindsight, I can see he might have done just that.'

Petra swallowed. Had he simply substituted the sperm of a very tall man for sperm from other fair, blue-eyed men? And if he had, *how* were they going to find that donor? She remembered the little key she'd just come across. Her father had shown her a small drawer he'd fitted under the desk in his study. It was possible he'd hidden a list there; names of donors whose sperm he'd substituted. She'd try the key on that drawer.

'I do know of a man I suspect might be the donor. Could we look for him?'

He nodded. 'So what's his name?'

'Bruce Traggard.'

'And his characteristics?'

'Fair-haired, blue-eyed, Caucasian, very tall – six foot four.'

Tom looked at her and shook his head. 'I'll run it through, but I'm afraid we wouldn't have accepted him. Too tall, you see.'

While Tom was running Bruce Traggard's name, a sudden thought flashed through Petra's mind.

'No luck, I'm afraid. I thought not.'

'Let's turn my premise on its head,' she said, breathless and eager. 'Do you have records of would-be donors who were turned down?' Her voice was grainy, her eyes bleak. 'From the early seventies, say? Would that be something you could put your hands on?'

He looked at her hard and long, then down at the list of codes he'd brought. He unlocked the top drawer of his desk, placed it inside and locked it again. 'Yes,' he said softly. 'Indeed. That is something that I *can* lay my hands on. And it won't take long.'

He opened the steel cupboard door and pulled out four large, foolscap-sized ledger books. 'No need for me to beat about the bush with these,' he said. 'It's just an old-fashioned list of names, with brief reasons why the men were turned down, and their Healthcare Trust. Not even in alphabetical order, I'm afraid. In order of dates. I've brought out the names of donors we rejected from 1970–1974. Those are the years you want to look at, aren't they?'

'My husband was conceived in 1973, so we can leave out 1974. You don't mind if I go through them?'

'David was a dear friend of mine. I never understood why he committed suicide; somehow it's got to be tied up with all this. So you think we're looking for this tall man you mentioned?'

'Bruce Traggard, yes,' she said, hissing the name.

He handed her the ledgers. 'Thanks,' she said, her voice husky as she took the books from him. 'I'd like to start with 1970.'

'Just one thing, Petra. I think *you* should bear something else in mind. Maybe you don't even know what name you're looking for. But you'll recognise it when you see it.'

'Yes,' she whispered, wondering what they'd find, almost too scared to look.

'I'll scan through 1973 for Bruce Traggard. Here's 1970 for you.'

The first books yielded nothing. Without a word they started on the next two, Petra taking the year 1971.

She ran her finger down the line of names, the T of Traggard in her mind, when she saw her father's writing of the capital letter O; it sent a cold chill of terror down her spine. Because it wasn't Bruce Traggard they should have been looking for. Tom Dryson was right; once she'd grasped that the man whose sperm was switched for the logged-in samples might be connected with a *rejected* donor, there was no special reason to look for Bruce Traggard.

The point was not who the particular donor was. The significant point – the horrifying point – was that Jack Oliver and David Jones were the ones who chose him. Spermfreeze had nothing at all to do with it.

38

'You've found Bruce Traggard?' Tom Dryson looked at her anxiously. 'You look as though you're about to pass out. I'll get you some water.'

'I've found a name I recognise,' she whispered. 'But it isn't Bruce Traggard. It's someone else I know, and the last name I'd have expected to find.'

'Someone you know?'

Her laugh ricocheted around the room, bouncing off the steel wall, harsh, loud. 'I know him very well.'

He walked over to her and put his arm around her shoulders. 'That's why we keep all this a secret. I shouldn't have lost sight of the fact that if you found a name, you'd know he was your father. I've broken all the rules. I'm so terribly sorry, Petra. Talking about David ... I suppose I miss him. I got carried away.'

She broke into a half-laugh, half-cry of despair. 'Don't worry, Tom. I don't mean he's my father. I mean he's the one who's behind all this!'

It was obvious enough, now that she knew. Jack was the one who actually told her parents about Edward's alleged genetic defect. All he had to do was lie, and falsify the DNA report to convince David.

'What's his name, Petra? I'm the one who allowed it to happen; that's unforgivable. I owe it to you – to the others like you – to help.'

She put her hands up to her face, pushed back her hair. 'That's why he was always at our house! Keeping an eye on me as I was growing up. He's arranged for a whole "family"!'

'Who, Petra? Who are you talking about? We have to have his *name*.'

'Jack Oliver,' she whispered. 'His name's Jack Oliver.' She thought back to how Jack and David would disappear for hours into David's study, watching videos of games, analysing them, enlarging sections of frames. 'He and David grew up together in a little village near Llandrindod Wells. Did my father – David – ever mention him?'

'Yes. He runs some sort of agency now, doesn't he?'

'A highly successful one.' She remembered standing outside David's study, hearing the laughter coming from inside, snatches of conversation: 'There's another one in Ealing, Dewi. Working a treat, is it.'

'The funny thing is,' she heard Tom Dryson say, 'that after all these years he's stuck in my mind.'

She frowned. 'You mean you know him?'

'Cocky little bastard; made one hell of a fuss when we turned him down. I was only a junior then – a glorified tea boy – but I clearly remember him standing there, all five foot of him, and really letting us have it.'

She thought about the photo she'd just seen. The gang of four – and Jack was the one who headed it. He'd always been the leader, the one responsible, the one in charge. He'd egged Ian on to steal, incited David and Gwyneth to set fire to incomers' cottages – perhaps as much to have power over them as anything else. David and Ian had protected Gwyneth. But why had David Jones allowed himself to be forced into such a scheme? Because of Gwyneth, Petra was sure. *That's* what Jack had used to blackmail David. Gwyneth's involvement – something the police knew nothing about, but which he could pin on her if he felt so inclined.

Tom Dryson was putting the records away again. 'He had a sort of point, you know. He was good-looking, with a remarkable grasp of language – and vocabulary! And we turned him down just because he was short. That's pure prejudice.'

'Not really; he's a pituitary dwarf. His GP would have pointed that out to you, and you would have had to turn him down in any case.'

The Jack Oliver Media Agency had started ten years ago, when Jack spotted Phil. How did Jack know so precisely where to look for his talent? Because he and David had been breeding basketball players? She felt sick as she thought of the terrible things Jack must have made David do.

'Mind you,' Tom said, looking pensive, 'I thought at the time that his reaction was extreme. There was something – I can't explain it – sort of not quite right about him. Very intense, somehow. Arrogant.'

Petra turned wet eyes on him. 'The Napoleon syndrome. He goes crazy about his lack of height. The sperm bank picked on the very reason which would have made him flip.' So that's where the money in the trust fund had come from. Jack had paid David – no doubt handsomely – every time there was a successful insemination, every time they cashed in with one of their 'family'.

She turned to Tom. 'I've had an idea. Would you be able to get his medical records from Powys, do you think?'

He frowned. 'What good would that do?'

'Maybe we can find the name of the doctor who treated him. If he's the brain behind this, maybe there's a record of some psychological problem. That would help tie him in.'

He shrugged. 'If they still have that information. Those records are likely to have been sent to another authority.'

'I don't think so. He's always boasting that he hasn't had a day's illness since he left Wales. Says the Welsh hospital mucked him about, and he's never going to let anyone mess about with him again.'

'Well, if they still have them, and we request them, they'd send them to us eventually. It would take time, though.'

'Could you give them a ring? Find out if they're still there?'

He looked at his watch. 'Four-thirty on a Friday afternoon? Not much chance, I'd say.'

'You promised you'd help, Tom. I'm thinking of my girls, and the many other children who might be at risk with this bombshell in their genes.' Her eyes were still wet with tears. 'There could be *hundreds* of them.'

'Baby roulette,' he said reflectively. 'I've often thought that we were a glorified gambling house. But this isn't just gambling – this is gambling with loaded dice, a whole cargo of faulty sperms projected into different ova. The laws of chance mean that there will often be a hit.' He picked up the phone.

'Llandrindod Wells Hospital,' Petra said. 'That's where he had the treatment, whatever it was.'

'Stella? Tom Dryson. Could you get me Llandrindod Wells Hospital? That's in Wales.'

He turned to Petra. 'D'you know which Healthcare Trust?'

'Powys.'

'It's Powys, Stella.'

'The chance of the faulty gene getting through could be as high as one in two, Tom. And we can't stop it happening even now. I can't *prove* anything.'

'Don't be too sure of that,' he said, the soft eyes now grim, his cheeks sucked in. 'I always knew there was something strange about David. He wasn't just shy and withdrawn – he was fearful, somehow.' He turned back to the phone. 'Sorry, Stella. Yes, I'm here.' He held the receiver to his ear, his face changing from anticipation to disappointment.

'Thanks, Stella.'

'Gone home for the weekend?'

'Their record file office was broken into recently. They haven't got it sorted yet.'

Ian. It was beginning to add up. *That* was why Ian had broken into the hospital, and why the medical record files were with the drugs! Now she knew who the second file Gwyneth had found belonged to. Jack had paid Ian to steal *his* medical record file as well as David's. A voice began to sound in her ear, a Welsh voice, lilting, halting – Gwyneth saying some phrase. What was it?

'We're never going to be able to prove anything!' she cried, almost reaching the highs of hysteria.

'We haven't even begun yet.' The dogged look of the true researcher showed in Tom's face. 'We've tracked down two men who might have been tampering with sperm; I think we've done quite well for starters.' He took her hand. 'I know we've only just met, Petra, but somehow I feel I've known you all your life. David was so very proud of you. If you'll let me, I'd like to help you get to the bottom of this.'

'But how, Tom? If Jack Oliver's involved, it's going to be very tough to pin him down.'

'We have one trump card, don't forget. If we can find evidence to link Bruce Traggard into this, the police can get hold of a non-intimate sample and test his DNA. If that correlates with yours and your husband's, that's proof.

Forget about the crimes; let's concentrate on identifying the donor.'

Suddenly Sally's small, retching figure came back to Petra. During their last night together in their room in Mardon, Sally had tried so hard to convince her that something really horrific was going on. 'I've got to get out of here before they kill me,' she'd said. And she'd thought Sally deluded, crazed by grief.

Sally had been right all along; she was the key. And Sally had always been convinced that Bruce Traggard was involved. Was that why she'd been murdered?

39

Louise was on the phone, making last-minute arrangements involving her bridge club. She was in her element, organising the end of the tournament. It meant Petra had most of the day to herself; it would give her the chance to track Beatrice Wheeler down. She'd been trying to do so ever since she got back from Spermfreeze last night, but her mother had insisted they meet up with some friends. She hadn't even had a chance to speak to Ed.

She tried to find Beatrice Wheeler's number in the phone book. It wasn't there. When she asked Directory Enquiries, they told her there was no number listed under that name. Had Mrs Wheeler moved, or simply decided to do without the expense of a phone?

She waited for her mother to finish her latest call, then rang for a cab. While she waited, she tapped in Gwyneth's number. The line was engaged. She tried Megan's number, allowing it to ring for a long time. No answer. Ed must be feeding the children at Gwyneth's place, she smiled to herself.

As she was about to try Gwyneth's number again the cabby rang the doorbell. Ed would be upset that she hadn't phoned him before she went out, but she'd ring as soon as she returned.

'I'm just off, Mother,' she called to Louise, now sitting at her desk in her living room.

'Bye, Pet. I'll be out when you get back,' she answered cheerfully, 'but I'll be home between half five and six.'

Petra shut the front door behind her and settled into the cab. It wasn't till then that she thought back to the papers in her briefcase, and the letter addressed to the IOM bank.

She pulled it out and opened the envelope. A deposit slip filled in for £25,000 was inside, along with two cheques, both from different IOM banks. She turned over the first one; it was dated the day her father committed suicide.

Pay Petra Penn Jones Trust Fund
The sum of: twenty-five thousand pounds only.
Signed: David Jones.

She turned the second cheque around, already knowing what she'd find. It was dated a week before the other cheque.

Pay David Jones
The sum of: twenty-five thousand pounds only.
Signed: Jack Oliver
Jack Oliver Media Agency

The 'only' was such a nice touch. David hadn't even bothered to put it into his bank. He must have lost heart; the question was – why? What had changed? What had made him suddenly decide he couldn't take it any longer?

'This it?' the cabby asked, stopping outside the flat where she'd helped an excited little Sally carry her duffle bag. That was the last time she'd seen her friend. She felt the tears begin to prick, and wiped them determinedly away. 'I'll get him for you, Sal,' she whispered to herself. 'I'll see he pays for it.'

She saw the cabby looking at her. 'Yes or no?'

426

'Yes, that's the one.' She paid him off, stared at the nameplate and saw that Beatrice Wheeler's name was still there. She pressed the bell, and waited.

After two minutes she pressed the bell again, tentatively. Beatrice Wheeler would be older now. Perhaps she found it even harder to manage the stairs.

'Who is it?'

'It's Petra, Mrs Wheeler. Sally's friend.'

The door opened and a much thinner, somewhat wizened Beatrice Wheeler held out her arms. 'Petra! It's so good to see you. I've been trying to get hold of you. I tried ever so hard, but I just couldn't find you. No one seemed to know where you were. Not even your mum!'

'I'm sorry, Mrs Wheeler. We should have been in touch.'

'You said you would be, when you'd settled down somewhere.' She pulled Petra inside and began a slow but steady climb up the stairs. 'I've lost a bit of weight; makes it easier to cope.'

'You're keeping all right?'

'I've got my brother's family to keep me sane. I told you about them, didn't I, dear?'

'Like your own grandchildren, you said.'

She beamed at Petra and pointed her towards the flat. It had improved; the furniture was new, there was a large television in the corner, and a VCR underneath. 'That nice Mr Oliver helped me out after Sally ... you know. Said she was as good as Phil Thompson's wife, and he wanted me to have a bit of the pension Sally would have got. I couldn't take it, but I didn't like to refuse the things he sent.'

Petra could feel the gagging in her throat, but forced her eyes to smile.

'You all right, dear?'

White anger made her hot. 'I'm all right, really. It's just that seeing you reminds me of Sally. It's funny how like you she was.'

Beatrice's eyes slid away. 'I'll get us a pot of tea. And you can see the tape I've been keeping for you.'

'The tape?' Petra stared at her. Could she mean the tape she'd taken of Phil's last game? Sally had always insisted that that tape would show how he'd been murdered. And Sally hadn't taken it to Jack's that day because she'd been too honest to pass off work which wasn't hers! 'You mean you've kept it?'

'She was always on about it. Said it was yours, that you took it. Ever so good it was, she said.'

She rummaged underneath her set, pulled out a tape and slotted it into the machine. 'I've watched it once or twice. I'm not being rude, love, but I don't know what she was going on about. Nothing much on it, really. Few minutes of that basketball game, and a few bits at the end with the camera at all angles.' She pressed play.

It all came back to Petra then; meeting Edward for the first time, being introduced to Phil, the way he'd refused to kiss Sally – had held her friend at arm's length. She watched, tears pouring down her face as she relived the action.

Phil Thompson, all six foot nine of giant man, was about twenty-five feet from the basket. She remembered taping him, centering the tall, athletic body in her sights, and pressing the firing button.

'I suppose she clung to it because it was her last sight of Phil.'

'Have you shown it to anyone else, Mrs Wheeler?'

She smiled. 'No. It didn't seem much to show them. And very sad.' Then her eyes lit up for a moment. 'I would have shown Mr Oliver, but he was in such a hurry when he came.

Asked if I had any more of Sally's tapes. I couldn't pretend this one was hers; she was always on about how you took it. Ever so strict about not taking credit for other people's work, she was.'

'Mr Oliver asked you about Sally's tapes?'

'Well, I'm not sure which ones he meant. Asked if I had a tape of when Phil was took bad. Maybe he meant that one – but then he kept talking, and it slipped my mind. He never came back no more.'

'You don't mind if I take it away with me?'

'It's yours, love; that's what she said. Ever so fussed about it she was, poor dear. But then, it was the illness, wasn't it? Terrible, that. And losing Phil, I suppose.' Beatrice smiled through her tears. 'Let's talk about you, instead. Did you marry that boyfriend you were so keen on?'

Petra laughed. 'I did, and we've got two little girls. Look, I've brought along some photographs. See?' She pressed them on her. 'I can get more done. You keep them if you'd like to.'

Beatrice stared at the pictures of the little girls. 'I suppose I'm getting old and silly,' she said, a sort of wonder in her voice, 'but I could swear that's the look Sally used to have as a baby. I'll show you.'

Before Petra could stop her she'd rushed into the small hall behind the living room, opened a cupboard and pulled out an old photograph album.

'This is my Sal when she was eighteen months. See that? Isn't that like your little girls?'

Petra stared, her heart pounding in her chest, the sweat beginning to bead on her forehead, moistening her underarms. Her little girls didn't have eyes like Sally's, but they had her impish smile, the crease around the eyes, the way the lids were set.

429

'Tell me about Sally, Mrs Wheeler,' she said, her voice soft and breathy. 'She *was* adopted, wasn't she?'

Beatrice's irises had the ring of age around them, but they were the same eyes as Sally's. 'That's what we put out,' she said. 'But Sally was mine.'

'Yours?'

'My own. Her dad was the infertile one.'

Petra felt as though an electric current had gone through her. She jolted upright. 'You mean you had her by donor insemination? You went to a centre?'

'Yes, dear, I did. Ever so secret it was in them days, but we both wanted her so much. My brother put me on to it. Said it were easier than trying to adopt.'

'A lovely idea,' Petra said, putting her hand on Beatrice's gnarled one.

'I'm not much of a one for secrets. I always told Sally everything, straight out. She was the one didn't want it known. She liked to put it about she were adopted.'

'She was always upset about her height. *Is* that why she was so small, d'you think? Her biological father passed that down to her – pituitary dwarfism?' Jack suffered from that, and it was an hereditary trait. Had David actually substituted *Jack's* sperm for one of the donors? Could he have been as irresponsible as that?

'Pituitary dwarfism? Sally were a midget, if that's what you mean. That's what Joe – that's my brother – said. One of her glands didn't have sufficient hormones; we had to have them injected into her. Nothing like that in our family.'

'Did your brother suggest you tell the sperm bank?'

'Oh, yes. They tested the sperm, traced it back all right. Wouldn't let the same stuff be used again. Lucky our Joe—'

She held her breath. 'Which sperm bank was it, Mrs Wheeler?'

The older woman looked at her, and frowned. 'Which sperm bank? Why do you want to know that?'

'My daughters; they've got a problem, too.'

Beatrice looked at the photographs again. 'I can't see nothing wrong, Petra. My Sally looked like a little Cindy doll. Your girls are on the large side, I'd say.'

She nodded. 'On the large side, yes. Too large; same difference.'

'But you didn't—'

'Not me, my mother.'

Beatrice Wheeler smiled. 'I don't mind telling you – I don't mind *who* knows. I'll never forget it, I was that pleased. Sperm Donors Ltd, it were... Are you all right, dear? You look that white!'

Petra drank some more tea. 'I'm all right, Mrs Wheeler. You were saying?'

'Funny thing is, that Mrs Thompson. Bit of a stuck-up so-and-so, but she came over special to see me. Soon as Phil asked Sally to marry him.'

That began to sound like a familiar pattern; another mother worried as soon as there was talk of marriage. 'On her own, you mean?'

Beatrice drew herself up. 'My Sal, she wasn't a one for telling lies. She told Phil straight off; told him what was what.'

'You mean, she told him she was a DI child?'

'Would you believe it? He was as well. That's why his mother come running, slumming or not!' She laughed, and Petra squeezed her hand. 'Said she wanted to make sure she knew the kind of dad I'd chosen for my Sal. Told her I wanted someone like her own dad – well, like my Burt, the one she called her dad. Not too tall, fair hair and blue eyes. Not what Phil's mum asked for. She asked for tall.' She looked sad. 'Sally had already let on to Phil about being a midget. Mrs Thompson wasn't too pleased with that. So I told her it wasn't in my family.'

Petra cleared her throat, but her voice still sounded breathy. 'And did she tell you which centre she'd used?'

Beatrice shrugged. 'Same one, would you believe. She wanted fair hair and blue eyes as well, but what she asked for special was tall.'

Petra rushed out, unable to stop her stomach heaving. She found the kitchen sink.

Beatrice padded after her. 'Whatever's wrong, dear? I'll find you a flannel.' She came back with one, and held it out for Petra. 'Not coming down with a bug, are you?'

Petra gasped, wiped her mouth, filled a glass and drank some water. 'The same insemination centre, did you say?'

'That's right, dear. That's why I remember it so well. Very same one – it's the best there is. Gone all modern, it has. They call it Spermfreeze now.'

40

'I'll make real Welsh Rarebit,' Megan said, bustling around Gwyneth's kitchen and feeding Jacintha spoonfuls of mashed banana. '*Caws Wedi'i Bobi*.' Sad eyes watched Edward giving Corilla a bottle. 'Are you quite comfortable here?'

'Everything's fine. It's very good of you to let us stay.'

'That's what family's for.' She kissed her little great-granddaughter. 'Poor Gwyneth was so fond of you all. She would have wanted...' She handed the dish with the banana to Angharad and wiped her eyes with her apron. 'I just can't seem to settle to it. First David, and now Gwyneth. Was it the cleft palate, do you think? Is that why they died young – they couldn't cope with it?'

'Nothing to do with that, Mam.' Angharad put the dish down and folded her arms around her mother. 'You know it was Ian who made her life a misery.'

'We shouldn't have let him come back!'

'You weren't to know he could have such a terrible thing in mind, Gran Megan,' Edward said, putting a hand on her arm. 'Think of the future, not the past. You've got your first great-grandchildren now. Think of that.' Petra and Edward had agreed not to tell Megan that David wasn't Petra's father. They were well aware that David's death had been a blow to Megan, but Gwyneth's death had left her devastated. She didn't seem able to get used to the fact that her daughter was no longer next door, popping in morning and evening, gossiping.

The tears wouldn't stop. 'I've got to go and get Dad's dinner. Bring the little ones round when they've had their nap.'

The phone in the hall began to ring just as Jacintha spilled her orange juice.

Edward felt excitement go through him as he rushed to answer it. 'I'll get it. Must be Petra at last; I wondered why she hadn't rung us yet. She knows I've got to get home.'

'Can't Gareth manage the farm?'

'He's getting old, Angie. He can't run it on his own for days on end.' He walked out into the hall and picked up the receiver. 'Hello?'

'What the bloody fuck are you playing at, Ian? Where the hell are—'

'Hold on there . . .'

'*Hen gythral* . . . you cunting *gythral*. Said you were going to send them—'

'*Jack*! It's Edward here.'

The line went silent.

'Jack? That is you, isn't it?'

'Hello, Edward.' His voice had taken on its normal honeyed tones. 'I thought I was ringing Ian Davies. Did I dial your number instead?' He laughed, a nervous, brittle sound. 'Must have pressed the wrong memory button!'

'You haven't heard? Ian's in prison.'

Another pause. 'In prison? Last I heard he'd been released.'

'I suppose you wouldn't know what's happened. Gwyneth's dead. They've booked Ian on suspicion of her murder.'

'My God, Edward!' He could hear Jack suck in his breath with a sort of hissing noise. 'Murder? They think he murdered her?'

Jack could be a cold bastard. He'd known Gwyneth all through his childhood and he didn't even react to the news of her death. 'She died in a car crash, Jack. They say he tampered with the brakes. Pengwyn Hill did the rest.'

'So our Gwyneth's dead, is she?' Jack's voice sounded shaken, then Edward could hear him clear his throat. 'How's the old lady taking it?'

'Badly. The kids and I are staying next door.'

'You're in the house?'

Something in the tone reminded Edward that he couldn't take anything, or anyone, for granted. 'Just for a day or two. Petra's in London with her mother.' He heard Petra's voice, warning him that they were all in danger, never to let the girls out of his sight. 'You know how women are. Now she and Louise are getting on again, she's collecting a few of David's things as mementoes.' He covered his anxiety with a laugh. 'And bringing Louise back with her to see something of her granddaughters.' Why was Jack ringing Ian?

'She's staying with Louise for the weekend?' The voice was as he'd almost always heard it; gentle, persuasive. 'Unlike her to leave her babies.'

Think on your bloody feet! Edward urged his brain. 'Well ... you know. Burying the hatchet, Jack. She'll be back tonight – tomorrow at the latest.'

'Thought you said Louise was coming back with her?'

Lying didn't come easily to him. He blew his nose and produced an imaginary cough. 'Sorry, frog in my throat. *They*'ll be back. I've got to go, Jack. Kids, and all that.'

'Quite the house-husband.'

'Anything I can do for you?'

'Do?' The voice sounded irritable.

'What were you ringing for?'

A chuckle – quite a convincing one, Edward felt, resentment against Jack now pounding blood through his neck. 'Just something Ian was meant to do for me. I like to put a job in his way every now and again. For old time's sake.' Another chuckle, not quite so easy. 'Should have known better. He's always let me down.'

Edward clicked the receiver into its cradle, an anxious feeling in his guts. He'd had the impression that Jack had not been in contact with anyone he'd known as a child since he and David had left home, nearly twenty-five years before.

'Petra all right?'

'It wasn't Pet.' Edward lifted Jacintha up and cuddled her. 'When did you say she rang last night?'

'I've told you, Ed – around six, just before you got back. She asked about the kids and you, then said she'd promised to go and meet some of her mother's friends. She said she'd ring again this morning.'

'Can't understand why she hasn't. Was she all right? She didn't sound worried?'

'She was fine, honestly, otherwise I'd have told you!' She took the empty bottle out of Corilla's mouth. 'Someone for Gwyn, was it? Glad you took it this time. There are so many calls, and I'm always bursting into tears.'

'Not for Gwyneth, no. Rather odd, really. Jack Oliver for Ian. I thought they hadn't been in touch since Jack left Wales.'

'Jack, was it? He'd heard about Gwyn?'

Now that he thought back, Jack had been sure that Ian would answer the phone. 'No; seems he had no idea. Just started in, lambasting Ian.' He swung Jacintha up and down and she crowed with pleasure. 'I'm not really in the know, but I didn't think they'd been in touch lately. Gwyneth would have mentioned it, I'm sure. I thought they

couldn't stand each other because Ian went to prison and
Jack got off scot free.'

'And Ian and Dewi protected Gwyn.'

'No thanks to Jack, apparently.' He put Jacintha down,
and held out his arms for Corilla. 'So why's he ringing Ian?'
He didn't like the feel of it, all back to front somehow.

'He asked for Ian?'

'He assumed Ian was answering the phone. When it
turned out to be me he said he'd asked Ian to do a job for
him.'

Angharad stared at him, her mouth open. 'My God, Ed,
what's going on? Gwyn did mumble something about Jack,
that he was up to his old tricks, that now she understood the
significance of the records.'

'Records? What records? Ian stole some CDs, you
mean?'

'The medical records stolen from the hospital. Gwyn
couldn't understand why Ian would want to steal from the
hospital at all. The equipment's useless, and there weren't
enough drugs to make it worthwhile. That left the records.
One of them was Dewi's, she said. She went on about Jack
being involved, something to do with someone called
Bruce...'

Edward handed the baby back to Angharad. 'I know I
sound over the top, Angharad, but I have to get hold of
Petra.'

He went back into the hall and tapped in Louise's
number. It was engaged. Why didn't she have call waiting,
for God's sake? This was the modern world they were living
in... He pressed redial. Still engaged.

'Look, Angharad. It's the most awful cheek but I know
something's really wrong – something to do with Jack and
Petra. Can you and Megan take over the kids today, and a
bit of tomorrow maybe?'

'You look terrible, Edward, *bach*. Whatever's going on?'

'Don't know yet; I'm going on gut feeling. Jack Oliver's at the bottom of all this. I don't know how I could have been so stupid for so long. I think Petra's in terrible danger, Angharad.'

'Danger?'

'Gwyneth's been murdered, Ian's the prime suspect. And suddenly Jack rings Ian. Two other people were murdered two years ago. Pet and I thought they died in accidents. We were wrong; I think he murdered both of them. He'll kill Petra if he gets a chance. I've got to go.' His voice was husky as he raced upstairs, pulled on a sweater and grabbed his anorak.

He pressed redial again. Still busy. 'He's a murderer, Angharad. He'll kill the girls as well.'

'You've forgotten, Ed. He's in prison because of Gwyneth.'

'Not Ian, for God's sake – Jack!'

She stared at him.

'Don't let them out of your sight for a single moment,' he told her urgently. He kissed his daughters, put an arm around Angharad's shoulders. 'I know I sound demented. Will you do it for me?'

'It's all right, Edward,' Angharad said. 'Gwyneth's been murdered, and I can see it now. It wasn't Ian; he hasn't got the brains to have worked it out.'

Jack slammed the receiver down, his eyes flashing. So petulant Petra had caught on that something was going on, and was up in London trying to work it out. What the devil had possessed the girl to start measuring her infants' lengths? And why hadn't the medical profession been able to convince her that that was no yardstick for eventual height? He kicked himself. It was *he*, of all people, who'd alerted her. How could he have been such a fool?

At least he'd had the intelligence to take Louise out to dinner, to find out what she'd told them.

'So they brought the children up to see you?' he'd asked her, sounding casual.

The refined hostess laugh. 'Well, hardly that, Jack. They came up to have the children checked out by some bigwig consultant in Great Ormond Street. You know how Petra fusses.'

He'd known right away that Louise was holding something back. Why was she suddenly on Petra's side?

'Worried about Edward's genetic heritage, I suppose?' he'd prodded.

'Not just Edward's . . .' she'd started out, then stopped. 'Well, maybe. I think they're worried that the Welsh doctors aren't up to the mark,' she'd waffled.

Had the bloody woman changed her mind and given a DNA sample after all? That would have made it easier for the damned meddling doctors. He had to know whether those DNA analyses had been done. If not, he could contain it all quite easily.

He picked up the phone and tapped in the number for Great Ormond Street Hospital for Sick Children.

'The Endocrinology Department, please.'

'Appointments.'

'Good morning. I'm checking on an appointment time for my two little girls: Jacintha and Corilla Dunstan. I'm very sorry, I'm afraid we've lost the slip.'

'Which consultant?'

Fuck. Should have checked out the top man before ringing. 'You'll think me very stupid, but the name has slipped my mind. It was the consultant in charge. The head endocrinologist.'

'Dr Planter?' The voice sounded dubious. 'He sees very few patients.'

'That's the one! Some time next month, I think it was.'

'What was the surname again?'

'Dunstan. Jacintha and Corilla Dunstan.'

'Address?' There was a hint of suspicion in the voice. 'Ochr-cefn Farm, Llansantffraed Cwmdeuddwr, Powys RA8 9UP,' he said smoothly. 'Bit of a mouthful. Would you like me to spell that for you?'

'That's all right, Mr Dunstan. I can hear you're from Wales! We have to be careful, you know. I'll just check the computer.' She was back within a remarkably short time. 'You're down for February the twentieth, but if there are any problems, just get in touch and I'm sure Dr Planter will see you earlier.'

He put on his best come-hither voice. 'Just one more thing, now you've got the file up. Did Dr Planter send the DNA analyses over to our GP?'

'Of course not, Mr Dunstan.' The voice sounded quite shocked. 'They'd be with Dr Planter's notes. We never send out DNA reports.'

Shit! So they knew they were half-brother and sister; and Planter would have found the mutated gene. And the reason that stupid bitch Louise and Petra had become close again was because she'd told Petra about the sperm bank. Could Petra have worked it out yet?

Not very likely. She'd have wormed the name of the centre out of Louise, but even if she'd traced it to Spermfreeze, what could she have found? That Ethel Dunstan had been to the same sperm bank, but that she'd had a different donor. Big deal; what were they going to do about that? He cackled as he realised that couldn't get them anywhere.

He dialled out. 'Louise! You're in. I was beginning to

440

wonder whether you lived there. Either you're out, or your line's constantly engaged.'

'I'm secretary of the club.'

He couldn't remember what she was talking about. 'Of course,' he said in his smoothest voice. 'That must keep you very busy.'

'You've forgotten the tournament was on all last week, Jack. You coming to lunch on Sunday? Petra's here...'

'A little bird told me that. Maybe I could take two beautiful ladies out tonight. Could I just have a tiny word with her?'

The miffed sounds came back. 'So you're ringing her, I see. Well, she's already gone out.'

'Out? I thought maybe she'd come to spend some time with you.'

'She's doing some sort of research – for her degree, I think she said.'

'Degree, of course.' He cleared his throat. 'So you're off to the club now, are you?'

'You didn't listen to a word I told you. Today's the cup presentation! I really have to run ... I'll be back about six. Why don't you come round then, and we'll have drinks? Then we can go on and—'

'That's wonderful,' he said, cutting off the flow. 'Know when Petra's getting back at all?'

'I've no idea, Jack. She went to see Sally's mother this morning.' She sounded put out. 'Bound to be home by the time I get back. You'll see her then, I promise you. We haven't anything planned for tonight. OK?'

'I look forward to it, my dear. Have fun.'

41

Petra took a cab back to Louise's house, let herself in and redialled Gwyneth's number. No reply. A cold sweat of fear spread through her. Had Jack found out what she was doing? Was he in Wales? She walked around the house, into David's study, and cursed herself for a fool. The girls would be at Megan's! She tapped in the number, reassured herself that her children were all right and asked for Edward.

Angharad took over the receiver. 'He started worrying about you up there on your own. He's left everything and driven off, Petra.'

'Left? For the farm, you mean?'

'Got into the car and rushed off to London.'

'When, Angie?'

'Around twelve, I think. We had a bit of a meal with the children. He'll be there as soon as he can make it.'

Edward had left the girls after what they'd agreed? Something must have happened. 'But why was he worried? Because I didn't ring?'

'Not just that. Jack Oliver rang Ian's number. Edward thought that very fishy. But don't you worry about the babies; we won't let them out of our sight. Ian's in prison, and Jack's up in London. They'll be fine.'

She walked back into David's study and switched on the computer. No one with whom to talk it through while she waited for Ed; she'd watch that tape, magnify the parts Sally had shown her and make notes on the computer.

The room was hot, the windows double glazed. Louise had left the central heating on and Petra was used to fresh, humid air and the Rayburn heating a couple of radiators upstairs. She walked out into the hall, up to the half landing, opened the lower part of the window overlooking the back garden, left the study door open wide and sat down in front of the monitor.

Her long upper legs made her knees bump against something hard under David's desk. She put her hand out, and found the secret drawer David had shown her. She was sure the key she'd come across would unlock it. It did, and she found just one item there – a small book with a list of names and addresses. She didn't doubt what they were. They would help Spermfreeze identify the children with the mutated gene. She put the booklet into her briefcase.

The tape; she got up, put the video into the machine and switched to play. She watched again what she'd filmed that fateful night. She saw Phil coil his whole body ready for the spring which would end in a jump shot. The lens zoomed towards Phil's feet. She remembered how irritated she'd been that Joss Black had blocked her view of Phil's legs with his own leather-braced limb. She'd tried to shoot round him, found she couldn't, moved the viewfinder and travelled slowly up the full six foot nine of sinew and muscle.

Even in retrospect she could feel the crowd's thrill of anticipation, their roaring for victory. The lens caught Phil's arms extended high, the basketball resting for a fraction of a second on the fingers of his right hand. She zoomed tight in on the uplifted hands and was surprised, just as she'd been that night, to see them waver. Instead of cocking forward like a trigger to follow through in the direction of the basket they seemed to hang there, motionless. The ball, allowed to travel without sufficient thrust, teetered upwards for a short distance, then faltered. None of the other players had expected that; it slithered between them.

She'd pushed the lens right in and focused on Phil's face. She watched the video intently, horrified to see the alert blue eyes grow vacant, the mouth grow slack, the jaw drop down. Working on instinct, she'd pulled out the lens, caught the whole body as it froze into immobility, then filmed it as it crashed, straight like a tree-trunk, on to the court. The referee's whistle shrilled; the remaining nine men on the court seemed turned to stone.

She wound the tape back and used the magnification facility to study the pictures of Joss Black's leather-braced leg near Phil. The memory of Sally gulping out Phil's last few phrases came back to her:

'...Said ss ... *can't* ... siss ... be wrong...'

That double ss sound. Sally had stressed again and again that she thought it meant Joss or Bruce, but Petra knew better now; it didn't mean either. As the implications of what Sally's mother had actually said began to filter through to Petra, she understood exactly what Phil had tried to say. 'Siss' meant *sister* – their marriage could not take place because of a mistake, because Sally was Phil's half-sister. And the only way Phil could have known that was because Helen Thompson had told him so.

Sally had insisted that Helen Thompson could not abide the idea of Phil marrying her. And finally Helen had found a reason, and she must have had proof, because Phil had believed her.

But how did she know? Who told *her*?

Phil must have told her that Sally was a DI child, Beatrice

had told her they'd used the same donor insemination centre. So no one had to tell Helen anything; all she'd had to do was have Phil's and Sally's DNAs analysed. She could have found a way to get samples without alerting either of the young couple.

But how *could* Sally have been Phil's half-sister? Sally was a midget, with her mother's dark colouring. And Phil had been a fair giant of six foot nine. It was much more likely that Phil was her and Ed's half-brother, and that Sally was Jack's daughter...

She thought back to Beatrice Wheeler's photographs of Sally as a baby. Was it possible? Were she and Sally related? Half-sisters, for instance? Was that why they'd had so much in common? But Sally had been a midget, and she had the mutated gene for height!

Mutated gene for height – that was the key. The phrase came back to her, hollow on the phone line during the storm, with Gwyneth mouthing the m. Petra's hands froze, in spite of the heat in the room. A mutated gene for height could mean gigantism *or* dwarfism – they were simply at the two extremes of the distribution curve for height. Was it possible – could it be – that David Jones had found a way of mutating sperm to carry the gene for gigantism? Were David and Jack deliberately breeding *giants*? She keyed the facts she knew into the machine:

Jack Oliver is short, and was turned down as a sperm donor because of it.

David Jones, his special friend, worked at a sperm bank. Had Jack persuaded – or blackmailed – David into substituting his sperm for stored semen? As a sort of revenge?

David knew Jack wasn't just short, he suffered from pituitary dwarfism – a mutated gene for height. He had access to Jorncy drugs; had he supplied Jack with extra growth hormones?

Mutated gene for height applied as much to gigantism as it did to dwarfism. Had David tampered with Jack's sperm so that his offspring might inherit the gene for gigantism?

Jack was quick to spot that Jacintha and Corilla were longer than average. Was he one up on the doctors?

Did David substitute Jack's mutated sperm in an attempt to breed giants?

Sally was older than Phil, and Phil was older than she and Edward. Was it really possible that they were all Jack's children? That David hadn't cracked it until the year Phil was conceived?

She shuddered as a further possibility occurred to her. Could David have substituted Jack's sperm for *all* fair-haired, blue-eyed donors? Was that how the Jack Oliver Media Agency had scored so easily on basketball players? Because there were so many of them, and Jack knew exactly where to look for them!

All Jack had to do was send his scouts round to check on the children David's records would identify. Then, when he'd pinpointed the likely ones, he'd send them for physiological testing. If they came through with flying colours, he'd sponsor them through Millfield or some equivalent. A licence to print money.

That's where David Jones' money had come from. Jack

had told her that David had been a bit of a gambler, that he'd taken an outside chance and it had come off.

Assuming her theory was right, both Edward and Phil were Jack's sons. And she was Edward's half-sister ... that meant she was Jack's daughter, too! Had David known that?

'I've never made any secret of the fact that I like tall, fair men with blue eyes,' Louise had told her. So Jack could have known Louise had chosen a fair donor, even if David didn't find out till later. And if David had substituted Jack's sperm for *all* fair-haired, blue-eyed donors, she would have had to be Jack's daughter. *That* was the reason for David's suicide. Somehow he'd finally found out his wife had opted for a fair-haired donor, and then he'd realised that that had to be Jack. No wonder he'd taken his own life. He'd found out that the daughter he loved more than anything else in the world was in love with her half-brother, and that they might both carry a mutated gene for gigantism. That's what the suicide note had been about!

'Tom Dryson, please.'

'I'm sorry, madam. He doesn't come in on Saturdays.'

'Have you got a home number for him?'

'I'm afraid we don't give out home numbers. Can I help you?'

She forced a smile into her voice. 'It's Petra Dunstan here, David Jones' daughter. Tom Dryson was a great friend of my father's.'

'I'm ever so sorry, Mrs Dunstan. I still can't give out that information.'

'I promised him some pictures of my children. I'm going back to Wales tomorrow, you see. Could you let me have his address?'

'You're the lady who thinks there was a problem with one of the donors?'

Would that count against her, or for her? She had no choice. 'Tom was sorting that out. He's so brilliant...'

'Can't hurt if I tell you he lives in Greenwich, can it? Can't tell you where, of course.'

'I appreciate that. I've left my Welsh number for him; if you could just ask him to be in touch?'

'I'll do that, Mrs Dunstan. Soon as he comes in on Monday morning.'

She put the receiver down and dialled 192. 'Name and town, please.'

'Tom Dryson, Greenwich.'

'And do you have an address?'

'I'm afraid not.'

'We're not really supposed to give out numbers without the address,' the modulated telephone voice told her. 'But there aren't that many Tom Drysons in the area.'

And then, the mechanised recording announced: 'The number you require is 0181 123 8976. I repeat, the number you require is 0181...' She put the receiver down and dialled.

'Tom Dryson speaking.'

'It's Petra Dunstan here, Tom.'

He was eating something and started to choke. 'Sorry about that. I'm eating lunch.'

'I'm sorry to disturb you. Tom – I've got another name.'

'Another name?'

She explained what had happened with Beatrice Wheeler.

'You mean you think they substituted Jack Oliver's sperm for some of the donor sperm?'

'And that it produced Sally – yes. That's why he kept an eye on her. But he hated the way she was a midget, like him. He wanted nothing to do with her.'

449

'This is getting out of hand.'

'Tom, I've had an idea. It may be completely crazy, but I told you I knew Jack was a midget, too. In other words, his gene for height had a mutation. You said David was something of a genius in the laboratory. Could he have changed Jack's sperm to carry a mutation for giants instead of midgets?'

'They say you can't change the germ-line cells.'

'But you do keep the sperm frozen for six months to test that the donor isn't HIV positive?'

'True.'

'That *is* assuming a change could take place in the germ-line cell. Otherwise why bother?'

'They do that in case the donor tests HIV positive in the meantime. But you're right! I think that's what David must have done – found a technique which allowed the alteration of genes in the sperm, and produced the mutation. If anyone could do it, your father could.'

Petra put down the receiver and stared at the computer monitor. She stiffened; she could feel a change in her surroundings. She glanced at the VCR which had switched itself off, at the windows, at the desk. All as it was. She turned to the computer monitor again and saw a reflection in it. Was she imagining things? A shape behind her head; another head. She gasped and gagged as her brain ordered her shoulders to whirl round. She already knew who it would be.

She felt the pressure on her shoulders; two vice-like grips which held her tight.

Pretend; pretend it was a game and humour him. 'Uncle Jack!' she said, forcing her voice into the tones of pleasant surprise, deliberately using the term Uncle. 'How on earth did you get in?'

His voice was languid, almost as she'd always heard it. Just a tiny edge of anger slipping in sideways. 'Always so careless, Petra. You left the back door unlocked.'

She put her hands up to try and undo the clamping on her shoulders. 'I put the cat out. And since I'm at home, I thought—' His strong fingers gripped her shoulders even harder, beginning to dig into her flesh, to hurt. Pretend it wasn't happening. 'Mother should be back by now.'

'Such touching devotion between mother and daughter.' This time the tone was tighter, as though his throat was being held and the voice box squeezed. 'No, she isn't back. And I've made sure we won't be disturbed. I've bolted both doors; you can never be too careful nowadays. But don't you worry, my little Pet,' he purred. 'I've got you all to myself for at least an hour. Thought we might have a little chat. Long overdue.'

She sat, staring at the screen, her voice now merely a whisper. 'Chat?'

'Patience, now. First we have to make a couple of adjustments.'

Before she could bring her mind round to what he might do he'd taken his hands from her shoulders, grabbed her arms and twisted them back and slipped his hands round her wrists, pushing her forward in the chair and hard against the desk. 'Busy little hands; we'll just keep them out of mischief for a bit.'

She was free to turn her head. She twisted her face around and tried to look at him. His hair, still thick and plentiful and blond – the colour of her own – was all she saw. She heard the ripping of tape. He was tying her wrists together with parcel tape. She felt him twist the tape around, over and over again. She wouldn't be able to get it off without some sharp instrument.

'Why are you doing this?' she snarled. Trying to charm him wasn't going to work. He was fighting for his life.

'Do you think I want to? You never listened to me. How often have I told you to leave well alone, Petra? Why couldn't you just—'

'You're the one who came after us!' she yelled at him. 'We tried to get away. You're the one who wouldn't leave Ed alone!'

'He's an outstanding player.'

Her head twisted round again and this time she caught his eye. 'Couldn't breed them fast enough, is that it? After you killed Phil, Edward was the best. With all those children to choose from, you haven't found a replacement for Phil Thompson yet.' She gathered saliva in her mouth and spat at him.

He cuffed her head; first the right side, then the left. Hard enough to make her reel, unable to think.

'Do that again and I'll take a razor to you.'

Her eyes faced the monitor again, her head heavy, tears beginning to run down her face. She felt him grab her right arm and tape it to the chair arm. After a few seconds she heard the tape tear, and he grabbed her left arm and taped that to the other side. He pushed the chair back on its casters, grabbed her ankles and taped them together. When he had finished he stood in front of her. Slowly, deliberately he wiped the spittle from his face. The action held more menace than if he'd threatened her with a knife.

'So you want to play games, do you? We've got plenty of time. Let's start with the computer, shall we? The Petra game is all set up.'

She put on her best smile, her most innocent look. 'What do you think you can achieve with this, Uncle Jack? If you kill me they'll all know it was you. It isn't like Phil and Sally, you know. Edward knows, and so does Tom Dryson.'

'Don't worry your pretty little head about my problems, my dear. I'll manage those all right.' Quite suddenly his face turned into a contorted grimace. 'And cut that Uncle Jack crap. You'll call me Father, or I'll fucking well cut out your tongue!'

She saw her little girls, saw Edward. Her innocent family. She had to use her brain to disarm this man; part of her brain was from his genes. Make use of that and read it.

'What do you want?' she said.

'Father,' he insisted, sharp teeth gleaming between scowling lips. 'You can start by calling me Father. All that Daddy crap with David Jones; enough to make me sick.'

'What do you want, Father? Where is all this leading us?'

His eyes narrowed as his head shot back. 'Going to play ball at last, are you? Let's see what you actually know.' He scrolled the text back on the monitor.

> *Jack Oliver is short, and was turned down as a sperm donor because of it.*

'You got on to sperm donors from Louise. How the hell did you connect me with it?' His eyes had narrowed into slits.

She laughed. 'I told you Gwyneth worked out that David wasn't my father. Then we found out Edward and I were closely related from the DNA analyses. We were stupid enough to tell you about that, so you must have guessed we knew. *And* that we shared a mutated gene for height; Planter said it meant we have a common biological father. So when Mother finally admitted to using a sperm donor, she told me the name of the centre.'

'It's changed.'

'I whittled it down to three possibles. Struck lucky second time.'

He grasped her face in his hands and shook it. 'Let's cut the crap. How did you get to me?'

She told him how Tom Dryson had recognised her as David's daughter, and that the Spermfreeze records showed Louise and Ethel had had different donors.

'Get to the point!'

'We knew that wasn't true. So Tom Dryson guessed David had substituted sperm; he said he'd always known it subliminally, but never wanted to admit it. That made me ask to see the list of rejected donors in the relevant years.'

She could see the admiration in his eyes. 'So you came across my name. How could that tell you anything?' His eyes held suspicion again. 'Can't have said anything except that I was under five foot eight; their fucking cut-off point. Who the hell do they think they are, playing bloody God?'

This wasn't the time to point out that he and David had played God much more successfully than any insemination centre had ever dreamed of.

'The Joneses told me about your dwarfism. And Gwyneth saw the phrase *mutated gene for height* in one of the medical records Ian stole.'

'Should have told him to get rid of that bitch years ago.' He sounded as casual as if he were talking about old newspapers. The blue eyes had turned to pinpoints of black. 'So I'm a fucking dwarf. You're looking for giants!'

'Scientific training; the Open University.'

He laughed, shaking the chair she was bound to back and forth, making her head spin. 'Come on, Petra. You've got to do better than that!'

'I worked out that *mutated gene for height* could mean dwarf *or* giant. Depends on the mutation.'

'That's not enough – what else?'

'Beatrice Wheeler told me that Sally was a DI child. I showed her pictures of my little girls, and she suddenly thought they looked like Sally when she was a baby. So she fished out some old photographs, and I saw she was quite right. That's how I eventually guessed Sally and I were half-sisters.'

'Very scientific! But that doesn't get you anywhere. What else?'

'Then Beatrice told me that Phil was a DI child as well.'

'Helen Thompson, I suppose.'

'Yes. That's when I finally put together that they were half-brother and sister; that's what Phil had found out before that match.'

'Bloody women.'

She might survive; she had to get as much information as she could. 'Did David genetically engineer your sperm?'

He grinned. 'One hell of a leap. Let's see what we've got next.'

David Jones, his special friend, worked at a sperm bank. Had Jack persuaded – or blackmailed – David into substituting his sperm for stored semen? As a sort of revenge?

'Do psychology at the Open University, do you?'

'Professor Dunstan's class, first term in Exeter. Did you blackmail Daddy?'

His face came up to hers, breathing hard, his teeth bared. '*Call him David.* He wasn't your fucking father!' He spun the chair, kicking at her legs each time she came round. She gagged.

'Just watch that bloody lip of yours. So you think your precious David couldn't possibly have done it without being pressured, eh? Well, let me tell you something. He did all right, and you got the benefit. And I didn't see you turn the trust fund down. Damn fool never spent a penny of it on himself. All went to Gwyneth and the trust fund.'

David knew Jack wasn't just short, he suffered from pituitary dwarfism – a mutated gene for height. He had access to Jorncy drugs: had he supplied Jack with extra growth hormones?

Mutated gene for height applied as much to gigantism as it did to dwarfism. Had David tampered with Jack's sperm so that his offspring might inherit the gene for gigantism?

Jack was quick to spot that Jacintha and Corilla were longer than average. Was he one up on the doctors?

He'd stopped the cursor at the end of the last phrase. 'You can say that again! They didn't even believe you when you pointed it out.'

'No,' Petra said. 'That's why I went to Planter.' An idea came into her mind. 'You don't really want them to be giantesses, do you ... Father? They're your granddaughters, you know.'

His face had lost some of its aggression. He perched on the desk, his feet dangling in the air, and stared at her. 'Can they treat them?'

'Because I went so early on, yes. They hope to keep them from growing to more than six foot.'

'Hmmm.' He moved the cursor again.

456

Did David substitute Jack's mutated sperm in an attempt to breed giants?

Sally was older than Phil, and Phil was older than she and Edward. Was it really possible that they were all Jack's children? That David hadn't cracked it until the year Phil was conceived?

'Good, very good,' Jack said. 'Not just a tall body and a pretty face, I see.'

'You *were* breeding giants for the basketball teams, weren't you?'

He shrugged. 'Once you spotted that David had mutated my sperm, that's hardly news.'

'Did you substitute your sperm for all fair-haired, blue-eyed donors?'

He grinned. 'Only at first, then the numbers got too large. We settled for *tall*, fair-haired, blue-eyed donors.'

'Why did you murder Phil?'

He shook the chair again so violently that she bit her lip. He saw the blood spurt and stopped. 'Come on, now. Work it out.'

'Phil's mother guessed that he and Sally could be half-brother and sister.'

'How?'

'She found out that Beatrice and she used the same insemination centre. I think she had Phil and Sally's DNA analysed; that's how she could have proved it.'

He flared his nostrils. 'That damned Sally blabbed about being a dwarf *and* being DI!'

'And Helen Thompson told Phil what she'd found. And Phil would have told the world, and it would all have come out. That's the only reason you would have killed the golden goose – well, gander.'

'Know how it was done?'

'Show me,' she said. 'The tape you tried to suppress; it's in the VCR. How did Joss Black do it?'

He picked up the remote control, pressed play, fast-forwarded to the shot of the players' legs, and froze several frames showing Joss's braced leg. Then he magnified a section of the frame showing the leather strap jutting out. Petra couldn't see anything wrong. 'Even with the magnification it's hard to tell. He had a small syringe with a fine needle. All it needed was a tiny prick. The poison can't be traced, even if they hadn't cremated Phil.'

He fast-forwarded the tape, scanned through, then stopped at the lopsided pictures the camera had taken when Petra had lost control of it. There was a shot of Joss's legs, and his hand beside the leather thong. 'There we go; he's retrieving the syringe. Always amazed Sally never spotted that.'

'I suppose you bribed him with Phil's place in the States.' He had begun to twirl her round again. 'And Sally – you killed her because she wasn't going to stop until she'd proved what she'd sensed.'

'Shouldn't have been allowed to live – a dwarf like that.'

How could Jack Oliver be prejudiced against a human being with the same defect that he suffered from? She shuddered.

'Wondering what I've got in mind for you? Don't worry, I'll explain it all in detail.'

'How did you make Sally ill?'

His eyes were flat. 'Salmonella in egg mayonnaise, deadly nightshade in Evian water. Almost too easy.'

'So that's why you paid for Sally's cremation.'

He grinned. 'You're very thorough – a real chip off the old block.' He laughed uproariously.

'So why are you going to kill me? Substituting sperm isn't

a serious crime as yet; at worst it's fraud. And David did that, anyway. And Joss Black killed Phil, and a mugger killed Sally. What can they pin on you?'

'Let's just say I don't like snoopers.'

'You really think Ed will let it go?'

He patted her cheek. 'Don't you worry about your old daddy, darling. I'll work it out.'

He quit the file, then erased it. He typed in the command to reformat the hard disk, waited until it had finished, then slipped a floppy into the floppy drive and transferred a file to the hard disk.

'Just to make sure it's got a nice virus,' he said. 'We don't want any clever hackers going through people's notes.'

Petra turned to look at the clock. Four-fifteen. Edward must be near London now. But even if he got here in time, could he get in? Both front and back doors were bolted.

She lowered her head as she remembered the window in the hall. Had Jack closed it? Would Edward notice it was open? Even if he did, would he be able to get to it? It was a good ten feet off the ground, maybe more...

'And now it's time for little Petra.' Jack grinned, taking a plastic bag out of his pocket. 'Nothing too fancy. Just put the bag over your face until your brain loses its capabilities. A lack of oxygen is very detrimental to the human brain. A warning to others!'

She heard the front doorbell. That had to be Edward!

'Someone at the door,' Jack said softly, laughing, as he tried to place the plastic bag over Petra's head. 'Wouldn't be the knight errant by any chance?'

She used all her strength to steer the chair away from him and managed to elude him by a few inches.

'Ed!' she screamed. 'Help me, Ed!'

Jack grasped her by the shoulders and placed the bag over her head. She knew she had to conserve her breath. He was using a large, black dustbin bag. Perhaps if she could get it in her mouth and bite...

She heard the rattle of the back door. He was in the garden now. Had he heard her? Would he know she was in the house? Would he notice the hall window?

She heard the tearing of the tape sealing the bag around her throat. 'I'll tell them you were just like your Daddy David, shall I, my little Pet?' she could hear Jack mocking her. 'Tell them you tried to commit suicide!'

Edward screeched to a stop outside Louise's house, saw Jack's E-type in the drive, parked the Range Rover next to it and sprinted out without even turning off the ignition. He pushed his finger hard on the doorbell. He could hear it reverberating in the hall, but banged on the knocker as well, and tried the door handle. The door was locked. He pushed the bell again; no reply.

He looked through the windows of the living room. No one there. Then he thought he heard a muffled cry... He rushed over to the study, saw the blinds were drawn.

Had he heard Petra cry out? He ran down the path beside the house leading to the back door, crashed the knocker up and down several times as he tried the handle, rammed against it to force it. It was a solid door, and locked.

He looked at the house from the back, saw that the lower sash of the hall window was slightly open. The sill was roughly ten feet above the ground – the height of a basketball hoop. Putting a ball through the basket with a dunk shot, that's what his training had fitted him for. And it was one of his strengths as a player. He flexed his muscles, pushed his feet against the ground, raised his arms up high, and jumped.

He only managed to get within six inches of the sill. The window must be further off the ground than he had realised.

He *had* to get in! He ran back into the garden, turned, began a run-up and tried once more. He managed to grasp hold of the stone sill, then slipped and landed on the ground again, his hands bleeding. Somehow he had to get into that house! He ran back, heard Bruce Traggard's voice nagging at him: '*Bend* your knees before you jump, Dunstan!' He took up the stride position again, landed on his right foot, bent his knees and took another leap. He managed two inches higher this time, grabbed the window frame as well as the sill and hung there.

Strong arm muscles inched his body upwards, massive shoulders pushed his head beneath the sash frame and pushed it up. He vaulted himself in, jumped down from the sill, listened for any noise. The study was down a short flight of steps and to the left.

'Petra? You there, Pet?'

The ticking of the hall clock, the firing of the boiler in the cellar. He strained his ears.

'*Mmm.*'

The muffled sound came from the study. He rushed towards it, tried the handle, found the door locked. That had to mean she was in there, and that Jack was trying to kill her.

He moved away, picked up the coat-stand in the hall and used it like a battering ram against one panel of the door. It made a hole. Then he used the bottom of the stand like a hammer, splintering the panel wide, crashing his body through.

Jack Oliver was by the desk chair, spinning it. Edward could see a figure held to the chair, a shiny black bag over its face. Petra!

The small man advanced towards him, holding a letter-opener in his hand. Edward lunged, caught him by the waist, flipped him up and crashed the blond head against the window.

He let go at once, turned towards the chair, ripped a hole in the black plastic with his hands, and freed Petra's head. As he turned back he saw Jack Oliver standing there, blood streaming from his face. He crashed his fist into the little man's body, time and again. It crumpled to the floor.

'Stop, Ed. Stop! You'll kill him and they'll charge you with murder!' he finally heard Petra scream.

He stopped, his hands bloody, the anger spent, terrified in case Petra was badly hurt. He grabbed the letter-opener lying on the floor, tore off the tapes binding her arms, her wrists, her feet. He carried her into the living room, laid her on the sofa and dialled 999.

42

'What on earth is going on here?' Louise walked through
the open front door of her house.

A police squad car and an ambulance were blocking
the entrance to her garage. She'd had to leave her car
parked in the road outside. As she'd walked past them
she was astonished to see both Jack's E-type and a
Range Rover with the driver's door open outside her
front door.

A young policewoman was standing in the hall. 'I'm
afraid you can't come in here,' she said, advancing towards
Louise with a grave expression on her face.

'This is my house!' She felt anger explode at this invasion
of her territory. 'And I am certainly coming in. Now: has
there been an accident?'

'I'm sorry, madam. I shall have to fetch—'

Louise stalked past the young woman and on through the
open door of her living room. The back of a blond head was
high above one of her easy chairs; there was a policeman
standing beside the seated person, blocking her view of the
rest of the room. The head turned, and she recognised her
son-in-law. 'Edward!'

He rose and came towards her.

'Has something happened to Petra?' She saw his drawn
face, the white lips, and focused on the bloody hands.
'Where is she?' Fear was beginning to make her legs feel

insecure and she stood, uncertain, staring at him. Why was he bleeding? Had he attacked her little girl?

'She's all right now, Louise. She's . . .'

If Petra had had a road accident she would be in a hospital emergency department. What had he done? 'Where is she?'

'She's here, Louise, on the sofa. We think she's all right, but we're waiting for the paramedics to see to her. They'll take her to hospital to check her over.'

'But what's *happened* to her?' Louise pushed past Edward and on towards the sofa.

'She's had a terrible experience. She's in deep shock.'

Louise brushed past the policeman and further into the room. She saw that Petra was lying still, her eyes closed, blood around her mouth. Was she dying?

She felt her jaw drop, her knees buckle. 'Why is her mouth all bloody? What are you doing to her?' She rushed to her daughter, knelt on the floor beside her, put her hands to Petra's head. 'What have they done to you, Pet? What is it?' She turned, eyes blazing. 'Is someone going to tell me what's happened to her?'

'It was Jack, Louise.' Edward stood towering above her. He sounded hoarse and strained. 'I only got here in the nick of time. He was going to kill her . . .'

'Jack? *Jack*'s here?'

'He's in the study, Mother.' The voice coming out of the bleeding lips was soft but determined. 'He found me there, and trussed me up with tape.' Petra's voice broke into a sob, but she controlled it. 'He was trying to turn me into a vegetable – by keeping oxygen from my brain.' She sat up, eased her legs off the sofa and rubbed her wrists. They were red, and swelling into puffiness.

'Jack?' Louise stared from Edward to Petra and back again. 'Why would Jack attack you, Petra? He was always so very fond of you. Almost as though you were his daughter!'

'That's the awful thing, Mother. I am. That's exactly what I've been finding out.'

Louise hauled herself on to the sofa next to Petra. 'Pet, darling. You can't know what you're saying. I can see you've had some sort of ghastly shock. It's all my fault. I should never have told you... That sperm bank business has upset you, hasn't it?'

'Jack attacked her, Louise!'

They had to be talking nonsense; Jack wasn't even there ... 'I thought you were all right, that you'd find out about the wretched donor.' Had they already taken Jack away? Is that what they were trying to tell her? 'How could *Jack* be your father?'

Petra put her hands up to her face. 'Because David Jones worked at Spermfreeze, Mother. That's what Sperm Donors Ltd is called now.'

'He worked at Jorncy!'

'Spermfreeze is part of the Jorncy group, Louise,' Edward said, sitting down in the chair, staring at his hands. 'David Jones was in charge of the storage unit of their sperm bank. He collected Jack Oliver's sperm at regular intervals, and substituted it for that of fair-haired, blue-eyed, tall donors.'

'He says he substituted it for *all* fair-haired, blue-eyed donors at the beginning.' Petra rubbed her wrists, and shivered.

Louise put her arm around her daughter's shoulders. 'But that means...' Louise felt her stomach drop, her jaw gape. 'That's what David got so upset about? Because I told him I'd asked for a fair donor, and not a dark-haired one? So he knew it had to be Jack?' The words came out in whispers, hardly audible.

'That's how he knew.'

'What else?'

'Three other women we know of were inseminated at Sperm Donors Ltd. Ethel Dunstan, Beatrice Wheeler and Helen Thompson. Jack fathered their children, too.'

'How can you possibly know that? They wouldn't have told you...' Her voice faded away.

'They all asked for fair donors,' Edward told her. 'That was the worst of it. David found a way to mutate Jack's gene for height from dwarfism to gigantism. They were playing at being God; breeding basketball players.'

Louise looked up and saw two paramedics carrying a stretcher with a body on it towards her front door. 'That's Jack?'

'I didn't have time for niceties, Louise. I knocked him out, cold. For all I know I killed him. Petra was sitting, bound to the desk chair, with a plastic bag over her head. I knew I had to act fast to save her. I didn't even know whether I was in time.'

'But...'

'If you'd like to come with us, Mrs Dunstan,' the policewoman coming into the room began.

'I'm all *right*,' Petra said. 'I can think, so my brain must be OK. I'm not going in the same ambulance as that man.'

'I'll drive her to the hospital,' Edward told them. 'My car's outside.'

'I'm sorry, sir. We have to detain you.'

'Detain me?'

'Ask you to come down to the station and help us with our enquiries.'

'You're charging *me*?'

'There's been a serious physical assault.'

Louise put her arms around her daughter. 'Jack tried to kill you?' she whispered.

'Put me out of action, yes.'

She turned to her son-in-law. 'I'll look after her, Edward. And I'll ring my solicitor for you right now.' She turned to the policewoman. 'You're not suggesting you're holding my daughter, are you?'

'Perhaps if we could interview her...'

'After she's seen a doctor,' Louise said firmly. 'I'll drive her to the hospital myself.'

Petra and Edward were sitting in Gerald Osborne's office, facing him, with Tom Dryson on a chair to the right of them.

'So you're telling me that Jack Oliver admitted that his mutated sperm, frozen in cryopreservation fluid, has been substituted for some of our donor sperm?'

'I think you have to assume that *all* sperm from fair, blue-eyed donors up to the time David Jones committed suicide is suspect.' Petra's lip was still puffy, but it was healing. She smiled at Tom. 'Don't you agree?'

'Indeed. We can prove that with samples presently stored, of course. We can analyse the DNA from each sample.'

'That would take months of work!' Osborne gasped.

'And be very expensive, yes. All we have to do is get rid of the entire stock of suspect sperm,' Tom explained. 'And start again from scratch.'

'So we'd be left with no donors who match that description.'

'You're quite safe with sperm donated after David Jones' death, Mr Osborne,' Petra said, smiling as well as she could. 'And I have some good news for you. I came across a key which opened a drawer in David Jones' desk. It held an address book with the names of all live births following insemination with Jack Oliver's mutated sperm. Spermfreeze will be able to contact each individual.'

Osborne looked at her, and sighed. 'It will be a start. We'll have to make our own enquiries.'

'The funny thing is,' Petra said, looking round the room, 'Edward and I were convinced the sperm donor was a man called Bruce Traggard. He's tall, and fair, and blue-eyed; and he looks quite similar to Edward and Phil Thompson, and a couple of the other basketball players.'

'You think he was involved in some way?'

She shook her head. 'Not for a moment. I think he was a useful fall guy. Poor chap; we all blamed him and he was the only innocent one in the whole lot!'

'So what's going to happen to Jack Oliver?' Tom Dryson asked. 'How are we going to stop him doing this again?'

'Recovered, has he?' Osborne looked enquiringly at Edward.

Edward grinned. 'He's alive. It'll take a little time for him to get back into action.'

'The safeguards are much more stringent now.' Osborne leaned back in his massive chair. 'And he needs an accomplice working in a sperm bank. I don't think there's any chance of it happening again.'

'He won't be in a position to do anything,' Edward hissed. 'At least I hope not. We're pretty sure the police will be able to nail him for conspiracy to murder Phil Thompson. They'll extradite Joss Black, the man who actually did it. He couldn't have had access to the poison he injected into Phil. I'm sure he'll implicate Oliver, if only to save his own bacon.'

Osborne stood up, and looked out of his window. 'There is a much more serious problem we have to solve. Do you realise we export sperm to the USA?'

Petra leaned forward. 'I know, I've been thinking about

468

that. I feel responsible, somehow. This quite horrific set-up was created by my biological father and my nurturing father. If you'll allow me to, I'd like to trace all US children born of this terrible mutation.'

'I know that Tom will do his best to follow up the ones in this country...'

Tom cleared his throat. 'Shouldn't be too difficult, Mr Osborne. The files are in perfect order, and the address book will corroborate what happened.' He sighed. 'I can destroy any sperm we suspect within a week. And of course I can prevent it being used from today.'

Osborne nodded at Tom, then looked towards Petra. 'I don't know that we can afford to research what happened in the United States...'

'All I would ask you for is travelling expenses, and phone costs perhaps.' She smiled at Edward. 'My husband will be playing professional basketball. He's hoping to be drafted by an NBA team – the Atlanta Hawks. Our family will be living in the States for a few years to come.'

Osborne nodded at her. 'The Chief Executive will be back from holiday next week. I'll raise your suggestion at a Jorncy board meeting. It's a most generous offer which I'm sure they'll be only too happy to accept.'

Petra put out her hand and found Edward's. They would have to give up their beautiful home in Wales. No one in the States would know that she and her husband were half-brother and sister. They would never be able to allow themselves to have more children, but at least they could live together. And they were blessed with two beautiful little girls they could raise without the shadow of the Jack Oliver Media Agency darkening their lives.

More Thrilling Fiction from Headline Feature

Emma Lorant

CRADLE OF SECRETS

HER DREAM OF TWINS TURNED INTO A NIGHTMARE

When Alex and Lisa Wildmore move to the pretty Somerset village of Lodsham, they anticipate a rural idyll. Newly pregnant, with one adorable toddler already, Lisa is confident that the countryside is the best place to raise her family; she embodies the good life of the caring 'nineties.

But the sun-dappled tranquillity of the Glastonbury moors is deceptive.

Childbirth brings identical twin boys, despite a scan showing only one baby. When it becomes clear that this is only the start of a terrifying chain of events she is powerless to prevent, Lisa realises she is in the grip of a phenomenon as sinister as it is inexplicable.

Of course she loves her children – blond, blue-eyed and enchanting – and is determined to protect them from any dangers that might attend their unusual genesis. And a rash of 'accidents' convinces Lisa that there are dangers indeed.

Whom can she trust with her cradle of secrets? Alec assumes she is suffering delusions brought on by post-natal depression. Previously friendly villagers adopt a hostile curiosity. Can she even trust her own maternal instincts? Or is Lisa Wildmore losing her mind . . . ?

FICTION / THRILLER 0 7472 4358 1

More Thrilling Fiction from Headline Feature

gone

Kit Craig

It's 10 p.m.

Do you know where your children are?

'A tightly wound psycho-thriller written with terrifying understatement . . . riveting and menacing to the last page'
Newsweek

When fifteen-year-old Michael Hale wakes up to find his mother missing he knows something is wrong. His older sister scoffs at his nervousness and his four-year-old brother Tommy is too young to know what is going on. But as the day wears to an end and their mother still does not return, it's clear Michael is right. Reliable, endlessly loving Clary Hale is

gone . . .

'Tantalizes and terrifies . . . a one-sitting book defying the reader to budge until the end' *Los Angeles Times*

'Genuinely frightening, unpredictable plot throbbing with menace and escalating horror . . . outstanding psychological thriller' *Publishers Weekly*

'Just the right mix of diverse characters, suspense and unpredictable twists' *New York Times*

'For those who like to be scared without having their stomachs turned, GONE is pretty close to perfect' *Booklist*

'The main characters . . . are complex, believable, and so wonderfully, humanly likeable' *Washington Post*

FICTION / THRILLER 0 7472 4021 3

A selection of bestsellers from Headline

BODY OF A CRIME	Michael C. Eberhardt	£5.99	☐
TESTIMONY	Craig A. Lewis	£5.99	☐
LIFE PENALTY	Joy Fielding	£5.99	☐
SLAYGROUND	Philip Caveney	£5.99	☐
BURN OUT	Alan Scholefield	£4.99	☐
SPECIAL VICTIMS	Nick Gaitano	£4.99	☐
DESPERATE MEASURES	David Morrell	£5.99	☐
JUDGMENT HOUR	Stephen Smoke	£5.99	☐
DEEP PURSUIT	Geoffrey Norman	£4.99	☐
THE CHIMNEY SWEEPER	John Peyton Cooke	£4.99	☐
TRAP DOOR	Deanie Francis Mills	£5.99	☐
VANISHING ACT	Thomas Perry	£4.99	☐

All Headline books are available at your local bookshop or newsagent, or can be ordered direct from the publisher. Just tick the titles you want and fill in the form below. Prices and availability subject to change without notice.

Headline Book Publishing, Cash Sales Department, Bookpoint, 39 Milton Park, Abingdon, OXON, OX14 4TD, UK. If you have a credit card you may order by telephone – 01235 400400.

Please enclose a cheque or postal order made payable to Bookpoint Ltd to the value of the cover price and allow the following for postage and packing:

UK & BFPO: £1.00 for the first book, 50p for the second book and 30p for each additional book ordered up to a maximum charge of £3.00.

OVERSEAS & EIRE: £2.00 for the first book, £1.00 for the second book and 50p for each additional book.

Name ....

Address ....

....

....

If you would prefer to pay by credit card, please complete:
Please debit my Visa/Access/Diner's Card/American Express (delete as applicable) card no:

Signature .... Expiry Date..............